WITCH

By M MacKinnon

Witch
Copyright © 2025 by M MacKinnon

All rights reserved. No part of this publication may be reproduced, distributed, or transmitted in any form or by any means, including photocopying, recording or other electronic or mechanical methods, without the prior written permission of the author, except in the case of brief quotations embodied in reviews and certain other non-commercial uses permitted by copyright law.

Without in any way limiting the author's [and publisher's] exclusive rights under copyright, any use of this publication to "train" generative artificial intelligence (AI) technologies to generate text is expressly prohibited. The author reserves all rights to license uses of this work for generative AI training and development of machine learning language models.

This is a work of fiction. Any characters, businesses, places, events or incidents are either the product of the author's imagination or are used fictitiously. Any resemblance to actual persons, living or dead, events or locales is entirely coincidental.

Printed in the United States of America
Paperback ISBN: 978-1-965253-49-6
Ebook ISBN: 978-1-965253-50-2

DartFrog Plus is the hybrid publishing imprint of DartFrog Books, LLC.
301 S. McDowell St.
Suite 125-1625
Charlotte, NC 28204

www.DartFrogBooks.com

DEDICATION

Màiri MacKinnon and Rory – Màiri, kinswoman and friend, has helped me since the beginning of my writing journey with the dialects and languages of the Scottish Highlands, and introduced me to one of the most wonderful dogs I've ever met. She is the inspiration for my female protagonist, and the reason there's a dog in this book.

ACKNOWLEDGEMENTS

Carl Dannenberger - My amazing husband. His tireless work to publicize, market, and promote the books allows me to live my dream. Because of him, I can just write.

Kenny Tomasso – Minister of Mayhem. Helps me to understand exactly where to stab someone in the most dramatic way, how to blow things up spectacularly, and where to hide the bodies. No matter the method, he's the expert.

Kathy Kiel – Unflinching beta reader, that greatest of friends who will be honest without worrying about the consequences.

Steve and Mary Maclennan – Highlanders for Hire and the inspiration for my Highland Players. They've taught me the right end of a sword, and what a *sgian dubh* really is.

Victor Cameron – The first friend I met in Scotland, he is always ready and willing to take me on another journey into the heart of the Highlands. This time it was a research trip to Dornach. He infuses his love for his country's history into everything he does. Author of Walk History and Time Facebook page: https://www.facebook.com/profile.php?id=100091411576014

Caomhìn MacFhionghuin (Kevin MacKinnon) – another kinsman I was lucky to meet in Inverness, he is a walking Highlands history book, always willing to share his huge knowledge base and love of his country's past. The inspiration for Wee Caomhainn.

Margaret and Graham Hastie – my landlords in Inverness, always willing to share their wonderful history with us. Margaret was my inspiration for Nessie in the first book—aye, she's that wonderful.

By *the River Café* at Highland Hospice, Inverness – Manned by volunteers, the cafe is one of my favourite spots for a lovely lunch. The ladies here were thrilled to help me with my research on the area. Home to Màiri's gran in the book. The facility is located on the River Ness in the heart of Inverness, and you can discover more about them here: https://highlandhospice.org.

ACKNOWLEDGEMENTS

Patricia Duff, Animal Helpline Acting Supervisor, SSPCA, Inverness – Told me how the adoption process works and thus helped Adam find his magical dog.

CONTENTS

Glossary	XI
Pronunciation of Gaelic Names	XIII
Prologue - Dornach, Scotland, 1727	1
Chapter 1 - Ballachulish, Scotland – Present Time	7
Chapter 2 - Fort William, Scotland – Present Time	17
Chapter 3 - Glen Coe, Scotland – Present Time	27
Chapter 4 - Aberdeenshire, Scotland, 1705	35
Chapter 5 - Dornach, Scotland, 1707	43
Chapter 6 - Inverness, Scotland – Present Time	51
Chapter 7 - Fort William, Scotland – Present Time	61
Chapter 8 - Glen Coe, Scotland – Present Time	69
Chapter 9 - Dornach, Scotland, 1716	79
Chapter 10 - Dornach, Scotland, 1716	87
Chapter 11 - Glen Coe, Scotland – Present Time	95
Chapter 12 - Fort William, Scotland – Present Time	105
Chapter 13 - Fort William, Scotland – Present Time	115
Chapter 14 - Dornach, Scotland – 1722	125
Chapter 15 - Dornach, Scotland – 1722	133
Chapter 16 - Ballachulish, Scotland – Present Time	141
Chapter 17 - Fort William, Scotland – Present Time	151
Chapter 18 - Fort William, Scotland – Present Time	161
Chapter 19 - Dornach, Scotland – 1726	171
Chapter 20 - Dornach, Scotland – 1726	179
Chapter 21 - Glasgow, Scotland – Present Time	187
Chapter 22 - Fort William, Scotland – Present Time	197

Chapter 23 - Glen Coe, Scotland – Present Time	207
Chapter 24 - Dornach, Scotland - 1727	217
Chapter 25 - Dornach, Scotland – 1727	225
Chapter 26 - Fort William, Scotland – Present Time	233
Chapter 27 - Fort William, Scotland – Present Time	243
Chapter 28 - Glen Coe, Scotland – Present Time	253
Chapter 29 - Dornach, Scotland – 1727	263
Chapter 30 - Dornach, Scotland – 1727	271
Chapter 31 - Fort William, Scotland – Present Time	279
Chapter 32 - Glen Coe, Scotland – Present Time	289
Chapter 33 - Ballachulish, Scotland – Present Time	299
Chapter 34 - Dornach, Scotland – 1727	309
Chapter 35 - Dornach, Scotland – 1727	317
Chapter 36 - Fort William, Scotland – Present Time	325
Chapter 37 - Glen Coe, Scotland – Present Time	335
Chapter 38 - Fort William, Scotland – Present Time	345
Chapter 39 - Dornach, Scotland – 1727	355
Chapter 40 - Dornach, Scotland – 1727	363
Chapter 41 - Ballachulish and Fort William, Scotland – Present Time	371
Chapter 42 - Fort William, Scotland – Present Time	383
Chapter 43 - Fort William, Scotland – Present Time	393
Chapter 44 - Dornach, Scotland – 1727	403
Chapter 45 - Dornach, Scotland – 1727	411
Chapter 46 - Fort William, Scotland – Present Time	417
Chapter 47 - Fort William, Scotland – Present Time	427
Chapter 48 - Dornach, Scotland – 1727	437
Chapter 49 - Fort William, Scotland – Present Time	445
Chapter 50 - Fort William, Scotland – Present Time	455
Epilogue - Dornach, Scotland, 1737	463
Author's Note	469
Books by M MacKinnon	471

GLOSSARY

arasaid – an 18th-century woman's draped garment worn in the Scottish Highlands
balaich seòlta (Gaelic)– lunatic
bealach – a narrow mountain pass
céilidh (Gaelic) – a Highlands gathering or party
choocter: a country bumpkin, rough, uncouth, or uneducated person
dewlally - anxious or crazy
dobber: A person who is seen as undereducated, with poor social skills
dreich – depressing, miserable, or cold. Often used to describe the weather
eejit: an idiot
feardie – a coward, a timid person
Haud yer wheesht – Shut up
kelpie – a seal
leannan (Gaelic)– sweetheart
meff – Scouse word meaning stupid or idiot
minger: a disgusting person
mo chridhe (Gaelic)– my heart
mo ghràdh (Gaelic)– my love
peely wally – pale, sickly, or unwell

plaid – a piece of tartan cloth, often gathered around the waist and belted.
radge – uncontrollably angry
Scots ell – the basic unit of length in Sìne's time, equal to 37 inches (941.3 mm).
scrambling –somewhere between hill walking and rock climbing: moving freely over rocky terrain and clambering over rugged ridges
scree – a slope covered with small, loose stones
scunnered – disgusted or annoyed
skunk – marijuana

PRONUNCIATION OF GAELIC NAMES

Sìne – **Shee**na
Doirin – **Door**-in
Maighread – Mer-**aid**
Màiri – **Ma**-rree
Caomhainn – **Koo**-van
Ronain – **Raw**-nan
Ailis – **Ã**-liss

PROLOGUE
DORNACH, SCOTLAND, 1727

The smell is an acrid, nauseating stench, like all the fetid odours I have ever smelled all mixed together into a stew of charcoal and scorched meat. It is like the odour of leather tanned over a flame, so thick and rich in its pungent abhorrence that I can taste it. Though I have not eaten in two days, I fight to keep my stomach from heaving, because I know what this smell is.

It is the burning body of my mother.

They called her Waghorn, Clootie, Auld Mistress Sandie—Witch. As if my gentle mother, a healer by nature and calling, would ever consort with the Devil or cast spells to harm. Naming her thus was an abomination, a mockery of justice for which they had no proof and no wisdom.

They made me watch as they paraded my mother through the town—this sweet, simple woman with no harm in her. Covered in an obscene coat of hot tar and goose feathers, forced to hold tight to the insides of a barrel while two mules pulled her along the muddy path.

WITCH

Mother's eyes widened when she saw me, her daughter, and incomprehensible sounds forced their way out through the gag in her mouth, as if to tear out her throat.

And then my captors yanked at the rope around my neck so I was forced to stumble where they willed. I could only hear the wretched screeches fade away as they dragged Mother to the place of her execution, but I would see that hideous sight for the rest of my life.

Short as it will be...for I am next.

They unbound my hands before thrusting me back into the tiny hut that has served as my jail since the travesty they called a trial, laughing as I stumbled and fell onto the earthen floor. None of my captors will look me in the eye, but they have no trouble hurling taunts and jeers before they turn away and leave me. People I have known all my life, neighbours whom I nursed, to whom I brought soup when they were ill. I watched over their bairns, taught them to read and to write letters.

The villagers had been kind when they needed me. No longer, not since the trial. Now I am untouchable, unclean, a child of Satan. A witch. My mother was Satan's plaything, and I her vile tool.

When Mother began to fail, to stumble in her speech and forget things, our kind neighbours reacted with repugnance and fear. They stopped bringing their bairns for her healing treatment, avoided us in the village, whispered behind our backs. Then they looked at me, and the whispers grew louder and more harsh.

"She bears th' sigil o' th' Devil's own."

"Look at 'er cloven hands 'n feet! Tis 'er mother's fault. She formed 'er own daughter into a beast o' burden."

DORNACH, SCOTLAND, 1727

"They pretend t' heal, but they'll turn our bairns into changelings."

And then the fever found our village. People sickened and died in days. The churchyard was full to overflowing, and grief ran like water through the town. Eyes red with weeping turned toward our cottage, where no one was ill, and tongues wagged like loose shutters in the wind.

My mother tried to help, but her words made less and less sense and our neighbours' faces darkened when she approached. When the son of the village headman was hurt and my mother was found crouching over his body, the whispers turned to roars, and they came for us.

"Witches!" they hissed. "Auld Harry's women. Why ye ken, I saw Mistress only last week, ridin' her daughter like a pony in the dark o' night."

The trial was short, presided over by the village headman himself. There was no hope of reason and no one to stand for us. It was a nightmare of accusation and vitriol that darkened our days and deepened Mother's confusion, and they cleverly pulled words from her that made their case and sealed our fate.

Tomorrow I too will be burned at the stake...alive. Not strangled first, as so many others before me during these times of horror and unrest. I will feel the fire, smell my own hair as it burns. Will I live long enough to see the skin turn black on my hands and arms, or will the smoke act as a merciful saviour, sealing my mouth and nose and stopping my breath before the inferno melts my skin and leaves only bone?

I cannot say I am unafraid, but it matters little now. I deserve this fate. I who was born imperfect,

WITCH

misshapen, marked by the Devil as his own. I am the reason for this monstrous perversion of faith, this deception of righteousness. I am different, so no matter that I have saved others and tried to ease their pain all my life. I am an abomination, cursed by whatever sin they deem fitting.

And now here I stand in my windowless prison, hearing the shouts and jeers that drown out my mother's shrieks. Mercifully for me, for I do not want to know when the screams stop, when the fumes fill her throat and steal her breath. I am a coward. I pray not to recognize the moment my innocent, lovely mother leaves this earth.

She will be with God, of that I have no doubt. There is little mercy in the world, but Heaven will welcome her with open arms. I will know she is safe, because I will not see her where I am going. I know not why the Devil wants me, but Hell is the only place for one who was born to cause her mother's death. I accept it. I have no choice...I have never had a choice.

The smoke drifts under the cracks of my cell and into my eyes. I taste the thickness of it, let it wrap around me as if it is intent upon filling our entire village with its poison. As if the fire itself seeks vengeance for my mother and me.

The voices have died down, and the smoke seems less bitter now. My mother is dead and gone to a better place. The villagers are likely returning to their homes, their lust for killing sated for the moment. They will be back tomorrow, refreshed by the sleep of the righteous, when it is my turn to face the unholy blaze.

My thoughts turn unwittingly to the men who swore they loved me. I think for one agonizing moment of

DORNACH, SCOTLAND, 1727

the one to whom I gave my own love unconditionally. He was not there when the sentence was pronounced. The others were there, but he was the only one who mattered. The one who betrayed me in the end.

A black rage fills what is left of my heart. God has forgotten me, but perhaps some other higher being will listen. I close my eyes and repeat the words of my curse...

CHAPTER 1
BALLACHULISH, SCOTLAND – PRESENT TIME

Death twitches my ear;
'Live,' he says...
'I'm coming.'
—Virgil

Adam MacArthur studied the proofs spread across his desk and wondered why his picture had to be on the damn brochure anyway. Glencoe Mountain Mystery was about the tours, not the tour leader. The mountains were the star of this show.

Daniel had made him pose for two hours yesterday, and these six shots were the result. The photos all looked the same to him—an average lad, perhaps slightly more fit than many his age. As he should be, considering he climbed Munros for a living and ran competitive mountain races for fun. There was nothing in the photographs to show more than a thirty-year-old man in the best shape of his life.

Nothing to show he was dying.

When would it happen...the Big One? Would he be running the trails through Glencoe's mountains, or riding his bike through the valley? Maybe he'd be sitting alone in a coffee shop, enjoying a scone in peace like all the other patrons. People like those he passed in the street every day, unaware that the young man they had just nodded to was a ticking time bomb who might go off at any moment.

It seemed stupid—the running—but his doctor had told him that in his case physical exertion wouldn't hurt him. Wouldn't help, either; it would happen when it happened, whether he exercised or not. His condition was so rare that doctors were baffled as to the cause and sceptical about treatment. "Just do what you're doing," Doctor Marshall had told him. "Enjoy your life."

If it didn't matter whether he was sedentary or active, he'd pick active every time. So he kept his business going, entered races once or twice a year, and hiked as much as possible. He'd had some scares, but so far nothing major. It was coming, though, just a matter of time. The knowledge was always there in the back of his mind like a malevolent ghost.

The condition might be hereditary; at least they thought they knew that much. It seemed to strike males in their twenties. If you had it, you had a one in four chance of passing it to your offspring. His father hadn't had it, nor did any of his brothers; they'd all gotten checked after his first attack two years ago. His uncle Seth had died at age thirty-five, and his grandfather at thirty-two. In his generation, he was the lucky recipient.

BALLACHULISH, SCOTLAND – PRESENT TIME

Everybody in his family knew about the Curse, as he called it. His older sister Iseabail knew, because Izzy knew everything. Of course Ewan's wife Fiona knew; his brother never kept anything from her. Their sister Sophie knew, so probably her boyfriend Brian did. He wondered about his brother Daniel's fiancée, Eve, and sighed. Probably her too.

None of them ever mentioned it, at least in front of him, but he could tell by the looks they gave him if he so much as coughed that it was always lurking in their minds, and he hated it. The idea that they were all pitying him was like acid eating away at his soul. And for some reason, today he was feeling its presence more than usual.

Curiously, his diagnosis had brought the siblings closer than they'd ever been. Not a stretch, that. "Loving family" was a phrase that would never be used to describe the MacArthur clan—at least not since his mother had died when he was nine. His father had checked out emotionally, abandoned his family as surely as if he'd walked out the door, leaving six children to rattle around the dark old house on Ardconnel that had once been a home.

He and Ewan had managed to stick together, likely because of their shared interest in the mountains and climbing. He hadn't seen Jonah in over a year. Despite being only a year apart in age, they had little in common. In truth they were more like polite strangers than brothers.

He'd had little to do with his troubled brother Daniel, four years his junior, until a year and a half ago when he showed up in Glencoe, met Eve in the local cafe, and stayed. Now Dan was the photographer for Adam's company, Glencoe Mountain Mystery, and it seemed as if they'd never been estranged. Life was like that sometimes.

The bell to the outer office jangled and Adam looked up to greet his brother, halfway through the door and struggling to juggle photography equipment and the case in which he kept his drone.

Daniel looked up. "A little help?"

"Why don't you just leave all that stuff here?" Adam asked as he grabbed the tripod case. "You'll pull a ligament hauling it all back and forth from Glencoe to Ballachulish every day."

Daniel grinned at him. "Well, I would, except this isn't the only place I go. And I don't just take pictures of mountains, y' know. I can't afford to duplicate all the equipment, so back and forth it goes." He offloaded his equipment to the worktable and threw himself into a chair. "Usually Jared's here to help. When's he getting back?"

"End of the week," Adam told him. "You know he's helping his uncle with some woodworking project, and it's taking longer than he thought. Said the old man's hopeless with tools and likely to cut off a hand if someone's not there to stop him. I'll be glad when he's back, though; running this business is rubbish without him. He's a wonder when it comes to marketing, and his computer skills are on another level. Shoulda been a hacker."

"Well, I'm glad we have him," Daniel said. "That lad's pure magic with a keyboard."

"Like you are with a camera," Adam said. He picked up the Canon DSLR from the table and thumbed through Daniel's recent shots. "Ahh, yes. Magic. Eve reading. Eve cooking. You and Eve...never mind that one. Hey, here's one of a mountain. Oh look—isn't that Eve climbing it?"

"Shut up," his younger brother said mildly. "She photographs well."

"Doesn't she get tired of you following her around like a paparazzo?" Adam asked. "I mean, I could never figure out what she sees in you anyway..." He managed to dodge a magazine winged at his head with admirable accuracy and laughed. "All right, I'll quit."

Daniel stood, grabbed his camera from his brother, and placed it carefully back on the table.

"So, what's on for today?"

Adam consulted his laptop. "There's a group of German botanists at ten, then some college lads from Nova Scotia at half one. That's probably the group Brian got in for us. I think I like him; a Canadian brother-in-law might be good for business." He fixed his brother with a gimlet eye. "Our company is being helped by the additions to our family," he said. He pasted a smirk on his face. "And speaking of additions..."

Daniel put his hands up in a warding gesture. "Whoa, not yet! It'll happen, trust me," Daniel told him. "We have time. We're not old fogeys like you." It was his turn to duck the pen that came flying over the desk. He went on as if nothing had interrupted. "When are you going to find your own Mrs. Right?"

The silence that fell in the room spoke volumes. "I'm sorry, Adam," his brother said. "I didn't mean to..."

"Stop *doing* that!" Adam spat the words. "I hate it when you all creep around me like cats." He softened his glare. "No, *I'm* sorry—it's fine. We all know there's no Mrs. Right in my future, so let's just leave it at that, aye?" He went back to the computer and tapped the keys until he could sense that Daniel had looked away.

Without taking his eyes from the screen, Adam said, "I'm thinking of getting a dog."

"What kind of dog?"

"A dog to run with. Look." He turned the computer to face his brother. "A retriever or a border collie. I'll run up to Inverness this weekend and check out the SPCA; stop in and see Ewan and Sophie. I haven't been home in a while. Want to come?"

Daniel shook his head. "Not this time. Eve has a job interview at the West Highlands Museum Saturday, and I'm going for support...you know, to hold her hand."

Adam snorted. "Don't you do that enough already?"

"Haud yer wheesht," Daniel said. "It's not worth talking to you about anything except mountains. This is the job she's been hoping for. She's mad about the history of this area and knows more about Glencoe than just about anyone else. She'll get the job—I'd bet on it, but she's that nervous."

The pride in his brother's voice had a smile crawling onto Adam's face, one that died just as quickly. He fought it, but it was hard sometimes not to give in to self-pity. *What would it be like to have someone you cared about more than yourself? Someone to plan a future with, to build a family?*

BALLACHULISH, SCOTLAND – PRESENT TIME

That wasn't in the cards for him. Even if he found someone who wouldn't mind if her husband had an expiration date stamped on his heart, he couldn't imagine one who would be willing to abandon the idea of having children. Women liked children—little lads and lassies to run around the house.

And he couldn't take that risk. He wouldn't sentence a tiny human being to a life with limits. Nope—a dog would have to do. He forced his attention back to the conversation.

"Is the position full time?" he asked. "Will Eve have to give up her job at the bookshop?"

"I don't know," his brother said. "The museum job is full time, but she loves the shop and all the crazy people there. She'd have to cut way back on her hours, but hopefully the museum would work with her on that." He laughed. "How 'bout we get her the job first, eh?"

"Oh, she'll get it," Adam assured him. "As you say, she's a walking history book on Glencoe. I guess we'll have to look for a new scheduler, though."

"Don't be surprised if she still manages to do some of that, too," his brother said. "She's a working fool, that one." Somehow, he made the word 'fool' sound like a term of endearment.

Adam snapped his fingers. "I forgot I have to go to the shop later. I want a book on dog breeds. I'll say hi to Eve while I'm there—oh. Is this interview a secret or can I wish her good luck?"

"Not a secret. She can use all the good luck she can get, aye?" Daniel gestured at the laptop screen. "You really want a dog?"

13

"I think so," Adam said. "I've been looking online, and apparently mixed-breed dogs make some of the best mates, so I'll start there. I want one that's a good runner, especially in rough terrain like ours. I figured I'd study a few breeds of running dogs and then look for a mix that blends the best characteristics. Adoption is all done online now. Once I pick a dog from their website, they'll set up a meet and greet at the centre."

"Well, good luck," his brother said. "Looking forward to meeting your new partner. I'll see if I can think up some valiant names for him. Angus or Brutus, or how about Crusher?"

As Adam parked in the car park off the High Street in Fort William that afternoon, his mind went over the names his brother had thrown out. Crusher wasn't half bad, but his dog needed a name that sounded fast, not fierce. Strider, or Sonic, or something Gaelic, like...*Cù beinne*. Mountain Dog. Simple, had a ring to it. Perfect name for a beast that ruled his domain. He could almost visualize the two of them running the Glencoe mountain trails. Adam hurried down the High Street, suddenly eager to learn more about his dog.

The woman at the front desk of the bookshop was someone he'd never seen before, but he hadn't been here in months. A lot seemed to have changed. He studied the person in front of him. Tiny, dressed incongruously in a brown gown and a checked arasaid, like the garments worn in the eighteenth century. She cocked her head to the side and regarded him with bright black eyes that reminded him of a small bird.

BALLACHULISH, SCOTLAND – PRESENT TIME

"Hullo, lad," she said. "Would ye be lookin' fer the Animals 'an Pets section, then?"

Adam blinked. "Umm...yes. I'm looking for a book on dogs as running companions. But...how did you guess?"

The woman's eyes crinkled. "I didnae guess, ye wee numpty. A good bookshop owner knows what 'is customer needs, aye?" She pointed to the back of the shop. "Last row on th' left, two aisles down. Off ye go."

Adam found himself grinning as he followed the directions to the back of the store. On his way, he noted another woman dressed in eighteenth-century costume, bright red curls springing from a white cap. She was talking to the tallest man he'd ever seen. The giant was dressed in the Great Kilt, the long sash thrown over one shoulder and fastened by an antique filigree badge. Not any tartan he recognized, but he wasn't an authority on the clans. If he were a movie director, he'd be casting that one as William Wallace or the Bruce.

Adam watched the man reach to put a book on the top shelf without the aid of a ladder. *Useful sort of lad to have in a bookshop,* he thought. *But why are they dressed in period costume?* Must be a new marketing scheme. Jared would probably approve.

He spied the section he wanted tucked into a corner in the back, and a few minutes later emerged with two books on dog breeds. He made his way back to the front desk, now manned by the plump red-haired woman.

"Find what ye need, lad?" she asked. Adam nodded and paid for his books, and then spied Eve arranging books on a table. She waved at him and he started in her direction—and froze. Standing next to her, obviously another employee judging by the period costume, was the most beautiful woman he'd ever seen.

Black curls framed a pale face with eyes as blue as the sky on a rare sunny day. She smiled at something Eve said and a dimple appeared in the corner of her mouth. Somehow the eighteenth-century attire suited her better than anything the modern era could produce. All the air left his lungs, and he gasped for breath.

Suddenly he realized what was happening. His throat closed; heat filled his lungs and moved toward his heart. It was as if he were fighting to get out of a burning building, struggling against the smoke that wrapped around his chest. Eve and the beautiful girl faded from his sight. His knees buckled and he sagged against a table and then folded to the floor, taking a stack of books with him.

In the distance he could hear voices calling out, footsteps running toward him. He tried to speak, to tell them it was no use. He knew his own body, and nothing anyone could do would help this time. This was the moment he'd been dreading for two years. The Big One. He closed his eyes and waited.

Soft hands cupped his face, fingers pulled at an eyelid. They moved down to his chest and stayed there. Adam opened his eyes, surprised he could do that much, and gazed into the blue eyes of the beautiful woman he'd seen across the bookshop. *Ahh*, he thought. *You're here. You found me. Isn't that the way it goes?* He smiled at her, closed his eyes again, and everything drifted away.

CHAPTER 2
FORT WILLIAM, SCOTLAND – PRESENT TIME

*All encounters in life are reunions
after a long time apart.*
—Bai Luomei

"Miss MacLachlan? Miss MacLachlan?"
Màiri froze, then fixed a smile on her face and turned slowly around to face the three young lads arrayed in front of her.

"It's the Three Musketeers, third time this week," Eve whispered behind her. "Seriously, that's what they call themselves. And I think somebody's got a crush, eh?"

"Shut it," Màiri hissed between her teeth. Her colleague backed away, but not before Màiri heard stifled laughter. She squared her shoulders.

"Hullo, lads, what can I do for you today?" She studied their eager faces. "Let me guess… You" — she pointed to the tallest of the three, a lanky young lad with shoulder-length sandy hair —"your name's Bastian, aye? And you want another book on swords.

And you"—she transferred her gaze to the one currently trying to brush the brown curls out of his eyes— "Donnie? You're just dying to read another biography of William Wallace. And you—"

The third lad, a thin boy with bright red hair and tortoise-shell glasses that made his blue eyes seem huge, pushed his way between the other two. "It's Cory, miss." There was a slight waver to his voice. "I want a book on firefighting." He stood up straighter. "I'm going to be one, you know—a firefighter. Who knows, someday I might save you from a fire!" His friends snickered, and the lad's face flushed to match his hair.

Màiri decided to take pity on the lad. After all, he did buy books. Besides, it wasn't the first time someone had developed a crush on her, although they usually weren't this young. She gave the three her best smile.

"How old are you lads?" she asked them.

Bastian, apparently the leader, spoke up. "Donnie and me are sixteen." He pointed at the red-head and smirked. "Wee Cory's only fifteen."

Màiri registered the angry flush that deepened the younger lad's already red face. "Donnie and I," she said in a crisp voice. "If you hang out in a bookshop so often, you ought to know that much, aye?"

It was Bastian's turn to flush. "Aye, ma'am," he said.

Màiri reached out and gave his arm a pat to show she was only teasing. "Well, you lads go find what you need. You know where everything is." She shooed them away from the table where she and Eve had been arranging the current bestsellers.

FORT WILLIAM, SCOTLAND – PRESENT TIME

"That Cory's in love," Eve said under her breath. "And I'm pretty sure the other two aren't far behind, even though they'd never admit it."

"Why me, though?" Màiri moaned. "I mean, you're gorgeous. Why don't they sniff around you?"

"Two reasons," her friend told her. She held up the hand that sported a diamond ring. "First, Daniel was here the first time those lads came in, and he has a very definite 'hands off' air about him." Eve laughed at the memory. "He gave them his best side-eye, and they backed right off."

"Hmmm," Màiri said. "You have a point there. And the other reason?"

"Well..." She studied her friend. "As a woman and therefore a reasonably objective source, I think part of the reason men swarm to you is your hair. It's a dark halo around your head, like a floating cloud. People pay lots of money for those curls you have naturally, and the rest of us straight-haired lassies just have to make the most of what we have." She smoothed her own sleek dark bob. "Put together with those bluer than blue eyes, you look like a goddess from the front cover of a romance novel—and then there's the gown."

Màiri opened her mouth to protest, and Eve grinned. "I know we all wear the costume, but in that eighteenth-century dress you look just like a Highland village lass who stepped out of the past, innocent and in need of protection. And all men need to protect, even bairns like those lads."

Màiri snorted and rolled her eyes, but she had to admit there was some truth in what Eve said. It seemed that ever since the new owners had taken over the bookshop and dictated that the employees should wear costumes from the eighteenth century as uniforms, more men seemed to be stopping in to browse. What was it about women in old-fashioned gowns? Maybe because less and less was worn these days, the mystery of a woman covered head to toe was what turned men on.

Màiri looked around the shop, marvelling at how much it had changed in just a few weeks. She'd worked here since high school, when the shop was called *High Street Books*, and had never laid eyes on the previous owners. They were some big outfit out of Edinburgh that ran four or five bookshops in Scotland, all with the same footprint. Tastefully decorated, very modern...rather boring.

She remembered stopping in at the store in Perth once, and it was exactly like this one. The same beige carpeting, the same IKEA-style bookshelves. A big central island with three or four cashiers in identical navy-blue polo shirts and khakis. Recessed fluorescent lighting. Useful and energy-conservant, maybe, but not very exciting.

Màiri had spent a lot of time dreaming back then about what she would do if the bookshop were hers. Then just recently it was sold to a couple named Duncan, and almost overnight it changed. The sign now read *HP Booksellers*, rendered in a filigreed Celtic font. The carpeting had been ripped out and distressed-looking wooden flooring put in. Tartan area rugs were placed artfully to look as if they'd been strewn about, and the shelves were a dark,

FORT WILLIAM, SCOTLAND – PRESENT TIME

pitted hardwood with ornate moulding that looked ancient and probably cost a fortune.

Comfortable brown leather armchairs graced every area, looking as if they'd been there forever, next to antique side tables with bronze reading lamps.

"Folks sh'd git t' ken a book before they take it home," the owner's wife told the employees in her heavy brogue. "A book isnae jist paper an' a cover, it's a companion."

The merchandise was different too. Now, along with the current best-sellers, Scottish travel guides, and modern books on Highland history, the shop boasted a large selection of used and rare books. A small cafe in the back of the shop sold espresso, scones, and shortbread, under the sign *HP Sweets*.

Màiri had no idea what HP stood for. The Duncans were a husband and wife named Mary and Henry, and they didn't seem inclined to share the secret. They dressed like eighteenth-century reenactors and brought others with them—a plump, cheerful, red-haired woman named Betty who seemed always to be smiling, a huge russet-haired giant of a man who wore a well-worn great kilt that looked as if he slept in it...and a small black cat. The giant was ridiculously called Wee Caomhainn, and the cat answered to Biscuit, when it answered at all.

Another thing these HP people brought was an aura of mystery that sent a shiver of delight through Màiri's romantic soul. It was as if they'd picked her brain, found all the touches she'd dreamed of, and put them into the shop. When they asked the employees to wear costumes like theirs for work, she was over the moon.

"Books 're timeless," the owner's wife told them. A tiny, brown-haired woman with bright black eyes like a curious bird's, she winked as she passed out the paperwork for their measurements. "Bookshops should be th' same, aye?"

They all talked like that, as if they'd sprung from deep in the Highlands somewhere...or some*when*. As if they'd time-travelled from the eighteenth century complete with kilts, arasaids, and a strangely modern business sense.

They handed out cards with the shop's name on them and the words, *Books are a door to the past and the future...where will you go?* On the reverse side was another quote: *The world is full of magic things, patiently waiting for our senses to grow sharper. W.B. Yeats.*

A couple of the employees had quit, muttering that they weren't going to dress like circus clowns for any job, but most had stayed. They put on the gowns, great kilts and homespun trews, and tried to thicken their brogues. It became a sort of contest, to see who could sound the most authentic.

Màiri spotted the three teenagers making their way toward her, each with a book in hand, and decided she'd had enough of their awkward courtship for one day. She whispered to Eve to take over and slid away toward the stockroom in the back of the shop.

The door swung shut and she was alone in the silent space. The smell of cardboard mingled with the musty odour of old books, giving the place a

FORT WILLIAM, SCOTLAND – PRESENT TIME

sense of ancient mystery. It was where she came to think, to plan, to escape the loneliness that never left her side.

Oh, don't be so maudlin! You're not technically alone. Stop whinging.

It was true. She had friends, and parents who loved her almost as much as they hated each other. And she had her beloved gran, who had taken over the raising of a confused three-year-old after Mum and Dad divorced. She had a job that surrounded her with books, and even if she sensed there was more out there she could be doing with her life, she was content.

Dad now lived in Germany with his new family, and her mother spent most of her time in Australia, studying the environmental impact on sea lion populations. Both of them were much happier apart than they'd ever been together. They didn't visit often and always seemed eager to leave. Her parents were generous with their money, as long as they weren't expected to stay in Scotland for any length of time, and Màiri and Gran were perfectly happy with the arrangement.

When Gran's memory began failing six years ago, Màiri hadn't told her parents. She knew she was in denial, but it had always been just the two of them against the world, and she was desperate to keep things the way they'd always been as long as possible. The Alzheimer's diagnosis had been devastating to them both, but they'd managed, until Gran began wandering away and forgetting her way home.

Twice she'd been found by the police and brought back, accompanied by a stern lecture on responsibility, and finally Màiri knew it was time to seek professional help. She'd settled on Highland Hospice, a lovely facility along the river in Inverness, because the carers treated Gran with respect and listened to her ramblings as if she made perfect sense.

It wasn't until she'd come back to the huge family home and heard the echoes whisper through the empty hallways that the realization sank in. She was truly alone. With her parents' agreement, she sold the house and moved into a tiny rooftop flat, where Gran's tales of fairies, witches and kelpies didn't live in the walls and whisper through the air.

Màiri looked at her watch. Wallowing wasn't healthy, and self-pity wasn't her nature. She opened the stockroom door and peeked to make sure the three young Romeos were nowhere in sight, then returned to the table where she'd been arranging new books to find that Eve had nearly finished the job. Guilt washed through her.

"Sorry, sweetie," she said. "I'll treat you to lunch."

The bell above the shop's door jangled. A man entered and walked toward the counter where Mary Duncan stood. Màiri watched as Mary launched into her spiel and smiled to herself at the man's delighted reaction to something the tiny woman said in her thick brogue.

She has a gift, that one. Almost like magic.

As if she sensed Màiri's thoughts, Mary looked up and smiled. She turned back to her customer and waved a hand toward the back corner where the books on animals and pets were shelved. The young man grinned again at the owner and went on his way with a light step.

FORT WILLIAM, SCOTLAND – PRESENT TIME

A few minutes later he emerged with two books and started toward the checkout counter again. He glanced around the shop until he saw Eve and veered toward their table. Then his eyes met Màiri's and widened.

Do I know him? she wondered. She didn't think she'd ever seen him before. Apparently he knew Eve, so maybe he was a friend of Daniel's. But why the look of shocked surprise?

Suddenly the man stopped in his tracks and a look of pain crossed his face. He clutched at his chest and seemed to be fighting for breath. Before Màiri's horrified eyes, his knees folded and he grabbed for the edge of a table, and then almost in slow motion he sank to the floor, taking a stack of books with him.

Màiri didn't stop to think. "Call 999!" she shouted at Eve. She raced across the small space and crouched next to the motionless man on the floor. She put two fingers to his throat and felt for a pulse. Nothing. She tilted his head the way she'd seen rescuers do on the telly, opened his mouth and felt for an obstruction. She pulled one eyelid up. His pupil was fixed, no contraction against the overhead lights. Panic exploded in her brain. *Is he dead?* She moved her hand down to his chest and rested it on his shirt. Nothing... No, his chest was rising against her fingertips. He was breathing.

Why are you doing this? her inner voice asked her. *You're not a doctor—you've never even taken a first-aid course!* She pushed the voice to the back of her mind. Self-doubt wasn't what was needed here. "Eve, go get a blanket or a coat!"

WITCH

The man opened his eyes. They were all the shades of brown—chocolate and walnut and peat—under long dark lashes. The shadow of a smile crossed his face, and then he closed his eyes again.

Màiri's mind stilled. She took his hand and waited with him as the sound of the sirens grew nearer. Somehow, she knew he'd be all right, that whatever the reason for his collapse, this wasn't his time.

This! her inner voice told her. *This is what you're meant to do.*

Màiri's hand tightened around that of the unconscious man beside her. *Thank you,* she breathed. *Whoever you are, thank you for being alive.*

CHAPTER 3
GLEN COE, SCOTLAND
– PRESENT TIME

A great fire burns within me, but no one stops to warm themselves at it, and passers-by see only a wisp of smoke.
—Vincent van Gogh

The fire was like a snake, flickering its yellow tongue as it grew. It worked its way through the small pile of twigs the lad had built for it, leaving charred black stumps. As the small fire moved on to the larger logs and became a raging blaze, it spawned more tongues—hissing in fury, insatiable in their need to destroy.

The wooden kindling crackled as it broke apart and died, forgotten under the conflagration. The fire leapt higher, sucking the air into its embrace. It was glorious. It was power, and he had made it.

The man stared into the fire, remembering the first time he had felt this power...

This kinship with fire had started when he was five years old. Sitting before the fireplace in his home, he watched the flames undulate as if they were alive, watched them char the strong wood his father had laid just moments before until it turned into ash. A cinder had escaped onto the hearth and lay there, sizzling angrily, and the boy felt a strange compulsion to save it, to return it to its rightful place.

He reached for the tiny bit of wood and it reacted with fury, spitting and hissing and burning his fingers before it turned dull and lay, still and dead, on the rug. But before it died it left its mark, a defiant black ring on his mother's prized carpet. And the boy knew that within this tiny ember was the secret of power, if only he could decipher it.

He began to pay attention—to the pilot light on the AGA, the small flame on the water heater, to any appliance that owed its life to fire. He didn't try to touch it; he remembered the pain of his burned fingers and knew that fire demanded respect.

In school he read about the Celtic gods and goddesses and his favourite was Belenus, the god of fire. The book said he was associated with healing, but the book was wrong. Belenus was greater than that. Why else did his followers light fires to honour him, say prayers in his name, and even offer sacrifices? That was much more powerful than healing.

Belenus should be honoured properly. A god deserved much more than small, secret fires in the woods. He needed a leader here on earth. Someone to bring others into his sacred circle, to teach them the ways of the fire god. And to punish—to destroy when necessary.

He would be that leader, but before he could do that, he had to begin at the bottom like any acolyte. He must master the art of fire-building. He found a secluded spot in the woods and practiced what he'd learned from the Boy Scout Handbook. He gathered small sticks for tinder and built a little tower. He added wood shavings and paper and then used the lighter he'd stolen from his mother's handbag to light his tiny offering.

The result was a tiny flame that burned along the edges of the tower of sticks, moving upward until it overwhelmed the small stash of kindling and sent tongues of flame into the air. The crackling sounded like laughter. Or maybe it was his own joy, freed by the knowledge that he had created something so beautiful.

He experimented with flint, rods, and strikers until he could start a fire without matches or lighter in any weather. His fires grew larger, more brilliant, stronger. Belenus was watching, and he approved.

At the end of every ritual the lad would spread his arms wide and pretend to embrace his fire, like in the images he'd seen of Belenus in a book in the school library. His favourite showed the god standing in a raging inferno, his hair and beard engulfed in flame. The god's arms were stretched wide, as if he wanted to wrap them around the entire earth. The boy had ripped out the page and taped it up on the wall of his bedroom, and every night he prayed to it before he went to sleep.

He never told anyone about his secret practice. They wouldn't understand. They'd think he was radge and shun him, and he needed them, even the stupid ones. *Especially* the stupid ones. They were the ones who would do the work.

He looked deep into the flames, and they answered him. They crackled and snapped at him, acknowledging him as Belenus' disciple. They were celebrating because he was the one who would set their creator free.

He knew why he'd been chosen for this honour. It was simple: he had the ability. He was popular, good-looking and friendly, and he'd discovered early on that he was adept at convincing people to do what he asked. Other lads wanted to hang with him, and lassies followed him around like midges. The teachers told his parents he was a born leader.

"He'll be on council one day," his history teacher said. "Mark my words, that lad will make something of himself. Look how he's revived Guy Fawkes Night and made it a neighbourhood celebration like it used to be."

Guy Fawkes Night marked another kind of victory. It was the first time he tried his power on a lass. She was in his class at academy, and her eyes lit when he invited her to the village bonfire. He stared into the flames and watched the effigy burn, while everyone else chanted, "Remember, remember, the fifth of November." He knew the lass was staring at him but he pretended not to see. Then, when the fire was at its zenith, he placed his hand on her arm and gave her the shy smile he had practiced before the mirror at home.

GLEN COE, SCOTLAND – PRESENT TIME

"Let's get away from all these people, aye?"

Without a word she let him take her hand and lead her out of the circle cast by the flames, and in the grass by the edge of the trees he discovered a new sort of power.

It was her first time, and his. He felt the power surge within him and knew he could do anything he wanted with her. The knowledge was magical. When it was over, he led her back to the bonfire and left her there. He never sought her out again, despite her sad eyes and pleading glances. She'd played her part, and he was grateful.

It was so easy, this binding of human will. As he grew older, he became more adept at seduction of both men and women. People were so easy to manipulate. A word here, an expression there, and he had them in the palm of his hand. The trick was to let them think he was just one of them. He was good at dissembling. The hardest work was to keep his contempt hidden.

His teachers tried to steer him into politics or the law, but he was adamant. "I want to work with fire," he told them.

"Oh, you want to be a firefighter—that's wonderful," they said. And he let them think so, because he needed them to believe.

He made his first sacrifice to Belenus when he was sixteen. His neighbour's old cat was sunning itself in a patch of sunshine behind the woodshed when he crept up on it, wrung its neck, and stuffed it into a sack. He carried his offering over his shoulder into the woods, to the new fire pit he'd readied, and built his pyre carefully, knowing that his god required concentration and care.

When the fire was blazing, he picked up the sack and held it high in the air. "*Tha mi a 'toirt urram dhut, Belenus!*" he chanted. "I honour thee, Belenus!" He'd looked up the translation online, and it sounded so much more impressive in Gaelic. The fire understood the auld tongue. It seemed to blaze higher in recognition of the boy's tribute.

He heaved the sack into the greedy flames and felt a surge of power as it caught and was consumed almost immediately. He watched until the fire died down to embers, and then made his way home, satiated for a while. He said his evening prayer and slept like a baby. He didn't dream—dreams were for the weak.

It was lonely, being the only worshiper, but that would change someday, and for now he was content. Belenus was right here with him, every time he lit a fire. A god could be patient, because time was nothing to him. Still, the lad could sense a growing eagerness every time he lit a fire.

By the time the boy reached the end of his school years, he'd decided two things: it was time to stop making small sacrifices, and he was ready to begin his real work. He briefly considered becoming a forest ranger but eliminated that almost immediately. Preventing fires was counterproductive and an insult to his god. Besides, it was a solitary job, and he liked people. He wanted to work among them. They were useful.

A career counsellor visited the academy and interviewed the graduating class. When she asked about his interests, he decided to be honest. "I like fire."

GLEN COE, SCOTLAND – PRESENT TIME

"Oh, you want to be a firefighter? That's a great career," she said, beaming.

I don't want to fight fires, I want to light them, he'd thought irritably. But he knew of no real jobs that required starting fires, so he kept the thought to himself. He nodded and smiled and allowed her to sign him up for a visit to the local fire station with a few of his classmates.

The station was a new world. There were huge fire appliances on site, with ladders and hoses and protective equipment. The firefighters told stories of harrowing trips into burning buildings and rescuing people from second storey windows. Best of all, there were the dangers of flammable liquids and explosive substances. Firefighters were the ones who entered a burning building and tried to put out the flames.

Being *expected* to enter a fire! There was so much possibility here. He would be close to fire every day. He looked around at the rapt faces of his classmates and a slow smile spread over his face. He doubted they were thinking along the same lines as he was, at least not most of them. They were sheep, mollified by promises of honour and adventure and glory.

But perhaps someone else was there for the same reason he was. He would find that person and befriend him. Then when he was ready, they could recruit others and begin their real task. He'd be working with people who worshipped fire, as he did. People who would be honoured to walk into the flames of Belenus.

He signed up for the training, and three years later stood with his peers to receive his Scottish

Vocational Qualification and his Apprenticeship in Fire and Rescue. He had found an apprentice, one man out of all those who'd trained with him. He'd found others outside the fire station: angry men who were dissatisfied with their jobs and yearned for more. They didn't know it yet, but they were going to be heroes.

With him, they made thirteen—a magic number. It was nearly time...

The man pulled his attention back to the inferno he'd created. He looked around the circle and saw the results of all the training, the practice, the pandering to lesser beings. He was no longer alone—thirteen men stood around the raging fire, chanting to Belenus, the god of fire. It had been worth every minute of the long journey, and it was only beginning.

He felt a stirring of something, a pull toward something bigger than this. It was not enough to build fires in the woods. If Belenus was to reclaim his position in the universe, it was up to his disciples to show the way, to strike fear into the hearts of weaker men and bring them to their knees. And there was only one way they could accomplish the task with the proper honour, to cleanse the world of its arrogance and pride.

That way was fire.

CHAPTER 4
ABERDEENSHIRE, SCOTLAND, 1705

DOIRIN

There was something not right with Lady Emily. Doirin studied her employer, trying not to be obvious. Her ladyship's complexion was usually ruddy, something she took great pains to conceal. Doirin should know; it took her more than an hour each day to apply the layers of blanc across Lady Emily's face and shoulders, and then the rouge that must be painted in a perfect circle on her cheekbones. Distilled alcohol was rubbed over the lips to redden them, and then the eyebrows were plucked carefully into a half-moon shape and darkened with kohl. The same routine, every day for the last ten years. No one knew Lady Emily Gordon better than her trusted maid.

Doirin Gilchrist had come to The Pillars when she was eighteen. There had been no suitors and no prospects in sight, and when Doirin's parents heard that Lady Gordon was looking for a maid after the death of her ancient nanny, they saw an opportunity to rid themselves of an unmarriageable mouth to feed. They told Doirin that the best thing for a clever girl like her was a position.

"Gilchrist means 'servant of Christ'," her mother told her. "Which means He expects you to serve." So off she went. She had never looked back.

Lady Emily Gordon was kind, with an engaging sense of humour and a quick wit. The two had developed a bond that was more friendship than employer to employee, despite the difference in age and class. Still, Doirin was under no illusion that they were equal. She dressed Emily, helped her bathe, read to her, and personally selected the ingredients for her meals. They were closer in some ways than sisters, and Doirin had developed a second sense where her lady was concerned.

"Are ye feelin' quite well, m'lady?" she asked as she pulled the nightgown down over her ladyship's ample frame. "Ye seem sommat pale."

"That's the idea, isn't it?" Lady Emily said. "Dinnae ye work hard t' make me pale?"

"Aye, but ye're no wearin' paint now, an ye're still pale." Doirin cocked her head and studied her employer. "Tell it true now, ye're no feelin' well, are ye?"

Emily sighed. "I cannae fool ye, can I?" She frowned. "I am feeling a bit poorly, if truth be told." She sighed again. "I suppose ye better call the doctor."

Doirin felt a shiver of apprehension slide up her spine. Lady Emily hated illness, thought it was a

ABERDEENSHIRE, SCOTLAND, 1705

sign of weakness. If she was willing to see a doctor, things were worse than she'd thought. She eyed her employer, but Lady Emily's eyes skittered away from hers. Doirin tucked her into bed and hurried out to summon the family physician.

An hour later, the doctor came out of the room, his expression dour, and closed himself into the study with Lord Robert. Doirin crept to the door and shamelessly put her ear against the wood panel.

"Tis her heart," she heard him say. "Ye need t' get yerself ready."

She couldn't hear what his lordship said, but the doctor's next words were like a knife to her own heart.

"I'll give ye some pills, bit they're just for show. Keep 'er comfitable; it willnae be long."

Doirin fled from the hall to the kitchen, where she made herself a strong cup of tea and sat staring at the fire. No! she thought. *I'm no ready t' say guid-bye!* The familiar loneliness washed through her, and she gave in to self-pity and cried silently until her tears were spent. Then she washed the cup and put it back on the rack, walked out into the hallway, and paced up and down for most of an hour, thinking about what life would be without Lady Emily Gordon to take care of.

Something stirred in Doirin's soul. As if propelled by an unseen force, her feet took her back up to the darkened bedroom, where she stood for some time gazing at the woman from across the room. Very quietly she approached the bed and peeled back the coverlet. She stood watching the woman's chest

37

rising and falling, listened to the slightly laboured breathing...and then it stopped.

She placed a hand on Emily's chest. "Milady?" she whispered. "Lady Emily? Breathe. Please breathe!"

Her lady's chest remained still.

"Please," she repeated, tears coming to her eyes. "Breathe!" She looked to the heavens. "God, please... let her breathe!"

But her prayers went unanswered. Grief surged through her body, and she stared in helpless misery, unable to move. Slowly a picture formed in her mind. A bluish tinge appeared around the edges of Doirin's hand, glowing through Lady Emily's nightclothes right where her heart would be.

It was cold...painfully so, but she held her hand in place and slowly the sensation dissipated. The colour changed to a soft pink, and warmth surrounded her hand. She listened. *Was Emily's chest rising?* Suddenly frightened, Doirin backed away, wondering what had just happened. Surely not...

But the next morning, Lady Emily rang for Doirin, just as she always did. Her colour was back to a ruddy glow and her eyes bright with health. When the doctor came to check on her, he came out of the room slowly, his brow furrowed. He closed himself in with Lord Robert again, and within hours the rumour began to circulate that some sort of miracle had taken place last night.

Doirin told no one of her nighttime foray into Lady Emily's sickroom. She didn't understand it herself, but she never forgot the sensation of cold, how it had warmed under her hand and turned pink.

ABERDEENSHIRE, SCOTLAND, 1705

Servant of Christ, came her mother's voice from the past. *Is that what I am? Has God called me to be his servant...to heal?*

As the days became weeks and weeks turned into months, the rumours died as rumours do. Life went on as usual in the Gordon household, and Doirin began to see the odd happenings of that night as a figment of her imagination. Surely Lady Emily hadn't really been dead; surely she hadn't gotten well because of *her*. The doctor was simply mistaken. Why on earth would God, with all the people in the world to choose from, settle on a mere lady's maid as His servant? It was beyond ridiculous, best forgotten.

"Doirin?" Lady Emily's voice broke into her reverie. "What's goin' on in that head o' yours? Didnae ye hear me speakin'?"

"So sorry, m'lady." Doirin forced her mind back to the moment.

"I said, I've a fancy for some fish t'night. See if ye cannae find a nice cod at th' market, aye?"

Doirin loved the market. The noise, the smells, the colours—all of it called to her heart. Shouts of the costermongers, with their melodic chants and singsong poetry extolling the merits of their vegetables, warred with the excited chatter of villagers catching up on news and gossip. Occasionally a fight broke out between women intent on seizing the best turnips or the largest tatties, and curses flowed without regard for the opinions of the other marketgoers.

The smell of roasting meat vied with the enticing scent of baked goods, but Doirin ignored it and

WITCH

followed her nose until the odour of fish told her she had reached her goal.

"Tell me, pretty lass, whit I can dae fer ye on this lovely mornin'?" came a voice in her ear, and she turned to find a man standing next to her. His broad shoulders and sunburnt complexion told her, more than the catch arrayed behind him did, that he was a fisherman. A fisher-*man*, and one who was standing uncomfortably close.

Doirin backed a step away and tried to put on her sternest face—the one she used when the younger maids skimped on the ironing of her ladyship's gowns—but it seemed suddenly as if there was something seriously wrong with her knees. She smiled weakly at the man and received a radiant smile in return that melted her heart into a puddle of treacle.

He waited patiently while she studied him. Wild black curls flew about his head as if they had a will of their own. A week's worth of growth did nothing to hide the chiselled face and perfect cheekbones.

But it was his eyes that held her in place like a rabbit facing a fox. A man had no right to have eyes bluer than the North Sea in summer, and those eyes had no business doing what they were doing to her stomach.

It was he who broke the silence. "Ye are so beautiful." He said it seriously, even though she knew it to be false. She wasn't beautiful, and she knew it. Plain brown hair, large brown eyes, tall for a woman; she was no one's idea of a dainty, desirable young lady. But one look into those eyes, one smile from that beautiful mouth, and she was ready to believe.

ABERDEENSHIRE, SCOTLAND, 1705

He swept off his bonnet and executed a courtly bow, to the delight of those passing by. "Cormac Jamieson, m'lady. Will ye nae gie me yer name?"

"D-Doirin Gil-christ." The words were hers. She heard them stumbling from her mouth, but she was helpless to stop them. She should be telling him in no uncertain terms to step away, to leave her alone. But here she was, giving a stranger—a *man*—her name!

An hour later, Doirin drifted between the huge round pillars that had given the Gordon's house its name, clutching a brown paper bundle in which nestled a large cod. Drifted, because her feet had not touched the ground since she'd met Cormac Jamieson.

He was indeed a fisherman. He went out every day in his dory and delivered the best of his catch to the market. From now on, he had whispered into her ear, he would be looking for a certain bonny brown-haired lass who had stolen his heart the first time he saw her, and he hoped she would be there to greet him.

From the mush her brain had become, Doirin pulled out one sure truth. The Gordons would be eating a lot of fish from this day on.

CHAPTER 5
DORNACH, SCOTLAND, 1707

DOIRIN

oirin Gilchrist put a hand to her back and straightened from the vegetable bed with difficulty.

"She'll be born today," she told the beans. They swung on their vines and ignored her, as if the birth of a daughter was nothing remarkable. "She's comin'."

Doirin's heart swelled with joy. To have someone to love, to give a piece of yourself to the world. Another human being with whom to share the beauty of the land and the power of healing. A new life to teach and protect. Hope reared; maybe her daughter would inherit the Gift.

If asked, Doirin would be unable to say how she knew her bairn would be a girl. She just knew it, the same way she knew the whitecaps on the firth heralded a storm or that the planting of a rowan tree would assure good luck. Or the way she knew she was being watched right now.

She glared down the dirt road at the smug sandstone cottages, all lined up like prim dowagers. Staring at her...judging her. Like the village wives who huddled together in the market and peered at her when they thought she wasn't looking and then put their heads together and bleated like a flock of sheep. She sighed and bent over the rows of vegetables again, ignoring the dull throbbing in her back.

She was thirty-two years old—an old woman. She'd come to Dornach five months ago, pregnant and alone, running from her disgrace. Told the villagers her husband was dead, that he had died protecting her from ruffians—that he was her hero.

The tears she'd summoned were real, but the story was not. Cormac Jamieson, may the bastart rot in Hell, was anything but a hero. And he definitely wasn't hers.

Doirin felt the bile rising in her throat at the memory. What an accomplished liar! For more than a year she'd met him faithfully at the market, spent hours listening to his tales of the sea, held his hand when he talked of the loss of his family to the flux, tears working their way down his cheeks.

He was the perfect man, in her opinion—although admittedly she had no barometer upon which to make that claim. He was gentle, patient—she supposed fishermen had to be patient—and she was just like a greedy, bulging-eyed fish, snapping at the bait he threw out and never knowing her mistake until

DORNACH, SCOTLAND, 1707

it was too late. One look into those eyes, one smile from that beautiful mouth, and she'd thrown caution out with the spent tea leaves.

When she fell pregnant, she'd been so happy to tell Cormac that he was going to be a father, that they would be a family of three. She'd run to the market to meet him, earlier than their usual time but unable to wait to share her news. She imagined those blue eyes widening and then crinkling at the corners as he realized the miracle they had made together.

Instead, the eyes that had widened were hers. She rounded the booth next to the fishmonger's and stopped, frozen in place, at the sight of Cormac and a strange woman locked in an embrace. A young woman, her hands fisted in Cormac's black curls as they kissed.

Doirin didn't know how long she had stood in the midst of the busy market, people parting to go around her as if she were an island in the river that ran by Dornach. Cormac's eyes met hers over his partner's shoulder, and a sheepish smile spread over his face. He pulled the woman's arms from around his neck and said something into her ear before patting her on the bottom and sending her laughing away down the path.

Then he stood still and stared at her, blue eyes wide and innocent. Doirin forced her feet to carry her to him, knowing even then that he was not the man she had thought him to be.

Still, she tried to hold onto the lie, the image of happiness that was already shattering into shards that cut their way down and into her heart. She would forgive him; he would forget that woman when he understood.

So she told him, and watched the blue eyes become flat, stagnant pools of still water, their depths hidden and obscure. He stared at her for a long time, and then he spoke.

"Well, lass, why'd ye go an' let yerself get wi' child? An' why would ye think it be mine?"

Doirin remembered the shock of that moment as if it were yesterday. Her mouth hanging open, gulping for air, her throat closing. She must have looked just like the catch he pulled in every day. Her gaze clouded and she thought she might faint, and when the air finally cleared, he was gone. She turned and stumbled home, barely able to see for the mist that shrouded her eyes.

As soon as her condition became apparent, she was let go. Lord Robert's valet told her to pack her meagre belongings and get out of the house and the village, lest people think less of the mistress for allowing such a person to tend to her.

Lady Emily had been kind, but helpless. The men made the decisions, she said as she slipped a small pouch into Doirin's hand. "Take care," she whispered, and then disappeared back into the cavernous house.

Doirin walked north, not for any other reason than that was where her feet were pointed when she set out, and when she could walk no further, she found herself in the village of Dornach, on the shores of a great firth.

Dornach had a castle, a huge stone monster of a building that loomed over the town and shrouded the road in darkness. To Doirin's tired eyes, the two towers on either side resembled the horns of the devil, and the black windows were diabolical eyes that seemed to know her sin. Across from the castle were the ruins of what once must have been a grand cathedral, although only its tower remained, a sad reminder of past glories.

She'd spent her first night in the shadowed remnants of the cathedral, unwilling to spend her small hoard of money. She huddled in her arasaid against the cold wind from the firth, and when wan daylight found its way through the broken stone walls, she ventured forth, armed with only the two serviceable gowns she owned and the lie she had made up during the long, restless night.

A familiar noise filtered into her exhausted brain, one that sent a shaft of pain through her heart. Costermongers, tartan weavers, butchers, all extolling the merits of their wares. This market, in the shadow of the cathedral tower, was much larger than the one in her hometown, but the sounds and the smells were the same. And so were the looks. Eyes met hers and then heads were turned away at her bedraggled appearance and protruding stomach.

"Are ye needin' help, lass?"

Doirin turned to face a small, rather round woman of indeterminate age. Kind grey eyes looked her up and down from a face wrinkled like a winter apple. "Ye're no from aroun' these parts, aye?"

There was something so—*right*—about this little gnome-like person. Doirin stared at the woman, and the answer slipped into place. For the first time in months, she was not being judged. Without warning, her eyes filled. Tears welled up from that frozen

WITCH

place deep inside, driving away the fear, the anger, and the self-disgust that had lodged there since Cormac's betrayal.

Without a word, the tiny woman stepped forward and put pudgy arms around Doirin's middle. She stepped back, eyes narrowing.

"Ye've got th' gift, have ye no?" she whispered. She grabbed Doirin's hand in her own. "Come wi me, noo."

As they walked down the path, the woman told Doirin her name was Maighread Arthur and she was a midwife. She had lived in Dornach all her life and had brought most of the village children into the light of day, as well as seeing to illnesses, broken limbs, and assorted rashes. Until now she turned no one away, but she had never before taken anyone in.

In the next three months, as Doirin's belly expanded, Maighread taught her all she knew of medicine. "Yer a healer, lass," she said. "A better one than me, b'cause ye have a magic I dinnae have. Tis a gift from God, but no everybody'll see it that way." She took Doirin's hand and gazed deep into her eyes. "People fear what they dinnae ken. Ye must take care."

Remembering those days, Doirin laughed to herself, and then winced. The pain that had started in her back was arcing through her whole body now, a throbbing, seething agony that took her breath away. She straightened as best she could and made her way to the cottage she shared with Maighread Arthur. The woman looked up as she stumbled over the threshold and smiled.

"Is't time then, love?"

DORNACH, SCOTLAND, 1707

"Aye." Doirin gritted the words out through clenched teeth. "Tis time."

Throughout the day, as the pain ebbed and then rose again to engulf her, Doirin clutched Maighread's hand and breathed.

"Push, lass!" The words came to her on a fresh wave of agony. "Push, now. She's almost here!"

Doirin gathered all her strength and pushed, and a moment later heard the squalling of a new life. It was the most beautiful sound she'd ever heard...the first cries of her daughter.

"Yer name is Sìne," she whispered to the bundle Maighread placed in her arms. "It means 'God is gracious'."

She looked up to find Maighread staring at her, eyes hooded. The woman was not smiling.

"What?" Doirin asked.

"Ye better see, love."

Doirin peeled back the cloth. A wee foot waved in the air. Three toes—no, five toes, but the two on each end were fused, giving the foot the appearance of a tiny bird's claw. As Doirin watched in horror, a hand emerged from the wrapping. Through welling tears, she saw that the fingers were fused in the same way.

"I dinnae care!" Doirin said fiercely. "I dinnae care. She's perfect, my Sìne."

"Aye," Maighread said, her voice low and rough. "She's perfect, but to others it'll no seem so. Ye need be prepared, love. Th' world is cruel t' those who be different."

CHAPTER 6
INVERNESS, SCOTLAND – PRESENT TIME

Once you have had a wonderful dog, a life without one is a life diminished.
—Dean Koontz

Adam stared at the driving rain as he made his way up the A87 toward Inverness. The wipers beat a rhythm as they scraped across the windscreen of his car, keeping time to the bleak thoughts that rolled through his head. He shook them away in frustration, but they had put down roots and refused to budge.

He should be happy he wasn't dead. A panic attack, the emergency room doctor had told him—not the Big One, after all. The man had looked put out that he didn't seem happier about the diagnosis, but to Adam it was just one more thing to add to the list. He'd never had a panic attack before. Brilliant.

"Do you have a family history of panic disorder?" the doctor had asked.

"Well, my brother Daniel used to have them, but they're controlled now. His doctor told him they can be caused by stress."

"Hmm. And what about you? Are you under any stress?"

Stupid question, Adam thought. *Well, doc, there's this curse...*

When he didn't answer, the doctor went on. "Or a sudden major change in your life?"

Adam thought about that. "I don't think so..."

But now he allowed himself to focus on the doctor's words. A sudden major change... There was that woman—the dark-haired woman in the bookshop. She was the last thing he remembered seeing before he passed out.

Words drifted out of his memory. *You found me.* His own voice.

The wipers beat a counterpoint to the words. *You found me...you found me.* And what the hell did that mean? Why had she had such an effect on him? Sure she was beautiful, but he knew a lot of beautiful women. None of them had made an impact on him, because he didn't allow that to happen. So why this one?

You found me. Found him? Had those words really been his? But the rhythm of the wipers had no answer, so he pushed the question to the back of his mind and focused on the road.

Loch Ness came into view on his right, its dark waters hinting of the mystery in its depths. The loch had been there since the last Ice Age, formed from the huge glaciers that covered the land. In his university days, Adam had studied the mountains and

INVERNESS, SCOTLAND – PRESENT TIME

lochs that formed his country's topography, and he knew Loch Ness was relatively young in geologic terms. It hadn't existed during the time of the dinosaurs—or had it?

Maybe the Nessie story was the loch's private joke at the expense of modern geologists who thought they knew everything. The thought cheered him for some reason, and as if the weather sensed the change in his mood, the rain dwindled and then stopped altogether and the sun worked its way out from behind grey clouds and sparkled on the dark water.

Re-energised, Adam made his way through Inverness to the A9, and shortly after parked the Peugeot in the Scottish SPCA's car park on Culloden Road. Suddenly nervous, he stood looking at the long, grey building and imagined the animal that was waiting for him inside.

Cù beinne was part Labrador retriever, part border collie. Adam had picked him out on the SPCA's website, and now he was here to meet his mountain dog in person. The dog's bio said he was two years old and had been found wandering in the woods. He had not been claimed, but he'd obviously been well cared for and showed evidence of prior training. *Needs space to run*, the bio said. *Prefers a house to a flat. Does not like cats.*

That was fine. Adam didn't have a house or a cat, but he hardly spent any time in his flat and he could give his dog plenty of space to run. He would have the whole mountain range of Glen Coe to exercise in, and Jared had promised to take him out whenever Adam couldn't. Jared had once been a footballer, and the man could still run with the best of them. *Cù beinne* was going to be the happiest creature in Ballachulish.

Adam straightened. He wondered when this dog had taken on such importance in his life. Still, he couldn't seem to make his feet move toward the entrance. Questions swirled like the sudden nausea rising in his stomach. Would his dog like him? Would the SPCA find him a fitting companion for *Cù beinne*? Was it irresponsible for a man on borrowed time to take on the raising of an animal?

Dark thoughts weren't getting him any closer to the answers, so he forced his feet to move. He opened the door with a hand that trembled only a little and went into the spacious lobby. A middle-aged man with thinning red hair held back in a ponytail smiled and extended his hand over the counter.

"Mister MacArthur? I'm Harry MacGregor. Are you ready to meet your best friend?"

Adam cleared his throat. "I think so. Yeah. Um... are people usually this nervous when they adopt a pet?"

The man grinned. "Aye, it's a normal occurrence, and a good one. Shows you're serious. Your dog will appreciate it." He opened a door behind the counter and disappeared.

Adam wandered around the lobby looking at the pictures of dogs and cats and their happy owners, the displays of cat toys and dog leashes, and the bags of pet food. He picked out a blue tartan leash, a bag of kibble, and a stuffed sheep. *Should appeal to his border collie instincts.* He carried the lot to the counter and deposited it, then returned to the pictures.

INVERNESS, SCOTLAND – PRESENT TIME

The door behind the counter opened again and Harry MacGregor reappeared, bent over as he talked to something out of sight. "Are ye ready, lad?" he asked. "Aye, he's nervous too."

Adam heard a loud wheezing sound as MacGregor rounded the corner, one hand holding the end of a leash. He waited, unable to control the huge grin that was spreading over his face in anticipation.

The grin died as soon as the man and dog emerged into the lobby, and a sense of shock set in.

Cù beinne was a bulldog.

Short, bowed legs held up a thick body and a huge head topped by ridiculous folded ears. The white furry face was wrinkled like a cranky old man's. This was not *Cù beinne*. It was not a mountain dog. It looked as if it would be happiest flopped on a couch in front of the television, watching a documentary on its doppelgänger, Winston Churchill. This creature was the farthest thing he could imagine from a runner.

"Th-that's not my dog!" The words exploded in a gasp.

MacGregor frowned. "What do you mean?" His tone was noticeably cooler than it had been a minute ago.

"The dog I requested isn't that...that...." He waved a hand at the bulldog. "My dog is a border collie-Lab mix."

"I'm sorry, but here's the paperwork you filled out online, and here's the photo of your dog." He held out the papers in his left hand.

Adam stared at the printout. The words swam up off the paper. *Loves to cuddle on the couch. Needs exercise, but be careful of over-extending. A three-mile jog will not happen, but a casual walk around the block should suit just fine. Likes cats.*

At the bottom of the form was a picture of the bulldog, and Adam's electronic signature.

"If you don't want the dog, you will certainly not be held responsible." MacGregor's tone was frosty. "That is, after all, the purpose of the meet and greet."

Adam looked at the bulldog. The animal looked back at him, brown eyes drooping. Then it waddled up, stuck out a huge tongue, and painted a coat of drool across his hand. It sat down and grinned up at him.

"What's its name?" Adam asked, to cover his embarrassment.

"Pearl."

The damned bulldog's name was Pearl.

"But I wanted a running dog." His voice sounded petulant to his own ears.

MacGregor glared at him. "Then why on earth did you pick a bulldog?"

"I didn't! I picked out a running dog!"

MacGregor nodded his head at the paper in Adam's hands. "Apparently not." He gave a loud sigh. "Well, I'm sorry things didn't work out, but..."

"I think she likes me," Adam said.

MacGregor straightened. "Pearl is a male dog."

"B-but...*Pearl*..." Adam was sliding further down the rabbit hole. He grabbed hold of the edge and tried one more time. "It's not a girl?"

"No, the eejits who brought him in thought he was a female, so they named him Pearl. I don't know how they missed the man bits; they're huge," he snorted.

INVERNESS, SCOTLAND – PRESENT TIME

"They found him in the woods just wandering around by himself and thought they'd adopt him, but they couldn't stand the snoring and the drooling. Shame," MacGregor said. "He's a nice dog. But no way a runner." He pulled on the leash. "C'mon, Pearl."

"That's all right," Adam heard his own voice saying. "I want him." He stared at the surprised MacGregor and straightened his spine, and twenty minutes later he was the owner of a bulldog named Pearl.

On his way back to Ballachulish, Adam kept looking in the rearview, surprised that the animal smiling at him out of its huge, wrinkled face was still there. *What have I done?* he asked himself. *What the hell am I supposed to do with this thing?*

"I wanted a running dog," he told it. "I hope you don't take it personally, but you were *not* what I had in mind, at all." A happy wheeze came from the back seat. Adam looked in the rearview again, to see drops of slobber plopping onto the leather seats of his precious Peugeot. Pearl grinned.

When he got home, Adam snapped on the new blue tartan leash and hauled the lump of canine matter out of the back seat. Pearl didn't seem to mind, but he didn't help, either. When they had made it into the foyer of his new building, the dog looked up the stairs with his head cocked and then waddled over to stand in front of the lift, tongue lolling from between crooked teeth. Adam sighed and pushed the 'up' button.

"I was kind of worried about living in a flat, since the bio said running dogs don't like flats," he told Pearl as he unlocked his door, "but somehow I don't think that'll be an issue with you." The dog gave him a sloppy smile and waddled over to the couch, jumped up with surprising agility, curled up in the corner next to the leather arm, and closed his eyes. In a matter of moments, loud snores filled the flat.

Adam made his way into the kitchen, poured himself a whisky, and downed it in two gulps. He returned to the couch, put his head back, and closed his eyes, which did nothing to drown out the noise from the buzz saw beside him.

He was running along the top of one of Glencoe's mountain trails, but something was off with his timing. He should have been much further ahead at this point of the race. A competitor passed him, laughing, and then another, and he looked down to see himself tethered to a lead that was attached to a waddling lump that coalesced into a bulldog who looked up at him with adoring brown eyes. "Come on," said the bulldog. "You can do this. You'll win, or my name's not Pearl!"

A loud knocking pulled Adam out of the dream, and he jerked upright, disoriented. There was a bulldog curled up next to him on the couch, snoring. The knocking repeated. He sighed, got up, and went to the door to greet Jared.

"Well? Where is he?" Jared demanded, and pushed his way into the flat. His dark brown eyes surveyed the small space and settled on the dog curled up on the couch next to a stuffed toy sheep.

"What is *that*?" he said.

"That's Pearl," Adam said, trying not to sound defensive. "My dog."

INVERNESS, SCOTLAND – PRESENT TIME

"What happened to *Cù beinne*?" Jared asked, but he had already moved to sit down next to Pearl on the couch. He laid a large brown hand on the dog's head and scratched him behind the ear. With a snort, the animal woke up and gazed into Jared's face. It cocked its head, and then swiped the new acquaintance with a warm, moist tongue.

"He likes you," said Adam. "At least, I think so. He might like everybody. I don't think he's picky."

"So, what happened?" Jared asked. "I mean, when you left, he was a border collie named *Cù beinne*, and now he's a bulldog named Pearl. Didn't you notice the difference?"

"Shut up," Adam said mildly. "He needed me, and I think I needed him. I have no idea why."

"Not a runner, though," Jared said, as he stroked the dog. "More of a lover, then?"

"Shut it," Adam repeated. "Oh. He likes cats, apparently. Should I get a cat?"

CHAPTER 7
FORT WILLIAM, SCOTLAND – PRESENT TIME

. . . love and attraction can take many forms. And if one is open to unexpected possibilities, there are no boundaries.
—Morgan Rhodes

Màiri sat alone behind the desk and sipped her latte without noticing the taste. The Duncans were off somewhere again. They often went away for an hour or two and never said a word about it when they came back. Caomhainn and Betty always went along, and the four of them looked like time travellers, walking away down the High Street in their eighteenth-century costumes. But this was Scotland. The tourists probably loved it.

There'd been a few customers in the cafe this morning, but the shop itself was nearly empty of people right now. It was a weekday, so business would be light until the afternoon when school and work let out.

Màiri shivered. For some reason the emptiness of the shop gave it an air of melancholy or foreboding, as if it had a dark secret that it wasn't quite ready to share. She chastised herself for giving in to her morbid imagination. Why was she so *dark* these days? Empty didn't have to mean bad; alone didn't have to mean lonely.

Usually Eve was there for company, but she and Daniel had gone to the museum for the all-important interview. Màiri hadn't allowed herself to think about what it would be like without Eve, but the time was coming.

No one knew more about daily life in 17th-century Glencoe than Eve MacDonald; she could trace her lineage all the way back to the MacDonalds of the Massacre.

"Not that that's anything to be proud of," Eve had admitted with a grin. "They were disliked by pretty much everybody, even other MacDonalds."

Màiri sighed. She'd get the job, for sure, and then she'd have to reschedule her hours and Màiri would only see her if she took an evening shift. Was that what was niggling at the edges of her mind today? She hadn't realised how important Eve had become to her, and now she was about to lose her.

She pushed that topic to the back of her mind and stood up, left the desk, and wandered around the shop checking for books out of place or sticky remnants of scones in the children's corner. Finally, she rooted in her handbag for the Kindle she always carried and settled down in one of the armchairs where she could see the door.

FORT WILLIAM, SCOTLAND – PRESENT TIME

It felt like sneakery, smuggling a Kindle into a bookstore, and it was totally out of place with the eighteenth-century costume and the decor of the place. She wouldn't have dared had the Duncans been on duty, but no one was here to see her crime and that was what made it fun. The hands of the grandfather clock in the centre of the store marched toward afternoon, the rhythmic ticking sounding like clucks of disapproval. Màiri grinned at the clock and waved her Kindle at it. *Dare you to tell, Father Time.*

She realized she'd read the same two lines four times and still didn't know what they said. *What's going on with me today?* she thought. *Why am I so skittery?*

But she knew. She'd been avoiding the subject since yesterday, and it wasn't working. She put the device in her lap, stared at the clock as if it must have the answer, and let the memories come.

That man with those beautiful brown eyes, looking at her as if he recognized her when she'd never seen him in her life. Who was he? Why had he just fainted like that, folding into a heap on the floor? What had he been so afraid of, in those last seconds before he lost consciousness? And why had he smiled when she touched him, as if he knew she could save him?

There. That was it—the crux of the mystery. *She'd been sure she could save him.* Why? And what was that strange feeling—that electricity—that had arced through her when she put her hand on him? How had she known to do that? She knew next to nothing about first aid. But what had happened yesterday hadn't had anything to do with medicine.

She'd run her hands down his chest, not knowing why she was doing such a thing, and he'd seemed to know what she was doing and relaxed. He'd understood what was happening when she hadn't a clue.

The memories brought another emotion with them, and now she looked it straight in the eye and recognized it for what it was. *Fear.* She'd been more afraid than ever before in her life, and she had no idea why. Was it simply concern that a human being might be dying right in front of her? Because he *had* been dying; she was sure of it. His heart had stopped and then started up again as she held her hand against his chest.

Màiri took a long breath and forced her mind to creep up to the memory she was suppressing. She tugged at it, and it floated up and out into the quiet bookshop. Under her hand, just visible around the edges of her palms, a light had appeared and spread. Soft blue at first, like a robin's egg, it had pulsed under her hand and then slowly warmed to a faint pink colour. Before she could wrap her mind around it, the colour had faded and disappeared. But it had been there.

It *had* been there. As real as the certainty that this was something important, in those few seconds as she knelt beside a stranger. *This!* a voice had said in her ear, and she'd looked up, surprised that no one was speaking. *This is a gift.*

So what was she supposed to do about it? She had no idea how to start or where to go to learn more about this new reality. Twenty-eight was way too old to start studying to be a doctor, and for some reason she didn't think nursing was where she should be.

FORT WILLIAM, SCOTLAND – PRESENT TIME

Problem was, she'd never even considered a career in medicine. Her visits to relatives in hospital painted a collage of bedpans, tubes, beeping machines, and smells she'd rather not know about. If her brain was going to finally offer up a calling, it would be nice if the message came with instructions.

Still, Màiri's memory kept returning to the colours and the electricity she'd seen and felt yesterday, and to the very real face of the man she'd helped. Brown hair, brown eyes that knew more than they were telling. Nice looking, about her age…

The bell over the front door played the first bars of "Flower of Scotland." Màiri shoved the Kindle into the cushion behind her and jumped up as a man entered. With the speed of an Olympic runner, the brown-eyed man disappeared from her head, to be replaced by a god. Blond hair perfectly combed, sharp blue eyes, a Harris tweed jacket, brown corduroy trousers. He looked like something out of an upscale sporting man's magazine.

She struggled out of the armchair. "May I help you?"

The man smiled. Perfect white teeth in a face that belonged in the movies, Màiri decided—not that she was interested in such things. She grinned at the weak attempt her brain was making to fool itself.

"Hullo," he said. God, even the man's voice was perfect. Smooth, like water as it made its way around the pebbles in a burn. *Enough already!*

"Hullo," he said again. "My name is Myles Grant. I have an appointment with Henry Duncan."

The name sounded familiar, but Màiri's brain had turned to sludge and refused to give up the information. She opened her mouth and forced words out. "Oh. Mister Duncan's not here at the moment. It's just me."

"There's no such thing as 'just me' with someone as lovely as you." The cheesy compliment slid off his tongue as if it were the most natural statement in the world, and Màiri could feel the heat rising higher in her cheeks. This man was good, and he knew it.

The bell jangled again and Mary Duncan sailed through the door, followed by her husband Henry. Caomhainn and Betty joined them in the foyer. A blur of black announced Biscuit, who appeared as if conjured and jumped onto Henry's shoulder.

"Myles!" Henry said, a smile breaking out on his usually taciturn face. "Sorry we're late. Have ye been waitin' long?"

Myles Grant extended a hand. "Not at all. Just got here. Your charming co-worker was on hand to greet me." He gestured to Màiri.

Mary rolled her eyes but reached up and patted the man's shoulder. "Let's meet 'n th' cafe, then, aye?"

Grant smiled down at her and followed the others obediently. Left behind, Màiri felt like the incomer at the wrong party—where she was the only one who didn't know the guest of honour. She turned to go back to the reception desk, but Mary's voice stopped her.

"Màiri! Come 'n join us! Caomhainn, git Murray t' cover th' desk, aye?"

Caomhainn nodded and loped over to the stockroom door. He stuck his head inside and bellowed something in Gaelic that was answered by a grunt,

FORT WILLIAM, SCOTLAND – PRESENT TIME

and then he returned to the group and shoved two tables together in the corner of the small cafe.

"What'll ye have?" Betty asked when they'd all taken their seats.

"Americano, thanks," Grant said politely, and the portly woman made her way to the small counter, returning with coffees and a plate of shortbread.

"Here ye go," she said, eyes fixed on the blond man, who winked at her and grinned.

"Thanks."

Betty's face flushed the colour of a tomato, and Màiri felt better. At least she wasn't the only one affected by the man's looks. But who was he, and why did he merit this star treatment?

"Ye've met Myles Grant, then," Henry said in her ear. "He's goin' t' do a signin' of *Death in the Cairngorms* here, an' we'll need everybody's help."

Màiri blinked. Myles Grant! The best-selling author of the *Death in the Highlands* series! Why was she such an eejit? Murder mysteries weren't her genre, but how could she forget a face like that?

Myles Grant's books were prominently placed on their own table in the front of the shop. Eve had recently bought a copy of one of them — *Death in Cruden Bay*? *Death on Loch Awe*? — and she remembered Daniel looking at the photo on the back cover and pretending to be jealous. Now she understood. Myles Grant!

She looked across at the author. Grant was looking back at her out of laughing blue eyes, and she blushed again. He probably thought all women had naturally red faces, if she and Betty were any judge. Only Mary seemed unaffected by the man's good looks, but Mary was unaffected by anything not controlled by herself. Màiri made a mental note to Google the author later.

"I want ye t' be 'n charge, Màiri," Henry was saying. He passed her a sheaf of papers. "His biography. Myles 's from right here 'n Fort William, but a lot o' people dinnae ken that. Yet. Ye'll have t' work close on wi' him, an' he'll fill ye in on anythin' special he wants people t' ken. Are ye all right wi' that?"

"Oh," Màiri said. "Oh. Right. I'm fine with that." She hoped that was what she said. She couldn't hear over the pounding in her ears. She was sure she sounded offhand and airy, as if she worked closely with ridiculously handsome superstar authors every day and it was nothing new in her world. She looked up and caught Myles Grant's eyes on her again. He was smiling at her. *Dammit*.

Henry filled them in on the date, time, and general logistics of the event, and Myles approved it all. He was really amenable, she decided, which couldn't be easy given the demands of such a high-profile career. Then Mary and Henry excused themselves to get back to the shop, Caomhainn wandered off to release Murray from duty, and Betty reluctantly pulled herself away to go through the catalogues. Màiri and Myles were left alone at the table.

"I think I'm going to enjoy this event," he told her. Then he leaned closer. "I'm wondering if I should change after this."

"Change?" Màiri gave him a puzzled look.

"From mystery to romance," he said. "We'll have to see."

CHAPTER 8
GLEN COE, SCOTLAND
– PRESENT TIME

When you aren't loved, you aren't real. Life is cold, like the stone against my palm.
—Richelle E. Goodrich

The woods at the base of Bein Nevis should have been filled with birdsong, the rustle of small animals, perhaps the death cry of a rabbit who had foolishly run afoul of a red fox. Instead, the air rang with loud, dissonant whacks of wood on wood, like a carpenter gone mad.

Two lads stood in the clearing, thrusting and parrying with wooden swords. A third, smaller than the others, sat alone on a log at the edge of the woods, a book in his hands.

"Cory!" shouted Donnie Chambers. "You're supposed to be judging! What the hell did we bring you for if you're just gonna read?"

Cory looked up and blinked. "What? Oh, sorry." He

folded down the corner of the page he'd been reading and closed the book. "Go ahead. I'm watching."

Donnie blew out a frustrated breath and swiped his brown curls off his forehead. He dropped his sword on the grass and ambled over to Cory.

"What're you reading, anyway? You've had your head in that book all day."

"It's a book on how to make an older woman fall in love with you," called Bastian Graham. "See? Look at the cover."

Cory tried to thrust the book behind him, but Donnie grabbed it out of his hands. "Hey, you're right!" he said. "Look, it has a flame on the front." He pretended to read the title. "*How to Light the Flame in her Heart*. Ahhh, adorable."

The colour rose in Cory's face. "Shut up!" he yelled. "You're such arseholes! Why don't you just leave me alone?"

Bastian joined them and squatted down next to Cory. He searched the younger lad's face, and something he saw there made him glance up at Donnie and shake his head slightly. After a moment's hesitation, Donnie handed the book back to Cory and flopped to the ground beside his friends.

"I'm sorry, Cory," Bastian said. "We are arseholes. Especially him." He poked Donnie in the ribs and was rewarded with a shove that sent him sprawling sideways in the grass. He rolled back to a sitting position, laughing, and lowered his voice.

"We know what the book's about, Cor. We were just teasing." He pointed to the image on the cover, a flame on the side of a bright red fire appliance. "But

GLEN COE, SCOTLAND – PRESENT TIME

why are you so obsessed with fire? I mean, even if you want to be a firefighter, like you say, you have to wait a long time, finish academy, go to uni and stuff. It'll be years!"

"I know." Cory's voice was low. "And I'm not obsessed with fire. I just want to help people *do* something." He let out a shuddering breath. "I want to make a difference."

"And you will," Donnie said quickly. "There's nothing wrong with being a firefighter. It's a very noble job. I just don't understand why it's so important to you. There are lots of jobs that help people. You could be a doctor, or a cop. Why does it have to be a firefighter?"

Cory's blue eyes darkened, and his small face wrinkled in on itself.

"Because of my mom." His words fell into the air of the clearing and hung there.

The other two boys shared a look but said nothing.

"I never told you guys about my family—about what happened to them." He stopped and considered, then seemed to make up his mind.

"We—we were on our way to Skye, on holiday." He began to talk faster, his words coming out stilted and automatic as if he were a wind-up toy. "Me, my mom, and my dad. I was six years old. I was in the back seat. A tourist driving a hire car was coming on too fast on the single-track road. He hit us head-on and the car flipped. All the doors were jammed except the driver's." He stopped, breathing fast as if he'd just run a race.

His friends were staring at him in horror. "Why didn't you ever say?" Donnie said.

"Because my dad's a coward." Tears were running down the boy's face now, plopping onto the cover of the book. Cory swiped at his eyes. "He jumped out of the car and ran away. The cops came and pried open the door to get me out, but th-the car—it caught fire and my mom d-died."

"What?" Bastian gasped. "But your parents are fine."

"The MacMillens aren't my parents." The words were acid, sizzling in the summer air. "They're some kind of cousins of my dad's. They took me in, I guess because they thought they had to. I don't know why. They hate kids." He looked up, eyes dull. "My last name is really Fraser, but the MacMillens made me use theirs, even if they never adopted me officially." His brows furrowed. "They mostly ignore me, which is better than when..." He stopped and pressed his lips together.

Bastian's brows had drawn together, and his mouth hung open. "So that's why you never invited us over? Why you hardly ever go home?" His eyes narrowed further, and he grabbed Cory's arm, pushing up a sleeve. His face darkened. "That's why you have bruises?" He released Cory's arm and flopped back on the grass. "That's why you stay with me and Donnie all the time, isn't it?"

"I should've known," he muttered to himself. "You're not clumsy."

Cory shrugged. "Your parents are nice. The MacMillens never even notice if I don't come home. They're drunk a lot."

"So..." Bastian hesitated, then went on. "What happened to your real dad?"

GLEN COE, SCOTLAND – PRESENT TIME

Cory gave him a look that was rimmed with bitterness. "Dunno. He never came back."

"What?" Bastian breathed. "Shite. That sort of explains the MacMillens. The whole family's full of bastarts."

Donnie reached out and gave the younger lad's knee an awkward pat. "Now I get the firefighter thing. I'm sorry we messed with you."

Cory stood up suddenly. "It's fine. It was a long time ago. I barely remember. As soon as I turn eighteen, I'll be out of there, and till then I'll just stay out of their way as much as possible. Plus," he said, a grin breaking over his face, "I have you two arseholes."

He grinned and picked up the sword Donnie had dropped on the grass. "Who wants to take D'Artagnan on?" He danced away toward the centre of the clearing.

Dusk fell, but the Musketeers hardly noticed. If their footwork was off, if their thoughts seemed to be elsewhere some of the time, if two of them seemed to go out of their way not to hit the third, it wasn't noticed by the trees, or the moon, or the few creatures that remained awake in the woods. They practiced until darkness fell and they could barely see each other in the dim light.

"We'd better stop before one of us gets knocked out," Bastian said. "Cory, you're actually not too bad when you put the book down and concentrate."

"Haud yer wheesht," Cory said without heat. Bastian grinned and drew his finger across his lips like a zipper.

"Look how late it is," Donnie spoke up. "My folks are gonna fuckin' kill me."

"Mine too," Bastian said cheerfully.

Cory watched his friends, wondering what it would be like to be able to say that and smile. What it would be like to have parents who cared enough to fuckin' kill you?

"Can I stay at your place tonight?" he asked Bastian. "I want to watch the slaughter." His laugh was fragile, a thin parody of humour.

"Aye, 'course, you're always welcome. And my parents think you're *so cute*"— he made his voice a falsetto —"they might just let us all slide if we're lucky."

Bastian stopped talking as Donnie grabbed his arm. "Shhh," he whispered. "Someone's out here."

All three froze and listened. "Who'd be here besides us?" Bastian said. He listened to the wind whisper through the trees. "Shee-ite, it's gotten really dark."

At first they heard nothing above the rising wind. Then a sound that was not a part of the woods came to them—a sort of shuffling that could not be an animal. There was no wind, but the air seemed to chill as they listened.

"Let's get out of the open," Donnie said. They made their way out of the clearing and into the woods, moving as silently as they could until they came to a large gorse bush, near the path but far enough from the clearing. They knelt behind the bush and waited.

"There's more than one!" whispered Cory.

"Shhh!" Bastian hissed. They shrank back deeper into the night shadows, holding their breath.

GLEN COE, SCOTLAND – PRESENT TIME

The footsteps grew closer. What had seemed like one set of steps became many more, walking in some kind of weird rhythm like a stealthy army.

The footsteps were accompanied by a humming sound that sounded like a hive of bees. As the steps came closer on the path, the sound resolved itself into a low chant, many voices speaking the same words in an oddly pitched cadence that rose and fell.

Being closest to the edge of the bush, Cory peeked out and strained to see through the darkness. What he saw couldn't be, but it was.

A ghost was walking down the path. A black, faceless being that looked like a picture he'd once seen of the Grim Reaper. It was followed by another reaper, identical in appearance, and then another. The chanting continued, monotonous and chilling in its uniformity, as they moved toward the clearing the boys had just been in.

Cory put both hands over his mouth to keep himself from crying out and screwed his eyes shut, as if not seeing the creatures would make them disappear. He reached behind him and clutched Bastian's sweat-soaked shirt. Cory's fear was a living thing, urging him to run for his life, but somehow he managed to say still.

He forced his eyes open and peeked around the edge of the rock again. The clouds had parted for a minute and in the dim light of the moon he could see that he'd been wrong. The reapers had faces after all; they were simply wearing masks, and their eyes were shrouded by the deep hoods of their dark robes.

Somehow, knowing they were human made the

scene worse. In Cory's life, people were always worse than anything nature could conjure. He wanted to stand up and run into the woods screaming, because evil was no stranger in his life and these people were evil on a level he felt viscerally. His body was vibrating with it.

But if he ran, he would put Bastian and Donnie in danger. His two best friends, the ones who had taken a younger lad in and given him a sense of family. They'd never know how much their friendship meant, and he'd never tell them. He hadn't even meant to tell them about his parents, but somehow it had forced its way out.

He turned back to the parade of reapers. They kept coming, three, four... He counted thirteen in all. Cory could just make out their eyes, staring straight ahead as if they were in a trance, mumbling the strange words over and over. Except for the last one.

Its eyes darted left and right, as if it sensed their presence. Suddenly the reaper's hood swivelled toward the place where they crouched, shivering. Cory saw its blue eyes widen, just for a second, and then it was past, shuffling along behind the others.

The chanting grew fainter as the men moved down the path toward the clearing. The night wind absorbed the sound of footsteps and humming as if it had never been there.

Bastian stood up. "Let's get out of here," he said in a tense voice. Donnie nodded and the two turned to head back to the edge of the woods, then stopped and turned around. Cory was standing at the edge of the path, staring at the darkness that had closed around the strange chanting figures.

GLEN COE, SCOTLAND – PRESENT TIME

"Cory!" Bastian hissed. When Cory didn't move, he grabbed the younger lad's hand and dragged him along. Just before the woods ended, the three stopped and stood staring at each other.

"What the hell was that?" Donnie said. "Some kind of cult?"

"I don't know, but they creeped me out," Bastian said. "I mean, we were just in that clearing, making all sorts of noise. What if they'd heard us?"

"I don't think they did," Donnie said. "They were too far away. We didn't hear them until after we stopped practicing. They seemed to be on something, didn't they? Like some kind of drug, maybe? I mean, the way they were all walking together like that, and chanting. I doubt they could hear anything over that."

"Well, we need to find another place to practice," Bastian said. "Those were men! Adult men! What the hell were grown men doing playacting like Druids or something in the middle of the woods at night? Let's meet at my house and figure out a new place, because I'm not going back to that clearing." He let out a breath. "In fact, why don't you both stay at my place tonight? I don't think I'll be going to sleep anytime soon."

"Okay," said Donnie. "All for one, one for all. Aye, D'Artagnan? ...Cory?" He swung to face an empty path.

Cory was gone.

CHAPTER 9
DORNACH, SCOTLAND, 1716

SINE

Clootie, Clootie, come 'n play
Willnae let ye hae yer way!
Who will gie on Clootie's back,
Ryde 'er doon th' village trak.
Waghorn, Waghorn come 'n play,
Gie us all some fun t'day.
Cannae hide 'er cloven toes,
Ride 'er till awa she goes!

Sìne Gilchrist faced the five children who surrounded her, chanting the words to their favourite song. Walter Ross the leader as always, with his odious little brother Ronain repeating every word even though he probably didn't even know what they meant. Archie Ross, the follower, desperate to gain favour from Walter in any way he could.

Then there were the watchers. Alan Grant, with his wide innocent eyes, and that mean little Ailis MacAllan. They didn't chant the words, but they laughed along with the tormenters and avoided eye contact with their victim. Wee cowarts; they were somehow the worst of all.

She should have been used to it by now, but it never stopped hurting. The words cut into her heart and twisted like a knife, as the chant grew louder and the laughter more gleeful.

They thought they were so clever. Did they imagine themselves safe from the Devil if they used that name? Her face turned red in mortification. Clootie meant cloven foot. Was it her fault her hands and feet were stuck together? Did it make her a bad person?

It was true; she'd been born with fingers and toes fused together. It hadn't made a difference to her; she could do everything as well as anyone else, except for writing. When she picked up a stylus and tried to mimic the schoolmaster's letters, the pen slipped from between her fingers and clattered to the wooden table, taking the ink pot with it.

That was the first time she'd heard the word "Clootie," whispered loudly by Walter MacKay to Archie Ross. The schoolmaster brought his stick down on Walter's head, earning Sìne a narrow look of hatred from the bully.

Walter made sure the nickname stuck. The chant had surfaced mysteriously not long afterwards and became a permanent part of village song whenever Sìne was unaccompanied by her mother or

DORNACH, SCOTLAND, 1716

Maighread—or Uncle Mungo. She wondered what *he* would do if he knew this was happening.

Mungo Murray was Mam's friend, or maybe more. He came for supper most nights, fixed things around the cottage, and sometimes walked Sìne to school on his way to the docks where he worked. He'd been around so long that he'd become a part of their little family, and he would have skelped Walter MacKay within an inch of his life. The thought cheered her.

Now, facing her worst tormenter, she brushed a hand across her eyes and glared. "Ye dinnae e'en ken what Waghorn means, ye big gowber!"

Walter's face flushed. He pushed Sìne roughly to the ground and squatted over her as if he were riding a pony, chanting, "Waghorn, Waghorn, come an' play!"

Something flew across the path and pushed Walter violently off his victim, rolling with him in the dirt. Even though smaller and lighter, the lad pinned Sìne's assailant to the ground and rained blows on his shoulders.

"Ye miser'ble piece o' shite! Wha' a great man ye are, hittin' a wee lass! T'day I'm gonnae give ye th' beatin' ye deserve!"

Sìne rolled over and sat up. None of the others noticed; their eyes were on the two lads now covered with dirt and grass, pummelling each other with all the force they could muster.

A roar of fury rose over the curses and cheers, and the children turned to see three adults approaching on the run. One of them, a tall man dressed in a buff waistcoat and linen trews, waded into the fray and yanked the lad off Walter.

"Hugh Alexander Gordon Sutherland!" he bellowed. "What d'ye thynk yer doin'?"

The lad raised his head and stared at his father with defiant brown eyes. "E's a cowart, Da! Hittin' a wee lass!"

His father reared back and brought the palm of his hand across his son's face, sending him sprawling onto the path.

"Yer a Sutherland," he yelled. "Ye have nae business mixin' wi' lesser folk. I'll no have ye makin' a foole out o' yerself just fer "— he turned and glared at Sine — "*that!*"

Hugh scrambled to his feet. "She's my friend, Da! A man should pr'tect his friends, shouldnae 'e? Especially a lass!"

His heroic speech was rewarded with another slap, one that left a large handprint on his face. His father grabbed him by the collar and dragged him away, jerking him to and fro like a stoat-weasel shaking a vole as he continued to berate his helpless son.

"I should never have let ye take lessons wi' th' village bairns." His angry voice floated back on the wind. "Tis made ye ferget who ye are!"

The others collected Walter from the ground and helped him to limp off in the wake of Hugh and his father, leaving Sine sitting alone in the dirt. Tears ran down her face and were lost in the dry packed earth of the path. Her best friend—her *only* friend—was being punished because of her, and there was nothing she could do.

Duncan Sutherland was the sheriff of Dornach, due in great part to his status as the largest

DORNACH, SCOTLAND, 1716

landowner in the area. He pretended to be just one of the lads and could be found often in the tavern raising his glass with the farmers and fisherman, but he wasn't really of their class. They all knew it but pretended not to because he was generous with his money and hired his 'friends' to work with the sheep and the cattle. Today he'd allowed his true feelings to come out.

I'll no have ye makin' a foole out o' yerself ...fer that! The hateful words burned into her mind and left a trail of ash. *That.*

Sìne stood up and swiped a dirty hand across her eyes. Hugh was really in trouble this time. He'd told her once that his Da beat him when he found fault with something he'd done, hoping to 'chase th' Devil out o' him.' He'd shrugged it off, saying it was all part of being a Sutherland, but Sìne had seen real fear in his eyes when his father dragged him off.

She brushed the dirt off her gown and set off in the direction the others had taken. Her determination kept pace with her fear. Hugh was her friend, and she would stand by him no matter what, even though there was likely nothing much a nine-year-old lass could do. She ducked behind the wall of the ruined cathedral and peered out.

Mister Sutherland had pulled Hugh to the town house on the market square, where a long-hinged frame made of two posts, one atop the other, rested across shorter posts at either end. A long wooden bench stretched behind the contraption. The frame was hinged at one end, and at intervals along each log pairs of half-circles had been carved to form holes. Sìne stuffed a small fist into her mouth to keep herself from crying out.

The stocks. No! He wouldn't, not to his own son! But Hugh's father, his face and neck bright red with anger, dragged his lad to the bench behind the frame and shoved him down on it. He signalled to two men standing nearby, and they raised the top post. The lad's skinny legs were stretched out before him and his ankles placed atop two of the indentions. The top post was lowered and a metal wire drawn through a loop at the end to hold the contraption together.

Sutherland stood in front of the small crowd that had gathered to watch. "My son has chosen t' engage in th' worst kind o' fightin' in public," he called out. "He will spend th' night here, 'an I hope..." — he looked around — "that ye good citizens o' Dornach will help me t' teach 'im th' lesson 'e needs. Am I unnerstood, friends?"

The villagers shuffled their feet and some tried to edge away, but Duncan Sutherland crossed his arms and glared at them until they bent to pick up clods of dirt and grass and began to throw them at the young boy in the stocks.

Hugh crossed his arms over his chest, looking like a small shadow of his father, and stared out at the adults who were being forced to abuse him. His eyes found Sìne, quivering in the shadows, and a small smile crawled over his face.

After another moment, Hugh's father stalked away without a backward look. As soon as he was out of sight, the villagers stopped throwing dirt and turned for their own homes, shoulders hunched in shame.

DORNACH, SCOTLAND, 1716

Walter, not to be denied his revenge, limped up and threw a tomato at Hugh's head. It splattered on the lad's forehead, and juice and seeds ran into brown hair already caked with dirt and sweat and dribbled down his cheeks. Hugh didn't flinch. He stared straight ahead until Walter hobbled away.

Dusk came and melted into darkness, and the square grew quiet. A small figure separated itself from the side of a stall and crept up to Hugh.

"Hullo, Sìne. What're ye doin' out here on this fine eve'nin'?" Hugh said, with only a small quaver in his voice.

Without a word, Sìne took off her apron and used it to wipe her friend's face. Then she sat down on the back of his stool and leaned her back against his. Braced this way, they sat through the long night, saying little. As dawn broke, Sìne left the stool and went back to the shadows of the market stall, where she watched until Hugh's father came and retrieved his unrepentant son.

CHAPTER 10
DORNACH, SCOTLAND, 1716

HUGH

Hugh Sutherland sat on the dock and dangled his legs in the water. The Dornach Firth was freezing, even now in summer, but just having the freedom to make his own decision about where to put his feet was worth the pain he'd endured last night.

His father wasn't speaking to him, and that was fine. Hugh's hero worship—he realized now it had been more fear than admiration—had turned to ashes and drifted away on the wind, and he was still reeling from the betrayal. It wasn't the public humiliation forced on him, or the slaps to his head. He was used to physical punishment from his father; he'd thought it a necessary part of growing up. No, it wasn't that.

Yer a Sutherland. Ye have nae business mixin' wi' lesser folk! The words kept repeating in his head like that horrible song those arses sang to torment Sìne. How could his father think it was mixing with lesser folk to fight for a girl's honour? And what were 'lesser folk' anyway?

Duncan Sutherland had released him from the stocks soon after dawn broke, hauled him home, and ordered the cook to give him a good breakfast. Then he'd disappeared into his study and slammed the door shut. Hugh had taken the opportunity to beat a retreat. He wanted to be anywhere but home right now.

"How're ye farin', lad?" came a rough voice behind him, and he turned to see Sìne's uncle, Mungo Murray, carrying a long pole and a tackle basket. Without waiting for an answer, the older man sat himself down beside Hugh, readied his line, and cast it into the waters of the firth. They sat for a long time, just watching the line drift back and forth in the choppy water.

"I wasnae wrong...was I?" Hugh said finally.

"Cannae say." Murray kept his eyes on his pole. "Wasnae there. Whyn't ye tell me aboot it?"

So, in a soft, shaking voice that grew louder and stronger with the telling, Hugh recounted his shameful experience the day before, and why he'd done it. Murray's gnarled hand tightened on the pole, but he said nothing.

"I dinnae thynk I was wrong...an' I'd do 't agin," Hugh finished on a surge of breath. He raised brimming brown eyes to the old man.

"Ye wasnae wrong," Murray said. The words came out in a harsh rasp and were swept away by the sea breeze.

DORNACH, SCOTLAND, 1716

Hugh gave a long sigh, and his body relaxed. They sat quietly for a long time.

"Ye like wee Sìne, eh?" Murray asked.

"I'm goin' t' marry 'er," Hugh said, and then clapped a hand over his mouth. But the words were out.

Murray sat very still for a moment that seemed an eternity, and then he asked calmly, "How old be ye, lad?"

"Eleven, month next," Hugh said.

"Weel..." Murray pulled the line out of the water and gave it all his attention. "She's th' best lassie 'n Dornach, o' course, bit ye might think aboot waitin' a wee while t' make sich an important d'cision." He stood and gathered his gear, then turned to walk off. At the last moment, he swung round and fixed Hugh with sharp blue eyes. "Ye wasnae wrong." And he was off, white hair flying in the wind.

Hugh sat a while longer, thinking about what had been said—and what hadn't. Then he squared his shoulders and started for home. On the way, he passed a group of children headed for the school. Sìne wasn't among them, of course. She was never invited to walk with the rest of the village children.

"Stocks!" called a derisive voice. Walter MacKay was surrounded by his usual minions and his adoring wee brother, Ronain. *Another bully in the making,* Hugh thought, and tried to keep his hands from curling into fists.

"Aye?" he said politely.

"Where ye goin'?" Walter jeered. "Did yer da d'cide ye were too good fer us *lesser* folk?" His eyes narrowed. "Ye didnae look too high n' mighty yestiday, wi all 'at dirt on ye."

Hugh said nothing. He didn't care what they said to him, as long as they left Sine alone.

"Did ye like th' t'mato I gave ye?" Walter continued. "Ye looked hungry, sittin' there wi' yer feet all propped up like a crim'nal. Ye should thank me."

Hugh shrugged and continued past the group, ignoring the trail of laughter behind him. MacKay would love to provoke another fight, and there was no way Hugh was going to give him the attention he sought.

He thought about what Walter had said. Da's last words before they got home this morning were, "Dinnae go t' school t'day. I havenae decided about it."

If Duncan Sutherland kept his son away from the school, he'd have to hire a tutor. Hugh would be no better than a prisoner, locked up in the huge house with some wizened old scholar pounding at him with numbers and facts—a fate worse than death. He was going to have to placate his father somehow. If he had to say he was wrong, well, he'd just do it.

Back in his room, he sat on his bed and let his thoughts circle in his head until they settled on Sine. She was the most beautiful lass he'd ever seen, although admittedly there weren't that many lassies in Dornach Village. Big, honest blue eyes, and blacker than black hair that floated around her face like a cloud. She was kind and funny and so smart. The smartest lass in the school, even if her penmanship was the sloppiest because of her hand.

Everything about Sine Gilchrist was a mystery, and maybe that was part of what made her so interesting. Her mam and her gran were the village healers. Hugh had been patched up by them once or twice. They were gentle and kind, asked him questions and listened to his answers, and they didn't treat him any differently just because his da was the sheriff and owned half the town.

Sìne's gran wasn't really her gran, she had told him, and her uncle Mungo wasn't really her uncle. He wasn't her da either...she didn't have a da.

"Everbody has a da," Hugh told her. "There has t' be a mam an' a da t' have a wean."

"I s'pose I have a da, then," Sìne allowed. "But I dinnae ken one. Uncle Mungo is better than a da, enyway." She'd treated him to that brilliant smile that made his day better just by seeing it. Then she'd leaned over and whispered in his ear, "I thynk Uncle Mungo *wants* t' be my da."

I wish Uncle Mungo was my da, Hugh thought, and wondered at the lack of guilt that thought evoked. It was the truth. His father was so very different from Sìne's uncle. Dark, and brooding and...mean.

It hadn't always been that way. When Hugh's mother was alive, the house had rung with music and laughter. His father had smiled more. "Ye look like yer mam, Hugh," he said fondly. "Ye have her eyes and her hair. Maybe th' bairn'll look like me." He ruffled his young son's brown hair and promised that they would all travel the world together someday—the four of them—when the baby was born and old enough.

But it wasn't to be. On a clear, beautiful morning, his mother and his baby sister died aborning, and his father retreated into work and away from Hugh. He probably looked at his son and saw Mam's face—but it wasn't fair.

Da drank too much. He wanted Hugh to grow up as fast as he could, and in order to see that plan to fruition, his words and actions became increasingly hard and uncompromising.

The worst part, though, was his duplicity. Hugh had at least thought his father cared about the village people and thought of them as equals. He'd been proud that da helped so many of them to make ends meet when times were tough, that he called them friends and treated them at the pub.

But it was all an act. *Yer a Sutherland. Ye have nae business mixin' wi' lesser folk.* Last night had shown him the truth. Hugh wouldn't have minded being punished; it was his father's right to discipline his son. It wasn't even the humiliation of being pelted with dirt and vegetables. It was the fact that the villagers picked up that dirt because his father made them do it. They were *afraid* of Duncan Sutherland.

Shame burned through Hugh at the memory of the sick helplessness in their eyes. He wondered what Uncle Mungo would have done if he were there, and his heart lurched. Mungo Murray wouldn't have stood for such abuse, not for a minute, and Duncan Sutherland's wrath would have been redirected to him—and to the rest of Sìne's family.

Sìne had once told him a story about a princess who was trapped in a tower by her wicked stepmother. He'd thought it a bit silly, but now he understood. Of course, he wasn't a princess, but he was trapped just the same.

DORNACH, SCOTLAND, 1716

He stood up, ran his fingers through his hair, and made his way downstairs. He'd do whatever it took to make his father change his mind about going to school. He'd put up with Walter and Archie, and he'd protect his friends. He wouldn't fight unless it was necessary. Sìne didn't mind the deformity in her hands and feet, so he'd try to be more like her. And one day they'd be grown up and could make their own decisions.

I'm goin' t' marry 'er. The words he'd said to Murray came back unbidden and took root in his mind. *I'm goin' t' marry 'er.*

CHAPTER 11
GLEN COE, SCOTLAND – PRESENT TIME

Hell is empty and all the devils are here.
—William Shakespeare

Cory MacMillen pulled the hood of his black fleece up to cover his red hair and huddled in the darkness. He couldn't shake the feeling that he'd made a terrible decision, leaving his friends in order to follow this strange group of chanting men. He'd listened to them talking about meeting up at Bastian's house and had decided two things. He had to be sure about the man he'd seen, and he had to keep his friends out of it.

There was something not right about this gathering of grown men—something primal and chilling and malevolent. And his father—if it *was* his father he'd seen—was a part of it. So he'd turned and gone back. Left his friends standing on the path and followed the reapers.

He knew they were just people—he was fifteen, for God's sake, not a bairn—but there was something otherworldly about these men that had the hairs on his neck standing at attention.

They weren't like normal people. There was something strange about their speech, for one thing. The masks muffled their words—foreign words, spoken over and over in a dull monotone like monks in those old movies about the Middle Ages.

They weren't reapers, of course. Reapers weren't real. They probably weren't monks, either, despite the chanting. Monks didn't wear masks. These were just a bunch of weird men who dressed alike and looked like ghosts. The illusion was compounded by the slow, ponderous march, every step in sync, and by the chanting.

They'd shuffled into the clearing and formed a tight circle around the dead firepit. The chanting continued until all were in place, and then they stood absolutely still like statues. He smelled smoke, and a few minutes later tendrils of fire snaked up into the air of the clearing.

He'd never paid much attention to that firepit before. It had been there when the Musketeers first found the clearing, and they'd just assumed it was the remains from an old campsite, like so many scattered throughout the woods. Due to its reputation as the UK's tallest mountain, Ben Nevis attracted locals and visitors alike all year. Some were hikers or mountain runners, but many just wanted the experience of camping at the base of the famous landmark.

In the flickering light of the campfire, he could see that what he'd thought were long black robes

GLEN COE, SCOTLAND – PRESENT TIME

were really the waterproof caped raincoats used by pipe bands all over Scotland, so common as not to be noticed. He counted. There were thirteen people, all dressed in black raincoats with hoods and masks that hid their faces.

He couldn't see the man he thought might be his father. He couldn't even be sure he'd seen correctly. It had only been a fleeting impression, lasting a second. All he had to go on was the eyes. Cory hadn't seen his father's face for seven years, but he knew those blue eyes...just like his.

And the man had seen him. For a second that was suspended in time, his eyes had found Cory's and widened. And then he had walked on, in step with the others.

Cory shook away that image and focused on the group ranged around the fire. There was something really off about these people. They didn't chat all together, like people did at a gathering. They didn't tell jokes, or laugh, or tease each other. They just stood still, waiting for something.

They were evil. If pressed to tell how he knew that, Cory would have been unable to put it into words. It was a word people used all the time, but it usually didn't mean much outside of the movies. These people though—they were evil. There was a reason for the masks, and the chanting, the odd walk, the order of it all, and it chilled him to his bones wondering what it might be.

A word swam to the surface, and Cory examined it. *Ritual.* Like in church. Cory hadn't been to church since his mother had made him go when he was little, but it had made a big impression on him because of the need to stay quiet and still. A vicar stood at the front and preached at you until your head was so full you thought it might fall off, and then you said prayers, all together, with words that didn't make sense. You sat together, stood together, knelt together, and at the end you paraded out silently together. He'd thought it was rather creepy.

Cory stood in the shadows, feeling the chill spread through his fleece and wishing he had one of those piper's raincoats. He rubbed his Musketeer's bracelet—the red, white, and blue braided band with a single bead that had the letter 'D' carved into it. 'D' for D'Artagnan. It reminded him that as long as he had Athos and Porthos, the world was still a safe and honourable place.

He should get out, find Bastian and Donnie. They might be mad, but they'd have his back. They would never tell the MacMillens or anybody else about the monks. When Cory showed up and they knew he was safe, they could all decide what to do. All for one, one for all.

He didn't want to be alone anymore. He'd been alone for most of his life, and it sucked. But still, he hoped Bastian and Donnie wouldn't try to find him. It was too dangerous. It was his problem to solve; it was *his* father—or it might be— and he wasn't about to drag his only friends into this mess he'd gotten himself into.

He was tired and hungry and cold. He needed to get out of the woods, go home and face his aunt and uncle. Not that they'd care where he'd been. If his

GLEN COE, SCOTLAND – PRESENT TIME

Uncle Ivor was drunk he might punish him, but otherwise they probably wouldn't even bother. At least he'd be warm. He had to think about what to do and where to go with this nightmare he'd stumbled into.

Tell a trusted adult. The words parroted by every teacher filtered through his head, mocking him. Great idea, that. A trusted adult. There was just one problem with that. Cory had never met an adult he could trust.

He forced his attention back to the problem at hand. The reapers gathered around that firepit were definitely not to be trusted. Any eejit could see that. They were up to something bad, but he had no idea what it was.

A man spoke suddenly, his words clear and precise in spite of the black mask he wore. The others repeated his words in that weird, dead-sounding monotone. The masked man must be the leader, so Cory decided to call him the Vicar. The man said something else, and the rest of the group repeated it after him, just like in church.

He recognized the language now. It was Gaelic, or some form of it. He'd studied the auld tongue in school and liked the rough, guttural pronunciation. He didn't know enough to keep up, but he could make out a word or two here and there.

Tighearna... That meant 'God', or maybe 'Lord'... *Belenus...a 'glanadh teine...* He was pretty sure *teine* meant 'fire.'

What the hell? What were a bunch of grown men doing out here in the wind and dark, chanting things about fire and God? He wished he'd studied harder.

WITCH

Instead, he stood stock still in the dark shelter of the trees and watched and listened until he thought he'd freeze.

His eyes snapped open and he gazed around, unsure for a moment where he was. His muscles had turned into hard plastic, and he was sure his fingers had fallen off. The reapers were still at it. The words were clearer now, not that it mattered. He still didn't understand much of it.

The Vicar was telling them something now, in English. "Remember...go back...next week..." Normal words. It made his previous fears seem ridiculous. These weren't strange beings, after all, just ordinary men meeting in the woods.

Thirteen ordinary people, dressed all alike in black cloaks and masks, chanting and swaying in front of a fire. *Aye, normal as pish.*

Everybody knew thirteen was unlucky. Once, when he was very young, his parents had taken him to London on holiday and they'd stayed at one of the newer hotels. He remembered counting the storeys out loud as they appeared on the display in the lift and asking why the numbers jumped from twelve to fourteen.

"Just a superstition," his mother had told him. "Even though they won't admit it, people don't like to stay on the thirteenth storey, so many hotels just skip that number. Daft, aye?"

"Why is thirteen unlucky?"

"I'm not sure," she'd said. "It just is. People believe bad things will happen on Friday the 13th, eh? And I think it's an important number in magic. Don't worry

GLEN COE, SCOTLAND – PRESENT TIME

about it," she said, ruffling his hair. "We're on the fifth storey."

Now here were thirteen people standing in a circle around a fire, repeating words in Gaelic. A chill unrelated to the weather slithered up his spine. *Evil. Fire. Magic.* He didn't want to admit it, but he was pretty sure what this was. A *cult*. Maybe a bunch of religious nutters who worshipped fire and practiced black magic. He knew he was being silly, but this had gone too far.

The reapers began to file out of the circle. The Vicar tapped a shorter man on the shoulder. "Stay back with me," he said. The man stopped walking and faced him without speaking, shoulders hunched and hands clasped in front of him. The others moved off down the path, but then a third man dropped back to join them. The three stood rigid and silent, watching the others move away down the path.

Cory stood frozen in place, not ten feet away from the three men. *Weren't they going to leave?* He was in over his head. It was time to go home. Time to find an adult, preferably one who didn't wander around in the woods at night in a black cloak and chant things about fire.

There was a rustling sound behind him, off to his left. Cory froze in place and strained to listen. Nothing. The rain dripping off the leaves, that was all.

The sound came again. Cory looked down and stifled a yelp. A black cat, almost invisible in the darkness, was standing right next to his foot, staring up at him with yellow eyes that radiated intelligence. It reminded him of Biscuit, the cat in the bookshop.

WITCH

The Vicar spoke suddenly, and Cory's attention snapped back to the three men on the path. He caught some of the words, uttered in a soft, gentle voice.

"Why...enough...chose to betray..."

The man in the middle stood between the two taller men like a child being scolded. His head was bowed and his hands kept clasping and unclasping.

The Vicar patted the man's arm. "Belenus says... forgive..." As he spoke, he raised his head and looked over the cowering man's shoulder.

He nodded, and Cory watched the third man ease a blunt, hammer-like object out of his cloak. He raised it high into the air and brought it down sharply on the other man's head. Cory gasped in horror as the man crumpled to the ground and lay still.

"What was that?" The Vicar whipped his head around and stared straight at the woods where Cory stood, fist jammed into his mouth. The third man took a step forward, still holding the hammer in his hand.

Something flashed out of the trees and raced across the path to disappear in the underbrush on the other side. Cory watched the man with the weapon whip his head around to face the path. "Just a damn cat," he growled, and returned to kneel over the motionless body.

"He's dead."

The two stared for a moment at the man sprawled on the path, and then the killer stowed his weapon in his cloak and bent down to hoist the body over his shoulders. Without a word they walked away down the trail toward the glen.

GLEN COE, SCOTLAND – PRESENT TIME

Cory turned and stumbled further into the woods. He rubbed his wrist, and his heart lurched. He brought his hand close to his eyes and stared at the empty place where his bracelet should be, but it was gone, along with the illusion of honour and safety and fairness that had carried him through fifteen years of life. He leaned against a tree, put his face into the crook of his arm, and sobbed.

CHAPTER 12
FORT WILLIAM, SCOTLAND – PRESENT TIME

*I don't have to outrun the bear;
I just have to outrun you.*
—Proverb

Myles Grant sat in his study and gazed out the window at Loch Linnhe. Usually this view relaxed him, no matter what was on his mind, but not today. He contemplated the whitecaps on the loch, envious that they knew exactly where they were going when his mind was such a mess.

He should be working. He was between novels, but his publisher expected the next book on time. Normally it wouldn't have been a problem. His *Death in the Highlands* series practically wrote itself now; seven crime novels so far, based on a tried-and-true plotline with characters who did what they were supposed to and behaved themselves as heroes and villains should.

He looked down at the laptop in disgust. Was it being home in Fort William that was unsettling him, after a long stint of research? Nothing new about that; he went out for months at a time, gathering the feel and the history of the place that would be the setting for his next book. Then he'd come home to turn his murderers loose and call up his protagonist, Detective Inspector Harper Beaton, to wreak havoc on their wicked lives.

Readers loved Inspector Beaton, a middle-aged, curmudgeonly fellow whose inattention to appearance was rivalled only by his clever brain. The crusty detective had ridden the *Death in the Highlands* series to worldwide popularity and made Myles Grant a wealthy man.

Myles didn't want to admit it, but he was tired of Inspector Beaton. Readers weren't stupid; if the author was bored with his character, they would be too. He'd been toying with the idea of killing him off more often lately...but to what purpose? He was a mystery writer—what else could he do?

I'm wondering if I'll have to change after this. The words uttered to that rather lovely lass at HP Booksellers came back to hover at the front of his mind. He hadn't really meant them. He'd just been flirting—something else he was rather good at.

Maybe he hadn't meant the words, but she *was* really very beautiful. Before he could pursue that thought further, he closed the laptop and returned his gaze to the waters of the loch. He was looking for a sign of the *each-uisge*, the water horse that legend said lived in Loch Linnhe and was reputed to prowl

FORT WILLIAM, SCOTLAND – PRESENT TIME

the waters in search of children. There was no sign of the monster. Of course not. There was never a sign.

Myles snorted. The water horse needed to do some serious marketing, like Nessie, the resident monster up in Loch Ness. Even though she'd never been seen and scientists were adamant that she didn't exist, Nessie populated gift shops all over the Highlands. She was a pro at sales.

The *each-uisge* didn't even have a name, much less a following, which could have been because its reputation was less than cuddly. According to legend, the water horse collected children on its back and then galloped off to the loch to drown and eat them. Not guaranteed to charm tourists, for sure. People didn't like it when their kids came home from holiday with nightmares.

Myles remembered being afraid of horses when he was a young lad, for fear that one of them might be the *each-uisge*. It might also be the reason he hadn't chosen fantasy when he began writing. But all the same, it was his loch, and his monster, so he was protective of the legend as only someone who lives by his imagination can be.

He sighed and stood up. All this introspection wasn't getting him anywhere, and it wasn't solving the problem of what to do with Detective Inspector Harper Beaton, either. Maybe he should drive into the town centre, walk the High Street, stop in at the bookstore to discuss the upcoming signing event. He might ask that pretty Màiri what she thought of offing his protagonist, and then slip in an invitation to dinner.

Considerably cheered, Myles drove round to the top of Fort William's High Street. He decided to take a chance on the Parade Gardens car park, even though it had only twenty-five spots that filled up quickly. He liked the walk to the High Street through the gardens and preferred the smaller lot.

Ahh, he said, as a car pulled out and he backed his Mercedes into the miraculously available space. *Things are looking up.* He paid for two hours through his app and walked the short distance to the historical park. Like all locals, Myles Grant had great pride in this park, home to the Peace Memorial that paid tribute to those who had died in two World Wars. He stopped at the monument to give his own moment of silence and then continued on through the park to the High Street.

HP Booksellers was in the middle of the pedestrian street, nestled between a chippy and a kilt shop, but somehow it gave the impression of age, as if the shop had been here much longer than the modern paved road. There was a bench under the bookshop window, and on the bench sat a black cat. Yellow eyes fixed on him, but the animal didn't move.

"Hullo, cat," Myles said. The cat swished its tail and blinked its eyes, and Myles passed through the door to the shop, wondering if he'd just been judged. *Was I supposed to pet it? Was I found wanting?* He didn't know why, but the answer seemed important.

Mary Duncan came around the reception desk to greet him. "Tis good t' see ye," she chirped. "Are ye here t' see Màiri, lad?"

"Oh! Is she here, then?" Myles hoped his answer sounded as nonchalant as he thought it did, but the

FORT WILLIAM, SCOTLAND – PRESENT TIME

look in Mary's eye told him otherwise. So did the unladylike snort he was sure he had just heard.

"Well, now, she isnae. She's down t' th' Museum, fer Eve's first tour. I dinnae think ye've met our Evie, eh?" At Myles headshake, she swept on. "She's part o' th' HP family, our Evie is, an' so's her Daniel, e'en though he doesnae work at th' shop. She's got herself a job at the Museum, an' we're that proud o' her. Ye'll meet her later."

Myles felt a curious letdown, as if these people shared a bond he wasn't a part of. Stupid, of course. He was a guest—a contractor. He'd never felt that way about any other venue he'd done book signings for, but the fact was that he was an outsider. He had no idea who this Eve and Daniel were, but he was envious. They were part of the HP family, and he wasn't. And what did HP mean, anyway? More irritating mystery.

He felt a pressure on his leg and looked down to see the black cat brushing his ankle.

"Biscuit seems t' like ye, an she's verra petickular," Mary said, as if she knew what he'd been thinking. He had a sudden strange idea that this little woman could read minds. *You're getting too fanciful today, Grant. Get a grip!* Still, he felt much better. He'd never owned a pet. He travelled too much, and if he had, it would have been a dog. He gave the black cat a wary eye. Apparently this creature's opinion counted here.

" Flower of Scotland" chimed behind him, and Myles turned to see a man about his own age pushing through the door. An average lad, brown hair, brown eyes. Nothing special about him, except for his physique. The stranger was fit—*very* fit—and for some reason it rankled. He suddenly felt like a pudding.

A hoarse, snuffling wheeze had followed the newcomer in through the door, and Myles realized the man was holding a leash in his right hand. At the other end of the leash was a squat, bow-legged bulldog.

Myles regarded the customer with mild distaste. Of course, it was perfectly fine for a man to have a dog, but if he did it should be a *real* dog like a retriever, not a wheezing ottoman on a leash.

The man had stopped in the entryway and was giving a wary look to the crowd that had now swelled to include Caomhainn, Betty, and Henry.

"Is my dog allowed in?" he asked tentatively. "I mean, your sign says well-behaved dogs are welcome, and he *seems* well-behaved. I'm not quite sure—I just got him."

"O' course he's welcome!" Betty was kneeling on the floor, both hands scratching the bulldog's ears. The dog's wrinkled face folded into a blissful grin.

Mary took the newcomer's hand in her tiny one and peered up into his eyes. "Are ye awright, lad?" she asked him. "Ye gave us quite a scare last week, but Màiri called an' th' doctor said ye were fine. I'm verra glad!" She pulled the leash out of his hand and handed it off to Betty. "Get the wee dug some water, aye?" She led the man over to the nearest armchair and pointed to it. "Sit."

"I'm fine," he protested, but he sat.

"Maybe ye should introduce yerself," Henry said, his tone dry. "I mean, we met ye under such

FORT WILLIAM, SCOTLAND – PRESENT TIME

harrowin' circumstances, and now ma wife seems t' have decided yer a part o' th' family."

There it was again—part of the family. Myles watched with growing irritation.

"Oh. Aye," the man said. "I'm Adam MacArthur. I'm a friend of Eve's. Her fiancé is my brother."

"An' who's this bundle o' p'fection?" Betty asked, her attention still focused on the dog.

"Oh. That's Pearl. And before you ask, he's a male."

"Well, o' course 'e is!" Betty looked astonished. "I mean, look a' th' size o'—"

Caomhainn burst into laughter. "Ah, Betty, yer th' best. Nivver change, lass." He joined her on the floor and began speaking in Gaelic to the dog, who grinned and drooled at the attention.

Myles had been standing near the reception counter while all this was going on. *Without a doubt*, he thought, *this is the weirdest group of people I've ever met. What have I bitten off, agreeing to work with them?* "Umm..." He cleared his throat, preparing to leave.

Mary gave him a sympathetic look. "I'm sorry, Mister Grant, we've fergotten t' introduce ye."

I don't want to be introduced! At least, not to him! Myles' inner voice protested. But Mary gave him another look, one that plainly said she knew what he was thinking...again.

"Adam, Pearl," she said, "this is Myles Grant, Fort William's own author."

Myles smiled politely. Then, deciding to be magnanimous, he reached down and patted the dog on the head. The bulldog smiled up at him.

The dog's grin died as Biscuit sauntered up and

gave him the once-over. Pearl studied the cat for a moment and then reached out a tongue and swiped it up her chest.

It seemed to Myles that the air had been sucked out of the room. The four proprietors were staring at Biscuit as if she were in charge of this situation and they were only there to watch.

The cat turned and walked away toward the children's section of the shop, tail high. She stopped and cocked her head, and Pearl lumbered after her like a huge minion, dragging his leash.

Mary let out a long breath and then looked at Adam as if he was responsible for this remarkable happening. "Yer wee dug has good taste," she said.

Myles wondered why he felt so grumpy. He opened his mouth to say something clever, but his words were lost in the sudden cacophony of sirens shrieking in the distance. Everyone stopped and listened as the wailing grew louder.

Myles stepped out onto the High Street and was nearly bowled over by a man running by the shop.

"It's the museum!" the man gasped. "The museum's on fire!" He broke away and continued toward the end of the street.

The museum? Hadn't they said Màiri was at the museum?

Fire trucks were pulled up to the old building, where black smoke billowed from a front window. Myles began running, not stopping to think why. He was halfway down the street before he realized that Adam was right behind him. For a second they ran side by side, then the man sped up and passed him easily. Myles increased his pace, but by the time he reached the barricades that had been put up by the firefighters, he had to bend over to catch his breath. Adam was standing behind a barricade six feet away from him, straining to see.

Myles let his thoughts whirl and re-form. What the hell was he doing? He wasn't a firefighter, nor was he a rubbernecker. He had no business being here. What had propelled him down the High Street as if he were training for the Olympics?

There was an answer; and he was pretty sure its name started with an 'M.'

Damn it.

CHAPTER 13
FORT WILLIAM, SCOTLAND – PRESENT TIME

*What is it about fire? So calm and peaceful,
but inside, full of power and destruction.
It's hiding something, just like people do.*
—George R. R. Martin

"You're a natural, Eve!" Màiri hugged her friend. "I've lived in this area all my life, and I didn't think there was anything I didn't know about Glencoe, especially the massacre. But you made me feel as if I was there in 1692. What a horrible night!"

Eve smiled. "Well, could be because I'm a MacDonald. It's in my blood. It's weird, though. I sometimes feel as if I remember being there that night, too. I hear the gunshots, feel the cold of the blizzard. It's happened more frequently since I met Daniel." She laughed. "Did you know MacArthur is a sept of Clan Campbell? Makes us a proper Romeo and Juliet, aye?"

Màiri looked around the central room of the West Highlands Museum. Maybe it was because they were the only ones left in the building, but the silence was profound. It seemed to have a life of its own.

"Well, you've certainly been obsessed with the past for as long as I've known you, and it's not likely to get better now that you work here. Am I right?" she asked the woman in a glass case next to her, who was resplendently arrayed in an eighteenth-century gown with a yellow and black checkered arasaid. Being headless, the woman didn't answer.

"There's a name for what you feel," she told Eve. "It's called *retrocognition*. People remember things from the past that they couldn't possibly know. What?"

Eve was staring at her. "How did you get so smart?"

Màiri blushed but waved her away. "I work in a bookshop, numpty. When business is slow, I look stuff up. I love scientific terms."

"Hmmph. I work there too, but I don't know all the little things you do. Nope—you're just smart. Didn't you memorize all the kinds of phobias once? I mean, who does that? You should've been a scientist...or a doctor."

Màiri's face stilled. "Why do you say that?"

"I don't know. I just think it's something you could have done, if you'd had the right guidance in high school. Too late now, I guess." Eve bent to straighten the stack of maps that guided visitors around the museum. When she looked up, Màiri was still standing there, staring into space.

"What's wrong?" she asked. "You're in another world."

FORT WILLIAM, SCOTLAND – PRESENT TIME

Màiri's eyes regained focus. "Oh. Nothing." She smiled. "Practicing retrocognition, I guess." *Should've been a doctor...Too late now.*

Suddenly Eve raised her head and sniffed. "Do you smell smoke?"

Màiri sniffed the air in the large room. "Yes!" She looked toward the door that led toward the exit. "But wouldn't the fire alarm have—"

The urgent wail of the fire alarm cut her off. It resounded in the space, reverberating off the glass exhibit cases in a harsh shrill of sound. The smell was growing stronger, and now they could see a thin trail of black smoke seeping under the door.

Màiri turned to Eve. Her friend's hands were shaking and her face had drained of colour. "M-Màiri, the museum is on fire! We're trapped!"

Eve's entire body was shaking. Her eyes were unfocused, and she seemed rooted to the spot. *Pyrophobia.* The word swam out of the back of Màiri's mind. *Fear of fire.*

"Eve, snap out of it! We have to get out of here!" She pointed toward a door that led deeper into the museum.

"The smoke is coming from the front. Come on, let's go that way!"

She grabbed her friend's hand, but it was like trying to pull a boulder. Fear had frozen Eve's limbs and given her the wrong kind of strength. Màiri was going to have to drag her full bodyweight, which was surprisingly heavy given her slight build.

Their progress was painfully slow. Màiri stopped and slapped Eve's face a couple of times, but she seemed to have gone somewhere unreachable, and there was no recognition in her wide grey eyes.

Suddenly Eve pulled her hand out of Màiri's grip and bolted for the front door—the one from which the smoke was pouring.

"Eve, no!" But it was too late. Smoke billowed into the room, filling the space with an acrid, stifling cloud of grey. Now Màiri could see tendrils of red and orange, licking at the edge of the doorway. Eve had disappeared.

Màiri looked for the exit on the other side of the room. Smoke was curling under the door there, too. She'd have to go after Eve. She could hear sirens in the distance, their wail growing stronger. Help was coming. She took a deep breath and regretted it as smoke filled her throat, then charged toward the doorway where Eve had gone.

The room was filled with smoke. A bookcase against the wall was on fire, the paper and glue sending poisonous fumes into the air. Flames worked their way around the edges of the room, as if they had been given a villainous mission and would let nothing stand in their way. Màiri dropped to her hands and knees and crawled, keeping to the centre of the room and as far from the burning bookshelf as possible.

It seemed as if time had stopped, holding her prisoner in a world of smoke and fire. Images danced in the flames that now engulfed the entire wall where the bookcase had stood. With a whoosh, the curtains on the window next to the case went up in a ball of fire.

FORT WILLIAM, SCOTLAND – PRESENT TIME

Across the room was a bundle of clothes on the floor. *Eve!* Màiri crawled across the floor to where her friend lay, eyes closed. Words came to her as if written on a piece of paper: *Get the victim out of the danger area first!*

Màiri saw that Eve had almost made it to the door leading to the museum's foyer, so she stood, reached down to take the unresponsive woman under her arms, and pulled. It seemed as if the exit was impossibly far away, but at last they made it to the door. Màiri felt for heat, relieved that there was none. She eased the door open and dragged Eve through and into the foyer.

The air was clearer here, but it wouldn't be for long. She pulled desperately, but Eve was a dead weight. A curious weakness spread through her own body, and her eyes were losing focus.

No! She was the only one who could get them out of here. She checked to make sure Eve was still breathing.

She wasn't.

A shaft of raw fear arced through her. *Eve! No!* Then she began CPR, dredging up the instructions from the online search she'd done after the incident in the bookshop. CAB, she thought. *Compression, airway, breathing.* She placed her fists in what she hoped was the right position and began pushing down on Eve's chest. *One...two... How many?* She fought the panic waiting to curl around her head and squeeze the reason out of her and kept going.

Airway. She tilted Eve's head back and checked to see that her airway was clear. She pinched her

WITCH

friend's nose shut and breathed into her mouth, *once...twice.*

Nothing. Eve's chest remained still. The panic tightened its hold, but Màiri pushed it ruthlessly aside and began the sequence again. Twice more, and still there was no response. *Where was the ambulance?*

She could hear sirens, off in the distance, but Màiri could see nothing beyond the tiny space in which she was fighting for Eve's life. She did the CPR sequence once more. Still no response. A memory was trying to make its way past the knot of panic in her mind, and she let it slide in.

What had happened in the bookshop had had nothing to do with CPR, and yet she'd known she could save that man. Maybe...

She took a deep breath and placed her hand on Eve's chest, as she had done with the brown-haired man. At first, nothing happened. Then a blue light appeared, very faint but definitely real, around the edges of her hand, and she felt the cold of a heart no longer beating. Her eyes welled and terror gripped her, threatening to take her into the abyss.

The blue light was fading. *Was her hand growing warmer?* The light changed to a light pink and spread out around her hand. Màiri forgot to hope, forgot the panic, forgot everything except the light, growing ever pinker under her hand.

Eve's chest rose, almost imperceptibly. Then it fell, rose, and fell again. She was breathing.

The wail of the sirens grew stronger. Help was coming. She took a deep breath and regretted it as smoke filled her throat and she began coughing.

FORT WILLIAM, SCOTLAND – PRESENT TIME

The door behind them crashed open, and a firefighter burst through. He took in the scene in seconds, scooped Eve up, and pointed to his belt. Màiri nodded and hooked her fingers around the canvas strip, and seconds later they were outside.

The firefighter pulled off his mask. "Can you wait here?" I'll be right back." Without waiting for an answer, he carried Eve to the waiting ambulance.

Màiri stumbled over to the flower bed at the side of the museum and vomited up the lunch she'd had that afternoon, mixed with soot and smoke. A hand touched her shoulder, and she spun around to see that the firefighter who'd pulled them out of the museum was back. He'd removed his helmet, and concerned grey eyes scanned her face.

"They'll take good care of your friend," he said. "But you've inhaled some smoke, too, and you need to get checked out. Would you like to ride with her?"

Màiri nodded. A piece of rough sandpaper kept scraping the sides of her throat, and she was afraid to speak. Their rescuer walked with her to the waiting ambulance and helped her inside.

"Th-thank you," she rasped, and he smiled before putting his helmet back on and racing back to the burning building.

Inside the vehicle, an ambulance technician fastened an oxygen mask to her face. Eve had a mask in place and had been hooked to an IV, so Màiri sat next to her and held her hand. It was warm, and a moment later her eyes opened. A sob of relief rose in Màiri's parched throat.

"It's going to be fine," she rasped. "We made it."

Eve nodded, but then a look of alarm flared in the grey eyes. "Th'—th'—museum—"

"Don't try to talk!" the technician cautioned. He adjusted her mask and smiled. "You're more important than a building, aye, lass?"

Màiri patted Eve's hand and tried to look hopeful. "The museum will be fine," she lied. "The firefighters got there very quickly. You'll be back to work in no time."

Eve sighed and closed her eyes. Màiri glanced at the paramedic, and he nodded. He knew as well as she did that the museum was not going to be fine.

Poor Eve, she thought. *She got her dream job, and after one tour, it's up in smoke. Literally.*

But she was alive. She'd live, and her dream would live within her. That was all that mattered.

At the hospital, Eve was whisked away and Màiri spent the next two hours in the emergency room, undergoing tests and having unpleasant instruments placed down her throat. She was assessed for soot and thermal burns to her airway. They listened to her lungs, nodded a lot, wrote things down on their clipboards, and finally a doctor came to see her.

"You were very fortunate, miss," the doctor told her. "You inhaled very little smoke, and your airways are clear."

"So I can leave?"

"Well...not quite yet. We want to keep you overnight, monitor your CO levels, and make sure there are no delayed repercussions. Fires are different from any other kind of accident," he added. "It's possible that you could have neurological issues" — he

FORT WILLIAM, SCOTLAND – PRESENT TIME

put up a hand at Màiri's frightened expression—"unlikely, in your case, but I have to inform you of the possibilities."

"Wh-what neurological issues?"

"Well, you could experience memory impairment. Again, unlikely. But we'll want you to come in after a week or two and we'll run the tests again." He patted her hand. "I don't want to scare you, but you need to know that the aftereffects of fire can be dangerous."

Later, lying in her hospital bed, Màiri stared at the darkening sky outside her window and ran over the doctor's words again and again. *Neurological issues... memory impairment.* She'd been afraid to ask, but the thought sat like a leaden balloon on her stomach. *What about Eve?*

Another thought filtered up, pushing the balloon aside. What happened back there? It had happened again, the sense of light and warmth, just before Eve started breathing. Was it the CPR, or something else? One thing she was sure about, though. She had saved Eve, just as she had saved that man. Shouldn't she be proud of that? So why this sense of terror?

CHAPTER 14
DORNACH, SCOTLAND – 1722

SÌNE

The screaming was relentless. Sìne pressed her hands to her ears, but with nothing but a curtain to separate the living space from Maighread's midwifery, it did little good. It was a woman's duty and privilege to go through this agony, again and again. From the time they were born they were destined to repeat the cycle of life, to produce an heir, or a farmer, or a fisherman. Their pain was necessary so that the village could go on. None questioned it.

Well, Sìne questioned it, but that mattered little. Her destiny was different. She would never marry, so she would never have to bear a child. No man wanted a malformed wife. No one wanted to hold a hand that resembled a goat's hoof. And where would they put the ring?

WITCH

When the screaming was particularly intense, like now, she thought it a blessing, but when the child was born and she was allowed in to see it, the love shining in the mother's tired eyes almost undid her. How quickly the birth erased the pain that had come before.

Sìne wondered why it was called a miracle, when it was merely the result of a man and a woman mating, no different from the sheep in the fields or the cat in the barn. Surely the mother had toiled, at the risk of her own life, to produce this small creature that nuzzled contentedly at her breast. But it was merely God's plan, and one that was particularly cruel to women.

No, the true miracle lay in her mother's gift. And that was something neither Maighread nor Doirin knew she was aware of. They thought her safe behind the curtain, ignorant of the truth. But she had seen. Her mother had told her once that 'Gilchrist' meant 'servant of God' in the old tongue, and she believed it. Surely He had blessed Doirin Gilchrist and called her to do His work.

She had been awakened one night, several years ago now, by screams of pain, accompanied by Maighread's low, soothing crooning. Another difficult childbirth, she thought. But suddenly the screams had stopped, replaced by a new urgency in Maighread's voice that had Sìne creeping to the door.

She peeked through the curtain that separated the bedrooms from the main room of the cottage. A woman was lying still on the bed, eyes closed, face white as chalk. Maighread and Mam were bent over her, whispering something Sìne couldn't hear.

DORNACH, SCOTLAND – 1722

She sucked in her breath. The woman was Finola Grant, Alan's mother. He'd just been talking about her yesterday in school, complaining that his mother was so fat and lazy because of the bairn in her stomach that she didn't even want to cook anymore. And now here she was, lying still, maybe even dying. Lads were like men, so stupid and selfish; they never thought about what women did for them.

As Sìne watched, her mother placed her hand over the bulging belly. A light, faint at first and then becoming a bright blue, emanated from beneath her hand and flowed over the mound. As it moved in a widening circle, the colour turned from blue to lavender and then to a light pink. The pink travelled up to Finola Grant's neck and then to her face, and her eyes opened.

"That's it, love," Maighread whispered. "Now, push!" Moments later a fuzzy head pushed its way into the midwife's hands, and Alan's wee brother was born. His skin was a translucent porcelain blue, but he was alive.

Mam slept the whole of the next day and night, looking almost as drained as Mrs. Grant had looked the night before. But when the sun rose over the firth on the second morning, she was up tending to the fire as if nothing unusual had happened.

Sìne began to pay more attention, but as she grew older, she failed to witness any more instances of her mother's odd ability. The blue light turning to pink, the remarkable recovery of a person thought to be dying. She never mentioned what she had seen, and her mother and gran never talked to her about it.

Alan's little brother Askill, whom Sìne privately thought of as 'the blue boy," was growing up to be a right twit just like his brother. He toddled after Alan, trying to join in the 'fun' when the others called her names because of her malformed hands. So many times Sìne wanted to pull him aside, get in his cherubic little face, and say "D' ye ken ye're here t'day because o' my mother, y wee rattie? "

She had come to terms with her deformity. Life was a balance, after all; God gave and He took away, the Bible said. Her fused hands were the price she paid for her mother's gift of healing. Had she never seen the miracle, she might have grown up bitter and resentful, but instead she thanked God every night in her prayers for the trust He had put in her wonderful mother.

She came to think He had something planned for her, too, and when He revealed it, she would not let Him down. She could bear the taunts of the other children, even odious Walter MacKay and Archie Ross and that prissy young Ailis MacAllan. They didn't know the honour that had been bestowed on her family. And she would never tell.

The screaming on the other side of the curtain stopped, replaced by the grunts of a woman desperate to be rid of the burden she had carried for nearly ten months.

"Push, love!" Maighread said, and soon the grunts were replaced by the strident cries of another newborn bairn.

"Ye can come on out noo, lass," her mother called. "Tis done. We have a newcomer t' th' village. Come see. Keep yer distance, ye dinnae want t' scare th' wee lad."

Keep yer distance. Not because she might frighten

DORNACH, SCOTLAND – 1722

the new one, but because the mother wouldn't want her near her precious bairn. Sìne kept her hands tucked under her apron, smiled at the woman, and made her way to the door and out.

Her feet took her, as usual, to the seaside. It was her favourite place to get away, to sit and think. It seemed as if none of her schoolmates ever came here...except for one.

"Sìne!"

She turned to see Hugh Sutherland loping toward her, a huge smile on his face. With his flyaway brown hair and multi-hued brown eyes, he was going to be so handsome when he grew to manhood.

Sìne frowned. He was already attracting the attention of the lassies at school, and the knowledge caused an odd lump of pain to lodge somewhere in the region of her chest. He was growing tall, filling out from the work he did in his father's fields, leaving the lad behind. How long would it be before he left *her* behind?

Hugh had left school last year, finished with the books and teachings of childhood. She didn't see him as often now, but when they met it was as if they were children again, just happy to be together. It would be hard to lose him, but she knew she must.

He plunked himself down beside her and they sat for a while in comfortable silence. He was her best friend—her only friend if truth be told—and silence was a part of their communication.

"What're ye thinkin', lass?"

Sìne turned to see him studying her, concern reflected in his eyes. They were such unusual eyes...

all the shades of brown and gold mixed together. She smiled at him and sighed.

"Twas another difficult birthin'," she said. She grinned up at him. "She may prance about th' village like a queen, but that Flora MacInnes can scream like a stuck pig when she's birthin'!"

Hugh laughed. "I cannae picture it, no." He shook his head. 'Why d' they make ye hide an' listen when there's a birthin'? Isnae there somethin' ye could do t' be o' help?"

"No." Sine's face fell. "They cannae let me near. Th' women arenae in their right minds, birthin', an' they're afraid their bairn might be cursed. It might come out like me." She gave him an embarrassed smile. "Can ye blame 'em?"

Hugh's face turned red, and he turned his head away to look at the sea. He turned back suddenly and picked up one of her hands, studying it.

"They're a pack o' fools, superstitious an' mean. Anythin' they cannae explain, they decide is bad. Look," he said, holding her hand up between them, "there's nuthin' wrong wi' yer hands. Ye have five fingers, just like everbody else. Ye just got em stuck sommat."

Sine laughed, but then the shadow crossed her face. "But they dinnae thynk th' same as ye, aye? Ye ken people allus thynk th' worst o' us, me an' Mam. They call us names, make up stories about Mam. They say she must o' been doin' summat wrong fer me t' be like this."

Bitterness oozed out of her voice. "Everbody kens I havenae a da, e'en though Uncle Mungo pertends t' be one." She looked up at Hugh, blue eyes shining with unshed tears.

"Yesterday, I heard some o' th' lassies at school talkin'. They said maybe my da isnae around b'cause he's th' Devil, an' that's why I look like this." Her voice was low, urgent. "I ken tis nonsense...I'm not a bairn. But it hurts, Hugh!"

"I ken it does, an' I wisht I could do somethin' about it," Hugh said, his voice low and rough. "I'll allus be here fer ye, ye ken 'at, aye?" He grinned. "Except right now, I have t' get back t' work." He stood and helped her up.

Sìne smiled. "It means th' world, ye ken?" She dusted off her skirts, patted his arm, and started away down the path.

Hugh watched her go, and then turned for his own home, whistling.

"Hugh!" A high-pitched voice hailed him, and he turned to see a girl coming from the trees at the edge of the path. She was very young, with long blonde hair and large brown eyes with lashes that fluttered like butterflies.

Ailis MacAllan.

He sighed and stopped walking. "Ailis," he said. "What brings ye here?"

The girl swayed her skinny hips and batted her eyelashes again. "Ye," she giggled.

Hugh frowned. "What?"

"I'm goin' t' marry ye," she announced.

"Dinnae be ridic'lous! Ye're nought but a bairn. What are ye...ten years?"

"Twelve." Ailis smiled at him. Then her expression

morphed into one of sulky displeasure. "I saw ye talkin' t' that Sìne Gilchrist again." She wrinkled her nose. "Holdin' her hand, too. How can ye bear t' touch it?"

Hugh's jaw tightened. He opened his mouth, then shut it again. Without a backward look, he strode off and away from Ailis MacAllan. She remained on the path, watching him go. A predatory gleam flickered in her eyes, and a sly smile crossed her young face.

"Jist ye wait, Hugh Sutherland. Jist ye wait."

CHAPTER 15
DORNACH, SCOTLAND – 1722

HUGH

Hugh jabbed the spade into the soil, pulled it out again, and thrust it harder into the ground.

"Hugh! What're ye tryin' t do? Kill th' earth? Move along!" His father's voice brought him out of the delightful daydream where each clod of earth had a name. *Walter MacKay, Archie Ross, Ailis MacAllan—*everybody who'd ever made fun of Sìne Gilchrist.

I'm goin t' marry ye. The words danced through his head, simpering, taunting. Ailis MacAllan was just a wee bairn, a nuisance. She followed him around, teasing at him like a whole horde of midges, and just like midges there seemed no way to get rid of her.

Ailis' father was the Sutherlands' foreman, an easy-going gentleman who was serious about his work and his leisure time in equal measure. He seemed a nice fellow; treated Hugh as an adult and even asked his opinion once in a while, if the subject wasn't too weighty.

Hugh felt sorry for Mister MacAllan sometimes. He seemed almost afraid of his wife—a sallow, pinched woman who might have been pretty if she took her nose down out of the air long enough. Thoroughly unlikeable, and it was obvious to Hugh which parent Ailis resembled. She and her mother were cut from the same cloth.

How can ye bear t' touch it? Hugh stabbed the spade into the soil again. *How dare she say that about Sìne!* The two girls were furlongs apart in social status, and yet Sìne was ten times better than that little minx, in every way.

I'm goin' t' marry ye.

O'er my deid body. Now, if it had been Sìne saying that it would be different. Hugh had decided years ago that once they were grown to marriageable age, Sìne would be the one he would choose to spend the rest of his life with. She was kind, generous, and smart. They would never run out of interesting things to talk about, not if they lived to be a hundred years old.

Hugh stopped punishing the clod of earth and moved to the next one, lest his father stick *him* with a fork. But his thoughts rolled around in his head and always came back to Sìne.

She was worried about her mother. Doirin Gilchrist was recognized as a healer, but it was a tenuous respect, balanced by the knowledge that she'd given birth to a daughter out of wedlock and had a suspect past. Truth be told, if she hadn't had Maighread

DORNACH, SCOTLAND – 1722

Arthur at her back, Doirin would have been dropped like a hot cinder by the women of Dornach.

But nobody wanted to tangle with Maighread Arthur. The old woman had helped to birth most of their children and she knew too many secrets, shouted out in the throes of childbirth or confided in relief when the bairn had come safely into the world.

Hugh wished there was something he could do for Sine. God had to like her at least as much as he himself did, so why had He marred her like that? How could He stand to watch as one of His own was maligned and abused for something over which she had no control? Hugh frowned at the dark clouds overhead. God had better have something big planned for Sine, or He was going to have to reckon with Hugh Sutherland!

A clap of thunder sounded off in the hills, and Hugh ducked his head. "Sorry," he mumbled. "I shouldnae take Yer name in vain, I ken 't. But please, Ye do have sumpthin' planned fer her, aye? Sumpthin' good?"

The answer was a large drop of rain that plopped onto his head and rolled down his nose. It was followed by another roll of thunder, still far away. A storm was coming. Duncan Sutherland called a halt to the work, and the men made for their own cottages, where supper was waiting.

Hugh stood for a while under the overhanging thatch of the gardener's hut, watching the lightning arc above the mountains to the west. It was beautiful, wild and angry and free. But not yet here.

He left his shelter and loped toward the village, his boots taking him along the road toward a particular

WITCH

cottage. His father wouldn't be all that surprised when he didn't show up for supper. It happened frequently, and Duncan didn't seem to care. He'd probably care if he knew where his son went, though. The thought both cheered and chilled him.

"What're ye doin' out in sich dreich wither?" called a familiar voice, and Mungo Murray came toward him out of the lowering gloom. Then he laughed. "Never ye mind; she's t' home. There's space fer ye at th' table; I'm fer supper in th' village t'night." He patted Hugh on the shoulder and continued down the road, headed in the direction of the tavern.

Hugh reached the Gilchrist cottage and knocked on the wooden door. The rain was coming on heavier now, dripping off the thatch and running down inside his shirt. He raised his hand to knock again and the door opened. Doirin stood silhouetted against the light from the hearth fire. For just a second it seemed as if she were standing in the fire itself, oblivious to the flames curling at her feet. Then the illusion passed.

"Hugh! Come in, lad. Have ye had yer supper?" Doirin pulled him in out of the rain and handed him a cloth to dry his hair. "Yer welcome t' stay, as allus."

"Thank ye, Mistress. I thynk I will then." Hugh bobbed his head, and Doirin smiled at him, seeming amused by the title. Doirin Gilchrist's social standing was not of a level where she would normally be addressed as Mistress; she, like most of the women of the village, was just called by her first name. Hugh's father would skelp him if he heard his son using the honorific.

But Doirin was different from the other women in Dornach. She would be his mother-in-law someday, so he owed her respect. And Duncan Sutherland would give him more than a skelping if he heard *that*.

Sìne turned from the tub where she was peeling neeps and gave Hugh a wide smile. "I didnae thynk we'd be seein' ye t'night, not wi' the storm comin'. Ye must be part kelpie, then," she teased, "happy t' be oot 'n th' wet. C'mon in afore ye catch cauld."

"Ye're more like a kelpie, what with th' black hair," he said. "Much prettier than a kelpie, though."

"An' I'm not wet." She turned back to her task, having won that battle. She always won. Hugh didn't mind. She could always have the last word, as far as he was concerned.

They gathered around the rough wooden table and Maighread said the grace prayer.

> *Some hae meat an canna eat, And*
> *some wad eat that want it;*
> *But we hae meat, and we can eat,*
> *And sae the Lord be thankit.*

There was no meat—this was a fishing village, and meat was for the wealthy. If he were home, he'd be eating venison, fruit, bread with honey, and cake with berries. But somehow, this simple meal of oats, neeps, and fish tasted better than anything he'd ever had at the lonely dining table in the Sutherland house.

Conversation flowed freely, the women teasing each other and including Sìne and Hugh in their jesting. Maighread pretended to be a cranky old woman, but the others saw through her and let her have her way.

Thunder sounded over the crackling of the fire, and the wind howled around the corners of the small cottage. The hiss of rain on the thatch grew stronger. But inside was warmth, and love, and a sense of family. *This*, thought Hugh. *This is what it will be like.*

A loud pounding that was not thunder sounded against the wooden door, and Maighread looked up and sighed. "I kent t'would be t'night. None o' Bridie Campbell's bairns have e'er come easy. She'll be all night about it, too." She stood and made her way to the door, while Sìne and Doirin began to clear the table for another kind of duty.

"I'd better be gettin' on home," Hugh said. Birthing was women's work, and he was glad of it. The very idea of a woman labouring to bring forth a child brought memories of his five-year-old self, listening in abject terror to his mother's screams, rising and falling and finally dwindling to a horrible silence. He would never forget that silence.

It was not Bridie Campbell at the door. A man stood in the rain, twisting his cap in his hands. Water dripped from his hair and ran down his face like tears, and for a moment he just stood still, mouth half open.

"I'm sorry t' tell ye," he began, and they saw that the water running down his face *was* tears. "I'm sorry t' tell ye," he started again, "but there been a accident. We was walkin' 'im home...an' lighting...an' then a t-tree fell, and...I'm sorry, but 'e's..."

He shuffled and turned slightly, and just at the

edge of the circle created by the light from the fire they saw a bundle of clothing. No, not a bundle. It was a man.

Four other men stood around Mungo Murray, who lay impossibly still in the muddy yard. Doirin screamed, a horrifying keening sound that sliced through the heavy air, and the circle of men parted as she ran to kneel at his side.

Hugh pulled Sìne in and held her face against his chest while she sobbed. He put his head back and looked into the black sky, and let the rain pelt down on his face.

What are Ye thinkin'? The rage bubbled up from some place deep inside him. *Are Ye tryin' t' see how much she can take?*

CHAPTER 16
BALLACHULISH, SCOTLAND – PRESENT TIME

Sometimes, reaching out and taking someone's hand is the beginning of a journey.
—Vera Nazarian

"They said it was arson."

Jared looked up from his laptop and blinked. "What was?" he said.

Adam blew out a breath. "You haven't been listening, have you?"

"Well...no." Jared wrinkled his brow. "Sorry, mate. I'm trying to finish this spreadsheet, and I'm behind on everything since the Liverpool trip." He looked at his partner under lowered brows. "As you know. So what were you saying?"

"How much did you hear?"

"Um, something about arson?"

"Ach, man, you're impossible!"

Jared put his hands up in self-defence and then

closed the laptop firmly. "Tell me again. I'll listen. Since you seem to think it's important."

Adam made an indeterminate sound under his breath. "Hmmph. You know the fire in Fort William yesterday?"

"Mmmm. Yeah, I caught a little bit on the news. The museum, wasn't it?"

"Yeah. They managed to save the building, but there was a lot of damage. A whole room went up, and there was smoke and water damage to several others."

Jared whistled. "Whew. That's a shame. So much history, just gone. I've been through that museum; it's pretty cool. Was." He studied Adam. "But why are you telling me about this?"

Suddenly he snapped to attention and his brown skin turned a shade lighter. "Wait. Eve just got a job there, didn't she? Was she in the fire? Is she okay?"

Adam waved him away with one hand. "Yes to both. There were only two people in the museum. It was after closing, thank God, and they were rescued and taken to hospital. Eve'll be fine, but she's still in hospital being treated for smoke inhalation."

"Oh, my God!" Jared said. "Daniel must be dewlally over it."

"Well, aye, he's anxious for sure. He's been at hospital most of the time since yesterday, but Eve's awake and alert, and more worried about the museum than herself." He rolled his eyes. "You know Eve."

"I wondered why Daniel wasn't here yet this morning," Jared said. He huffed out a breath. "Poor bird. That was her dream job." He paused. "What about the other person?"

BALLACHULISH, SCOTLAND – PRESENT TIME

Adam went quiet. Jared waved a hand back and forth in front of his face. "Adam?"

Adam blinked. "I...kind of... know her too. She's the lass from the bookshop."

Jared's dark brown eyes widened. "The one you told me about on the phone last week? The one who helped you when you had that panic attack?"

"She didn't help me. She saved me." He frowned at the disbelief on his partner's face. "And it wasn't a panic attack."

"But didn't the doctor tell you it was?"

"He was wrong." Adam's words fell into the room with a finality that ended all discussion. Jared stared at him, his brows furrowed.

Adam sighed. "I've never told you this... Nobody knows, except my family."

Jared waited. After a moment, Adam began to speak. In a few terse words he told his partner about his medical condition and its ramifications. As he spoke, Jared's face grew still, and when he finished, the room was heavy with unspoken thoughts.

Finally, his partner spoke through tight lips. "Thanks for telling me," he said in a low voice. "I understand why you don't talk about it, but I'm glad you told me. How do you feel now? Are you all right?" Concern was etched on his features.

"That...right there...is why I don't tell people about it," Adam said. "I don't want to be stalked by my friends and family, asking me how I feel all the time. Please don't." The last was a plea, and after a moment Jared nodded reluctantly.

"I'll try," he said. A long moment passed between

them. "So, then, back to bookstore girl. Why do you think she saved you?"

"I was dying," Adam said simply. "I knew I was. This girl was there, talking to me, and then she put her hand on my chest and I—I woke up in hospital with the doctor telling me I'd had a panic attack."

"But..." Jared stopped, and Adam knew he was picking his words carefully. "But how do you know it *wasn't* just a panic attack?"

"It's hard to explain," Adam said slowly. "For the last two years I've known I was on borrowed time. I've paid attention to my body; I know the signs it sends me. I had another attack a few months ago, and my doctor said it's getting worse. Every attack damages my heart a little more, until one day it just won't start up again."

He looked up, eyes narrowed. "And I've never, in my whole life, had a panic attack. Wouldn't I have had one when I got the diagnosis, if I was ever going to?" He threw his hands up in the air. "I wasn't even worrying about the Curse, in the bookstore. I was thinking about dogs, and about the woman across the shop who was drop-dead gorgeous. I wasn't anxious!" He looked up. "What?"

He watched his partner's reaction. Jared's lips were pressed tightly together, and his dark eyes were full of pity. *Ugh*. But he cared, and he had a right to know what was going on. He was co-owner of the business and had become Adam's closest friend. Funny how here, at the end of his life, he'd found not only a brother but a friend that he could trust.

"Anyway," he said after a minute. "In the bookshop last week, I felt another attack coming, and I was sure it was the Big One. I felt my heart stop, Jared. I'm not being dramatic, but I knew I was going to die this time." He shivered, remembering.

"I passed out, and when I came to, that girl was bending over me, and all I could think about was how beautiful she was and that I knew her from somewhere. Isn't that weird?" He appealed to Jared, who hadn't moved since he'd started talking. "I mean, I knew I was dying, and *that's* what I was thinking about?"

"I believe you." Jared's voice was ragged, and he looked as if he were about to cry. "I don't understand it, but I believe you felt what you thought you did." He met Adam's eyes squarely.

"You're an athlete, Adam, and an athlete knows what's going on in his own body. I believe you, because I knew on the practice field that day, when my leg was twisted under me. I knew it was over. I felt it in my leg, in my heart, and in my mind."

Adam stared at his friend. Jared *would* know. He'd had his own life-altering tragedy, although it hadn't been a death sentence. Still, an athlete knew.

Eight years ago, Jared McGovern had been a footballer in uni, good enough to be picked up by the Rangers. He'd come up from Liverpool to Glasgow and done well enough to make the second team. The money was better than good, and he'd saved most of it.

He was on his way to realizing his dream, he'd told Adam, until one day a teammate landed on his leg during a practice match. In a microsecond, his future was gone. He was dropped from the team and found himself alone in a country not his own, with no career and no prospects.

When Adam had asked, he'd insisted he wasn't angry; it was the nature of the sport. It had happened to hundreds of athletes before him and would happen to hundreds more.

The problem was, he had never planned for this. His eyes had been on the gold cup, blinded by his own talent and the praises heaped on him. He'd told Adam and Daniel that he'd stood in the station holding his ticket to Liverpool and glanced down at a rack to see a tourist pamphlet extolling the beauty of Glen Coe. With nothing else to do, he'd picked it up and begun to read.

His train had come, and he'd looked up at all the people hurrying to board. "But my feet stayed planted to the stone floor of the station," Jared had told them. "I watched my train pull out of the station, and then I walked to the bus station and bought a ticket to Fort William."

Jared had backpacked around for a few months. "One day I found myself in Ballachulish, in front of a shop called Glencoe Mountain Mystery. A sign in the window announced that you were looking for a computer specialist. Five years later here I am, a co-owner of the business. Who would've thought?"

Now, watching the emotions play across Jared's face, Adam thought about the vagaries of life. He couldn't imagine the business without Jared; his gift with numbers and technology was nothing short of amazing. He would never be able to understand the passion the man had felt for football or the agony he'd experienced at its loss, but fate was a funny thing. Maybe God had been telling him that his genius was more needed than his legs.

BALLACHULISH, SCOTLAND – PRESENT TIME

Adam stood up suddenly. "I'm going to Fort William," he said. "No more tours today, and Pearl wants a walk."

Jared glanced down at the bulldog, snoring contentedly on his rug, and raised one eyebrow. "Yeah, he looks pretty eager. Better wake him up."

"He's dreaming of walking." Adam grabbed the leash from the rack in the corner and fastened it to Pearl's collar. The dog opened one eye, snuffled, and then struggled to his feet and lumbered out the door behind his owner.

Forty minutes later, Adam and his dog stopped outside HP Booksellers while Pearl slurped water from the bowl placed conveniently near the door, and then made their way inside. Adam looked around the crowded shop.

"Aft'noon, Adam," Mary said from the reception desk. "Are ye bringing Pearl t' visit Biscuit or d'ye wannae check on how our Màiri be doin'?"

How the hell did she figure that out? His face heated. "Um, well, I was concerned..."

He was saved by the appearance of Biscuit, who sauntered over and gave Pearl a smack on the jaw. Pearl grinned and swivelled his huge head to look hopefully up at Adam. He grinned and unhooked the leash, and the two animals wandered off in the direction of the children's section.

"My dog is in love with your cat," Adam said. "I hope he doesn't make himself a nuisance."

Mary gave a ladylike snort. "Biscuit'll let 'im ken if 'e does, aye?" She fixed Adam with those little black bird eyes. "The lass is o'er yonder."

But Adam's eyes had already found Màiri, standing alone behind a table of books. He wandered over, trying to make his progress look nonchalant, and paused to pick up a book for support.

"Are you interested in women's issues?"

Adam looked up to see Màiri grinning at him. "What?"

She gestured to the book he was holding, and he looked down to see the silhouette of a woman holding an old-fashioned scale and the words *Understanding Menopause* emblazoned on the cover. A flare of embarrassment and then a flash of irritation sliced through him, and he dropped the book as if it had burned him.

Fight or flight. He glanced over at the children's corner, where Pearl and Biscuit were curled up together on a beanbag chair, sleeping. Flight was out of the question, then.

"How do you feel?" he asked. "I mean, after the fire?"

She gave him a smile that took his breath away. "Oh, I'm fine. Thanks for asking." She gave him the full power of those blue eyes, and then her brow wrinkled. "But, how did you know? I don't think they gave names on the news."

"I was there. I saw you."

"Oh," she said. "Well, it was Eve who got the worst of it. She's lucky, though; they said she'll be fine."

A silence fell between them. Then Adam, his eyes locked on hers, said, "Did you save her, too?"

The colour drained from Màiri's face, and she dropped her eyes to the stack of books in front of her. "I don't know what you mean," she mumbled.

BALLACHULISH, SCOTLAND – PRESENT TIME

All in or go home. Adam reached across the table and touched her hand. "I mean," he said in a low voice, "did you save her like you saved me?"

CHAPTER 17
FORT WILLIAM, SCOTLAND – PRESENT TIME

*Everything burns...you just gotta
know what kind of fire to set.*
—Obie Williams

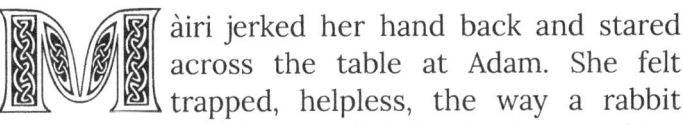

Màiri jerked her hand back and stared across the table at Adam. She felt trapped, helpless, the way a rabbit caught in a snare knows that the hunter reaching toward it carries death in his gloved hands.

Don't be such an eejit! she told herself. *He doesn't know. He can't know.* She schooled her features into a semblance of calm.

"I'm sorry. You startled me. I'm not used to strangers touching me." *And what century are you from, lass?* The thought brought a smile, and the fear subsided.

"My name's Adam," the man across from her said. "Adam MacArthur." He wore a stubborn look that wrinkled his forehead and made him look like a small boy about to stamp his foot. "I'm sorry I touched you," he said, his voice stiff. "But we're not exactly strangers."

"What do you—" Màiri bit the words back and changed direction. "My name's Màiri MacLachlan."

Adam stared her down. "What I *mean* is, Màiri MacLachlan, you saved my life last week. I only wanted to thank you."

"O-oh."

"But naturally, it wasn't as important to you as it was to me." His voice was petulant now, the small boy on full display. Would he throw a temper tantrum if she didn't acknowledge his pique? Suddenly, without warning, a laugh burbled up and spilled out between her pursed lips. Adam stared at her, his face reddening.

"I'm sorry—I really am," she said, but another giggle ruined the effect. "Are you *mad* at me?"

He looked affronted. "Of course not. I just...you... Oh, never mind. Can you take a break?"

"A break?" she said. "Why?"

"I'll buy you a coffee and a scone." He pointed toward the cafe. "I promise not to touch you." The snark was there, accompanied by a challenge.

"Oh." She thought for a moment. At least, she tried to look as if she were thinking; he didn't have to know that no thoughts of any consequence were rattling around in her brain. "Why?" she said again.

"Why what?" The dark cloud was back. Màiri decided that if she kept this up, he really would have a tantrum. The sulky look did nothing to obscure the fact that he was really very handsome, with his brown hair just touching his shirt collar and his

FORT WILLIAM, SCOTLAND – PRESENT TIME

multi-shaded brown eyes glaring a hole in her face. And it didn't help whatever was fluttering around in her stomach.

"Never mind," he said tersely, and turned to go.

"Wait." *Was that her voice? Wasn't that what she wanted, to make him go away and take his difficult questions with him? How did 'wait' fit into this plan?*

"Wait," she said again. Adam was looking at her in confusion. She looked at her watch. "I can take a break in five minutes. I'll have a coffee with you, as long as you promise not to talk nonsense." The order sounded prissy and ridiculous, but he nodded.

"Okay." The sun came out and the brown eyes sparkled. "I'll go get us a table, aye?"

Màiri's stomach flipped. She watched him walk away, and then turned to finish her task, trying not to look at her watch.

Out of the corner of her eye, she saw that two of the teenage boys who called themselves the Three Musketeers had entered the shop. She hadn't seen them for a few days, and now she realized she'd missed their awkward attempts at flirting. It was a difficult time of life for anyone, the cusp of adulthood. She should be kinder. She waved, and they made their way over.

"Hullo, lads. What're ye lookin' for t'day? An' where's yer third sword?"

"Oh, hi, miss," said the lad she remembered as Bastian. The leader. His face clouded. "Um, that's what we were wondering. Has Cory been in?"

"Well, no, he 'asn't." She hadn't noticed, but now that they pointed it out, it was odd. He was usually here every day, with or without his compatriots. She smiled. "Have ye misplaced him?"

They didn't return the smile. Bastian's shoulders drooped. "Thanks anyway," he said, and the two turned and made their way back onto the High Street. They looked worried, Màiri thought, but what teenagers didn't, most of the time? They were all convinced they carried the weight of the world on their young shoulders, and were quite surprised when they reached their twenties and discovered they didn't. Poor lads; they'd figure it out.

The five minutes were up, so Màiri put the Musketeers out of her mind and made her way to the cafe. She didn't know why she was doing this; there was something that drew her to this man and at the same time frightened her to her bones. Something that cried *Danger! Stay Away!* Like the smoke, licking at the moulding of the museum. He looked up and smiled, and the illusion evaporated.

They were the only ones in the cafe at the moment. Adam stood and pulled a chair out for her. He seemed unsure, as though he'd read how to do this in a book and needed to practice. But surely, a man who looked like this had women scrambling to be with him. He should know all the moves.

The man who doubled as baker and barista came over and took their orders. He was dressed in an eighteenth-century kilt, sporran, and hose, like all the other men who worked here, and he spoke in a mangled version of Scots that he must have gotten from YouTube, because it was truly awful. Màiri grinned at him.

FORT WILLIAM, SCOTLAND – PRESENT TIME

"Getting better, Bernard," she lied, and he rolled his eyes.

"Where's he supposed to be from?" Adam asked when the man had returned with their scones and coffee and retreated behind the counter.

Màiri laughed. "He's from London. Mary and Henry want everybody to speak in an old-fashioned brogue to match the costume," she explained. "Bernard goes along, but he's taken it way too far. Nobody can understand him, and he has to repeat himself at least once every time. I honestly think it's his own little joke. Nobody can be that bad without trying."

"I like the costumes and the accents," Adam said. "Goes with the shop, gives it a sense of history." He looked out at the main room, where a corner of the children's alcove could be seen. "I think Pearl likes it too."

"You should be proud. I've never seen Biscuit tolerate another animal—and that includes most humans—like she does your dog." She laughed. "If she meant that swat she gave him, he'd be running for the door."

"I don't know if you've noticed, but Pearl does not run," Adam said. His voice was dry, but Màiri could hear the affection in it.

"Adam!" Both turned at the voice. A young woman was crossing from the doorway of the cafe. She reached the table and leaned down to place a kiss on Adam's cheek, completely ignoring the other person at the table. Rude, but it gave Màiri a chance to study the disruptor.

Young, very pretty, probably in her mid-twenties. Artfully tousled blonde hair, large brown eyes and very fair skin. *Too much makeup, and that blonde is straight out of a box*, Màiri thought, and wondered at her snarky reaction.

"Hi, Laura," Adam said. He rubbed at his face where the girl had kissed him. "What brings you in here?"

"We're covering the fire at the museum," she said. "Jared said you might be here." She turned to Màiri. "Who's she?"

Adam frowned. "This is Màiri. My friend. She works here."

Laura sniffed. "I can tell that by the old-fashioned costume." She fixed Màiri with a look of thinly veiled hostility. "Hi. I'm Laura Macallan. Adam's girlfriend."

"You're not—" Adam's face flushed. He shrugged off the hand the girl had placed on his shoulder.

Her pretty face assumed a sulky pout. "Come on, don't be like that."

"Laura's a reporter for the *West Highland Times*," Adam said, to cover the awkward pause.

Màiri took another look at the blonde girl. She seemed young to be a journalist. Maybe there was more to her than eyeliner and hair spray. She supposed she shouldn't judge, but too bad. She wanted to.

"We're covering the fire at the museum," the girl said again. "The police think it was arson."

"Arson?" It was the first time Màiri had heard that. "But why would anyone—"

Laura cut her off. "Exactly," she said. "It's only a museum. Nothing valuable there, right?"

Nothing valuable? Tell that to Eve! Màiri fumed to herself. *She'd reduce this twit to rubble if she heard that.*

FORT WILLIAM, SCOTLAND – PRESENT TIME

"Màiri was there, Laura, and so was Eve. In fact, Eve almost died." Adam forced the words through tightened lips. "Don't people count as valuable these days?"

Laura narrowed her eyes and regarded Màiri. "Of course they do." Her voice was a purr. "People are the reason for arson, aye?" She looked down and studied her manicure. "I heard there's a fire investigator coming up from Glasgow. He'll probably be talking to you, since you were on the scene." A predatory gleam glinted in her eyes. "Hey! Maybe I should be interviewing *you*."

Màiri had had enough. She stood and picked up her plate and cup and turned to Adam. "I have to get back to work. Thanks for the coffee, Mister MacArthur. Nice to meet you, Laura." She straightened her spine and walked to the counter to deposit her dishes, then left the cafe without glancing back. At least until she got into the main room; then she turned her head just in time to see Laura slide into the chair she had just vacated. *Like a snake*.

She continued toward the front counter, passing the children's corner where the two animals were still sleeping. Pearl had his stubby front legs curled around the cat, and Biscuit had tucked her head under his right ear. It looked as if Adam MacArthur was going to be a regular, if his dog had anything to say about it.

And did it mean more visits from that Laura? *Ugh. I'm Adam's girlfriend...People are the reason for arson...Maybe I should interview you...Bitch.*

Lost in her thoughts, Màiri almost missed the wave from Mary Duncan at the front desk. The little proprietor was standing next to a tall, muscular man in his forties, and she had an unusually serious expression on her face. Màiri took in the man's appearance and hurried her steps.

He had bright red hair, trimmed neatly, and a short beard. He wore a blue shirt, tartan tie, and tweed jacket, and was carrying a worn leather briefcase in one hand. Lawyer? Accountant? As Màiri reached the desk, she saw that he had penetrating blue eyes rimmed with dark circles. He was not smiling.

Mary said, "Màiri, this is Mister Fraser. He's here to—"

"*Inspector* Benedict Fraser," the man cut her off smoothly, earning himself a poisonous, black-eyed glare from Mary. "I'm from the Fire Investigation Unit in Glasgow. May I have a few words, please?"

"You may use the office," Mary said. Her voice dripped ice pellets. "Màiri, would you like to have someone accompany you?"

Màiri noticed that Mary's accent was gone, which meant she was firmly entrenched in the here and now. The ramifications of that sent a shiver down her spine. Mary *never* broke character.

She smiled at her boss and shook her head before leading the inspector into the small office behind the counter. He immediately took the leather chair behind the massive wooden desk, leaving the visitor's chair for Màiri. *Used to being in charge.* She sat down gingerly, smoothed the folds of her gown, and waited.

"I understand you were in the museum at the time of the fire," Fletcher began. "I'm glad to see you're safe and well."

"Thank you."

FORT WILLIAM, SCOTLAND – PRESENT TIME

"I'd like to run over the incident with you, from the beginning." He took out a notebook and pen from his jacket pocket and leaned forward, elbows on the desk. "Your name is Miss Màiri MacLachlan, correct?" At her nod, he scribbled something in the notebook. "Who was in the museum at the time?"

Màiri cast her mind back to the minutes before everything went to Hell. "It was just Eve and me. Eve just got a job there as a docent and was practicing her talk on me. We smelled smoke, and then we saw it coming under the door that led to the front of the museum, and—"

Fraser put up a hand. "Wait. It was just you and"—he consulted his notes—"Miss Eve MacDonald in the museum? No one else? A janitor, or cleaner, perhaps?"

"No," Màiri said. "There was no one else, as far as I knew. Eve said we were alone."

She took him through the harrowing time they'd been in the museum. Minutes, probably, but it had felt like hours.

"She wasn't breathing, so I performed CPR. I heard the sirens, and then a firefighter came from the back and led us out, and the ambulance came and took us to the hospital," she finished. No way was she going to tell the inspector about the blue light.

"Where did the firefighter come from?" Fraser's pen had stilled.

"From the back, I guess."

Fraser frowned and jotted something else in his notebook. "Thank you," he said. "I think that'll be all for now, but I may want to interview you again.

When there's arson with a death involved, we can't leave anything to chance."

Màiri stared at him, eyes wide. "D-death? But I told you...I performed CPR. Eve's fine." *How does he know about Eve?*

Inspector Fraser pinned her with a blue-eyed gaze. "Oh, I'm sorry." He didn't sound sorry. "I neglected to tell you. There *was* someone else on site. A badly burned body was found in the basement. So now it's not just arson. It's murder." He drew the word out as if savouring it. *Muurrder.*

CHAPTER 18
FORT WILLIAM, SCOTLAND – PRESENT TIME

Pain is poison to the body. Worry is toxic to the mind. Yearning is venom to the heart. Lust is poison to the soul.
—Matshona Dhliwayo

He's pulling away from me. Laura Macallan stood in the shadows across the street from HP Booksellers. She was supposed to be working right now; what the hell was she doing, standing out on the street, spying on her boyfriend like a jealous bitch? She eyed the pub down the High Street and wished she were there right now, with a double dram in front of her.

He wasn't her boyfriend. He hated it when she told people that, but she'd always told herself it was probably because he was embarrassed and didn't want other people to tease him. Now, a cold hand clutched her heart and wouldn't let go. She was losing him.

You never really had him. The words were like ice in her mind. *He was never yours.*

No. She couldn't accept it. There wasn't anyone else in Adam's life. He didn't date at all, except for her—once in a while when she forced it. God knew she'd tried to make it more in the five years since she'd met him.

She remembered that first day as one of the brightest in her life. It was her first real assignment. She was twenty years old, just finishing up her internship at the *West Highland Times* in Fort William. She already had a job lined up there, but no one at the paper took her seriously because her dad was the managing editor.

When she first arrived, the whispers started almost immediately. *She's Mister Macallan's daughter, what do you expect? Parachuted her way in, didn't she? Wonder if she can even write? Too much makeup, in my opinion—where does she think she is? This is Fort William, not New York.*

That was from the women, of course. The men didn't trust her newspaper instincts either, but most of them came around in time. Batting her eyelashes always worked with men.

And they were wrong about her skills. She was good. Her instincts for a story were top of the heap, and her writing better than average.

And why wouldn't it be? Didn't it make sense for a newspaperman's daughter to have it in her blood? What about all the families with generations of doctors or solicitors? Did they all parachute their way in? It took work, and Laura was willing to put in the effort.

FORT WILLIAM, SCOTLAND – PRESENT TIME

She wanted to be a crime reporter and make a name for herself. But all she got was the fluffy shite-stories about pets, or the latest shortbread baking contest, or the opening of a new beauty parlour. Looking back, she should've been grateful, because that was how she met Adam.

Unfortunately, Laura lived in Ballachulish. The editors thought she should cover whatever managed to happen there, and apparently the opening of any business was considered newsworthy. The village only had 620 permanent residents, although the population swelled during the summer, with hikers, scramblers, and tourists flocking in to experience the site of the famous Glencoe Massacre.

Laura could care less about history. She'd been raised in the shadow of some of the most beautiful mountains in the world, but they'd long since lost their appeal. The newspaper was a stepping stone to greater things. Maybe she could be an anchor at a TV channel in Glasgow. She had the looks; it was a matter of time.

Her hometown was a dead end. The only businesses that seemed to do fairly well in Ballachulish were restaurants, holiday lets, and pubs. Tourists and hikers were always thirsty, and sales of the local whisky soared during the short summer. Everything else failed to thrive. Small businesses popped up frequently, only to close a year or two later due to lack of customers.

"Laura, there's a new place that's opened up on Albert Road. Some sort of tour company. Get over there and check it out." The bored look on the senior editor's face probably matched her own. But an assignment was an assignment, so off she went.

And that was how she met Adam MacArthur. He was going to run a small tour business for serious hikers and runners, he told her during their first interview. It would be called Glencoe Mountain Mystery, and would offer races, tours of the mountains, and scrambling adventures. His older brother ran a similar business out of their hometown, Inverness, he said, and now it was his turn to try it out.

It was a good thing she'd brought her tape recorder, because she remembered little of what he said. She'd been too busy cataloguing his assets. Flyaway brown hair, lovely brown eyes that sparkled when he talked about his mountains. Muscles in all the right places.

People who said there was no such thing as love at first sight were dead wrong. Laura had experienced it many times. It never lasted, but this time was different. This one was a keeper.

Unfortunately, the keeping was all one-sided. He had no idea how she felt, but for her, his disinterest added fuel to the fire and gave her a purpose. She'd asked him out to dinner, and he'd said yes. She'd waited, but when he didn't ask her out in turn, she decided to take the leadership role in this relationship. She knew she was forcing it, but she didn't care. They went out a few times, had fun, and never discussed a future.

Lately he'd begun to make excuses—always just about to do an event or work a tour. Laura Macallan was no quitter, though. She invented new reasons

FORT WILLIAM, SCOTLAND – PRESENT TIME

to interview him, even though most of her follow-up stories went into the trash.

Then she saw the advertisement for a computer technician in his window. Some black lad from Liverpool got the job, and that gave her another chance to hang around Glencoe Mountain Mystery.

She'd interviewed the new hire, Jared McGovern. He'd been a footballer, quit due to injury. Boring. She didn't like him. He always seemed to know what she was thinking, and she was sure he was blocking her access to Adam.

And last year Adam's brother Daniel showed up and took over the photography part of the business, so she interviewed him, too. Daniel was cute like his brother. He was closer to her own age, but taken. Some girl from Glencoe Village, Eve MacDonald, he told her proudly. She remembered Eve from secondary school—pretty enough, could've been prettier if she bothered to wear more makeup. She was welcome to him; Laura preferred older men.

Adam was seldom available, though, even though now he had a partner and a photographer to shoulder some of the load. How could he always be busy when she tried to arrange a meeting? She took to following his Facebook page, showing up where he was—all right, she supposed some would call it stalking, but it was her only option. She didn't mind him thinking they were just friends, as long as there was no one else.

Then two days ago she'd seen him enter the bookshop and followed. He was sitting in the cafe with some black-haired woman who obviously worked there, judging by the stupid costume. Whole place was weird, and that little woman at the front desk gave her the creeps—always watching. *As if she knew exactly what I was thinking, the old hag.*

Laura frowned, remembering. Adam had been so annoyed when she claimed him as her boyfriend, even more than usual. All her competitive instincts rose up and she wanted to scratch the witch's eyes out.

What did he see in that woman? Aye, Laura supposed she could be called beautiful, with those goddam blue eyes and that naturally curly hair. She didn't wear much makeup either—what was wrong with women these days?

Laura was an expert on makeup. It was a woman's armour. But in front of the older woman, she felt overdone, artificial...wanting. So she'd reacted with snark and spite. She'd looked her rival up on the newspaper's database and knew where the bitch lived—some attic flat in an old house a few streets over from the High Street. If you wanted to defeat your enemy, you had to study everything you could about her.

Her mobile rang. Laura looked at the screen and frowned at the name. *Not Adam. Dammit.*

Where are you?

On the High Street, she typed.

Meet me at the Celtic Cafe. Now.

Laura grimaced at the screen. She should have trusted her instincts with this one. There was something off about him, and she had the sinking sensation she might be in over her head.

FORT WILLIAM, SCOTLAND – PRESENT TIME

He was a firefighter. They'd met when she was covering a community event at the Fort William fire station and hit it off right away. She was tired of always doing the chasing, and when this lad asked her out to a local pub, she was happy to go. Their first date had been fun, and when he invited her back to his flat, she went.

He was an amazing lover. That was probably why she'd let it get this far, why she'd gotten herself in so deep. When he asked her for a small favour, she was happy to help.

Just do this little thing for me, love, and I'll pay you back. You scratch my back, I'll scratch yours, aye?

By the time she realised she was being used, it was too late. He had too much on her now. She was caught in a trap that she'd walked right into, eyes wide open.

She'd known about the museum fire before it happened. She was the first on the scene, and her story made the front page because of the details she had. Her colleagues were amazed and jealous, but there was nothing they could do about it. She was just lucky. Isn't that what news reporting is—luck?

She was on the fast track now. The editor had assigned the arson case to her, giving her exclusive rights to the story, and it was all because of him. Because of what she'd done for him. *You scratch my back, and I'll scratch yours.*

She gave the bookshop a last look and made her way to the cafe at the end of the High Street. *So close... Had he been watching her?*

He was waiting, his eyes undressing her as she walked in. Against her will, Laura felt her body begin to quiver.

Everything about this was wrong. She didn't love him. She didn't think she even liked him. If Adam ever found out about this, her dream of a life with him was over. If *anyone* found out what she was doing, her career was over. She didn't want to think what kinds of charges might be levied at her. This man held the key to her freedom, and she was trapped like a beetle in a spider's web.

The spider smiled at her and her legs went weak.

"Found a new place," he said. "We're going to try it out tonight." Her opinion wasn't required. He reached out and stroked her arm lightly.

They never went to the same hotel twice. They checked in under assumed names and left in the early morning, before most people were up. At first Laura had thought it was exciting, like a spy movie, but now it just seemed sinister and dirty.

"I don't want to do this anymore," she mumbled, too aware that she was not in control. She'd never been in control.

His face hardened, but then he smiled. His fingers continued to stroke her arm. "Why," he said, his voice like silk, "do we have to have this conversation every time?"

"I'm taking all the risks," Laura said. "I don't like that fire investigator; he's too smart."

His hand moved beneath the table and began to stroke her bare leg. Her breath caught and she shuddered.

"You're my own pet reporter," he said, his voice soft. "I'll tell you what to say, and you write it. *Exactly* as I say. Do you understand?" His hand moved upward.

FORT WILLIAM, SCOTLAND – PRESENT TIME

"Y-yes," she said. "I understand."

"The next place is the Three Sisters Tavern, on Fassifern," he said. "Tuesday, right after closing."

"Why that place?" she asked, surprised. "It's a dump."

His brows bunched and he pursed his lips. His fingers pinched the tender place on her thigh and she squeaked.

"It's none of your business," he said. "Don't be difficult, love. It's tiring. Just be there at the scene and write what I tell you, like always." He narrowed his eyes. "Now, let's go."

He stood and held out his hand. Laura took it, and his fingers tightened around hers like a vise. A *lamb to slaughter*, the phrase whispered through her brain. *He's the wolf, and I'm the lamb. How did I let this happen?*

CHAPTER 19
DORNACH, SCOTLAND – 1726

SÌNE

It should have been raining. Sìne glared up at the clear sky and cursed it for its spitefulness. White, puffy clouds moved lazily across a sky as blue as a robin's egg, heedless of the pain clutching at her heart.

She watched the casket through misty eyes as it was lowered into the ground in the cathedral churchyard. Most of the town was present to say goodbye to Maighread Arthur, the woman who'd birthed their bairns and taken care of their illnesses for so many years, but all of them stood conspicuously apart from the two chief mourners.

Doirin, dressed in the black gown she'd made three years ago for Mungo's burying, stood immobile next to Sìne, her eyes blank. She had never recovered completely from Mungo Murray's death, and sometimes, like today, it seemed as if she had gone elsewhere in her mind.

Gran had been the one who anchored their little family. She was a second mother to Sìne, and together she and Doirin had taught the young lass the medical knowledge Maighread had compiled through years of seeing to the needs of Dornach village.

"Ye have an agile mind, lass," Gran had told her. "There's things ye cannae do wi' yer hands, but ye have all the knowledge o' healin' in yer heid, an' who kens when it might come in useful?"

Maighread had continued her work as the village's midwife, but the years and the responsibility had taken their toll. Once red-cheeked and round as a wild apple, Maighread had shrunk in on herself. Her once rosy skin became shrivelled and sallow, and her sharp blue eyes were faded and red-rimmed.

If on'ly I could o' helped! Sìne thought as the first bits of earth were shovelled onto the casket. *I kent what t' do—I could 'o been there! She wouldnae had needed t' work so hard.* But no one wanted the lass with 'Clootie hooves' to touch them. They were afraid their newborn bairns would die aborning or be cursed by deformity. So Sìne had to take long walks along the rocky shore, until Maighread called it clear and she could return.

Sometimes Hugh came and walked with her. He would tease her and hold her arm so she wouldn't stumble on the rocks. He couldn't be around much—he was twenty-one years now, a man, and he had responsibilities on the farm—but he came as often as he could.

DORNACH, SCOTLAND – 1726

Sìne looked around the churchyard, but Hugh was nowhere to be seen. Duncan Sutherland was there, standing with some of the villagers who worked his land, but his son was absent. Probably punished again, Sìne thought. Even as old as he was, Hugh could not escape his father's ire if he did something Duncan didn't approve of. He'd come to her later. He always managed.

She would never wed. She was nineteen, well past marriageable age, but no one had come to Maighread and Doirin to ask for her hand. There were lads who wanted her, despite her disfigurement, but not for marriage. Alan Grant had sought her out more than once. He spoke sweetly, told her she was beautiful, an angel, and then tried to worm his fingers down the neck of her gown.

Sìne held no illusions about herself. The village lads favoured lassies like Ailis MacAllan: young, pretty, with long blonde hair and lovely white hands that fluttered in the air when she talked. Not an aging spinster with deformed fingers.

Ronain MacKay was staring across the churchyard at Ailis with grey eyes that were lit with young love. He must have felt Sìne's gaze, because his eyes shifted to her and his lip twisted. No love there for her, but she would have been shocked if there had been. After all, he was Walter MacKay's brother, raised at his brother's side to be just like him—maybe worse.

Ronain had been only seven years when his brother and Archie Ross tried to ride her down the path, chanting the words to that horrible song she would never forget. Ronain had probably grown up hating her—and Hugh, who had beaten his precious brother because of her.

She turned away from the contempt on Ronain's face and forced herself to close the door on the memory of that horrible day. She was here to bury her gran, not to moon over past injustices.

"There'll be plenty more, so dinnae dwell on th' ones 'at are done and gone, lass." Sìne turned to see Maighread standing next to her, watching the men heap dirt on her own casket. Gran looked hale and hearty, round and rosy-cheeked.

"I was wonderin' when ye'd come," Sìne told her, smiling through her tears.

"Couldnae miss th' goin's on, now, could I?" Maighread said. "Such a fuss o'er an auld woman!" But she puffed out her ample chest and looked around at all her mourners with a gimlet eye.

Probably to see who's missing, Sìne thought. She smiled inwardly and then sobered. She watched the clods of earth being shovelled onto the casket. "What am I t' do without ye?" she asked.

"Ye'll get on," said the old woman. "Ye have a brain smarter n' most men. Use it."

"But..." Sìne protested. She turned to Maighread, but the woman was gone. Sìne sighed. "Thank ye, ye auld trickster. That didnae help a'tall."

Sìne was no stranger to ghosts. She'd been seeing them since she was five, though they seldom talked to her. Gran had spent long hours over the heaving body of Eilidh Gordon, cajoling, wiping the sweat from the woman's brow, but in the end the bairn was born still, with blue lips and eyes that would never open on this world.

It was the first time Sìne had seen death. She'd peered through the curtain separating the sleeping room from the midwifery, unable to look away from that tiny, still figure or to block the wailing of the grieving mother. And then the bairn had opened its eyes and looked straight at her. Two pairs of blue eyes stared at each other, for just a moment, and then the newborn closed its eyes again.

No one else had seen what she saw, and Sìne had forgotten. Until it happened again, when she was seven. Young Hector Cumming had fallen into the firth when his brother left him alone for just a few minutes, and the whole town gathered to watch the men bring the sad little body to shore.

Sìne, holding tight to Doirin's hand, had watched with the others as they laid Hector on the beach, but only she seemed to see when he stood up from his body and walked over to her.

"Dinnae go swimmin'," he'd told her, his voice quivering with urgency. "Tis too cold." Then he'd turned around and gone back to his body, without a backward look.

The last time had been four years past, when Archie Ross' father Alasdair had collapsed and died in the field where he worked. Sìne hadn't been there, didn't even know it had happened, but suddenly the elder Ross was standing before her in the market, hands folded over his chest.

"I'm that sorry, lass, fer th' harm my son done t' ye," Alasdair said. "I tried t' raise young Archie fair, but he had t' go 'is own way." He'd fastened sorrowful dark eyes on her. "I wish ye well."

"Tis all right. Thank ye, sir," Sìne said. Alasdair Ross had nodded, and the next second he was gone.

The ghosts weren't frightening, though she had no idea why they'd chosen her for their last message. She knew, even at a very young age, that it was not a good idea to tell anyone else about their visits—people already avoided her because of her deformity, and some crossed themselves when she passed, as if to ward off some sort of evil. It wasn't until that day she'd been attacked by the gang of lads and rescued by Hugh Sutherland that she understood. They feared her.

The rain finally came, all in a rush as if it had been holding back until Maighread Arthur was gone. The villagers pulled their plaids and arasaids over their heads and hurriedly left the churchyard. Sìne and Doirin stayed for a few minutes, looking at the mound of earth, and then Sìne took her mother's arm and they walked back down the path and away from the one who had held their small family together.

There was a man standing at their door, dressed in black from head to boots. He hadn't been at the burial, and he was a stranger to Sìne. He had white hair and thick white brows that were knitted together over a large forehead. Water dripped off the tip of his sharp pointed nose.

"Hello, sir. Can we help ye?" Sìne asked him.

"Ye can ask me in, instead o' just standin' there." The man's tone was brusque and raspy, as if he had a cold.

"I'm sorry. Are ye feelin' poorly?" Sìne opened the door and the stranger pushed past her and into the house. He divested himself of his cloak and hung it on the rack without asking, and then turned to face the two women, hands on his hips.

"I'm feeling fine," he said. His accent was broad and flat, marking him as an inlander. "Now that I'm out of the rain." His dark brown eyes glinted, and an unpleasant smile formed on his lips. "So, when will ye be leaving?"

"I'm sorry?" Sìne's brow furrowed. "This's our home."

"Not anymore." The man looked at the small cottage and his lip curled in a sneer. "Believe me, I wish it weren't so, but there we are."

Shocked into silence, the two women gawked at him.

"Oh, I suppose I should introduce myself." Sarcasm dripped off the man's tongue. "I'm Doctor Albert Wilson, and I've been sent up from Edinburgh to provide medical care to this...place. This is the home I've been given. For what it's worth."

"By who?" Sìne gasped. "Where 'r we t' go then?"

"By Mister Sutherland," Wilson said. "And I don't care where ye go. Just not here."

CHAPTER 20
DORNACH, SCOTLAND – 1726

HUGH

"Da, how could ye!" Hugh stood in front of his father, fists clenched so tightly that the knuckles showed white. Blood pounded in his ears, and the urge to strike out at the older man was so strong he could almost taste it.

Duncan Sutherland narrowed his eyes. "Take care who ye're talkin' to, son," he said. "There's a line ye dinnae want t' cross."

Hugh took a deep breath and forced his fingers to relax. His father was right; he wasn't doing Sine any good by picking a fight. Duncan had all the power here and always had.

"I'm sorry, Da, but why did ye bring that doctor up from Ed'nburgh? Th' missus Gilchrist can handle th' midwifery an' doctorin', just like they allus have."

His father put down the ledger he'd been reading and gave his son a level gaze. "Th' village is growin' an' so are its needs. We have two bookshops now, an' three taverns—why not another healer?"

Hugh might have believed that his father truly meant what he said had his eyes not flicked away from his son's as he spoke. "I dinnae see th' problem, son."

"Ye threw them out o' their house!" Hugh said. "Did ye give 'em no thought?"

"I put Doctor Wilson in *my* house," his father said. "I take care o' th' needs o' this town as I see fit." He glared at his son. "Ye have no place interferin' wi' my decisions. B'sides, aren't those women stayin in th' potter's shed out back o' th' midwifery? Tis big enough." He snorted, a contemptuous exhalation of derision. "An' they'll be on hand in case th' doctor needs em.'" He picked up the ledger again. The discussion was over.

Hugh stood rooted to the carpet. A red haze threaded up and tangled in a knot in his throat, choking off his words. His fists clenched again, and he dug his nails into his palms to keep from screaming. His father thought to dismiss him? No. He couldn't let this go. Not this time.

As he watched, a small smile quirked the edge of Duncan's mouth. There was more to this than seeing to the needs of a growing town; did his father think him a bairn? And suddenly it all became clear.

"Ye—ye," he sputtered. "Ye planned this, didnae ye? Since e'en b'fore Mistress Maighread passed. Ye allus planned t' toss 'em out. Why? Wha'd they ever do, 'sides keepin' th' people o' this village alive?" He hurled the words into the air between them. "Maighread Arthur birthed most o' th' lads an' lassies in Dornach! She birthed *me!*"

A frown chased the smirk off his father's face. His colour rose and he slapped the ledger down into his lap again. When he spoke, it was low, hoarse, as if his words were propelled by some force inside himself.

"Aye," he said. "Aye, Maighread Arthur birthed ye." His eyes were hooded, hiding something dark and pernicious in their depths. "She healed all th' ills o' th' village. And she's gone." He stood and began to pace the room. "But did ye ken?"

He turned suddenly on his heel and fixed his son with a glare. "Two years after ye were birthed, that... that *woman* came. That vile woman who gave birth t' an abomination!"

Hugh stood still, transfixed in the face of his father's hatred.

"That *woman* who was here—right here 'n this house with Maighread Arthur—*helping*—when yer sister was born dead an' took yer mother with her!" His eyes shot sparks and spittle flew from the sides of his mouth.

"But—"

Duncan Sutherland rounded on his son. "There's somethin' ye never kent, somethin' I didnae thynk t' ever tell ye." He crossed to stand a foot away from Hugh, the muscles of his jaw moving as if something crawled beneath the surface of his skin. He lowered his voice to a whisper.

WITCH

"That woman, that Doirin Gilchrist, was here. An' when yer sister came int' th' world, she wasnae breathin'...an' she wasnae whole." The words slid into the space between them like a snake.

Duncan was looking at something beyond Hugh now, as if an image from the past had come to taunt him with the memory of that day. Tears welled in his eyes, and his voice was choked with grief.

"She had no fingers." Duncan looked up and his face twisted. "Yer wee sister had nothin' at th' end o' her hands but stumps." He let out a shuddering breath and covered his face with his hands. "She was an abomination—just like that lass ye're so keen on—only *that* one lived, didnae 't?"

Hugh found his voice. "But Da, surely ye cannae think Mistress Doirin—"

His father grabbed him by the shoulders and shook him like a rag doll. "She's not a mistress!" he shouted. "She's a hoo'er! She came t' this village wi' child, an' nobody kens who th' father o' that brat be! Maybe t'was th' Devil! Why else would her own daughter be born like that?"

Hugh stared at his father. Duncan Sutherland stared back at him, eyes dark and as murky as the waters of the firth in winter. He dropped his hands from his son's shoulders and stuffed them into his pockets.

"I didnae like her from th' beginnin'," he said, and now his voice was steady and calm, as if he and his son were having a talk about fishing. Somehow this was worse than the anger had been.

"I didnae trust her—a strange woman from who knew where? An' I would have driven 'er from the village as soon as she came. But then Maighread took 'er in an' taught her medicine. She kept t' herself, an' I thought maybe..."

He spoke softly, almost to himself. "The lads were right, back then, t' call the lass those names. They had th' right of it, and ye were wrong." He was nodding to himself, affirming his own beliefs. "Why'd ye thynk I was so harsh t' ye? Why d' ye thynk I put ye in th' stocks an' let those village chookters throw dirt at ye? At my own son!"

Hugh said nothing. He stood impaled by his father's angry gaze and let the hateful words rain down on him.

"Ye thought I was cruel, I kent it," Duncan said. "But now ye ken the reason. That woman an' her foul seed are evil. I never said it t'others, but I wonder did she cause th' tree to fall on Mungo Murray. I wonder did she have somethin' t' do with young Hector Cumming drownin'." He took a long breath through his nose and exhaled. "Aye. I wonder things like that."

Hugh tried to process the words he was hearing. He looked into the dark, angry eyes of the man he called father—eyes shining with an unholy passion he had never seen before.

Could his father truly believe that Doirin Gilchrist had something to do with his mother's death? That she was the cause of his sister's malformation? Of her own daughter's deformity? It was madness!

"I had t'wait till Maighread was gone." His father's calm voice reached him through the howling in his mind. "Now it's time others kent what is squirming in their midst." He smiled, a bitter twist of the lips that had no humour in it.

"I brought Albert Wilson here. He's a magistrate, a justice of the court in Edinburgh. He'll keep watch on your *Mistress* Gilchrist, an' on her vile spawn. They dinnae b'long here in Dornach, an' when they step out o' place, I'll be ready."

Duncan looked at his son with disgust. "Yer a man grown now, son. I cannae keep ye from seein' who you want, going where ye want. I cannae put ye in th' stocks anymore, an' I cannae choose yer friends fer ye."

He turned his back on his son and strode to the door. At the last moment he turned, his hand on the handle. "But I can tell ye one thing," he said. "Ye'll be doin' that wretchit lass no favours by bein' on her side. Ye'll only make it worse fer her."

The slam of the outside door resounded through the quiet house. Hugh Sutherland stood alone and listened to his father's poisonous words reverberate through the empty space.

He had promised Sine that he would protect her, that he'd see to it nothing could harm her. How was he going to keep that promise now? How long had his father held these thoughts? When had his mind begun to spiral down into darkness? Perhaps it had started all those years ago, when his mother and sister died.

The face Duncan Sutherland put on for the villagers—those *chookters*, he called them—was a mask behind which contempt seethed like a pit of vipers. Hugh had always known it, but now he knew something more.

DORNACH, SCOTLAND – 1726

His father truly hated Sìne and her mother...and he was insane.

CHAPTER 21
GLASGOW, SCOTLAND
– PRESENT TIME

*There are things known and there
are things unknown, and in between
are the doors of perception.*
—Aldous Huxley

Fire investigator Benedict Fraser leaned back in his leather desk chair at the office in Yorkhill. Something was tickling the edges of his mind...something about that woman Màiri. He sat up and pulled his notebook over, then turned his laptop on and transcribed the notes to a file.

Something she'd said? Or something she *hadn't* said? It would come to him; it always did.

He'd surprised her with the information about the corpse in the basement, which had been his intention. Unless she was the best actress in Western Scotland, she hadn't known about that. Her expression had transitioned rapidly, from shock to horror to sympathy. Her questions had been typical—Who was it? Was it a man or a woman? And then, would he have suffered?

There had been real concern in her voice. She cared. But was it because she knew the person and wasn't saying, or because she was an empathetic human being who had experienced being trapped in a fire herself? Remained to be seen.

He picked up his mobile and tapped the music app. Scrolling down the list of titles, he pressed the playlist for classical new age, and soon "Song for Sienna" rolled through the office. He leaned back in the chair again and closed his eyes, letting the piano and cello carry him away.

Suddenly he sat up again. Something about Màiri MacLachlan. She was a beautiful woman, but one he suspected had no real appreciation of her looks. Thick black curls falling into a pale face anchored by the most compelling blue eyes he'd ever seen. They radiated intelligence—and often humour, he thought. Although in his line of work he rarely saw much of that in the people he interviewed. A good listener, but nervousness might have accounted for that. Calm.

No, it wasn't her expression. It was something she'd said...

He went over his notes again, and then once more...and found it. The little piece missing from the puzzle, the ghost in the machine. It hadn't had anything to do with his revelation of the body in the basement.

...I heard sirens, and then a firefighter came from the back.

GLASGOW, SCOTLAND – PRESENT TIME

He'd noticed it the first time. *I heard sirens...and then a firefighter came from the back.* The fire appliances had pulled up in the front, so why was a firefighter coming from the back? Of course, sometimes volunteer firefighters joined the professionals at the scene, and they drove their own vehicles. But the timing of the sirens and the arrival of the firefighter seemed strange.

Fraser decided to let it go for the moment. He stood, turned the music off, and placed his mobile back into his pocket. For now, it was enough. But Miss Màiri MacLachlan was interesting. He'd wait a while and then see her again. Maybe at her home this time. He had no desire for another run-in with that wee terrier of a woman at the bookshop.

He took the lift down to the basement of the building and walked the grim, grey-painted hallways until he came to the mortuary. Steeling himself against the smell, he entered the room where a white-coated woman was hunched over a microscope.

"Wha' d'we have, Morag?" he asked.

The woman looked up from her scope, brushed a lock of grey hair out of her eyes, and gave Fraser a grim smile. "It's not pretty, but when is it ever, in our line of work?"

She walked over to a table with a body on it. A human being, although there was little left to indicate that. The body looked like a mummy that had been covered in charcoal. Nothing to reveal sex or age, although the corpse was relatively small in stature. A short man, or a tall woman?

"Male or female?" Fraser asked.

The medical examiner looked at him out of tired brown eyes. "Male. The hair and face and fingertips were burned away, so I can't tell if he's black or white, his age, or what his hair colour might have been. We're going to have to go with the dental records and hope for the best. Worst case, it'll be DNA." She brushed the errant lock of hair back again and looked back at Fraser.

"He didn't die in the fire. He wasn't in the wrong place at the wrong time," she said, her voice tight. "He was murdered."

Fraser looked up, startled. He'd thrown that bit out at Màiri MacLachlan just to get a reaction, and a part of him had regretted the statement. Now he felt vindicated, and his guilt abated somewhat.

"How do you know for certain?" he asked, though he should have known better. Morag Dunbar was one of the best in her profession—exacting and thorough, and on top of that she worked for the deceased, not the government. She talked to them, promised them results, and worked tirelessly until she got them.

He wondered what had led her to this line of work. Something in her past, perhaps? He had his own demons, his own reasons for choosing fire investigation as a career. Reasons he'd never shared with anyone. Memories washed through his head. He'd thought the past was dead and buried, but now... *What if—*

"Look." Morag's voice jolted him out of his reverie. She was pointing at the charred body. "Do you see how he's lying prone, as if he's asleep?" Fraser shook his head to clear it and nodded.

GLASGOW, SCOTLAND – PRESENT TIME

"If he had died in the fire, he'd be curled up, knees pulled up to his chest, hands clenched—the pugilistic position. You know all this, of course. Also, there's no soot in his lungs."

"Aye," Fraser said. "I just wanted to hear it from you. So he died elsewhere and was transported to the museum. I don't suppose we'll be able to find a cause of death?"

"Ach, ye of little faith," Morag said. "Do you see this indentation on the skull?"

Fraser bent over the body. "He was hit with a heavy object?"

"Aye. Enough to kill him. There might be more injuries as we go along, but that's not bad before the autopsy, eh?"

"So, this lad was struck on the head and killed somewhere else and was then brought to the museum and placed in the basement." Fraser paused, thinking. "The killer is probably a man. A woman would be unlikely to have the strength to move a man's body any distance. Also, arson tends to be a man's crime."

"Maybe, maybe not. A strong woman could have managed it. There are cases where it's happened. Or she could have had help. But you're right, arson is usually a man's choice. Little lads who dream of being firefighters, and then grow up to be fire starters, instead." She shook her head. "He didn't have to have been killed elsewhere, either. He could have been lured to the museum and killed there, and then the killer started the fire hoping to cover up the murder."

"You been reading those crime novels again?" Fraser asked. "Who's that author you like so much? Graham or something?"

"Grant. Myles Grant. And I don't have to read crime novels to see the underbelly of our society. I see it every day, right here," Morag said. "Besides, Myles Grant comes to *me* for information." She wagged a finger at him. "Maybe if you read one of Grant's books, you'd pick up some clues from Inspector Beaton." She grinned at the look of disgust on Fraser's face. "Just sayin'."

Fraser snorted. "I think I can manage without resorting to fiction, thank you very much." He gave an exaggerated bow and left the basement, bypassing the lift and heading for the stairs.

Inspector Beaton. Hmmph. Morag Dunbar knew how to push his buttons, that was sure. He took the stairs slowly, allowing the echo of his footsteps to beat time to the questions swirling in his head.

Who was the body in the mortuary? Why had someone gone to such lengths to get him to the museum? Whether he'd been coshed somewhere else and brought there, or killed in the basement, the key was the museum.

Had the victim been a criminal himself? Was he looking for something in the basement? Or had he been lured there by the arsonist? Until they knew who he was, those questions would remain unanswered.

Fraser turned left at the street level landing and left the building just as a bus pulled up and disgorged a horde of tourists. The bus was emblazoned with the image of a book and its author, a handsome blond man in his early thirties.

GLASGOW, SCOTLAND – PRESENT TIME

Myles Grant. Benedict Fraser snorted. He would never let Morag Dunbar know, but he *had* read some of Myles Grant's books. He was a decent author, paid attention to his research and the finer points of forensic science. His Inspector Beaton was a man Fraser would have liked to meet, were he real.

He looked at the advertisement on the bus again. *Death in the Cairngorms.* He hadn't read that one, but he'd seen it somewhere very recently.

He pulled out his mobile and searched 'Myles Grant.' The Wikipedia article said he'd been born and raised in Fort William, and his first book in the series — the one that had propelled him to fame — was *Death in Glen Coe.* Inspector Beaton's first case.

Something pinged in his memory. *That* was where he'd seen the book. At the bookshop on the High Street, HP Booksellers. The shop where he'd interviewed Màiri MacLachlan, just yesterday. The poster in the window had said Myles Grant would be doing a book signing for *Death in the Cairngorms* this month. He'd only glanced at the notice, so he couldn't remember the date.

The museum, HP Booksellers, Myles Grant, and Màiri MacLachlan. Everything was circling around that bookshop, like a whirlpool being sucked into a vortex. Reenergised, Fraser turned around and went back into his building, taking the stairs two at a time. In his office, he crossed to the blank whiteboard on one wall and picked up a black marker.

In the middle of the board, he drew a circle, and in its centre, a stick figure with a question mark over its head. Then he drew more circles around the victim and labelled them *West Highlands Museum, Màiri MacLachlan, Eve MacDonald, Myles Grant,* and *HP Booksellers.*

He picked up a green marker and drew a line connecting the unknown victim, and one each for Màiri MacLachlan and Eve MacDonald, to the museum. He stepped back and squinted at the board, and then connected Màiri, Eve, and Myles Grant to the bookshop, using a purple marker this time.

He stood back again and studied his work. It looked more like a lopsided spider with multi-coloured legs than anything else. He was sure there were more legs on that spider, but to find out where they began and ended, he'd have to make another trip to Fort William.

He couldn't do much more here in Glasgow anyway, not until the body was identified. Another visit to the museum wouldn't go amiss, and he could check out the bookshop and the fire station while he was there. He had to interview the firefighters who had been on the scene, and he wanted to speak with Màiri MacLachlan's friend Eve, the one who'd been given CPR. She'd be out of hospital by now.

Surely Miss MacLachlan would have met Myles Grant, if he was going to do an event at the shop. But had they known each other before? What kind of relationship did they have? A pretty woman, a handsome man... He knew he was stretching, but experience had proven that truth could be stranger than fiction, and speculation often led to discovery.

Did Myles Grant have a connection to the museum? He was an author, and he used a lot of history in his books. His Inspector Beaton was a history buff, always drawing parallels between past and present in his cases. The West Highlands Museum would be a natural place for Grant to start his research for a book, to ground his fictional character in reality.

Fraser picked up the green marker and drew a dotted line from Myles Grant to the museum, and two others from Grant to Màiri and Grant to Eve. His spider was morphing into a tangled ball of yarn.

From the centre of the board, the stick figure and its question mark taunted him. *Who were you?* he asked it. *What did you do to deserve an ending like this?*

CHAPTER 22
FORT WILLIAM, SCOTLAND
– PRESENT TIME

If there is someone who has saved your life, remember his name as long as you live, even if you forget your own.
—Mehmet Murat ildan

Màiri pulled the collar of her rain jacket up and bent her head against the wind coming off the firth. Scotland in July—one minute a cloudless blue sky and warm temperatures, and the next minute grey clouds came from nowhere and covered the sun, usually bringing a gift of rain with them.

It was hard being the sun in Scotland. Màiri grinned, remembering a meme she'd seen on the internet that showed a beautiful loch under a blue sky with the mountains in the distance and the words, *I love summer in Scotland. This year it was a Wednesday.* Funny, but definitely some truth in it.

She felt the first plop of rain and looked up. "Try not to be so predictable, aye?" she told the grey sky. As if it had been listening and wanted to be amenable for a change, the weather changed its mind—again. The clouds parted, and the sun struggled back out. The wind ignored all this and continued as it had been. Wind was a constant in the weather game of Fort William.

Màiri studied the building in front of her. She'd elected to walk to the Fort William Fire Station, as it was only thirteen minutes from the bookstore, up the High Street and through the pedestrian tunnel under Belford Road, and then the roundabout that led to Carmichael Way. Now she stood before a long, modern building constructed of concrete and sandstone, with a dark grey slate roof and three large red doors.

She was here to thank the firefighter who had rescued her from the museum fire last week. She hadn't been able to stop thinking about those few minutes, sitting helpless next to Eve. They had planted themselves in her nightmares, reminding her over and over that she might have died, but for that one stranger.

What must it feel like, to save a life? Doctors and nurses knew. So did the men and women who climbed Munros to find and rescue hapless tourists who had thought challenging the mountains a fine idea until they found themselves stranded on a hillside with a broken leg and no way to get down.

What must it feel like? She knew the answer. She hadn't had to climb a mountain or brave a blazing fire. She'd merely laid a hand on Adam MacArthur's chest and listened as his heart lurched back into action. She'd watched the pink colour spread under

FORT WILLIAM, SCOTLAND – PRESENT TIME

her hand as it lay against Eve's heart, and felt her friend's chest as it rose and fell once more.

How had it felt? It felt exhilarating, unreal, impossible even—and it had scared her to death. Maybe because, unlike the men and women in this building, she hadn't trained for it. She hadn't set out to do what she did; she'd just done it. Twice.

Beside the first door, a sign proclaimed the site as the town's Fire and Rescue Service above a logo featuring a flame between two thistles. Màiri spied a brown door under the sign, dwarfed in comparison to the red fire appliance doors, and pushed it open.

She was standing in an empty foyer. Two doors led off to the right and left, and behind one of them she could hear muffled voices. She waited a few minutes, scanning the small room. There was a PC on the desk, and three green plastic chairs against the wall. Across from her, behind the desk, was a grouping of photos under a plaque that read *We remember*. Each photo had a plaque under it, listing the owner's name.

Firefighters killed in the line of duty. It could have been her rescuer, up on that wall. It could be any of the brave men who had responded to the museum fire that day.

She forced her thoughts away from the sad gallery of photos and tried the knob on the door that must lead to the apparatus room. Feeling like an interloper, she eased the door open.

A man lay on the floor, surrounded by people in black T-shirts with the logo she'd seen on the side of the building. He wasn't moving, and one of the men was performing CPR on him. It took a few frozen seconds for Màiri to realize that the body was a dummy and they were practicing. This was a class, and she was trespassing. She backed out hastily and went to sit on one of the chairs in the foyer.

The door opened again, and one of the black-shirted men came out. His brows lowered as he stared at Màiri. He might have been handsome, she thought, if his face wasn't twisted in a scowl.

"We're training today," he said, sounding impatient. "Can I help you with something?" His look said plainly that he hoped not.

"Um," Màiri said, unsure how to proceed. This had been a stupid idea; she should have called and made an appointment. She'd had visions of shiny red fire appliances standing out in the sun, being washed by cheerful firefighters.

"Aye?" the man said. "What do you want?"

Now he was just being plain rude. Màiri set her shoulders back and gave him a level gaze. "I was rescued from the fire at the West Highlands Museum the other day, and I wanted to thank the man who saved me."

"It's our job," the man answered shortly. "No big deal."

"Well, it was a big deal to me!" Màiri snapped. "I only have one life."

The door opened behind the man, and a woman came through. She glanced at her colleague and then smiled at Màiri.

"Do we have a visitor, then?" she asked cheerfully. "Did I hear you say you were rescued from a fire? What an awful experience!"

FORT WILLIAM, SCOTLAND – PRESENT TIME

She turned to the man beside her and gave him a cold look. "You can get back to the training, Peter. It's your turn."

The man harumphed and went back through the door, mumbling under his breath.

"Sorry," the woman said. "I'm Meg MacInnes. Don't mind Peter; he's not always that rude. Sometimes he's worse." She rolled her eyes.

Màiri laughed. "Màiri MacLachlan. Did I come at a bad time? It was just a spur of the moment decision. Should I make an appointment?"

Meg waved a hand. "Nae, you're fine. The training'll be over in a few. What were you looking for?"

Màiri told her about the rescue at the museum. "I can't describe him, really. He was in full uniform, with a helmet and mask and everything. But he was very kind, and I wanted to thank him. All of them, actually. They're so brave. I never realized it before."

Meg nodded. "I think that's normal, really. All little boys — and some girls, like me — want to be firefighters when they grow up. But then they do grow up, and very few of them still want to do it as adults." She gave Màiri a contemplative look. "It's very nice of you to come just to thank us. Most people never do." She patted Màiri's hand. "Come with me."

Meg opened the door again and led Màiri into the small room off the appliance bay. Six men were clearing up the materials, and one had the training dummy slung over his shoulder. They all turned when the two women entered. Five pairs of male eyes regarded the newcomer with appreciation. The one called Peter looked annoyed.

Is it a requirement that firefighters look like film stars? Màiri thought. They were all tall and muscular like the grumpy one, but unlike him, they regarded her with frank interest.

"Lads, we have an esteemed visitor this morning. Miss Màiri MacLachlan was in the museum when it caught fire three days ago, and one of you lot was kind enough to rescue her." She looked around at the surprised faces. "C'mon, fess up. Which one of you was it?"

The men looked surprised. "Not me," said one. He eyed Màiri again. "But I wish it was."

"Wasn't me."

"Me neither."

There was a silence. Then a man at the back of the room, the one carrying the training dummy, spoke up. "Guess it was me," he said. He dipped his head toward Màiri. "Was just there at the right time, miss," he said, diffidently. "Glad I could help."

"Ach, Mackie, ain't you the lucky one!" one of his colleagues said. "Shoulda been me."

"Well, come on over and meet your grateful citizen," Meg told him. "Don't be shy. I don't think she bites." The men laughed and shoved the man toward Màiri. He set the dummy against the wall and stood in front of her, hands clasped in front of him. For the first time she was able to see what her rescuer looked like out of the bulky suit and PPE.

He seemed young, but it could be partly because of the stubborn cowlick that stuck up at the top of his forehead, making him look like a small boy whose mother had unsuccessfully applied the spit and

FORT WILLIAM, SCOTLAND – PRESENT TIME

hanky method on the way to church. His grey eyes were the eyes she remembered, full of concern and kindness.

"You're younger than you seemed at the museum," she said, and could have bitten her lip when his face flushed and several of his colleagues laughed. "I mean...I guess it's because of the uniform."

"I-I'm Alexander MacKay," the man said. "Everybody just calls me Mackie, though." He rocked back and forth on his feet and twisted his hands. "I'm glad I was there," he said, and despite his embarrassment there was a gleam of pride shining in his eyes.

A rush of affection for this young man coursed through Màiri. *All little boys want to be firefighters... very few still do as adults.*

"Well, Mackie, I'm very glad you're one of the ones who still wanted to be a firefighter when you grew up." She shot a look at Meg, who beamed.

"I'm grateful to all of you," she said, through a throat that was suddenly thick. "I couldn't have gotten myself out of there without you." She turned back to Mackie. "I heard the sirens outside, but I didn't think you'd get there in time. You must be very fast."

Mackie looked confused, and then he laughed. "Well, we train for it."

A derisive voice rose from the back. "Well, this is all very lovely and all, but don't we have a job to do?"

"Shut it, Campbell," one of the other men said.

Màiri looked for the man named Campbell, although she'd already made an educated guess. The man Meg had called Peter was staring at her with undisguised hostility. *What's his problem?* she thought. *Is it me, or is this just the way he always is? I've never even seen him before.*

Another thought presented itself. *I'm glad he wasn't the one who rescued us.* Then she gave herself a mental slap. *Don't be judgemental. He's one of the good guys.* She gave Peter Campbell a warm smile and was rewarded with another scowl.

"Well," she said, "I've got to be going. I just walked here, and I have to get to work. I know you're *busy*" — she was delighted to see a flush mount on Campbell's swarthy face — "so I'll get out of your way."

Màiri smiled again at Alexander MacKay and gave Meg a little wave before turning for the door. Then she pivoted and included them all in her smile. "If you're ever on the High Street, stop in at HP Booksellers. I'll treat you all to coffee at the cafe." She grinned. "And an extra scone for Mackie."

Well, that went well, she thought as she made her way back to the shop. It was amazing how a uniform full of impressive equipment made such a difference in a man's appearance. Or maybe it was the job itself. MacKay—Mackie— couldn't be more than twenty-six or seven, and yet in the uniform, carrying her out of a burning building with no effort, he seemed older, larger. A hero.

A strange feeling—a mixture of joy and trepidation—spread through her. Maybe that was what she was meant to do. Rescue people. Save them. It had to be the best feeling in the world to do that for a living.

"It is."

Màiri turned, surprised to see a middle-aged man walking next to her. He was dressed oddly for the

FORT WILLIAM, SCOTLAND – PRESENT TIME

unusually fine weather, in a black rain cape like those worn by bagpipers in competitions. An Inverness coat, it was called. The hood was pulled up, but he turned his head and she saw that he had blue eyes and a fair complexion. The coat was unbuttoned, and underneath it he wore the same sort of polo shirt as the firefighters at the station.

"Oh," she said. "Are you a firefighter?"

"I was." His smile seemed regretful. "I didn't realize what I had until it was too late." He seemed to be talking more to himself than to her. "It was all so stupid, and I don't even believe in that shite, but I let myself be pulled in. Then when I tried to leave, it was too late." He gave her an anxious look. "Don't believe everything they say, aye?"

Màiri felt a sense of unease spread through her. *Who is this guy? Why is he telling me this?* She gave the man a polite smile, broke eye contact, and edged away, and when she looked back, he was gone. She turned around and gazed down the High Street, but the strange man was nowhere in sight.

Strange. She shrugged and walked on. *I hope I wasn't too rude, but that was creepy.*

She hurried her steps and burst through the front door of the bookshop. The door banged into the wall, rebounded, and hit her in the head. Four pairs of eyes looked up at her dramatic entrance. Then Mary shook her head and went back to her paperwork, Caomhainn resettled himself on his ladder, and Biscuit blinked her yellow eyes once and sauntered away. Betty came up and held out a list of books.

Màiri rubbed the side of her head. Life in a bookshop. Nothing ever changed except for the displays on the tables. She held up her right hand and looked at it, flexed her fingers, and smiled.

There *was* a calling. She just had to figure out what it was.

CHAPTER 23
GLEN COE, SCOTLAND – PRESENT TIME

Suddenly, I'm burning up and terrified,
scared I'll be too weak to resist.
Scratch that – I'm petrified I've already given in.
—Amanda Bouchet

"Why didn't you get her number, then?" Jared asked.

"I was about to ask her when Laura showed up." Adam's voice was tinged with frustration. "She sailed in and acted like a proper nyaff—said she was my girlfriend! And the next minute Màiri was out of there like a bat out of hell." He huffed out a breath. "And I don't blame her."

The two had finished a run and were sitting on a rock on the slope of the mountain, looking down over Glen Coe. Jared looked out at the River Coe and let out another breath, this time one of awe. It didn't get old, this view, and it never failed to soothe his soul. Looking sideways at Adam, he saw his own emotions reflected on his friend's face.

Adam turned to see Jared watching him and grinned. "These are the times when I truly believe God has a plan. We're sometimes just too stupid to realize it."

"I know what you mean," Jared said. "I never would have found this place if it hadn't been…" He paused, uncertain whether to go on.

"If it hadn't been for your accident," Adam finished for him. "You're right. What kind of Englishman decides to chuck it all and live in the wilds of Scotland, eh? Do you miss Liverpool?"

"Sometimes. I miss the noise, and the crowds—oh, and there's traffic. Definitely miss that." He smiled and looked out again over the glen. "Seriously, I was never in the right place. I had my heart set on something I wasn't meant to have, so God stepped in and put my head on straight." He turned suddenly. "What about you?"

Adam kept his attention on the view. "I don't know how much time I have left. Not much, according to the doctor." He turned back to face Jared's question head on. "The Curse would have found me no matter where I was, aye?"

Jared nodded slowly.

"So, it's best to spend that time here, in the most beautiful place in the world." He paused. "You know I'm from Inverness."

Jared nodded again. Adam shuffled his feet in the dirt for a minute. Then he said, without looking up, "Inverness is beautiful. Everything about the

GLEN COE, SCOTLAND – PRESENT TIME

Highlands is beautiful. But Inverness is also where I grew up, in a family that made living a normal life extremely difficult."

He stopped and cleared his throat, and Jared waited, a little anxious about what might come next. Adam didn't talk about himself much, although he'd opened up more since the day he'd shared his awful secret.

Jared's throat grew thick, and he fought back a wetness that suddenly dimmed the view of the glen. He was convinced that Adam MacArthur had saved him, back there on a Ballachulish street. He'd given him a job, a home, and a family when months earlier he'd considered throwing himself onto the railway tracks in Glasgow station.

He owed Adam more than he'd ever tell him. The man sitting next to him, looking in the peak of health, was on borrowed time, and was doing everything in his power to make that time brilliant. Jared admired him for his courage.

He looked at Adam, wondering where that courage had come from. Apparently, he'd grown up in a dysfunctional family, and now there was a death sentence hanging over his head. *Why is life so goddamned unfair sometimes?* And yet the man persevered.

Jared remembered a father who always had time for him. His home had been filled with love, and when Da died, his mother had picked up the pieces and carried on. Jared missed his father, but the memories were all good. Because of that, he cursed the man who'd made the first few years of Adam's life lonely and frightening, no matter the reason.

"My brother Ewan had it the worst," Adam was saying. "Dad wasn't a bad man, but he was so bitter after my mother died that he retreated from us. We were all so messed up because of that. Izzy, Ewan, Sophie...Daniel was a complete wreck for a while, and Jonah hasn't come out of his books in years."

He laughed, a hollow sound that fell like a rock into the glen. "But people can't live like islands forever. I was lucky. I had Ewan, and we had scrambling. And now Ewan has Fiona, Sophie found Brian, and Daniel has Eve. We're slowly coming into the world, leaving the past behind. And for me, that past includes Inverness."

He looked up and a smile broke out on his face. "I have Ballachulish, and Glen Coe..." He batted his eyelashes. "And you."

"Ugh!" Jared pretended to gag. "I can't take any more of this! I think the air up here is too thin. Your brain cells are evaporating." He stood up.

"Shut up," Adam said equably, rising to join him. "That's the last time I tell you anything, you fuckin' dobber." He punched Jared in the shoulder, and his friend danced away, grinning.

"Divvy," Jared said.

"Bampot."

"Melt."

"Bawbag."

The insults continued for a while, Adam pulling out his best Scots slurs and Jared answering with Scouse. Since both Scots and Liverpool English had no shortage of rich vocabulary when it came to insults, this game could be quite educational.

GLEN COE, SCOTLAND – PRESENT TIME

Eventually they ran out of offensive terms and stood grinning at each other on the hilltop.

"So," Jared said. "Now that we've gotten that out of the way, let's talk about this Màiri bird. Why are you here, letting me pick you apart, when you could be with her?" He looked around and lowered his voice to a whisper. "I don't see Laura around."

Adam snorted. "This is the only place I feel safe from that one," he said. "Maybe it's the real reason I spend so much time in the mountains."

Jared pinned him with a glare. "Don't dodge the subject, mate. When are you going to visit Fort William again? Pearl's been pining away for that cat in the bookshop. Are you going to break his flabby little heart?"

Adam shook his head and assumed an expression of disgust. "Pearl will be fine. You, I'm not so sure."

"You're doing it again," Jared said calmly. "Answer the question."

Adam's eyes darted away. "I told you she was in that fire that burned part of the museum, right? I saw her ride off in the ambulance with Eve, and Daniel said they're both okay, but I figured I should give her some time..." He trailed off.

"Really?" Jared asked. "She shouldn't be meeting with people or doing anything because she experienced something traumatic? What does that have to do with you?" He moved to stand directly in front of his friend. "So what's the problem?"

"I think I like her." Adam's voice held a note of fear. "I think I like her, and I shouldn't. I can't!" The eyes that met Jared's were glassy with panic. "There's no future with me!"

"You are truly a coward," Jared told him. "I see I'm going to have to step in." He shook his head. "You don't have to propose to her. But we are going down this mountain, you are jumping into the shower, and then you will take yourself and Pearl to Fort William. You need a book on guts. Or spleen. Or something."

"Stop trying to run my life—"

"Oh hullo, Laura. What brings you all the way up here?"

Adam flinched, swung around, and fixed Jared with a menacing glare. "I'll get you for that." He sighed. "All right. Let's go. I hear Pearl howling from here. I think he needs a book."

⁂

Two hours later, Adam was walking up the High Street with Pearl lumbering happily along beside him. The bulldog was interested in every bit of rubbish, every crumb of shortbread that might have fallen onto the pavement, every human being perceptive enough to stop and tell him what a good dog he was.

"I should have left you at home," Adam told him. "At this rate, the shop will be closed and you'll miss your chance to see your cat."

Pearl's ears went up and he increased the pace of his waddle to its top speed, his little bowed legs carrying him ahead to the end of the leash. Adam grinned and caught up. He bent and scratched the dog behind his ears, and Pearl closed his eyes and drooled.

"At least you're honest about your love life," he said to the dog. "Jared's right; I'm a coward." He straightened up and sighed. "Come on, let's get this over with."

"Flower of Scotland" chimed as they passed through the doorway of HP Booksellers.

"Hullo, Adam, hullo Pearl," Mary said from behind the desk. "Biscuit's waitin' for ye, 'n th' bairn's corner." Adam unclipped the leash from the dog's collar, and Pearl waddled away as fast as his stubby little legs would carry him.

"She's t' th' back," Mary said. "Betty! Can ye nip into th' back room an' tell Màiri some 'uns here fer her?"

"No, I'm not...I just need a book." *What the hell book do I need? Damn it, forgot to figure that out.* He looked desperately around the shop for inspiration and saw Eve.

"I'm sure Eve can help me," he said to Mary, who was watching him like a robin eyeing a tasty worm. He hurried over to the shelf where Eve was standing on a ladder next to a stack of mystery novels.

"I need a book," he said, forcing himself not to look over his shoulder to see if Mary was still watching him. He knew she was.

"Hullo, Adam."

He turned to see Màiri standing behind him, her arms around a large cardboard box. Without allowing himself to think, he reached out and took the box from her. "Where are these going?"

"Oh. Just over here. Thanks." She led the way to a table in the back alcove behind the cafe, and he offloaded the carton. "These just came in and Mary asked me to unbox them. They're for a new display she wants on that round table in the front."

"That box is heavy! Isn't there someone else who can carry that stuff?"

"Aye, Caomhainn usually does it, but he's off today. It's not that heavy, really. We've all gotten used to doing some lifting, and I'm not a shrinking violet...ye ken?"

She smiled at him, and his heart did something strange and skittery. It occurred to Adam that she probably wasn't good for his condition. He should avoid her.

Except that she's the reason you're standing here gawking like an eejit in the first place, ye pudding. She's the reason your damn heart's beating at all.

"Adam? Are you okay?"

He focused on the blue eyes, now clouded with concern. "Oh, aye." He shook his head to clear it. "Do you have something to open this thing?"

"Oh, aye, right here." She produced a box cutter from the tabletop and he took it from her, snapped it open, and ran the blade down the length of tape holding it closed. The flaps sprang apart.

Màiri recoiled from the box as if it might hold a snapping turtle. Her eyes were huge, and the colour had drained from her face. "Smoke! It's on fire!" she gasped. "Get out!"

Adam looked at her in surprise. "I don't smell anything," he said. He pushed her behind him and stepped up to the box, pulling the flaps open carefully.

"It's just books," he said. He reached for the book on top and held it up for her to see. "Just books. No smoke."

The colour had returned to Màiri's face, and now it heightened. "I'm sorry. It must be one of those residual things the doctor told me about. Neurological sequelae, or whatever." She took the book from him and turned it about, opened it, and rifled the pages. "I don't smell anything now." She looked at him, her eyes hooded. "You must think I'm mad."

"No, I think you're somebody who went through something scary and dangerous. Being caught in a fire isn't something most people put on their bucket list, you know." He thought about it. "Have you talked to Eve about it?"

Màiri nodded. "She doesn't remember anything except when we first smelled smoke. She was unconscious most of the time." She shrugged. "They said these weird things'll go away with time; I just have to wait." She closed the book and put it on the table and began to unload the carton.

Adam peeked in. "There's one more here." He pulled it out. "It's different from the rest. Don't they come in lots? Why would there just be the one book?"

Màiri didn't answer. He looked up curiously and saw that she was staring at the cover of the book. Her colour had gone pale again and she looked ready to bolt.

Adam gave the cover a closer look. The title, *The Witch's Daughter*, was rendered in a Celtic font. The cover art featured the stylized red-orange image of a flame, centred by a tall pole to which was bound the silhouette of a woman. Smaller flames danced at her feet, and her long hair flew out on both sides of her head.

There was something…repulsive…about this book. Adam resisted the urge to throw it down on the table and opened it to the first page. *Chapter One*—WITCH was written in the same Celtic font.

He sniffed. An almost imperceptible odour drifted up from the paper. He put his nose closer to the book, and his own eyes widened.

Smoke.

Màiri hadn't been imagining things, and it wasn't sequelae from the fire...at least not *her* fire.

CHAPTER 24
DORNACH, SCOTLAND - 1727

SÌNE

"Ye'll go t' hell fer this!"

Sìne dropped her bag and hurried over to where Doirin stood, hands on her hips and eyes flashing fire.

"Mam!" she cried. "Tis not important." She pulled at her mother's arm and gave Bearnas Graham an apologetic look.

"I'm so sorry, Mistress Graham. She doesnae mean 't," she offered.

The woman behind the costermonger's cart narrowed her eyes and sniffed. "'At's all well an' good," she said, "but she cannae be goin' about accusin' honest folk o' cheatin', now can she?"

Sìne bobbed her head twice. "Yer right. I'll have a talk wi' her, eh?" She dragged her mother away from

WITCH

the cart and pulled her in the direction of home.

"She was tryin' t' sell rottin tatties," Doirin muttered. "Tellin me they was fresh. I willnae have enyone cheatin' me, aye?" She glared into her daughter's face. "Wha?"

Sìne patted her arm. "Yer right, o'course, Mam," she said. "Tis just that th' marks on the tatties are s'posed t' be there," she explained.

It seemed as if she was doing a lot of explaining these days. Mam had always been fierce in the face of injustice, but lately it was getting worse. She was picking fights more often with the neighbours, accusing them of stealing from her garden or spying on her through her window.

Doirin was forgetting things more and more, overreacting to innocent comments. She was angry most of the time. Sìne's gentle, brilliant mother was turning into someone else—someone she didn't know—and it left a hollow pit in her stomach where fear squirmed like a nest of snakes.

She settled her mother and made her way to her favourite perch on the rocks above the rolling firth. Within minutes, a familiar figure appeared in the distance and made his way toward her. Hugh was like one of the tonics Maighread used to make in her kitchen, Sìne thought—a magical elixir. What would she do without him?

Hugh reached her and threw himself down onto the bank. He pushed an errant black curl out of her face and looked into her eyes, reading them as he always did. Every time they met, he studied her with those lovely multi-hued eyes as if she were a book he needed to commit to memory, a precious artifact to be marvelled at. It gave her a warm feeling that seeped down into her heart and melted the ice that had gathered there since their last meeting.

"So what's botherin' ye?" he asked, and cocked his head to the side, waiting. "Is 't yer mam, again?"

Sìne sighed. He always knew.

"Aye," she said. "She got into another fight t'day at th' market. She's getting worse, Hugh. This mornin' she called me Emily."

"Who's Emily?"

"She was an auld lady back in Ab'rdeen Mam took care o'. Verra kind. Mam said Lady Emily didnae want her t' leave, but 'er husband would have none o' it."

"So, tis this Emily's husband I have t' thank fer bringin' ye here?" Hugh grinned. "I'd like t' thank the man one day."

Sìne laughed. "I'm sure he's dead by now, ye numpty."

He looked up into the cloudless blue sky. "Thank ye, Miss Emily's husband, fer bringin' Sìne Gilchrist t' Dornach."

"Hugh..."

"Aye?"

"Why d'ye like me? I mean, th' way I am. Th' way people talk. Why does it nae bother ye?"

He slanted her a sideways glance. "Well, yer sommat presentable, when yer hair's not flyin' in yer face, an' yer not as stupid as th' other lassies, I guess..." He ducked away from Sìne's fist before it could make contact with his arm and laughed. Then he scooted close to her and whispered, "I dinnae ken. I like ye b'cause ye're you."

"I'm presentable?" She tried and failed to look affronted.

"Ye're more than presentable," he said, seriously. "Ye're th' most beautiful lass in th' world."

"An have ye seen a lot o' th' world, then?" Sìne tilted her head to look at him.

"Enough. Doesnae take th' whole world t' ken somethin' so simple."

Hugh took one of Sìne's hands in his own and caressed it with his thumb. "I heard yer Gran say once't that God made ye more beautiful than th' other lassies, so t' keep them from gettin' jealoos He took a wee somethin' away." He grinned. "I'm not sure about that, but I do thynk He put his own mark on ye."

Sìne looked up, her brow furrowed. "What d' ye mean?"

Hugh reached out gently pushed Sìne's thick black hair off her neck. "There's His mark, real an' true, right here on yer shoulder."

Sìne craned her head to see. She could just barely make out the tiny mark on the top of her shoulder—a tiny line bisected by another, smaller line near the bottom. "What is it? I cannae see it clear. It's just lines, isnae 't?"

Hugh put on a shocked expression. "Just lines? Ye cannae see 't proper, lass. It's a cross. An' if that isnae God's own mark, I dinnae ken what is!"

Sìne laughed and swatted his hand away. "Yer a numpty. Why would God draw a cross upside down? Tis just a mark."

Hugh shrugged. "Who'm I t' question th' decisions o' th' Lord? An' maybe tisn't e'en a cross." He leant back and studied the mark. "Looks more like a wee sword t' me." He made a swishing motion with his arm. "Th' sword o' God."

Sìne laughed again. She knew he was just telling stories to make her feel better, but it was working. She wasn't one for self-pity; it took too much work to feel sorry for yourself. She pulled her hand out of his and jumped to her feet.

"Well, I have t' see what trouble Mam is up to." She started away, then turned back. "Hugh?"

"Aye?"

"Thank ye." She stepped forward and gave him a peck on the cheek.

She turned toward home, leaving Hugh Sutherland standing at the water's edge, staring after her.

"Sìne! Wait!"

Sìne turned back at the words. Hugh walked slowly up to her and stood still for a minute. Then he cupped her face in both hands and bent down to kiss her full on the mouth. Just for a second, but it was enough to change Sìne's world. For just that flicker of time, she forgot Mam's failing memory, forgot the suspicious glances of her neighbours, forgot her loneliness. She stood in the path, afraid to open her eyes lest the image be a lie.

I'm goin' t' marry 'im. The words drifted into her mind and hung there, fluttering like the wings of a moth when it sees the candle flame. Then they evaporated, as quickly as they'd come. Sìne opened her eyes. Hugh was gone.

"What're ye doin' standin' in th' path like a wee sheep?" Alan Grant was walking toward her from the other direction. He stopped in front of her and gave her his practiced smile, the one he used on all the village lassies.

"N-nuthin'," Sìne said. "Just on my way home."

"Can I walk wi' ye?" Without waiting for an answer, he stepped up beside her. "Such a bonny lass shouldnae be out here alone," he said. The words slid off his tongue like honey.

Normally it would have been nice to have a handsome lad walk her home, but today Sìne wanted to be alone with her thoughts. She wanted to examine Hugh's kiss, to turn it over in her mind and study it from all angles. Had Alan seen it? Was that why he was suddenly paying her attention?

Sìne studied Alan Grant out of the corner of her eye as they walked. He was very handsome, with that sun-bleached blond hair, clear blue eyes and ready smile. The problem was, he knew it. And why was he being nice to her now, when he'd always stood by and watched when the others made fun of her? To be fair, he hadn't joined them, but he hadn't stood up for her, either.

Alan seemed oblivious to her preoccupation. He slowed his walk to match her pace and made conversation that went in and out of her ears as fast as he said the words. He kept a respectful distance and his hands were carefully shoved in his pockets, but all Sìne could think was, *Please go away. I want t' be alone*.

"Mister Grant, is it?" A rough voice jolted her out of her thoughts, and they both spun around. Albert

DORNACH, SCOTLAND - 1727

Wilson stood on the path, hands on his hips and a frown of disapproval twisting his lined face.

"Mister Grant, I would have a word with my tenant, if ye dinnae mind. Please be on yer way."

Alan's face reddened, and he opened his mouth as if to say something. Then his shoulders drooped and he gave Sìne a look of apology. "Later, then, aye?" he mumbled, and walked quickly past the doctor and away.

"How can I help ye, sir?" Sìne said politely. She eyed Alan's retreating back enviously.

"I've been noticin' that yer mother doesnae seem well lately," the doctor said.

Sìne squared her shoulders. "She's a bit tired, is all. Thank ye for askin'." She could feel the hairs rising on the back of her neck as they always did in this man's presence.

"That's as may be," Wilson said, "but I thynk it's time t' make a change in the surgery."

"What kind o' change?" The hairs on her neck were at full attention now. This man had some kind of purpose, she'd always felt it. He never stopped watching.

"I thynk ye should take over from yer mother now." He watched her from under hooded green eyes. "She's taught ye th' basics, aye?"

"Aye, but what about—?" Sìne held up her hands. "Dinnae ye mind? There's things I cannae do, an' th' villagers willnae have me touch them."

The man's face twisted. The veins on his forehead stood out against his pale skin and his lip twitched. Then he cleared his throat.

"We'll accommodate for that," he said brusquely. "They willnae mind when they have need o' ye." He

223

waved a bony hand in the air. "So we're settled, then." And without waiting for her response, Wilson strode off toward the house without a backward look.

Sine was left staring after him, a sick feeling crawling in her stomach. This man had barely tolerated the Gilchrist women since he'd come to Dornach last year. Other than taking over their house and leaving them to make do with the garden shed out back, he'd done nothing to justify his lofty title of 'doctor,' either. Doirin had shouldered the burden of care left by Maighread's passing.

Wilson allowed Doirin to use the midwifery—the 'surgery,' he called it—but he did nothing to help. And now he wanted Sine to shoulder the burden of care for the women of Dornach, whether they willed it or not? There was more to this than he was saying, and the nausea swelled. What did *Doctor* Albert Wilson want?

CHAPTER 25
DORNACH, SCOTLAND – 1727

HUGH

Hugh walked into the parlour of his father's home—he had ceased long ago to think of it as his—and froze.

"We have visitors," his father said, and Hugh saw a warning look in his dark eyes. Two women sat on the tufted couch, each with a cup of tea in her hand. The elder's narrowed eyes roved over his body from head to foot, as if sizing him up as a possible brood bull. The younger studied him over the rim of one of his mother's porcelain cups and smiled. Her blue eyes were wide and innocent, but Hugh knew better.

"Hello, Mistress MacAllan...Ailis." Hugh nodded. His head seemed stuffed with cotton wool, and he probably looked like a sheep, too—a brainless sack of wool.

"Sit down, son." His father's words were calm, but Hugh sensed an undercurrent in them that made his skin crawl. He sat down in the only other chair in the room and clenched his fists in his lap.

He had been watching his father more closely during the last year, and nothing he'd done or said had been unusual or untoward. There had been no outbursts, no threats or diatribes aimed at the Misses Gilchrist, no talk of the devil.

Hugh didn't trust it for a moment. He would never forget the look on Duncan Sutherland's face when he'd faced him that day, the spittle flying unheeded from his mouth.

Nobody kens who th' father o' that brat be! Maybe t'was th' Devil! Why else would th' creature be born like that?

The poisonous words had replayed themselves countless times in his memory. The thought that Sìne and her mother could be the cause of a bairn being born dead was madness.

He'd thought his father insane that day, but now he wondered if he'd read too much into it. Could an insane person manage to hide his condition for so long? Could he continue to mix with the people he despised and not have his disdain noticed by anyone? Was his father that good a dissembler?

And if Duncan wasn't insane, that left another possibility, one too frightening to accept without proof. Hugh knew his father's keen intelligence. The farm he'd inherited from his own father was thriving, due to his brilliant management. If he wasn't mad, then what purpose could he have for the words he'd uttered that day?

DORNACH, SCOTLAND – 1727

It had something to do with that odious Doctor Wilson his father had brought up from Edinburgh, of that he was sure. Da said he was a magistrate, not a doctor, and according to Sìne the man did no healing at all, leaving the work to Doirin. In fact, other than stealing their home and relegating the two women to the tiny back hut, nothing really had changed since his arrival.

Wilson had been to this house frequently. His father would take the doctor into his study, and they spent hours in conversation, and no amount of listening at the door produced any knowledge of their subject matter. But there was something insidious and underhanded about these meetings, almost as if they were secret...

"Hugh!"

He looked up to find his father's dark blue eyes glowering from beneath furrowed brows.

"Aye, sir?"

"How old are ye now, lad?" his father said, never taking his eyes from his son.

"Twenty-two," Hugh said, automatically. His father *knew* that. What was this about?

"Ahh, time does flit awa from us, aye?" Duncan chuckled. "I remember when ye were just a wee lad in short trews, and here ye are a grown man." He shook his head and sighed. "An' Mistress MacAllan has been telling me that her Ailis has already reached seventeen years." He smiled, but his eyes remained opaque. "An' I've been thinkin...we cannae let such a lovely lass become an auld maid, can we noo?"

Hugh could feel the blood draining from his head. What in the name of God was going on here? Auld maid? Surely not... He stole a look at Ailis and saw that she was smiling at him like a barn cat who has cornered a rat and is waiting for it to realise that all hope for survival is gone.

"April is a lovely month, aye?" the elder Sutherland continued.

"Fer what?" The words burst out of Hugh's mouth. He knew he sounded rude, but this was ridiculous.

Elizabeth MacAllan frowned, and his father's eyes narrowed in warning.

"Fer a wedding, o' course. Ye'll be takin' over th' farm one day. It's not too soon t' start yer own family. Ye could live here..."

"I'm not gettin' married." Hugh stood up quickly. He turned to the two women, whose mouths were round circles of surprise. "I dinnae mean t' run, but I have t' see t' the coos. Thank ye fer visitin'." He bowed his head quickly, then bolted.

"Hugh!" His father's furious voice followed him, but Hugh was already out the door. As soon as it closed behind him, he began running, lest something reach out and yank him back into that pit of vipers.

When he was well within the woods that ran between his home and the village, he stopped and flopped down onto a fallen log. His breath pounded in his ears.

Marry? Marry that little bitch? Never, not in a million years. She's a bairn, a wee harpy. She's vicious, and calculating...

...and she isnae Sìne.

He should have seen it coming, though. Dornach was a small village, and the lasses near his age weren't so abundant. He'd never cared about that, anyway. He'd always known that if he couldn't marry Sìne, he wouldn't marry anyone. He'd thought they had all the time in the world.

He was a fool. He'd deluded himself into thinking that when he came of age, he'd be free to make his own decisions. He'd built a wall between himself and his father's hateful prejudice and hidden behind it while he spun gossamer threads out of his imagination and constructed a fantasy world for himself and Sìne.

Hugh remained in the woods until he saw the MacAllans' coach carry the two women away from the house and then made his way slowly back. This would probably be ugly, but better to face it and get it over with. His father could yell, but he couldn't drag his son in front of the preacher, could he?

He stopped with his hand on the knob and listened, but there was no sound on the other side. Maybe his father had already gone up to—

The door was yanked open and an iron grip latched onto Hugh's arm. Off-balance, he stumbled into the room and went sprawling onto the hardwood floor. He was pushing himself up when the kick came, hard and furious. He rolled into a ball around the pain that exploded in his stomach and tried to make himself as small as possible.

Duncan kicked his son again, this time in the head. Through the roaring in his ears, Hugh heard his father slide the leather belt from around his waist. And then his world narrowed to a shaft of pain. The stinging end of the strap crossed his back over and

WITCH

over, leaving a searing fire that subsided into throbbing agony.

At some point, he must have passed out. When his mind cleared, the room was silent. He opened his eyes slowly and found himself looking at the cracks of the wooden floor. He turned his head to the right, and nausea overtook him. He retched, the breakfast he'd had hours ago rising in his throat and spewing out onto the floor.

"You're awake. Good."

Hugh forced his limbs to move and pulled himself onto his hands and knees. He gave it all he had and raised his head. His father sat in his leather armchair, one leg crossed over the other, and watched his son with flat, emotionless eyes.

"If ye want t' be called a man, ye need t' be able t' take a thumpin'," Duncan Sutherland said. His voice was calm. He lifted one hand and studied his fingernails. "An' ye need t' be a man t' get married."

Hugh pushed back and sat on the floor with his knees bent and his hands over his face. He heard the words come out of his mouth as if they belonged to someone else. "I'm not gettin' married." He braced himself for the next blow.

It didn't come. When he took his hands away from his eyes, his father was still sitting in the chair, no expression at all on his face.

"Ah, but ye are, lad." The voice was low, almost a whisper. "Ye'll be marryin' wee Ailis MacAllan in th' spring. Tis been decided."

"I willnae." Hugh looked defiantly at the man he called Father. "Ye cannae make me do such a thing."

His father put the hand he'd been studying back in his lap and looked straight at Hugh. A slow smile spread over his face. The late afternoon light came through the window behind him, bathing his face in light as though he wore a halo. The irony of it made Hugh want to vomit again.

"Ye see, lad, I ken what ye *want* t' do. I ken where ye go, and who ye keep company with when ye think ye're alone." A muscle in his jaw jumped. "I'm the sheriff. I have ears an' eyes everywhere 'n this village. There's nowhere ye can go, nothing ye can do, that I willnae hear about."

"Ye-ye have people *watchin'* me? S*pyin'* on me?" The colour drained from Hugh's face. "Why?"

"How else would I keep my son safe?" his father said, a look of surprise crossing his face. "Ye're the future o' Dornach, lad. My only son. Ye'll have a proper wife, a fine family ye can be proud of."

Hugh struggled to his feet. "I. Will not. Marry. Ailis MacAllan." He drew the words out and watched his father's face, wondering if he could move fast enough in his condition to get to the door before the man reached him. But Duncan didn't move at all. He held his son's gaze until Hugh dropped his eyes and then sighed.

"Well, I'm thinkin' there's somethin' ye're not clear about," he said. "Ye see, yer wee hoo'er spawn an' her wicked mother are dependin' on ye. If ye dinnae wed wee Ailis in th' spring, I cannae promise their safety." He paused. "Let me say it sommat diffrent. I *can* promise 'at they *willnae* be safe." He pinned his son with sharp brown eyes, and Hugh saw something gleam in their depths. "Their miserable lives are up t' ye, lad. Do ye ken my meanin'?"

Hugh felt the walls closing in on him, but his father wasn't finished. "Ye're never t' see that creature again, ye hear? If ye do I'll ken, and ye willnae like th' consequence. This is a God-fearin' village, and tis up to those of us who watch over it to keep it that way. Th' Devil has his minions, but we willnae have them here." His voice rose. "Satan is not welcome in Dornach!"

CHAPTER 26
FORT WILLIAM, SCOTLAND
– PRESENT TIME

What is fame? The advantage of being known by people of whom you yourself know nothing, and for whom you care as little.
—Lord Byron

Myles glanced up at the queue in front of his table and sighed. It wound around HP Booksellers and out the door to the High Street, and his hand was already aching. The upside of fame for a writer was getting to sign hundreds of your own books for excited strangers who wanted to read what you wrote. The downside was having to sign hundreds of books for strangers you didn't care anything about.

He flexed his fingers and smiled at the middle-aged tourist in front of him.

"My first trip to Scotland and I get to meet my favourite author!" she said in a soft, southern American accent. "I was bowled over when I saw the sign about this event. Left my hubby at the hotel and ran as fast as my legs would carry me! I hope you're working on your next novel. That Inspector Beaton is a real character, isn't he? Bless his heart."

"Well yes, he is a character, after all." Myles winked at her, signed the book she thrust at him, and handed it back. "I'm glad you like him." *You'll probably be fair scunnered when I kill him off.* For some reason, he was cheered by the thought.

He caught Mary's eye, and she came over immediately to plunk a small placard on the desk that read *Our author is human, too. Back in fifteen.* Myles stood up and stretched.

The queue remained where it was; none of them wanted to lose their place in line. Most of them were reading *Death in the Cairngorms*, but a few had picked up a book from a nearby table and were deep in another world. Book people were like that; never bored waiting, because they always had a door to a different time or place at hand.

Myles wandered over to the table in front of the window, opposite the one where his *Death in the Highlands* display had been set up. It featured a large display stand with a placard that read *Who Were the Witches of Scotland?* in the shop's signature Celtic font.

Several books by different authors were arranged on the table, grouped into fiction and nonfiction. The novels featured nubile young women with flowing black hair and red lips, dancing about under the moon or stirring something into a cauldron. Myles ignored these in favour of the non-fiction offerings.

FORT WILLIAM, SCOTLAND – PRESENT TIME

The History of Witchcraft in Scotland, Scottish Witch Trials in the Seventeenth and Eighteenth Centuries, The Legacy of the Scottish Witch Trials.

Nonfiction book titles always seemed to want to bore the reader to death before he even opened the book, Myles thought. So prosaic, as if a little imagination would sully their lofty subject matter. His eye was caught by another book and he picked it up because of the author's name. *The Witch's Daughter* by Simon Grant. Not bad for a nonfiction title.

He smiled to himself. There were thousands of Grants in Scotland, most of them related in some way or other. He turned to the biography in the back of the book. *Simon Grant was born and raised in Dornach, Scotland, and has always been fascinated by the rich history of his village. His latest work is based on a manuscript found in the attic of his great-grandmother's house, which chronicles the events of 1727, culminating in the trial that became the last of its kind in Scotland.*

Myles looked closer at the book in his hand. The cover art featured the stylized red-orange image of a flame, with the silhouette of a woman in its centre. There was something about this book; something that called to him and repelled him at the same time.

Mary Duncan appeared at his side and reached for the book in his hand.

"I'll put it at th' front for ye, lad," she said. "Yer readers 'r waitin.'" She nodded toward the queue that hadn't diminished at all in the last fifteen minutes.

Myles took a deep breath and made his way back to the table, but as he scrawled his name and made automatic conversation with his readers, his mind kept going back to the book on witchcraft. Why had Mary Duncan assumed he wanted the thing?

"I'm going to do it," he said suddenly.

"Excuse me?" The man in front of him said. "Do what?"

Myles waved his hand. "I'm sorry. I was thinking about my next novel." He winked. "My next victim."

The man beamed. "Oh brilliant!" He took his book back and winked. "Does this mean you're going to kill off a middle-aged bald man in it?" He ran a hand over his bare pate. "Should I expect royalties then?"

Myles laughed. "We'll have to see, won't we?"

The man left, still chuckling.

Well, Inspector Beaton is balding, Myles thought. Considerably cheered, he took the book from the next person in the queue and signed his name with a flourish.

What seemed like hours later, he looked up from the last customer and heaved a sigh of relief. *So many people*, he thought, *and all of them eager to read about Inspector Harper Beaton's next case.* Did he really have the nerve to kill off a character that caused so many people happiness?

Of course he did. He was the author, and it didn't matter if they were happy. *He* wasn't happy. It wasn't Beaton's fault, but good things had to end sometime. He remembered the Inspector Morse series on TV, from back in the nineties. He'd watched it in reruns because the curmudgeonly inspector from Oxford had reminded him of his own crusty detective, and like everyone else he'd

FORT WILLIAM, SCOTLAND – PRESENT TIME

been saddened by the death of the iconic character that ended a beloved series.

The point was, it *had* ended the series. There was no coming back from death, not unless you were Sherlock Holmes. Fans couldn't lobby the story's creator for one more season or an author for one more book. He was dead, done. On to the next.

He decided to celebrate his new plan with a scone and a coffee and headed for the cafe. Unfortunately, it was crowded today because of the signing, and every table was full. Turning to leave, he spied Mary at the reception counter, waving urgently. He worked his way over, ignoring the unease coiling in his stomach.

"That man 's here agin," she said.

"What man?"

"Th' fire investigator. He came in yestiday an' wanted t' talk t' Màiri an' Eve about th' fire in th' museum, an' now he's back. Just came in and whisked our girl away."

Myles wrinkled his brow. "I don't understand. What can I do about that?"

Mary blew out a breath. "Go in there. Say I sent ye. Say ye're a copper. Ye can come up with sumthin'; ye're a writer, are ye no?"

"But..."

"I dinnae want my employee bullied, ye ken?"

Myles knitted his brows. "Is that okay? I mean, am I allowed to do that?"

Mary's look was stubborn. "This 's my shop, an' nobody's goin' t' barge in an' push my people around." She pushed him toward the door behind the desk. "Now, git."

He got. With no earthly idea of what to expect, he put his hand to the knob and his ear to the heavy door. His author's imagination conjured up images of a hot light hanging over a hapless victim's head, of beady little eyes boring into her frightened face, a sharp voice rattling off questions like a machine gun.

Myles eased the door open. Two sets of blue eyes met his; one narrowed in annoyance, the other wide with surprise. Myles studied the owner of the former. The man had taken the high ground, commandeered the one comfortable chair in the room and positioned himself behind the desk.

The man had red hair, tired eyes, a rumpled tweed jacket in dire need of dry cleaning, blue shirt, brown tie. The jacket had suede elbow patches that gave its wearer a dated look, as did the dark circles under the blue eyes. The eyes themselves weren't dated, though. They were shrewd, almost piercing. *He would've made a great detective in a mystery novel*, Myles thought.

"I'm sorry, I was asked to sit in on anything to do with the fire," Myles lied, the words sliding quickly off his tongue as he made them up. He sat down beside Màiri, giving her a conspiratorial wink.

"And who exactly are you?" the red-haired man snapped.

"I'm her friend," Myles said. "Also her solicitor, in case she needs one." He crossed his fingers and kept his eyes on the man across the desk. "Does she need one?"

The man blew air through pursed lips. "No, she doesn't need an attorney. I'm investigating an arson,

FORT WILLIAM, SCOTLAND – PRESENT TIME

and she's the only one who was there right after the fire started. I need her help." He sat back in the leather chair. "Inspector Benedict Fraser," he said, without offering a hand. "And you are...?"

"Myles Grant."

Fraser looked surprised. "Aren't you the author?" He narrowed his eyes and folded his arms over his chest. "An author *and* a solicitor? Impressive." His tone said *Tell me another one.*

Another downside to fame. His face was plastered all over the High Street, on all the tour buses, and right on the door of the bookshop. Myles could feel the heat in his face. "I guess you got me there," he said.

"The owner sent you in, didn't she?" Fraser said, and now his lips were twitching. "The one who looks like a wee brown bird?"

Myles deflated. "Aye."

"Don't worry, lad. She scares me too. Rest assured, I haven't used the thumbscrews yet on your lass. She's just"— he dropped his voice to a lower pitch and intoned — "helping me with my enquiries."

Myles and Màiri looked startled, and Fletcher laughed. "Sorry. I always wanted to say that." He looked across the table at Màiri. "Can you please tell your friend that I mean you no harm, lass?"

Màiri nodded. "It's true. He's been very nice, Mister Grant."

"Myles," he corrected. "As your solicitor, we should be on a first name basis, aye?"

"Myles," she said, and gave him a smile that had his heart beating a little faster. "Anyway, Mister Fraser is trying to find out about the man in the basement, and he was hoping I'd seen something during our tour." Her face was rueful. "I wish I had."

"The man in the basement?" Myles looked at Fraser. "There was a man in the basement? So, didn't he see... Oh. He was dead?"

Fraser gave them both an irritated look. "We haven't released that information yet. Please don't tell anyone."

"Who was he?"

"We don't know yet," the investigator said. "He was burned beyond recognition. We're waiting now for DNA results."

Myles had a sudden vision of the cover of *The Witch's Daughter*, the silhouetted image of a woman. Black, as if she were burning. *Burned beyond recognition.*

"I was telling Mister Fraser," Màiri was saying, "Eve's the one who might know him, but she was unconscious most of the time and doesn't remember much. She did say no one was supposed to be working at that time. That's why she was practicing her tour on me."

"And you're absolutely sure that there was no one on the scene during your tour with Miss MacDonald?" Fraser said. "Sometimes when you think about it later, something occurs to you. The reason I ask is, someone had to start that fire, and unless there was a timer involved—and we haven't found one—he must've been there while you were going through the museum."

Màiri shivered. "I can't think of anyone," she said. "I'm sorry. I really do want to help, Mister Fraser."

FORT WILLIAM, SCOTLAND – PRESENT TIME

"Call me Ben," the investigator said, and smiled. "Everybody does."

Myles looked at the sharp blue eyes. *I really doubt everybody does.*

The door opened again and another man entered. The lad called Adam, Myles remembered. Adam MacArthur, the one with the dog. The dog wasn't with him now, and the man's brown eyes held the same surprised look he himself must have had moments ago, when he'd been bundled into the office by Mary Duncan.

"I'm—I'm—" he stuttered.

"Another solicitor friend of Miss MacLachlan's?" Ben Fraser asked, his tone wry. "I see I'll have to stop the torture for the moment. The lady has too much backup."

Myles wasn't listening. He was watching Màiri's face. She wore a broad smile and her eyes were bright when she looked at Adam MacArthur. Her face shone with a light that hadn't been there before. *Was something going on between them?* The thought left a sour taste in his mouth. He didn't like it. And he didn't like the fact that it bothered him, either.

CHAPTER 27
FORT WILLIAM, SCOTLAND – PRESENT TIME

Adventures are only interesting once you've lived to see the end of them.
—Holly Lisle

Adam watched Myles walk out of the office, his hands stuffed in the pockets of his khakis. There was something bothering the man. He seemed angry. Had that fire inspector been bullying Màiri?

He turned his attention to the man seated behind the desk. "What did you mean, torture? Are you giving her a bad time?"

Fraser put his hands up as if to ward off a blow. "Whoa, lad. I was just joking, aye? Don't get your knickers in a knot." He hefted himself out of the leather chair and came out from behind the desk. "I was only going to advise you to be careful, miss," he told Màiri with a smile that softened the lines under his eyes. "But I can see you already have two guard dogs on duty, eh?"

Màiri blushed and then gave him a puzzled glance. "Why should I be careful, though? Am I in danger?"

"Probably not," the inspector said, but the smile had left his eyes. "It's just a formality."

"But why?" Adam echoed Màiri's question. "Even as a formality, do you need to scare her?"

Benedict Fraser sighed. He leaned back on the edge of the desk and regarded them both under hooded eyes. "Your girlfriend was in a building where a fire was deliberately set, and where a man was found murdered."

Adam looked at Màiri. Her blue eyes were wide, and the colour had drained from her face. His own face reddened, and he opened his mouth to speak, but the inspector put up a hand to ward him off.

"I'm not in the business of scaring people for no reason." He focused on Màiri and his voice gentled. "But you need to realise something. Just because you didn't see anyone doesn't mean he didn't see *you*."

Fraser moved to the door and stopped with his hand on the knob. "I'm sorry if I've frightened you. That's not my intention. But someone was there. He's killed once; he's not likely to hesitate to do it again, if he feels threatened. So please, be careful." He pushed himself off the desk, and disappeared out the door.

Màiri stood and then swayed on her feet, and without hesitation Adam put an arm around her to steady her. "Here," he said. "Sit down." He stepped to the open door. "Mary? Can you get her a cup of tea?"

FORT WILLIAM, SCOTLAND – PRESENT TIME

Mary reached under the counter and brought up a bottle of Tomatin single malt and a whisky glass. "I c'n do better th'n that, lad," she said. She poured a generous dram and handed it to Adam. "Here ye go, lad. This'll help."

He returned to Màiri, closed the door behind him, and gave her the glass. She downed the whisky in two gulps. "Good lass," he said approvingly, and watched as the colour returned to her face.

"He's right, though," he told her. "The inspector."

"About you being my watchdog?" She smiled. "Just kidding."

"If you like," Adam said.

She stared at him. "I said I was just kidding. No need to get all serious on me."

"I *was* serious, though," Adam said. "If it bothers you, just consider it repayment for you saving my life."

She searched his eyes. "You really believe that. That I saved you."

"Don't you?" he asked. "The way you reacted when I told you..." He reached for one of her hands and held it. She didn't pull back. Adam watched as her eyes changed from humour to uncertainty to acceptance. Finally, she nodded.

"Okay. Yes, I believe it. Something happened when I touched you that day. Something maybe only you will understand." She gave him her full attention. "I didn't believe it at first. I knew something strange happened—I mean, your heart stopped, Adam, and then it started up again!"

Adam watched as she took a deep cleansing breath and let it out. He sat very still. Something important was happening, and he was afraid to move, lest he ruin it. So he held her hand, the hand that had started his heart up again that day when he was sure he was going to die, and watched the battle going on behind those amazing eyes.

"But the reason I believe it now is..." She stopped and swallowed. "Is there any more whisky?"

Adam turned and opened the office door. Mary Duncan stood there, holding out the whisky bottle. He gave her a grateful smile, closed the door again, and poured Màiri another dram. This time she sipped it, taking her time. He waited.

"The reason is, it happened again," she said finally.

"What? When? How?" *Who?* Adam wondered at the stab of jealously that brought.

"At the museum, in the fire. Eve is afraid of fire—I mean she has a real phobia about it. It's called—"

"*Pyrophobia.*"

Màiri blinked and Adam gave her a wry smile. "I'm sort of an expert on phobias and weird diseases. Don't ask why; it's just me."

"Oh," Màiri said. "Well, anyway, she went into a trance or something, didn't know where she was or what was going on. And she ran the wrong direction...right into the fire."

She shuddered at the memory. "She was unconscious by the time I found her in all the smoke, and she wasn't breathing."

Màiri's eyes were glassy and unfocused as she fought through her story. Adam's heart hurt, but there was nothing he could do for her. She needed to get it out. And he needed to hear it.

FORT WILLIAM, SCOTLAND – PRESENT TIME

"I gave her CPR. The internet's good for something, after all." She gave him a wan smile that disappeared like a wisp of morning fog. "It wasn't working and I was panicking. Then I remembered what happened that day with you. I put my hand on her chest, like I did then. I felt her heart beating, and she started breathing."

"Did she know?" Adam asked. "I mean, like I did. Did she understand what was happening?"

Màiri shook her head. "She was unconscious the whole time. She didn't remember anything about it when she woke up in the hospital."

There was a perverse pleasure in being the only one to know about Màiri's gift. Because it was a gift. She didn't seem to think so, but from his viewpoint it could be nothing else.

"I think most of the book signing crowd should be gone, now that their hero has left," Adam said. "Let's forget about all this for a while and go get a coffee."

"But what if your girlfriend shows up again?"

"What?" *What was that tone? Was she jealous?* Adam allowed that idea to sink in. The thought brought its own kind of satisfaction. "Who? Laura?"

Màiri gave an exaggerated shrug. "I guess. I didn't really pay much attention."

"She's not my girlfriend. She's just a friend who lives down the street from me in Ballachulish." He sighed. "We went out a few times, and I guess she read more into it than there was."

He stood up and opened the office door. Mary was gone. "Coast is clear," he whispered. "I think we're safe, but do you want to go somewhere else?"

WITCH

Màiri laughed. "I only have a few minutes. Mary is very generous about breaks, but the Inspector ate up most of mine, and I *do* work here." She frowned, then gave him that heart-stopping smile. "I was just teasing, before. You can have all the girlfriends you want. It's none of my business."

Adam decided the better part of valour was to ignore that and led the way to the cafe. Shortly they were sitting at a corner table with two lattes in front of them.

"Um…" he said, after a moment. "Do you have one? You know, a partner?"

Màiri looked surprised, and then she grinned. "See those lads out there?" She pointed to two teenagers who were standing in the centre of the shop, scanning round as if looking for someone. "I have my own following, ye ken?"

"Are they looking for you?" Adam asked. "They look kind of grim."

"They do, don't they?" she said. "Usually they're full of vinegar, but they seem a wee bit dour today. Come to think on it, they haven't been in for a couple of days. Wonder what's up?"

She caught the eye of one of the lads and waved. He poked his friend in the shoulder and they wandered over.

"Hullo, lads," she said. The two boys shuffled their feet and mumbled something. "This is my friend Adam." They nodded vaguely toward him. "And these are two of the Three Musketeers," she told Adam. "Bastian and Donnie." She looked behind them. "Where's your third sword? Seems wrong, just the two of you."

FORT WILLIAM, SCOTLAND – PRESENT TIME

Her smile was not returned. The glum expressions on the lads' faces deepened.

Adam studied the two. Teenagers, in his limited experience, tended to be mercurial and moody much of the time, but these two were taking it to a new level. The taller one seemed on the verge of tears. He sighed. This was not the way he'd planned to spend the few minutes he had with Màiri.

"What's wrong?" she was asking. "Where's Cory?"

Bastian let out a huge sigh. "We don't know."

"What do you mean, you don't know?" Màiri threw Adam a glance. "Cory is their friend. They're always together."

Adam took in the lads' demeanour and Màiri's worried expression. *Well, in for a penny...*He got up, pulled over two chairs, and gestured to the lads. "Sit."

The two fell into the chairs with the natural gracelessness of preoccupied teens.

"Now," Màiri said, "tell us."

"We haven't seen him for three days," Donnie said. "He hasn't been to my house, or Donnie's either. It's weird."

"Did you call him?" she asked.

"He doesn't have a mobile," Bastian said. "He's not allowed." The words were laced with acid.

"Have you been to his house?" Adam asked. "Maybe he's poorly. Can't you ask his parents?"

"Them?" The word exploded out of Bastian. "They don't care where he is."

Adam suppressed a flash of irritation. *Ugh. Teenage drama.* He took a breath and let it out. "What did they say?"

"They said they don't know what he's up to," Donnie said, "and they slammed the door in our faces. They're mingers, just like Cory said."

Adam looked at them, surprised. "His parents did that?"

"They're not his parents." Bastian spat the words. "They're his aunt and uncle, but he only lives with them because he has to. His mom's dead and his dad's...another minger. Most of the time he stays with me or Donnie, and those bastards never care if he comes home or not."

"You were looking for him a couple of days ago, weren't you?" Màiri reached out and put her hand over Bastian's. "I'm sorry, I should've paid more attention."

Bastian pulled his hand away and mumbled "'s okay" under his breath.

"When did you see him last?" Adam asked them.

"Saturday. We were practicing in the glen."

"Practicing?" Adam asked. "Practicing what?"

Both boys flushed. "Swords," Bastian said. He gave Adam a challenging look.

Adam caught Màiri's eye and she shook her head slightly. "Then what?" she prompted Bastian.

"Then something weird happened," Donnie said. "We heard singing or something. You know, like monks on telly do?"

"Chanting?" Adam tried to keep the disbelief out of his tone, but this was just getting stranger by the minute. "Oh, come on. That's just weird."

"Aye." Bastian glared at him. "It *was* weird... So we hid."

FORT WILLIAM, SCOTLAND – PRESENT TIME

"I'm sorry," Adam said. "That sounds like a smart thing to do. Then what happened?"

"The singing—chanting—got louder, and then these guys started walking by, and they really *were* monks. Or maybe reapers—you know, like the Grim Reaper. They had long black robes with hoods and everything. They kept chanting, and they walked right past us."

Màiri said, "So what did you do?"

"We got the hell out of there," Donnie said. "As soon as they were gone, we ran like rabbits!"

"All three of you? Cory was with you the whole time?"

"Aye. I could hear him breathin' behind me," Bastian said. "But when we got out of the woods, we turned around and he was gone!"

"Gone?" Adam asked. "What do you mean, gone?"

"Gone! Like gone!" Bastian's face crumpled in on itself, and a choking sob burst free. "We-we went back a ways up the path, but he wasn't there. He just disappeared! We went home and waited at my house, where we were supposed to hang out, but he never showed up." He raised bleary eyes to Màiri. "What if the reapers got him?"

"Have you been to the police?" Adam asked. The two lads looked at him as if he'd grown an extra head, and he suddenly felt as if he'd aged twenty years in their eyes.

"We've asked around, but nobody's seen him," Donnie said, evading Adam's eyes.

"So," Màiri said slowly. "You haven't seen him for three days. He hasn't been in touch, and he hasn't been home." They nodded. "Well," she said, "it's past time to report this to the police. You lads know that," she told them.

The boys looked at the cracks in the wooden tabletop. "Aye," Bastian muttered. "But Cory'll hate that."

Adam nodded. "I know, but the police can help." He sat up straight. "I have connections with Search and Rescue. If Cory's up on the mountain, we need to find him as soon as possible."

He glanced at Màiri, and her look told him she was thinking the same thing. Three days in the wild, even in summer, was a long time for a child to be alone, maybe injured. He wasn't ready to believe much of their story, but Glencoe wasn't someplace to be messing about—with or without chanting monks.

The rule of three: *three days without water, three weeks without food...* If young Cory was out there somewhere, they had no time to lose.

CHAPTER 28
GLEN COE, SCOTLAND
– PRESENT TIME

When all the details fit in perfectly, something is probably wrong with the story.
—Charles Baxter

They pushed their way through the thick underbrush that lined the lower slopes of Bein Nevis. Adam held tight to Pearl's leash as the dog wandered from side to side on the overgrown path, sniffing at everything and getting the leash tangled around his stubby legs.

Adam's curses were increasing in frequency and creativity as he not-so-patiently untangled Pearl from each bush, wondering what on earth had occurred in his brain to suggest that bringing a bulldog on a search was a good idea.

"It's all your fault," he muttered to Jared, who was walking next to him on the path. In a singsong voice he recited, "'*English Bulldogs were originally bred for hunting and other working roles, such as herding, guarding, and catching livestock. All dogs are hunters.'* Where did you look that up, anyway? You know you can't believe everything you read on the internet, right?"

"Well, it makes sense," Jared said in defence of his research. "Dogs were originally descended from wolves, so they're all natural hunters."

Adam looked at the bulldog, now urinating on a patch of heather. "Well, I think some of them have travelled a long way from that heritage," he said.

"Here," Jared said. "Let me take him for a while. You go up with the lads." He pointed ahead to where Bastian and Donnie were waiting, rocking back and forth on their feet in their impatience to be doing something. "They're going to lose it if we don't find anything soon."

Adam jogged up the path, remembering what Bastian had said about Cory's parents. *They don't care…they slammed the door in our faces…they're mingers, just like Cory said.* He'd thought the lad was exaggerating, but then he'd gone to see the MacMillens himself.

The aunt—a thin, overly made-up woman in black leggings and a crop top that exposed way too much wrinkled skin—had held the door open six inches while she listened to his questions. *No, she hadn't seen Cory…No, he didn't sleep at home most nights… He had some friends he hung out with…No, she didn't know their names…No, of course she wasn't worried; he was fifteen, for God's sake, not a bairn.* The woman had promised to let him know when Cory came home and closed the door firmly in his face.

GLEN COE, SCOTLAND – PRESENT TIME

Adam could feel the anger building as it had when he'd stood on that doorstep, staring at the MacMillens' front door. How could someone care so little about the child they'd adopted? Cory had already lost his parents, and now he was living with this excuse for humanity?

If—no, *when*—they found Cory, Adam was going to be putting in a call to Child Protection Services. It was bad enough that they were negligent caretakers. Bastian and Donnie had said Cory always wore long sleeves, even in summer, and they knew it was to cover bruises. If that was true, the MacMillens were guilty of abuse as well as neglect.

He didn't know Cory, but even if the lad was disobedient or talked back, as teens frequently did, there was no excuse for physical harm. Adam's face darkened. His own childhood had been less than stellar, what with a father who was checked out emotionally, but even in the worst of times Father had never raised his hand to his four boys. And they'd had each other, although he hadn't appreciated it until he'd grown up.

He reached Bastian and Donnie and shook his head to clear the ugly thoughts. None of this was going to help. He needed a clear head here, and these poor lads were on the verge of mental collapse.

There were sounds further up the slope as the group from Search and Rescue spread out and went about their tasks. As soon as Cory was reported missing, Adam had called them with the few details he had, and they were already out and searching, along with the Ballachulish police. The police hadn't much cared for the idea of civilians out doing their jobs, but they knew Adam and trusted his insights. So here they were.

Adam's job entailed a fair amount of rescue, what with outlanders who thought they knew the mountains and overextended themselves, earning a broken ankle or a sprained wrist for their stupidity.

The 'search' part hadn't come into the equation too often in his tours, since Adam insisted on grouping, and they were all connected by an app on their mobiles. *Never alone* was the rule he held sacred. It wasn't good for business if your clients went off and got lost in the mountains.

He followed it himself, even more strictly. Since his diagnosis, he'd made sure never to spend much time alone. He missed it, running the trails with only the wind and the trees for company, but he couldn't take the chance on another attack coming while he was out of sight and earshot. No matter where and when it happened, he didn't want to die alone.

He had no illusions that Màiri's touch had cured him, that day in the bookshop. She'd saved him; that much was true. For the moment, at least. But yesterday his doctor had burst the bubble of hope. The tests showed the abnormality in his heart was still there...the Curse was waiting. And he couldn't drag Màiri MacLachlan around with him like a first aid kit. *Although that idea...*

"It's here." Donnie's voice broke into his thoughts. "This is where we always practice."

The trees had opened onto a clearing about a hundred feet in diameter. Shadows reached out from

GLEN COE, SCOTLAND – PRESENT TIME

the surrounding trees to cast an otherworldly gloom over the place. Grass and occasional gorse bushes covered the flat area, and there were the remains of a campfire in the centre. A faint odour of smoke rose into the still air from the charred wood in the pit.

"Did you lads make that?" Adam asked them, frowning.

"No, it was here when we found it. We know better than to start fires in the woods."

"And you haven't been back here since that night?" Adam asked.

Bastian gave him a horrified look. "Shite, no! What if those reapers came back?" He looked around nervously. "What if it's their meeting place?"

Adam put his hand on the lad's arm. "Keep the heid," he said. "If they come, we'll simply ask them if they've seen a red-haired lad." The look the two teens gave him told him exactly what they thought of *that* idea, but Adam still hadn't come to terms with the whole reaper thing. It was just too bizarre.

Jared and Pearl arrived at the clearing. Bastian looked at Pearl doubtfully. "Does that dog know how to hunt?" he asked.

Adam rose in defence of his animal. "All dogs know how to hunt," he said. "They were originally descended from wolves." He avoided looking at Jared.

"If you say so," Donnie mumbled. "What's he doing?"

Pearl was lumbering around the edge of the clearing. When he made it around once, he did it again. Occasionally he stopped and lowered his head to sniff something. After the third time they'd rushed over to find him looking intently at a stick or a mushroom or any other tidbit of nature's wonder, they ignored him...until he barked.

Adam spun and gaped at his dog. He'd never heard Pearl bark. He sniffled and snored, wheezed and sometimes slurped, but he never barked. Adam had actually wondered if he could do it at all.

But he was barking now. It was such an odd sound, short and higher-pitched than one would expect from such a deep-chested animal. And continuous. Pearl was looking at something on the ground at the edge of the clearing next to a tree, never taking his eyes off whatever it was that had caught his attention.

Jared strode over to the dog and bent down beside him. "What is it, mate?" He picked up something and waved it in the air. "I think he's found something." He patted Pearl on his wrinkled head. "You did good, lad."

The rest of the group had stopped searching the clearing and moved over to join Jared and Pearl.

Adam took the object and held it out for them to see. It was a braided circle about nine inches long, made of three wide woollen threads in red, white, and blue. Twisted into the centre was a bead embellished with a handwritten letter D. It looked as if it was meant to be joined by tying the two ends together, but one end was frayed and the knot was gone.

"Some sort of bracelet," Adam said. "Not old."

"It's Cory's."

They turned to Bastian. He was standing rigid, feet apart as if he was attempting to keep himself anchored to the ground. His right arm was extended

GLEN COE, SCOTLAND – PRESENT TIME

and bent upward at the elbow, and round his wrist was an identical red, white, and blue bracelet.

Donnie extended his own arm. On his wrist was a third bracelet.

"What's the D for?" asked Adam. "Shouldn't it be a C, if it's Cory's?"

Bastian dipped his head and stared at the ground. "It's for D'Artagnan," he mumbled. He looked up and held his arm out full length. "Mine has an A for Athos, and Donnie's is a P for Porthos. Cory was supposed to be Aramis, but he wanted to be D'Artagnan, so we let him."

"Well, you said you were here that day, together, so I'm not sure it's much of a clue," Adam said doubtfully. "Probably fell off while you were practicing."

"It didn't," Donnie said. "I grabbed Cory's hand when we were running away. It was getting dark, but I remember brushing up against his bracelet. He still had it on then."

"Okay," Adam said. "Tell me again what happened when you got out of the trees."

"We talked for a few minutes about the reapers," Bastian said. "About how weird and scary they were, with all that chanting shite. Then we decided to go back to my place. Cory didn't answer, and when we turned around, he was just...gone."

"Then he came back here, to the clearing." Jared wrinkled his brow. "But why would he do that? That's where your reapers were headed, aye? Wasn't he scared too?"

Donnie nodded vehemently. "He was. He was petrified, just frozen beside the rock, staring after those reapers. That's why I had to grab his hand."

"Okay," Adam said. "So it is a clue. For some reason Cory left you two and went back to the clearing, where there was a group of grown men wearing robes and hoods and chanting. Why?" He looked at the lads. "Is Cory reckless? I mean, is he the curious type? Would he deliberately put himself in danger for any reason?"

Both boys shook their heads. "No," Bastian said. "He's sort of a feardie, really. We tease him about it all the time. He was really scared." His voice wavered. "We all were."

"Then there had to be some compelling reason for him to come back to this clearing alone, in the dark. Something greater than fear." Adam looked at Jared. "I'll admit it, I'm baffled."

"And none of this is helping us find him," Jared said. "Adam, you keep the bracelet. Let's go back to Ballachulish and fill the cops in, aye?"

"No," Adam said. "You go. I'll be along later. I promised Màiri I'd let her know how we got on, so Pearl and I are going to check in at the bookshop." He turned to the lads. "You two go home and see if he's been there. You said he doesn't have a mobile?"

"We were going to put our allowance together and get him one, but then you have to pay for a plan and all." Tears shone in his eyes. "I wish we'd just gotten him a burner."

They took a last look around the clearing, then Adam picked up Pearl's leash and followed the others out toward the glen, where the lads had left their bikes. "Be careful now," Adam said. "Don't go back to look by yourselves, you hear? I—"

GLEN COE, SCOTLAND – PRESENT TIME

His mobile rang and he looked at the display. "It's Màiri." He wandered a few feet away to answer the call. "Aye?"

"Did you find him?" Her voice sounded tense.

"Not yet. I'll see you in a few and tell you what's going on."

"Adam…" She stopped. Adam waited, but all he could hear on the other end was her ragged breathing. "I-I've been thinking…"

"What's the matter?" he prompted. "Have you heard something?"

"No." She stopped again, and he waited.

"I've been thinking," she began again. "The body in the museum basement…it hasn't been identified yet. They said it wasn't a woman, but it was small for a man."

Adam gripped the mobile harder to keep from dropping it.

Màiri's voice trembled over the line. "Adam, what if…what if it's Cory?"

CHAPTER 29
DORNACH, SCOTLAND – 1727

SÌNE

The woman thrashed and screamed, her arms flailing. Perspiration ran down Sìne's forehead and dripped onto the muslin cloth that covered her patient. She wiped her face with the cloth she kept nearby and continued to knead the woman's stomach, but a sick feeling of foreboding was pushing at the edges of her mind, telling her that this time she was going to lose the battle against Death.

Aoife Campbell was too old to be giving birth, and her body was ravaged from the bearing of eight bairns. Last year when she'd struggled through the birth, Sìne had heard her mother telling her that it must be the last. The woman had looked at Doirin with tired eyes and said, "But I cannae say nay. Ye dinnae ken what th' bastart's like when he's in his cups." And sure enough, here she was, a year later, trying bravely to bear her ninth.

If Aoife Campbell survived this time, Sìne was going to have a word with her husband. It was not something she looked forward to, but it had to be done. Hector Campbell was a churlish lout at the best of times, and a hundred times worse when drinking, but surely he cared for his wife. Yes, Aoife called him a bastart, but it was said in a moment of stress, wasn't it? And would the man want to raise nine children on his own? Perhaps if she approached it that way...

An agonized scream rent the air in the cottage, and Aoife's body arched as if she was convulsing. She subsided into soft moans and lay still...too still. She was spent, and Sìne knew she couldn't last much longer.

A throat-clearing grunt came from the corner, but Sìne didn't look up. Albert Wilson was watching. He was always watching. Ever since he'd put her in charge of the midwifery of Dornach Village three months ago, he'd made sure always to be there, watching from the shadows.

He was waiting for her to fail. Of course he'd never said as much, but it was obvious. When a bairn came safely into the world and the mother burst into tears of gratitude and clutched Sìne's sleeve, Wilson would stand up, growl something under his breath, and stalk out of the cottage. As if he were disappointed.

Sìne had been lucky in these three months. Five healthy bairns had been born under her care. When the birthing pains came and Sìne was all they had, the mothers didn't see a monster with cloven hands; they saw a saviour. They brought gifts when they came to show off the bairn—gifts that Albert Wilson confiscated for himself.

She didn't mind. It was enough to be gazed upon with gratitude instead of curiosity or repugnance. Of course, they would forget as time went on, but in those moments Sìne basked in the unusual warmth of acceptance.

This good fortune wouldn't last, and Sìne knew it. Birthing was never absolute, and sooner or later she would lose a bairn, or the mother. Then Albert Wilson would pounce. The proof was lurking like a giant spider in the corner, always watching.

Another moan filled the space, weaker than before. Aoife Campbell's luck was running out. She no longer had the strength to fight the waves of pain rolling through her aging body, and if she couldn't summon the strength the bairn would die, and its mother with it.

The room grew ominously quiet. Aoife's face was white as the sheet that covered the table, and her eyes were closed. Her breath came in shallow gasps, each growing weaker and fainter than the last. She was dying.

A rustle came from the corner, and Sìne glanced up to see Albert Wilson, sunken eyes gleaming with an unholy light. A frisson of fear worked its way up Sìne's spine as she looked into those eyes. He *wanted* this woman to die. He called himself a doctor, but he was watching, hoping, waiting for a patient to perish under Sìne's hands.

She straightened her back and willed herself to go on. This woman and her bairn were not going to die, not while there was a spark of life left in her body.

Brave words, but as she thought them, a last gasp whispered from Aoife's spent body and she relaxed into an ominous stillness.

An image formed in the back of Sìne's mind. A memory from years ago. Maighread and Doirin, working over a woman who was no longer breathing. Doirin laying her hand on the woman's chest. A blue light emanating from under the hand, turning pink, and then a soft breath from the mother.

Sìne had almost forgotten in the last years. She'd only seen it once, and had almost convinced herself that she'd been dreaming. She'd surely never thought that she... But she *was* Doirin's daughter. Maybe... And now there was no time left for self-doubt or fear. Two lives—she looked at the hulking shape in the corner—maybe three lives depended on the next few seconds. Her life couldn't really get any worse than it already was, could it?

She drew a long, calming breath into her lungs, and laid her own hand on the woman's chest. Nothing happened. The chest was still, the only movement from the helpless bairn below, squirming to be let free. Sìne pressed harder.

A faint blue light appeared between her fused fingers and spread out like the ripples of the sea when it was calm. Ever so slowly, the light changed from blue to a pearly white, and then to a blush of pink. As Sìne watched, eyes wide in wonder, Aoife's chest moved. It rose, fell, rose again. The pallor in her face eased, and she opened her eyes.

"Push now, love." She echoed the words her mother had breathed years ago, and the woman gathered herself and pushed. "Again!" Minutes later, Aoife Ross' ninth bairn was expelled into the world, and the mother lay back, exhausted. Alive.

"Ye have a lovely wee lass," Sìne told her. "I'll have her cleaned and wrapped an' ye can hold her anon, aye?"

A sharp exhalation of breath drew her eyes to the corner. She'd forgotten Wilson was there, and suddenly the ramifications of what she had done overwhelmed her. How much had he seen? What would he do? She had no illusions that he would embrace the miracle that had just taken place in his cottage. He'd wanted the woman and her bairn to die, and he wouldn't allow Sìne to thwart him.

His eyes met hers, and she shivered under the malice in them. They were blacker than night, with glints of red light like small fires burning deep within his soul. If he had one.

He hated her. She'd always known it. He despised Sìne and her mother, and it seemed his passion might burn into her bones and turn her soul to ashes. She put her hand to her mouth to keep from whimpering.

The gleam in Wilson's eyes sharpened in triumph, like that of a hunter when his prey is trapped with nowhere to run. Then he turned on his heel and stalked out of the cottage, slamming the door behind him. Sìne found herself panting, as if from an arduous run. Every nerve in her body was screaming, *Go! Get out!*

Instead, she took care of the afterbirth and cut the bairn's cord, and soon the wee lass was nuzzling at her mother's breast. Sìne watched the love blossom between mother and child, but her memory kept returning to the miracle she had witnessed under her own hand.

She wasn't religious. She and her mother had never been welcome in Kirk, but she believed in God. Her mother had told her that Gilchrist meant 'servant of God' and now she understood. God didn't care a whit that her hand was malformed; He had given her the gift of healing, as He had her mother. He'd made her His servant.

He put his own mark on ye. Hugh's words floated out of her memory. Sìne twisted her head in an attempt to see the purple mark on her shoulder. One line crossed by another at the bottom. An upside-down cross. Had God really marked her like that?

Hugh. A weight descended onto her chest and squeezed it. She hadn't seen Hugh Sutherland in three months. At first she'd thought him busy on his father's estate, but then the whispers had begun to flutter like moths in the market.

Did ye hear? Hugh Sutherland's courtin' our Ailis! Th' lucky lass, she's allus had her heart set on 'im, an' now they say there's to be a weddin' in April. The whisper was just loud enough to reach Sìne where she stood in front of the costermonger's, as it had been intended to.

She hadn't believed it. But he hadn't joined her on the rocks overlooking the firth or come to her door of an evening to see if she wanted to catch fireflies. And then one day she'd seen him coming toward her on the path in town, and her heart had taken flight.

He looked the same: flyaway brown hair and homespun jacket over his brown cord trews. His hands were stuffed deep into his pockets and his eyes were focused inward, as if they searched for something within himself. Her heart soared at the sight of his beloved face.

"Hugh!" she called out.

He blinked. His multi-hued brown eyes, those eyes she loved so much, found hers. For a long moment he stared at her as if memorizing her face. Then he turned away from the path and struck off into the woods without a backward look. And Sìne knew, with a pain that sliced deep into her heart, that it was all true.

He'd abandoned her. He was like all the others, after all. She turned and went home to the small shed in the backyard of Albert Wilson's cottage, to a mother who no longer knew how to comfort her, and cried herself to sleep.

CHAPTER 30
DORNACH, SCOTLAND – 1727

HUGH

He'd almost turned back. The pain he saw in her eyes was more than he could bear and he wanted to run to her, take her in his arms, and tell her the truth. That she was the only one, that he would never marry Ailis MacAllan, that this was all just a horrid nightmare caused by small-minded, hateful people.

People with power. People like his father, and that repulsive excuse for a human being, *Doctor* Albert Wilson. Hugh doubted Wilson was even a doctor. Hadn't his father said he was a magistrate in Edinburgh? A magistrate *and* a doctor? Not very likely. And why would such a learned man come to a village like Dornach? Did his father have that much influence, that he could call such a man to do his bidding?

No, there was a hidden purpose in his coming, and until Hugh found what it was, he could not risk being seen anywhere near Sìne Gilchrist. It was the only thing he could do to keep her safe, though it had torn his heart out and left it in shreds on the forest floor.

Three days had passed since their meeting on the path. He avoided the market, the seaside, all the places he might run into her. He spent his time working the fields, under his father's watchful eye, or in the tavern.

He was drinking too much. Whisky and ale were his best friends these days. They dulled his mind and chased his memories away. Curiously, his father didn't seem to mind. He took Hugh with him and made him watch while he playacted as benefactor and friend for the very people he'd encouraged to throw rubbish at his son all those years ago. It sickened him, but there was nothing he could do about it.

Maybe he should try another way. If he pretended to accept his father's orders, went along with his fantasy about a wedding, perhaps he would relax his vigilance and let go the stranglehold he had on his son's life.

He looked at Duncan Sutherland across the rough wooden table, forced a smile, and raised his tankard in a salute. His father's eyes narrowed, but then he answered the smile and raised his own mug. Half in their cups already, the villagers around him—those *chookters*, Duncan called them—grinned and slammed their tankards down on the table, splashing ale on the already filthy tabletop.

DORNACH, SCOTLAND - 1727

Bastart, Hugh thought as he fought to hold the smile. If pandering would keep Sìne and her mother safe, he could do it. He had to. His father was a monster, and he made monsters out of others. It was an obscene sort of gift, and sometimes Hugh thought he was alone in a world where no one knew the truth but him. He took a small sip, and another.

What seemed like hours later, he stood up from the table and swayed, grinning like a fool. His father wouldn't bother to set someone on him if he thought he was too drunk to cause trouble, would he?

"I'm for home," he said, deliberately slurring his voicc. "I cannae hauld a light t' ye, and I need my bed." Amidst good-natured jeers and catcalls that made him want to vomit, he staggered out the door of the tavern.

It wasn't entirely an act, the drunkenness. He'd had just enough ale to blur the edges of his memory, which was the only way he could stop thinking. He looked up, surprised to see it was still light. Now, in midsummer, the days were long and the sun set after most folk were abed.

He had no idea how long he'd spent in the darkness of the tavern. Sometimes he wished for winter, when the days were short and the nights long. There was little to do in the fields and he could avoid his father by going to bed early. But a long night was no better than endless daylight, because then he would dream of Sìne.

He didn't want to dream of Sìne. Every time he closed his eyes, he saw the stricken look on her face when he turned away from her on the path, the shock and the hurt at his rejection. Her mother was failing, she'd been kicked out of her home by that rotter Wilson, and when she needed her best friend most, he'd betrayed her trust.

He tripped over a rock in the path and nearly pitched forward onto his face. He straightened, and there she was, as if he'd conjured her with his wayward thoughts. She was sitting on the log in front of the bookshop, reading. Riveted on the path, he watched as a man came out of the shop and joined her on the log. Her companion smiled at her and reached to push an errant black curl off her forehead.

Alan Grant. The village philanderer, who had all the lassies pining for him. All he had to do was toss that golden hair and widen his blue eyes, swing his plaid a little, and they'd fall at his feet. He'd courted most of them and eventually left them crying into their aprons, but they didn't seem to care.

He and Sìne had laughed about it. "I dinnae ken what they all see 'n him," she would say. "Tis sure he's most in love with himself, an' no lass can compete wi' that."

So why was she with him now? Sìne was too smart to fall for a lad like that...wasn't she?

She smiled and replied to something he said, her musical laughter hanging in the late evening air. Then Alan offered his hand to pull her to her feet, and she took it. *She took it!* Grant didn't seem to mind her deformed fingers. He tucked her hand in the crook of his arm and they walked off together, Sìne's black curls a perfect foil for his blond hair.

DORNACH, SCOTLAND – 1727

He thought he might die right there, but he didn't. That would have been too easy. Instead, he staggered to the side of the path and heaved up the alcohol and tatties he'd had for supper. He swiped his hand across his mouth and moved away from the mess to sit down at the edge of the road, his head in his hands. Shock raced in waves through him, threatening another bout of vomiting.

How could she? She was his—he was going to marry her! Well, he hadn't told her, but surely she understood. There was no one for him in this world but Sìne; how could she not know that?

The truth fell on him like a trencher of cold water. He'd done this. He'd driven her right into Alan Grant's arms. Frustration and self-pity swamped him, and he could feel tears building behind his eyes. Never mind that he was doing it to keep her safe, never mind that this was only temporary... S*he* didn't know that. She thought he'd abandoned her, thrown her away.

She must believe he was marrying that simpering bairn, Ailis. The news was all through the village, so of course she'd have heard it. They would have made sure she heard. What she must think of him! Well, it couldn't be any worse than what he thought of himself.

He was a fool, an ignorant, selfish gowk, and he deserved to lose her. How could he have thought Sìne would just wait while he pranced about with that little peahen on his arm, pretending? It was killing him—the pretending—but she couldn't know that.

He sat until dusk began to settle on the village and then struggled to his feet. It wouldn't do to be out at night when he'd said he was going home. He turned

WITCH

to start back, and then turned again when he heard a footfall on the path.

Alan Grant was coming back, walking toward him with his plaid swishing across his knees as if it had a life of its own. Even at a distance, Hugh could see the self-satisfied smirk on the bastart's lips. He waited until Alan was abreast of him and stepped in front of him.

"Ach, Sutherland, ye scairt th' life outta me just noo!" he said. "What's yer problem?"

"What's yer business wi' Sìne?"

Alan blinked, and then a slow smile worked its way across his face. "Weel, noo, an' I'm wonderin' just what that has t' do with you."

"Answer th' question, ye bastart," Hugh said in a low, measured voice.

Alan glanced up at the darkening sky as if he were pondering the wonders of the universe.

"Since ye're askin' so nicely, I s'pose I might's well tell ye. I like 'er."

Hugh's stomach clenched. "What?"

"I've allus liked her. I mean, what man wouldnae? She's a beauty, aye?" His eyes narrowed and he laughed. "And I'm goin' t' make sure she kens how I feel."

Through a throat suddenly so thick he could taste the sourness, Hugh forced out words. "And how *do* ye feel?"

Alan shrugged. "I said, I like her. I thynk she's smart, an' interestin'. We could have fun."

"Fun?" Hugh's mouth twisted. "So ye're no thynkin' o' marryin' 'er, then?"

Alan's brow creased into a frown and a look of disgust crossed his face. "Whoa, laddie! Marryin'? Let's no get ahead o' ourselves, aye? I said she could be fun, not that I want 'er t' have my bairns!"

He stared at Hugh and shuddered. "Wha' if they turnt out like her?"

A red mist rose in Hugh's eyes. He reared back and let fly with his fist, right into Alan Grant's handsome face.

"Dinnae ye...dinnae ye ever say...just ...*dinnae*!" he sputtered. He stood heaving, legs braced apart, and waited for the other man to scramble to his feet. Then he went for him again, landing two blows to his chest before Alan managed to grab his forearms. The two circled in the path, each trying to get the better of the other, until Hugh finally shook off his opponent's hands and danced back and away.

He shook his finger. "I mean it. If ye thynk that o' Sine, ye dinnae deserve 'er." He turned away and then turned back again. "I dinnae deserve 'er either, but least I ken she's th' best this rotten village has t' offer." And he stalked away, trusting his feet to get him home because he could hardly see for the tears welling in his eyes.

CHAPTER 31
FORT WILLIAM, SCOTLAND – PRESENT TIME

Of course it's very hampering being a detective, when you don't know anything about detecting, and when nobody knows that you're doing detection, and, in short, when you're doing the whole thing in a thoroughly amateur, haphazard way.
—A.A. Milne

"It's not your friend," Inspector Fraser said. "The body has been identified. He's Charles Fletcher, aged thiry-eight years. A local, from Fort William. Ever hear of him?"

It wasn't Cory. Màiri looked at Adam and wondered if he felt the same way she did—as if she'd been holding her breath forever and it was finally safe to let it out. Then she remembered that this poor man was someone who'd been alive a week ago. Someone who probably had a wife, maybe lads or lasses who were waiting for their dad to come home.

WITCH

"No," she said. "I never heard that name before." She caught the investigator's gaze. "Did he—did he have a family?"

"No, far as we know he wasn't married. Next of kin's his grandfather, who has dementia. He's a patient at a hospice in Inverness."

Màiri sat up. "Highland Hospice?" At the inspector's nod, "My grandmother's there. It's a lovely place, has a wee cafe staffed by volunteers. I worked there myself when I was in uni." *And if he's like Gran, he'll never understand what happened to his grandson. Maybe it's a blessing.* She sat back. "That was his only family?"

Benedict Fraser nodded. "As far as we've been able to find out. Ironically, though," he said, "he was a firefighter."

"Oh, no!" Màiri's face paled. "Where did he work?"

Fraser consulted his notes. "He was out of the local station, just up Carmichael Way. Why?"

"I was just there the other day," she said. "I wanted to thank the man who saved me from the fire." She thought of the photo gallery under the plaque. *We remember.* Soon they'd be adding another portrait, for the man called Charles Fletcher.

She thought of Mackie, his handsome young face flushed with embarrassment at being hailed a hero. He would have known this Charles Fletcher; maybe they'd been close. How awful if her rescuer had been upstairs saving Eve and her while his friend was lying dead in the basement!

Adam had been quiet during this conversation. Now he spoke up. "Why did it take so long to identify him? I'd think the other firefighters would have noticed he was missing and made rescuing him a priority, right? Didn't you talk to them?"

Fraser narrowed his eyes. "Of course we did, though we didn't know who he was at the time. He was never reported as missing." He let the words hang in the air.

Adam looked confused. "Why not?"

Fraser gave him a sharp look. "That'll be my next question for the lads at the station."

Màiri remembered the inspector's words when he'd first interviewed her. "You said somebody killed him."

Adam turned quickly and gave her a questioning glance.

"He said the man had been murdered," Màiri told him. "Wouldn't a firefighter know how to get out of a fire?"

Fraser sighed. "All right. I did say he was murdered, which I'm beginning to realise was probably a mistake on my part, but he wasn't killed in the fire. And that's all you'll get."

"Wait!" Adam inserted himself back into the conversation. "This man was a firefighter, but nobody knew he was there?" He gave Fraser a sceptical look. "Isn't that awfully coincidental? Where did they think he was, if he wasn't there with them fighting the fire?"

"You two should come interview in Glasgow," Fraser said, his voice dry. "We could use some more investigators."

Màiri flushed. "There's no need to be sarcastic," she said, and crossed her arms over her chest. "You're the one who keeps coming to *us* for information."

The inspector sighed. "I'm sorry, lass. And I wasn't really being sarcastic—at least, not entirely. Your questions are actually quite helpful, even though I've usually already thought of them. They do confirm what I'm thinking."

"Hmmph," Màiri said. She caught a movement in her peripheral vision and rounded on Adam, who tried to hide a grin. "He was talking about you, too, you know."

Adam put his hands up in self-defence, and she gave him the full power of her icy blue eyes before turning the same glare back on the inspector. "Fair enough. If our questions are helpful, here's another one. If this Fletcher fellow was killed somewhere else, why was he there? Where did he come from?"

"I've created a monster," Fraser moaned. "I don't know, lass. We only just found out his identity, and speaking of which, *you're* the ones who called me this time. Because you thought it might have been your friend. Remember?"

Cory. Her fears for the young, red-haired lad rushed back and she forgot the hapless Charles Fletcher. Her shoulders slumped. She'd caught Adam sneakily checking his mobile every few minutes, but it was stubbornly dark and silent. The rescuers were still out on Ben Nevis' flank, searching.

Adam had said they'd found his bracelet, so they had a starting point, but there was so much territory to cover. She glanced over toward the children's corner, where Pearl and Biscuit lay nestled together. *Good dog. You've been the best detective of all so far.*

She'd seen that bracelet. Red, white, and blue, the

FORT WILLIAM, SCOTLAND – PRESENT TIME

colours of the French flag, they'd told her with pride. Athos, Porthos, and D'Artagnan. They were such nerds. So innocent, in a time when it wasn't cool to be. Innocence didn't keep you safe.

If Cory was lost, or hurt... No. There was no use giving in to those fears. She had to keep her worries to herself, at least for the other Musketeers' sake. Right now, Bastian and Donnie had gone with Adam's friend Jared to the Three Wise Monkeys climbing centre. It was kind of Jared to step in like that, but it was a temporary fix. And it wouldn't keep their worries at bay for long.

Cory was out there somewhere, and so was a monster. Someone who had killed another human being and set him on fire to cover his crime. The chances of Cory running into the murderer were probably next to none, but so were the chances of a firefighter being burned in the same building where his colleagues were fighting a fire.

What if Cory had seen something he shouldn't have? What if he'd recognized someone who was desperate to hide that fact? Adam had told her that the lads said he'd been frozen in place staring after the 'monks'—or whatever they were. And now they knew he'd gone back to the clearing. Had he been seen? Was he being held somewhere...or worse?

"They'll find him," Inspector Fraser said. There was an odd note in his voice and his eyes didn't meet hers. Probably because his words didn't mean anything. He didn't have a clue, any more than she did. Still, she appreciated the effort.

"I know they will," she said, her words as empty as his.

Fraser's mobile rang. He glanced at the display and raised the device to his ear. They watched the colour heighten on his ruddy face, then drain out so that his freckles stood out like sentinels. "On my way," he said. He stood up and reached for his rain jacket.

"There's been another fire. The Three Sisters, off Fassifern."

Màiri knew the place. It was an old tavern, popular with the locals partly because of its apparent state of decay. To tourist eyes it was a seedy, run-down relic with a car park that was fighting a losing battle against the weeds that sprang up through the cracks in the pavement. But that was its allure. It was one of the best-kept secrets of Fort William.

"Why would anyone want to burn down a place like that?" she wondered aloud.

Fraser stopped with his hand on the door. "We don't know that anyone did. It could be an accident. But..." He seemed to be trying to decide something.

"The museum wasn't the first case of arson in this area," he said finally. "We've had two others just outside Fort William. We've tried not to make a big story out of it, but if—and this is a big if—this fire was set deliberately, it would be the fourth case of arson in two months. And *that* is all you get." He pursed his lips and was out the door.

"I wouldn't want to be him," Adam said, looking at the closed door of the office. "He has a rough job."

Màiri was quiet for a minute. "Adam," she said.

He turned those warm brown eyes on her, and for a few seconds she just let herself admire them. She gave herself a mental shake.

FORT WILLIAM, SCOTLAND – PRESENT TIME

"Something's weird."

"Weird?"

"About what you said to Fraser. You asked him where Fletcher came from, if he wasn't there with the other firefighters, and then you asked, 'Where did they think he was?' And that made me think."

"About what?" Adam gave her his full attention.

"About the timing. I was giving Eve CPR for just a few minutes, and I heard the fire appliances pull up, because the sirens got louder and then stopped." She closed her eyes and thought. "But it was only a few seconds later that Mackie came through and carried us out."

"I don't get where you're going with this," Adam said. "That's their job. They train for it. They have to be fast."

"That's what he said." Màiri shook her head. "But he would have had to teleport to get into the building that quickly." She gave Adam a puzzled look.

"Well, maybe some of the firefighters drove separately, and his group got there first and parked in the back alley. I don't know how many firefighters can fit on a lorry, but we can look it up if you want."

"I think I do want," Màiri said slowly. "But first, let's look up arson. I really don't know much about it, and we should be prepared, aye?" She ignored Adam's side eye and reached for the laptop on the desk. "We can find out more about it from the internet than we can from Inspector Fraser." Adam pulled his chair closer to sit beside her.

"Okay, according to the Cambridge dictionary, *'arson is the crime of intentionally starting a fire in order to damage or destroy something, especially a building.'* Well, we knew that much."

"Look up 'arsonist,'" Adam said.

Màiri tapped the keys. "*'An arsonist is a person who intentionally starts a fire in order to damage or destroy something, especially a building.'* Well, that wasn't very helpful, was it?"

"Dinnae ye give up, lass," Adam said. "Fraser said there've been several fires in the last couple of months. Look up 'serial arsonist.'"

Màiri tapped more keys. The dictionary definition was as dry as the first two, so she scrolled past the definitions and scanned the titles of articles on the subject.

"Look," she said. "Here's a study of serial arsonists. It says most are young white males, and most of them are under thirty." She read aloud, *"Their mental stability is poor*—well, duh—*and only about one-third have regular jobs. Oh, this is interesting: Nearly all of them use unsophisticated methods to set fires."* She looked up. "Is there a sophisticated way to start a fire?"

"I'm sure there is," said Adam. "All the arsonists on TV are clever and use unique methods."

"Be serious," Màiri said. "But knowing that doesn't do us any good, because Fraser didn't tell us how the fire was started." She looked up again. "We could find out, though."

"How?" Adam gave her a narrow look. "Ask Fraser? I think he's told us everything he's going to. He only talks to us when *he* wants information."

"No, not him. Mackie." Màiri batted her eyelashes.

FORT WILLIAM, SCOTLAND – PRESENT TIME

"How's this? 'Oh, Mackie, I wanted to thank you again for saving my life. Have a biscuit.'"

Adam shook his head. "What self-respecting man would fall for that line, even from you?"

"We'll visit the fire station again, take them some sweeties, tell them I'm doing an article on my experience or something…" She waved her hand in the air. "And that I'd so love to pick their brains. You'll be there, and you can watch their reactions to my questions."

Adam looked unimpressed. "Why are we doing this, again?"

Màiri's look was stubborn. "Because I need closure." Suddenly she slapped her hand on the table. "You don't have to help if you don't want to. I can ask Myles."

"Why?" The word came out like a gunshot, and Màiri jumped.

"He's an author. We could talk him into saying he's doing arson as the crime in his next book."

"No!"

"Why not?"

"Because we don't need to tell more people about this gommy-brained idea of yours." He put the back of his hand on his forehead as if checking for a fever. "And because I'll do it."

"Really?" Màiri beamed at him. "Grand."

"Aye," he mumbled. "Grand."

CHAPTER 32
GLEN COE, SCOTLAND
– PRESENT TIME

You only live twice:
Once when you are born
And once when you look death in the face.
—Ian Fleming

The tour group consisted of eight men and six women, ranged around Adam in the car park that led to Beinn a' Bheithir. He knew most of them; they were members of the Ballachulish Running Club, or locals who had done this trail almost as many times as he had but never tired of the climb.

He was glad of the distraction the tour would provide. Cory hadn't been found yet, and hope was fading. He'd been missing for almost a week now, and unless he had somehow found water and shelter, he wouldn't survive the elements.

Tomorrow Adam would be visiting the fire station with Màiri, and he had a feeling it was one of the stupidest things he'd ever do. What on earth could they accomplish by trying to trick information out of a stranger? The idea of firefighters being involved in a murder of one of their own was ludicrous. But if...

That was what had little anxiety-bots running around in the back of his brain. If Màiri accidentally set off some sort of alarm in a murderer's head, then she'd be in danger, and she might not even know it. Why had he agreed to do this?

You agreed because you couldn't stop her, and because she would've asked the author gowk to do it instead. That's why.

A throat cleared, and Adam blinked at the group standing expectantly in front of him. He'd better get his mind on the job, instead of falling into a distraction from a distraction.

He launched into his prepared speech, fully aware that some of his runners today could likely have given it for him.

"Now, I know some of you have heard this all before, but you know I have to say it again, aye? It's my job, and for you new to Glencoe, it could mean the difference between the most exhilarating day of your life and a trip to the hospital." The veterans nodded without really listening. They were on their mobiles, plotting out the route using one of the many apps available online.

The three he didn't recognize looked to be in good physical condition, which was a plus. Occasionally someone signed up for this tour having ignored all the warnings on his site about fitness levels and required equipment, and tours had to be abandoned because they weren't prepared and couldn't finish.

GLEN COE, SCOTLAND – PRESENT TIME

The newcomers stood slightly apart, looking with awe and some nervousness at the mountains that ringed Ballachulish. Adam gave them an encouraging grin. They looked fit enough, but he'd have to keep a close eye on them until he could be sure of their skill level.

"The trail is eleven miles from start to finish, a loop that'll end right back here in the car park. All of you seem to know what you're doing"— he nodded approvingly at the sturdy mountain running shoes they all wore — "and I presume you all have alpine experience, aye?" He looked at the newbies for confirmation and they nodded vigorously.

"That being said, no amount of experience is going to help if you don't pay attention on the trail. A part of this tour is over terrain that can be difficult, even hazardous. I'll let you know where that is, but just remember, this is not a race. Take your time and enjoy the experience. And don't wander off the trail, whatever you do."

Another car pulled into the lot, and Daniel climbed out with his camera bag slung over his shoulder. Adam waved and he jogged over.

"This is our photographer, Daniel MacArthur. Smile and try to look happy when you see him pointing his camera at you. You might wind up on one of our posters." Most of the runners grinned at Daniel, and some struck a pose. One of the new group of three was frowning, as if humour had no business on a running tour and should be squelched immediately.

"I didn't sign the waiver," he said to Daniel. "Don't point that thing at me."

Adam checked his paperwork. Sure enough, all the waivers but one had been signed. Next to the name Peter Campbell on his list, the box allowing photos was unchecked. He caught Daniel's eye, and his brother shrugged and grinned. The photos would be sorted later to make sure Campbell wasn't in any of them. *There's always one...*

Daniel started out ahead so he could arrange his equipment at the second peak and be ready with his camera when the runners arrived. Adam consulted his list and called out the names in his group, ticking them off as they answered. The three newcomers were Peter Campbell, Joshua Cameron, and Calvin Lewis.

He checked the list. Peter Campbell had listed 'firefighter' as his occupation. The man named Cameron, who had written 'bar owner,' had a Canadian accent, which Adam recognised because he sounded like Sophie's fiancé, Brian. The last man was definitely English. He'd listed his occupation as 'accountant.' Adam hoped the three would partner up for this experience, for safety's sake.

"Good. Everyone who should be is here, and we don't have any extras," he said. "Everybody ready? Let's go!" He took the lead, and they were off.

The first part of the trail was easy, through the forests that formed the bottom of the mountain. Then the forested slope steepened, and suddenly they were through the trees and at the base of a rocky slope.

"Boggy area," Adam told them. "Navigate carefully. We'll check our progress when we reach the bealach."

"What's a bealach?" asked the Englishman.

GLEN COE, SCOTLAND – PRESENT TIME

"It's a mountain pass, or a ridge," Adam explained. "You'll hear a lot of the auld tongue, or Gaelic, in these parts. All the Munros have Gaelic names."

"I do know what a Munro is," the Englishman said. "A mountain over 3,000 feet high, right?"

"Aye, good," Adam said. "There are 282 Munros in Scotland, named after the man who first listed them, Sir Hugh Munro. He didn't manage to climb them all, but to date, nearly 8,000 people have. They call themselves 'Munro baggers.' And now"— he winked at them — "enough stalling. Let's gie on." He led them upward to the bealach.

Once atop the ridge, Adam looked over his group. The Canadian and the Englishman had paired up. Most of the runners had listened and managed to avoid wet feet. This was looking to be one of the good days.

Or maybe not. The firefighter was missing. Adam waited for a few minutes, but there was no sign of the man. Anxiety bloomed in his gut. Climbers, especially experienced ones, did sometimes strike off on their own, even though he'd stressed the need to stay together. The hardest part of the climb was ahead, and it didn't do to be overconfident.

"Micah?" he called to one of the runners from the club. "Can you take over and get this lot to the top? We'll meet you there." He looked the group over and found another club member he knew well. "Andy, come with me, aye?" *Never be alone.*

The two began walking back down the trail, scanning the brush for the missing climber. Adam's heart was racing, and he was thinking of myriad

293

vile punishments he'd like to inflict on this Peter Campbell lad if they were legal, when the man suddenly appeared on the path twenty feet ahead. He looked surprised to see them, as if there was nothing amiss at all.

Adam's jaw clenched and he fought to keep his voice even. "Did you get lost?"

"Of course not. Saw a red squirrel and I wanted to get a photo. Did I miss anything?"

"No, but just stay with the group for the rest of the tour, please." Adam's teeth were definitely grinding. "You don't want to give your leader a heart attack because of a squirrel, aye?" He smiled to take the edge off his irritation and was rewarded with a frown.

"They could've told us sooner about the boggy part. These shoes aren't cheap," the man grumbled. He pushed past and strode up the path toward the summit of Sgòrr Dhearg, where the others were waiting. "Is this it?" he said. "That wasn't so tough."

Adam forced down the urge to punch the man. "Ach, no, lad, you're only halfway there. Now we're on to Sgòrr Dhonuill." He looked around and raised his voice so all could hear him above the swirling wind. "Does anybody"— he looked at the members of the running club — "not you lot—I mean anybody who hasn't done this tour before—know what 'Sgòrr' means?"

"The peak," said Cameron. "Or high, pointed hill." The others looked at him with respect. "I'm from Cape Breton Island, in Nova Scotia," he said. "I've taken a few Gaelic classes...aye?"

Campbell muttered something under his breath, and Adam decided enough was enough. "Good job,

GLEN COE, SCOTLAND - PRESENT TIME

lad," he said to Cameron, earning himself a grin from the Canadian. He turned back to Campbell. "Do *you* speak the auld tongue then, laddie?"

Campbell's glower intensified, and Adam chastised himself for letting the man get to him. He was a paying customer, after all. *Be professional. You know better.*

He turned a smile on the rest of the group. "Everyone ready for the last leg?" he asked, and they all nodded eagerly and retraced their steps to the bealach to continue the run.

Daniel was waiting at the peak of Sgòrr Dhonuill with his camera. He busied himself taking pictures of the various members of the group with the magnificent views of the glen behind them. "I'll compile these and send them to your email," he told them, and began packing his equipment. "Meet you below, aye?" He shouldered his pack and worked his way down the trail.

Adam faced his tour group. "The return might seem easier than the climb because it's all downhill, but you still have plenty of scree and boulders to contend with. Be careful, and I'll meet you in the car park. You've all done a great job, and you who are new to the trail can go home and tell your friends you've bagged your first two Munros."

He dropped back and followed at a walk, enjoying the uncustomary solitude. Something was tickling his brain and he let the thoughts roll around in his head, trying to figure out what it was. Something about this group seemed familiar, something that reminded him of Màiri...

A lot of things reminded him of her these days. Even without the fact that she'd saved his life, Màiri MacLachlan was impossible to forget. Beautiful, with that wild hair and those huge blue eyes, she'd moved into his memories and staked a claim without his realizing it.

She had a whip-crack brain and a dry sense of humour, and he already knew from her concern for Cory MacMillen that she was kind and empathetic. He realized that he'd never seen her out of that eighteenth-century costume she wore at the bookshop. *Wonder what she'd look like in a jumper and jeans?*

He stumbled over a rock and pulled his thoughts back. This wasn't the time and place to let his mind go all peely-wally over a beautiful woman. He picked his way along the trail, more carefully now.

The voices of his group had disappeared along the path ahead, and Adam picked up his pace. Allowing himself to become distracted was risky behaviour. But Màiri's image rose up in his mind again, despite all his efforts to send her away.

She wasn't for him. No woman was, but this time the realization was unusually sharp and painful. He'd long given up on a future, a family, the idea of love. He was the embodiment of 'carpe diem,' and he thought he'd come to terms with it. The Curse dictated his life.

Màiri had other admirers; that Myles Grant was one. He was always lurking in the background, famous and handsome and rich. She worked in a bookstore and loved books, and Grant wrote books. A perfect match.

GLEN COE, SCOTLAND – PRESENT TIME

It would be folly to try to compete when he had no ammunition for the fight. She'd saved his life, but she had no idea that it was a temporary fix, and he had no intention of telling her. Why should she care, anyway? They had built a friendship in a short time. He seemed to be visiting the bookshop more frequently than before and not buying anything, but that had to be enough. Another fleeting acquaintance.

Except he was doing things he wouldn't do for an acquaintance. He'd agreed to her little detective expedition to the fire station to cajole information out of that firefighter, Mackie, and he realised he was actually looking forward to it.

Wait. Something clicked. *Firefighter...* One of the members of today's tour group had been a firefighter. That miserable one—Peter Campbell. Did he work with Mackie?

He blinked and looked ahead to where the group had long since disappeared from sight and sound. How long had he been standing here on the trail, lost in his thoughts? He'd broken his own rule, *never run alone.* Time to catch up. He jogged faster and didn't slow until he stood among the trees at the bottom of the slope, trying to catch his breath.

He was having trouble doing that. His lungs were burning, and his feet seemed unwilling to pick themselves up off the trail and move. A strange lethargy was spreading through his gut and a shaft of fear arced through his heart, bringing an anxiety with which he was all too familiar.

He was having another attack. Alone on a mountain trail, where no one knew he was in trouble. He felt a weakness crawl through his legs and up to his chest, and his knees sagged. Was this the one? It was the same question he had with every attack—was this the Big One? He folded to the ground and lay face up on the path, staring into the darkness of the fir trees. If this was the Curse's last laugh, he'd die alone and never have the chance to say goodbye to Daniel or Jared. Or Màiri...

The wind whistled through the trees, and he gave his mind up to it and waited. It rose to a roar and then receded until it was only a whisper. Maybe this was the best way, after all... Everyone was alone in his last moments.

Out of the growing darkness in his mind, an image appeared. Màiri. She was dressed in a blue turtleneck jumper and jeans that fit her long legs as if she'd been born in them—just the way he'd imagined her. Perfect.

Adam smiled. *Aye, this was the best way to go, after all.* As his mind shut down, he had one last thought.

I was wrong. She *is* for me. The sadness swept in and pushed everything out of its way.

Was.

CHAPTER 33
BALLACHULISH, SCOTLAND – PRESENT TIME

There is no reality, there is only hallucination.
Reality is hallucination we agree on.
—Abhijit Naskar

Images swirled in Adam's head. Small, thatch-covered cottages along a dirt path. Horses tied up to posts in front of the ruins of an ancient church. A crowd had gathered on the lawn, talking over each other in their excitement. Their words were uttered in some language that was English but not, peppered with Gaelic. The people were pointing toward a square in front of a larger building, two storeys high. It seemed an important structure, with a roof of slate instead of thatch, and in front of the building stood a strange frame made of two long wooden beams, hinged at both ends.

In the centre of the square was a tall pole with stacked piles of wood spread around its base. A Guy Fawkes celebration, perhaps? Surely not; it was much too warm. And where was the effigy of the mad plotter? Why were all these people dressed in long gowns and great kilts or old-fashioned trousers? If they were reenactors, they were very good. He could read the feverish passion on their faces and in their frenetic gestures. This exhibition must have cost the town a lot of money.

As he watched, the images began to recede, the air around him becoming misty and blurred. New sounds intruded on his consciousness. The voices were more familiar, speaking in a cadence he understood. The air around him was still, and he could hear a soft beeping noise somewhere in the distance, like that of a bin lorry or construction vehicle backing up.

He kept his eyes closed while he tried to sort the changes in his environment, and slowly the memories crept back. A mountain trail. People running, the wind swirling around the peak. Daniel, with his camera, taking pictures of the people. A pain gripping his heart, sapping the energy from his body. A woman crouched over him. Màiri. She'd come to him, laid her hand on his heart, and saved him...again. And he remembered his last thought, before he passed out.

She is for me.

He wasn't in love with her. Of course not. The part of his heart that allowed such an emotion had been irrevocably broken with the doctor's diagnosis. *You have a one in four chance of passing the disease to your offspring.* No, he didn't—couldn't—love her, but he needed her.

He started to open his eyes, eager to see her again in her jeans and jumper. Then, suddenly fearful, he

BALLACHULISH, SCOTLAND – PRESENT TIME

screwed them shut again. The murmur of voices continued. Three people. Daniel, and Jared—he would recognise that rich Scouse accent anywhere—and a woman. He opened his eyes.

He was in a hospital room, and Laura MacAllan was sitting in the chair by his bed, talking to Jared and Daniel. Màiri was nowhere to be seen. The surge of disappointment that washed through him was so strong he could taste it, and he closed his eyes again, desperate to return to his illusion.

"He's awake!" Laura shrilled and grabbed his hand. "Go get the doctor!" Too weak to pull away, Adam had no choice but to allow her to cling to his hand.

"Laura, can you lower your pitch?" Adam could hear the exasperation in Daniel's voice, but it was no match for the frustration in his own mind.

A nurse swept in. "Good to see you back in the land of the living," she said, and the next few minutes were given over to poking and prodding and the taking of vitals. "Everything looks good. The doctor will be here when he finishes his rounds." She straightened his pillows and left the room. The others gathered round again.

A sudden urgency gripped Adam. "Where's Màiri?" The words came out rusty and garbled, but they must have been coherent. Laura's face flushed with colour, and she tightened her hold on his hand, her nails digging into his flesh like a raptor's talons. He grimaced.

"You're hurting him." Jared's voice was sharp. "Jaysus, Laura, let the man go."

Laura released Adam's hand and sat back in the chair, a petulant frown wrinkling her forehead.

"Sorry, love," she muttered. "I was so excited to see you awake."

Adam ignored her and focused on Jared. "How long have I been here?"

"Two days," Jared said. "Longer than last time." His face was creased with worry, and there were darker circles under his liquid brown eyes.

"What day is it?"

"Sunday," his brother said.

"Wait. Last time?" Laura's voice broke in. "This has happened before? Why didn't anyone tell me?"

Jared and Daniel exchanged looks, and then Daniel said calmly, "Calm down, lass. He just fainted once before, that's all. Dehydration on the trail. " His eyes met Adam's.

Laura's frown intensified. "Still, you should have told me."

"Why?" Jared's words were a challenge. Laura glared at him and opened her mouth, then she shut it again and stood up. She turned her back on Jared and smiled at Adam. "Well, since you're apparently going to be fine, I'll be off. Don't worry, I'll check in later." She pushed past the two men and left the room, back stiff.

"What was she doing here?" Adam asked.

"*Someone...*" — Jared jerked his head toward Daniel — "let it slip yesterday, when she came into the office on her usual stalking mission. You're going to have to do something about her," he added. "She doesn't seem to understand English."

"Never mind her," Adam said. "Where's Màiri?"

"Evie's friend from the bookshop?" Daniel's voice

was puzzled. "How would we know?"

"Didn't she come to the hospital with me?"

Daniel's brow furrowed. "Uh, and why would she do that?"

Adam looked back and forth between the two. They didn't know what he was talking about; that much was clear. But did that mean...?

"She-she wasn't with me?" he asked. "When you found me, I mean. She wasn't there?"

"When I found you," Daniel said, "no one was with you. You didn't show up in the car park, and the group said you were right behind them, so I doubled back. You were just inside the trees." He shuddered. "Just lying there on the ground. I thought you were dead."

The last word was thick, as if Daniel was speaking through a wad of wool caught in his throat. His face was pale. "I'm not gonna lie. I was petrified. Why the hell did you go down the trail alone?"

"Màiri wasn't there?" Adam persisted. "You didn't see her at all?"

Daniel blew out a breath. "Look. Don't you think we'd notice something like that? There was nobody there. Just you."

"Has she been in to see me?" Adam sat up and looked around. "Where's my mobile?"

Jared picked it up off the side table and handed it to him. Adam checked the display, then clicked the 'messages' icon. There were no texts. None. He lay back against the headrest and let the depression sink in. It had all been a dream. The weird, old-fashioned village, the vision of a woman with black curls and blue eyes running toward him in jeans and jumper.

Just a dream. He dropped the mobile onto the bed covers.

"Does she know what happened to me?" he asked, reluctant to let it go. "Did anyone tell her?"

Daniel still looked confused, but Jared spoke up. "I'm sorry, mate," he said. "I didn't know you two had that kind of relationship. You neglected to tell me," he added, narrowing his eyes. "Last I heard, you were trying to work up the courage to go see her again at the bookshop. Apparently I missed a few episodes."

Daniel said, "Are you two talking about Màiri MacLachlan? Evie's friend?" He looked from Adam to Jared and back again. "Is there something going on between you two?"

Adam had stopped listening. Màiri hadn't been there. She hadn't saved him. His thoughts picked up steam, like the old tourist train up in Aviemore. She didn't even know about it. Two days had gone by and she hadn't texted him, hadn't called to find out what was going on. The train slowed, belched out a last puff of steam, and died.

"Can I get out of here?" he asked. "I feel fine now."

"I'll check at the desk," Daniel said, and left the room. Jared was watching him closely, his dark eyes worried.

"That was a bad one, wasn't it?" he said quietly.

Adam nodded. "I thought it was the end. I mean, I think every one is the end, but this time..." He trailed off, lay back against the pillow, and stared at the ceiling. "Are you sure—" He stopped. Why was he beating a dead horse here? Màiri hadn't been there. It had all been a part of the hallucination.

BALLACHULISH, SCOTLAND – PRESENT TIME

Still, an unwillingness to give up without a fight gripped him. He picked his mobile up off the blanket and looked for Màiri's number in his contacts. He hovered his finger over the button for what seemed like eons and then took a breath and tapped it.

"Hullo?" Her voice came over the line.

"Màiri? Um...it's me. Adam. Adam MacArthur."

"Yes?" Her voice was chilly. "How have you been?"

"I'm better now," he said. "I'm sorry I couldn't go to the fire station with you..."

"No apology necessary. Well, I have to... Wait. Better?" Her tone changed. "Were you poorly?"

Adam looked up and saw that Jared had left. He was alone in the room. "Um, well, can you come?" He hadn't meant to say that; he hadn't wanted to seem clingy.

"Of course." The word was a balm. "Are you home? I don't think I have your address."

"I'm in hospital. Ballachulish Medical."

"What?" Her shocked gasp resonated through the mobile. "I'll be right there." She rang off without another word.

Adam lay in his bed letting the short conversation play through his mind.

Can you come?

Of course.

I'll be right there.

She did care. There had been surprise and real concern in her voice. He felt his heartbeat speed up and then slow down again. Another thought filtered through the syrup his brain was serving up. She hadn't known what happened to him. She really hadn't been there on the trail, like Daniel had said. It had been an illusion. Yet it had seemed so real.

It didn't matter. She cared. She was coming. A smile spread over his face.

Daniel and Jared came back into the room. "You can go home tomorrow, if all the tests come back negative," Daniel reported. "We're going to go now and let you get some rest. I'll go to your flat and get you some clothes." His voice was cheerful, belying the worry lines around his eyes that were always there. He gave his brother a salute and left.

Jared stepped up to the bed. "Are you sure you don't need company?"

Adam waved him off. "I'll be fine." He paused. "Anyway, Màiri's coming."

Jared gave him a thumbs-up. "You're doing better than I expected, mate." He grinned. "Should I stay and meet her?" He laughed at the look on Adam's face and put both hands up. "Sorry, had to." He turned for the door.

"Wait," Adam said. "How's Pearl?"

"Fine. Missing you though. And more importantly, missing his cat." He gave a dramatic sigh. "You'd best get back to the bookshop soon and take care of that, aye?" He laughed and was gone.

Adam must have dozed off, because when he opened his eyes, Màiri was sitting in the chair by the bed, concern written on her lovely features.

"Hi," she said, softly.

"Hi."

"I'm sorry. I didn't know. I thought… Never mind. I would have come."

Adam shook his head. "It wouldn't have mattered. I've apparently been unconscious for a couple of days. I just woke up this morning."

He stared at her, wondering what was different. His brain felt like sludge, and the answer was slow in coming, but finally he grasped what it was.

Instead of the ubiquitous eighteenth-century gown, she was wearing a blue turtleneck jumper and jeans that fit her long legs as if she'd been born in them—just the way he'd imagined. A smile found its way onto his face.

CHAPTER 34
DORNACH, SCOTLAND – 1727

RONAIN

From his place of concealment, Ronain MacKay watched the two men brawling in the middle of the path. The dandy and the dandy's lad. Disgusting. They didn't even know how to fight like men. God, how he hated them.

He watched them grapple, growing ever more embarrassed for both, until they finally broke apart, winded, and went in opposite directions. *Thank God. That was an awful thing t' watch.*

When they were both out of sight, he stepped out from behind the tree in time to glimpse the back of Alan Grant disappearing toward his home at the other end of the village. Should he follow Grant? Or—his head swivelled toward the direction Hugh had taken—that one?

Alan was a libertine. He played with lassies' hearts and left them strewn all over Dornach. He'd worked his magic on Ailis two years ago, when she was just fifteen, and when he was done with his fun, she'd come crying to Ronain, her best friend.

He didn't want to be her best friend. He'd been in love with Ailis MacAllan for as long as he could remember, and someday she'd come to know it. Meanwhile, he had to watch bastarts like Alan Grant toy with the heart that should be his.

One day Alan Grant would pay for breaking Ailis' heart, but he wasn't the real problem. Ronain looked north again, where the other man had gone, and his fists clenched. That was the one he hated most.

The sins stacked up against Hugh Sutherland were many and unforgivable, starting with that day eleven years ago when Hugh had beaten Ronain's beloved brother in front of the whole village. Oh, he'd paid for it then. Had to sit in the stocks all night and have rubbish thrown at him. It should have felt good, but it didn't.

Ronain had only been seven when it happened, and his arm too weak to hit his target. While Hugh sat helpless, his feet stuck through the holes in the stocks, Ronain had hidden behind his brother and thrown little clods of dirt that landed pitifully short of the mark. *I was a wee cowart then, too weak and tim'rous to step up fer my brother.* Shame coursed through him at the memory.

He spat on the dirt of the path and swiped his hand across his mouth. *But not now.* Not anymore. He was a man now, and it was past time to pay Sutherland back for everything he'd done.

DORNACH, SCOTLAND – 1727

He'd waited that night, shivering in the cold, hoping Hugh would fall asleep in the stocks. Then he'd creep up and bash him with a stick. He knew that was cowardly too, but he didn't care. As long as he got revenge for Walter's shame—and his own.

But then that crippled lass crept back out and started wiping the dirt off the bastart's face. Ronain waited, but she'd stayed with him, leaning her back against his to prop them both up. Walter had come back and dragged him home before their mother came looking for him herself.

Ronain hadn't known then what 'clootie' meant. But now he knew, and she'd deserved the name. In a way, everything that happened that day was her fault.

His mam had given Walter a skelping when they got home and called him a numpty for letting Hugh get the best of him. "Them lads was just playin' with 'er," she'd snarled, and told Walter he should've done more. He should have given the little witch the beating a child of the Devil deserved, instead of just making up songs.

Mam hated Hugh Sutherland, too, for what he'd done, but she was a woman, and all women seemed to do to get even was gossip with other women. Besides, she knew as well as anybody else that Hugh's father owned half the village and was the sheriff. It didn't do to run afoul of him.

The Gilchrist women were fair game, though. Ronain's mother had told both her sons, every time they saw the two in the market, that those who'd been marked by Satan would have their day in court.

"Matter o' time," she would say, and many of her listeners nodded in agreement.

The fact that Hugh had stuck by Sìne was another tick against him. Ronain rather liked that; it proved he was every bit as bad as she was. But that wasn't the worst thing about him.

He could feel the blood pounding in his ears. No, the worst thing was, the bastart was marrying Ailis. And that, more than anything else, was the match tossed into the powder barrel for Ronain.

When Alan moved on from Ailis, Ronain was angry at him for giving her pain, but glad at the same time. *He* was the one she turned to, the one who comforted her. The one she told her secrets to. Someday soon she'd come to love him as much as he adored her. He just had to be patient.

Then Duncan Sutherland and Mistress MacAllan put their heads together and ruined everything. Ailis had danced into the market and started telling everyone who'd listen that she was to marry Hugh Sutherland, the sheriff's son. He'd stood in stunned agony as she told him how she'd always liked Hugh, but he hadn't noticed. And now he was to be her husband! Ronain had looked into her shining face and felt his heart dry up.

It couldn't be! It was impossible that Ailis could have feelings for that bawbag. What could she see in him? Aye, his family owned half the village, and Ronain supposed he wasn't bad to look at, but what about it?

He didn't feel any better when Hugh refused to marry Ailis. Nobody stood up against Duncan

DORNACH, SCOTLAND – 1727

Sutherland; the man breathed power and privilege. He was the law in Dornach, and no one dared to take a stand against him. His own son was still wearing the bruises to prove it. If he hadn't detested Hugh so much, Ronain might have felt sorry for him. *Ach, no. Never.*

He moved onto the path and set out in the wake of the man he despised most in the world. If he could get rid of Sutherland, Ailis would be bereft. She'd turn to him, and he'd be waiting to console her. Heartened, he increased his pace.

Torchlight danced on the path ahead of him. A shadow coalesced and morphed into a man, dressed all in black. Ronain started for the side of the path, sensing that this man was dangerous—he couldn't say why.

"Young Ronain MacKay, is it?" an oily voice reached him out of the darkness. Ronain stopped, surprised.

"A-aye," he said. "Who are ye?"

The man came closer, and now Ronain recognized him. That new doctor Sutherland had brought to Dornach last year. Wilson. In the light of the torch he looked like a death's head, all angles and sharp points and white skin. "Are ye a friend o' young Mister Sutherland?" he asked.

"We're not friends!" Ronain glared at the man.

"Ahhh," Wilson said. "And would ye be friends with his betrothed, then?"

Why was he asking these questions? It was none of his business. But Ronain's mouth opened and words came out as if the man had attached a string to his tongue.

"F-friends, aye."

"Ahhh," Wilson said again. "Do ye ken they're t' be married, then?"

"Aye." All the misery in Ronain's soul must have been evident in that one word, for Doctor Wilson nodded in commiseration.

Ronain pulled himself up and tried to take control of his tongue. "Why? What business is 't o' yours?"

"My business..." — he drew out the word like a spider spins a length of silk — "...isnae wi' yer friend. Nor is it wi' young Sutherland."

Ronain blinked. "Wh-wha'?"

Wilson studied him for a long moment. "There is evil afoot in Dornach, lad," he said finally. "The Devil has come t' our village."

Ronain gawked at him. It occurred to him that were he asked to draw a picture of the Devil, it might look very much like *this* man. Tall, gaunt, with bony fingers and long, yellowed nails. Maybe it was the light from the torch, but an odd light glinted in his dark eyes. Ronain shivered and leaned away from him. Suddenly he wanted very badly to go home.

"Satan looks for the weak-willed among us," Wilson continued, pinning Ronain with that otherworldly glare. "Give up on th' lass, son," he said softly.

Ronain felt trapped, caught in this man's spell. There was something unnatural about him, something frightening and raw. "Wha d'ye mean?"

"Take care, young MacKay," Wilson said, by way of an answer. "Dinnae ye get caught in the Devil's spell." And he was gone, his coat tails flapping against his skinny legs.

Give up on th' lass.

DORNACH, SCOTLAND – 1727

Ronain clenched his fists and stared after Wilson. *Fuck that*, he thought. He was going to have Ailis, and there was only one way to do that.

He was going to have to kill Hugh Sutherland.

CHAPTER 35
DORNACH, SCOTLAND – 1727

SÌNE

"**M**am!" Sìne rushed to the fireplace and yanked her mother's hand away from the simmering kettle. "Ye cannae touch it!"

Too late. Angry red welts were already spreading over four of Doirin's fingers. Tears ran down her face and she backed away from the fireplace, whimpering. "I'm sorry, I'm sorry!"

Sìne took her mother's hand in her own and studied it. There would be blisters. She reached for a clean cloth and soaked it in the vinegar that was always kept next to the fire. Wrapping the wet cloth around the burned hand, she gave Doirin a severe look.

WITCH

"How many times 'ave I telt ye, dinnae come near th' fire!" She could hear her own voice, repeating the same words Mam had said to her so many years ago. Their roles had reversed and now she was the mother, Doirin the child.

I s'pose tis right, she thought, wearily pushing a curl out of her eyes. *Tis my turn.*

"Dinnae come near th' fire," Doirin mumbled. "Dinnae come near th' fire." She looked up and gave her daughter a sweet smile. "Fire is bad."

Sìne wanted to cry. The tears had gathered, and it took all she had to keep them from spilling out.

Doirin Gilchrist—her brave, intelligent mother—was lost. Sìne remembered how it had started. She'd forget where she put the ladle or wander into the midwifery and seem surprised to find herself there. At first, they laughed about it. "I'd forget my heid if t'were not attached," she'd say. "I reckon tis part o' growin' old, aye?"

But it wasn't. Maighread had noticed it, and she was far older. She said nothing at first, but her worried eyes followed Doirin as they worked together. Finally, just last year, she pulled Sìne aside.

"I dinnae thynk I can let yer mam help with the birthin's much longer."

"Is she makin' mistakes?" Sìne had asked.

"Nae, tis not so much 'at," Maighread said. "She's usin' her gift more often, e'en when she doesnae need t'. She's gettin' reckless."

The fact that Maighread was talking about the gift with Sìne was proof that there was something wrong. Sìne wasn't supposed to know about that.

DORNACH, SCOTLAND – 1727

Maighread and Doirin had taken great care to keep it from her. And Sìne had never told them what she'd seen that night.

But there was Maighread, talking as if she'd known all along. Sìne nodded. It was no use pretending she didn't understand what the old woman was talking about.

That had been a year ago, not long before Maighread passed on herself, leaving Sìne with the burden of her mother's failing mind...and her gift. In a way, it had been a blessing when Albert Wilson forced Doirin out of the birthing room. Her mother had protested, but she was afraid of the man, too, and there was no going around him. It was his home now, and a word from him would see them both set adrift without any shelter at all.

They'd get no help from the sheriff if that happened. He was nothing like Hugh.

Hugh. The pain came flooding back, and the tears that had been building let loose. Would she never get over his betrayal? Would she ever stop missing him? She pulled a hand angrily across her eyes and when she looked up, Doirin was gone.

Sìne sighed and left the tiny hut. Her mother was nowhere in sight, but Sìne knew where she'd be. Mam had developed a sweet tooth lately and could usually be found at the taffy stand in the market, gazing longingly at the sweets on display.

Dorcas Munro was a kind woman, sweet like her wares, and she kept a ledger of Doirin's 'purchases' underneath the cash box so Sìne could pay up later with money she could ill afford to lose. But even Dorcas' patience was growing thin.

Her feet came to a halt, rooted in the pathway. Not twenty ells away, Hugh Sutherland was sitting on a log, reading. A flood of emotion threatened to engulf Sìne, and she nearly turned around to go back the way she had come. He hadn't seen her; there was time.

But Mam was still out here somewhere. The market would be closing soon, shopkeepers rolling down the curtains over the front of their stands, packing their wares for the evening. The men would be eager to get to the tavern, the women to their kitchens. There would be no time to deal with that crazy Gilchrist woman, and not everyone was as kind as Dorcas Munro.

Hugh was still deep in his book, but the daylight was fading and he was sure to look up soon. Then he'd see her, and she'd have to put up with his cold rejection once more. Sìne stepped behind the closest tree, thinking to go round through the woods and resume her search for Mam.

Something moved in the trees behind Hugh. Sìne squinted and saw a figure separate itself from the darkness. Ronain MacKay was sneaking, ever so slowly, toward the log upon which Hugh sat, unaware. Before Sìne could react, a twig snapped, and Hugh's head jerked around.

Too late. Ronain brought a thick branch down on Hugh's head with such force Sìne could hear the crack from where she stood, frozen in mute horror. Hugh's body folded and rolled off the log to lie motionless on the path. Ronain stared down at him for a brief second, then he threw down the branch and melted away, back into the trees.

DORNACH, SCOTLAND – 1727

For a long moment, Sìne was unable to move. Then she started toward the place where Hugh lay, blood pooling under his head. She made it to within ten ells and stopped again.

Doirin Gilchrist appeared from the direction of town and raced to Hugh. She knelt on the ground next to him and ran a hand behind his head, pulling it back covered with blood. She put a finger under his nose, shook her head, and put her head near his heart, listening.

Sìne watched, amazed. Gone was the vacant, forgetful woman her mother had become in the last year. Here was the old Doirin, the healer. With precise efficiency, she tore a piece off the bottom of her muslin gown and wrapped it quickly around Hugh's head. Then she pulled up his shirt, put her hand over his heart, and splayed her fingers. Within seconds a blue light appeared and spread.

Voices could be heard in the distance, but Sìne didn't move. She watched in awe as the blue turned to a soft pink and moved in a wave across Hugh's chest. Doirin continued to hold her hand in place, a small smile playing about her lips.

"Stop!"

Sìne's attention was wrested away from Hugh and her mother. Six men had gathered on the path and were staring at Doirin with her hand on Hugh Sutherland's chest.

"Stop! Get ye awa from th' lad, ye witch!" bellowed Albert Wilson. He raised his hand and two of his henchmen raced to drag Doirin away from Hugh. They pulled her over to stand, held by both arms, in front of the doctor, and then one of them returned to kneel next to Hugh's body.

"He's breathin'!" he shouted. "We stopt 'er in time."

"I kent I'd catch ye at yer wicked ways, ye spawn o' Satan!" Wilson's voice trumpeted. "If we hadnae come in time, ye would have kilt th' lad."

Sìne ran to stand next to her mother. She pulled at the arm holding Doirin fast, but it was like trying to move an iron bar. The man brushed her hand away as if he couldn't bear to be touched by her.

Doirin's eyes were wide and frightened, and she had begun to whimper incoherently.

"She's not tryin' t' hurt him!" Sìne said. "She just saved 'is life!" She faced Wilson, her eyes blazing with anger. "Ye ken she has th' gift; ye've seen it. I ken ye have. Why are ye tryin' t' twist th' truth?"

Wilson smirked. He nodded at the man holding Doirin's arms, and he produced a set of iron cuffs with which he bound her hands in front of her.

"Stop!" Sìne choked out the words. "What are ye doin'? Leave her be!"

Wilson signalled again. The man who had been holding Doirin rounded on Sìne and forced her hands in front of her. Within minutes, she was shackled like her mother.

"Can ye no see she bound his heid?" Sìne sputtered. "Why would she do that if she was tryin' t' hurt him?"

Wilson bent over until his face was inches away from hers. She could smell his fetid breath and feel the heat of his anger. Spittle landed on her cheek and rolled down to her chin.

"Ye best be thinkin' o' yerself, lass," he hissed. "There's nuthin' we want t' hear from the witch's daughter."

He gestured to his men. Two of them picked up Hugh's body and carried him between them, and the others herded Doirin and Sìne toward town, pushing them roughly and laughing when they stumbled.

They came knowin', she thought. She looked down at the iron cuffs binding her wrists. *This was planned from th' beginnin'*. Horror slid into her heart. She looked into her mother's eyes, wide and vacant, and was grateful that she didn't seem to understand what was happening. Then Sìne's eyes sought Hugh. He was still unconscious, but his chest rose and fell in a steady rhythm as the men carried him.

Thank ye, Lord, she sent a prayer to Heaven. *Whatever happens, he'll be awright*.

CHAPTER 36
FORT WILLIAM, SCOTLAND
– PRESENT TIME

Every world has its villains, every universe has its saints, every era has its heroes.
—Matshona Dhliwayo

Meg MacInnes met them at the door of the fire station. She backed up so they could enter the small foyer and smiled at Màiri.

"Welcome back. I was disappointed when you called to cancel the other day, but I'm glad you're here now and thrilled to be able to help you in your research."

She looked over Màiri's shoulder at Adam and gave him an appreciative once-over that seemed just a wee bit excessive in Màiri's opinion. "Meg MacInnes, station manager." She extended a hand. "I hear you run mountain tours for a living. It certainly shows."

Was that really necessary? If she were a man, I'd expect a wolf whistle right about now. Màiri ignored the voice in her head that said, *And why do you care? He's not your property, is he?* But her senses seemed fine-tuned to Adam's reaction. She could feel her jaw aching from the effort to keep her teeth from grinding.

Adam smiled. "Er...thanks, Ms. MacInnes. But I'm sure your training is much tougher than mine."

"It's Meg, please. And yes, our training is pretty comprehensive. But we don't usually fight fires while running up mountains, aye?" She gave Adam a light punch on his arm.

The teeth gritting was turning into grinding. Màiri searched her mind for something innocuous and clever to say, but all she could see was Meg's hand on Adam's arm. The other woman was quite pretty and way more fit than Màiri. She and Adam looked like advertisements for *Sport and Fitness Magazine*. This was turning out to be a bad plan, in a way she'd never imagined.

She pulled her gaze away from the two fitness specimens and found herself looking at the photo gallery behind the desk. A new photo had been added, the name plate underneath reading *Charles Fletcher*. The firefighter who had been murdered and burned in the museum fire.

Màiri stared at the man's picture with an odd sense of recognition. *Do I know him?* He had brown hair, blue eyes, and he was smiling for the camera. A man in the middle of a life, who had no family except for these colleagues. A man who'd had to be identified by DNA.

And then it came to her. Her heart skipped a beat, and she felt sweat breaking out on her palms. *I didn't know what I had until it was too late...*

FORT WILLIAM, SCOTLAND – PRESENT TIME

She didn't know him, but she'd seen him before. Walking beside her on the High Street, wearing an Inverness coat...*a week after he was found dead in the fire at the museum.* There one minute, gone the next, like a ghost.

And that was simply impossible. *Brilliant,* she thought. *First a magic healing power, now I'm seeing ghosts. Gran would be so chuffed.*

No, it had to have been someone else. She wrenched her gaze away from the new photo on the memorial wall as the outer door opened again, and her mouth dropped open in surprise.

Myles Grant stood in the doorway, dressed in khakis and a blue chambray shirt that matched his eyes perfectly. Meg dropped her hand from Adam's arm and gaped at the newcomer.

Màiri stared at Meg, and then at the object of her interest. For the first time, she saw Myles Grant through another woman's eyes. *He's really very handsome,* she thought, *though not really my type.* She glanced over at Adam. His brown eyes when they met hers seemed to reflect relief that Meg's spotlight was no longer on him. *My type is more subdued. Not flamboyant. A comfortable kind of handsome.* She grinned at him and was rewarded with a brilliant smile.

"My goodness," Meg exclaimed. "This is my lucky day! I mean, there's never a lack of handsome men in a fire station, but we can always make room for more, aye? Meg MacInnes, station manager," she said to Myles. "Are you here for research, too?"

Myles seemed startled by the question, but he

recovered quickly and smiled back at Meg. "Why, yes, actually." He extended his hand. "Myles Grant."

"The author? Oh, my! What an honour!" Meg took his hand and held it almost reverently. "I've read all your books! Inspector Beaton is my favourite character!" Suddenly she gasped. "Don't tell me you're planning a book with a fire theme!"

Màiri caught a frown from Adam and shook her head. *It wasn't me!* she mouthed. *I didn't tell him anything!*

"Well..." Myles said. Then he leaned closer. "Shhhh! It's a secret for now." He straightened and looked around the room, which was now filling with people who had heard Meg's excited voice. "I guess not so much of a secret anymore."

"Hullo, Miss MacLachlan," said a soft voice behind Màiri, and she turned to face Alexander MacKay. The young man smiled shyly. "Why are you here again? I mean" — his face turned a flaming red—"I'm happy to see you, but why—I mean..."

Màiri launched into her prepared speech, hoping it didn't sound as lame to him as it did to her. "I want to write an article about fire rescue. Oh, this is my friend, Adam MacArthur. Adam, meet Alexander Mackay, my hero."

"Mackie." He shook hands with Adam and then turned a puzzled look on Màiri. "Are you a writer, too, then?"

She could feel her heart pounding. "Well, sort of. It was a very traumatic experience for me and I want to write about it. I suppose to you it must have just been another day on the job, though, right?"

"Well, in some ways, I guess," Mackie said. "I mean, we're trained for that, but every rescue is different, and we never know the outcome. You were one of the lucky ones."

"That's why I want to go through the whole process, from the time you arrived at the scene until we were outside and safe," Màiri said, warming to her topic. "When I came before, Meg said nobody ever comes back to thank you for your service. People should know what heroes you are." She stole a look at Adam and he rolled his eyes.

Mackie looked even more embarrassed, if that were possible. "I'm not special. Any one of us would have done the same."

"Oh, of course! I'm hoping to interview as many of you as I can." She gave him a wide smile. "Of course, as *my* rescuer, you are *very* special." *Am I really batting my eyelashes right now? Does this stuff really work?*

Apparently it did. Mackie shuffled his feet and gave her a weak smile. "Well, I'm on shift now. Let me ask Meg." He stepped away.

"How'm I doing?" Màiri murmured to Adam. "Does anything I'm saying make sense?"

Adam laughed. "Not sure. Maybe. So, you're a 'sort of' writer, eh? Do you have a magazine in mind, or a blog or something, in case they ask?"

"Of course. It's Eve's blog, called 'History and Heroes of Fort William.'"

"Eve has a blog?" Adam asked.

"She does now. I already talked to her, and she's ready to lie on demand."

Adam wrinkled his forehead. "You're impressive. What are you going to do if he asks for a copy of the article? Or checks the internet for Eve's blog?"

"I guess I'll have to write something then." She glanced over and saw that Myles Grant was watching them over Meg's shoulder. "Or maybe Myles would do it. I still think we should enlist him. He could probably spit out an article in minutes. I don't know how much he'd charge, though. I'm sure his time is precious."

"Hmmmph," Adam said. "He'd probably do it for free…for you."

Màiri gave him a sidelong glance. *Was he jealous?* Interesting. She decided to explore that later and felt for his hand. "Thank you," she said. "I don't know why this is so important, but it is. There's just something strange about that day, and it's driving me mad trying to figure out what it is."

"I heard a little bit of what you were saying." Myles had appeared at her side. "Do you mind if I sit in? Maybe we can help each other out."

Adam said nothing, but his silence spoke volumes. Màiri outlined her plan quickly, leaving out the real reason behind her interest and the fact that there was no actual article planned. "Are you really going to do a novel with a fire theme?"

"Yes, I think so." Myles hesitated. "But not modern fires. You know the new display at the bookshop? The one on witches?" He laughed and rolled his eyes. "Of course you do. You probably arranged it."

"Actually, I didn't," Màiri said. "That was all Mary. To be honest, there's something about those books that creeps me out. I find myself making a wide

FORT WILLIAM, SCOTLAND – PRESENT TIME

circle around that particular table." She shivered. "It's weird."

"Witches?" Adam asked. "Like the Devil and spells and magic?"

"Aye," Myles said. He turned back to Màiri. "I know what you mean about being creeped out. There's one book there, called *The Witch's Daughter*, that got me that way. It was written by a Simon Grant, and I wondered if we were connected somehow. So I bought the book, and I thought maybe I should investigate it more."

"I remember that book!" Adam said. "It smelled like smoke, as if the publisher added something extra. Remember, Màiri?"

She nodded. "It gave me a sick feeling, but I don't know why."

"That's the one," Myles said. "The last witch in Scotland was burned alive in 1727, up in Dornach," he said. "It was a superstitious time, and the poor woman was probably just senile, but nobody was up on mental illness in those days."

"Miss MacLachlan," said a soft voice behind them, and Màiri turned to see Mackie standing behind them. "Meg says it's fine to talk with you, as long as you understand we'll have to drop everything if we get a call."

"Brilliant," Màiri said. "Is it all right if my friends sit in on the interview? Mister Grant thinks it might be useful for his next book, so we can kill two birds with one stone, aye?"

Mackie gave the two men a nervous look. "Sure, I guess." He led them through the side door into the larger room where the fire trucks were housed and to a small round table in the rear. "This is as good a place as any, eh?"

They arranged themselves around the table and Myles pulled out his mobile. "Do you mind if I record this?" he asked. "That way, I won't forget the details."

Mackie's brow furrowed, but then he smiled. "No worries."

Màiri began. "How many men can fit on this appliance?" She pointed to the truck behind them.

"Five for this one," he said. "It used to be however many could hang on to the sides of the truck, but now the rule is as many as there are seatbelts. Guess they decided it was best if the men got to the fire in one piece, aye?"

"How many appliances were there at the museum fire?" Màiri asked.

"Two," said Mackie. "But the other one" — he pointed to another truck — "is smaller and fits only two or three."

"Does everybody at the station respond to the fire?" Adam asked him.

"Usually," Mackie said. "We're a small station, so only five of us live and work here. We all fit on these two trucks. But volunteers can join us if it's a big fire, and they drive their own vehicles."

"So, did all of you ride the fire appliance to the museum fire?" Màiri asked.

Mackie hesitated. It was a very small flicker in his clear grey eyes, gone immediately.

"Well, now that you mention it," he said, "Peter Campbell came in his own car. But that's not unusual if one of us is offsite for some reason. We get the call wherever we are. Why do you ask?"

FORT WILLIAM, SCOTLAND – PRESENT TIME

"I was just wondering," Màiri said. "I'm just grateful you got to us so fast."

"That's what we're trained for," Mackie said. "Um, was there anything else you needed? I think I'd better get back to work." He stood up. "Thanks for coming to see us, but like I told you before, it's not necessary." He smiled and disappeared through another door behind the table. Myles turned off the recorder on his mobile.

"Well, that was interesting," Màiri murmured. "He seemed suddenly eager to get rid of us, don't you think?"

"I think you're reading too much into this," Adam told her. "A lot of people get nervous when they know they're being recorded." He looked to Myles, and the author nodded in agreement. "Let's talk to some of the others and see if they all say the same thing, eh?"

They talked to the other firefighters but learned nothing new. Finally, they stood up and made their way out to the reception area, where Meg was waiting for them. The second door off the foyer was standing slightly ajar, and Màiri registered two people in a small room, heads bent together. One of them was Peter Campbell and the other was a blonde woman—Laura Macallan. Campbell's eyes met hers, and he crossed to close the door firmly.

As if I was spying on him or something, Màiri thought. *Jerk.*

"Get everything you needed?" Meg said. She gave Myles and Adam another once-over, and grinned. "Come back anytime."

"Thanks for your help," Màiri said. "I don't think

I need any more. I brought sweeties and biscuits. Please share them with everyone and thank them again for me. Oh! And don't forget to come to the bookshop cafe, aye? Everybody's welcome. My treat."

"Will do," Meg said. She held the door open for them and waved as they left.

"I'll type up the recording and send it to your email," Myles told Màiri. He hesitated. "See you soon?"

Màiri smiled. "Aye."

Adam said nothing until they reached the car. Then he turned to face her.

"There's something wrong, isn't there?"

"I don't know," she said. "But there was one firefighter missing—a nasty lad named Campbell. And he went to the fire in his own car, according to Mackie." She frowned. "Did you see the lad Laura was talking to?"

"Laura?" Adam gave her a startled look. "Laura Macallan? No, I didn't. But she's a reporter, right? I think she's been put on the arson cases, so it wouldn't be unusual for her to be talking to a firefighter."

"You're right," Màiri said. "I'm probably imagining things, but it seemed personal."

"Would that it were true!" Adam gave a short laugh. "Then maybe she'd leave me alone."

Màiri didn't answer. There had to be a clue here, something they were missing.

Mackie...Peter...Laura. There was something odd about all of them.

Something there...or something not there that should be, she thought. The thought danced away, just out of reach, and finally she gave it up. *It'll come, if it's important.*

CHAPTER 37
GLEN COE, SCOTLAND – PRESENT TIME

There was a place inside me carved out for him; I didn't want it to be there, but it was.
—Elizabeth Berg

Maybe they wouldn't come tonight. The weather was dreich; the kind of wet, cold misery that sinks into your bones and leaves you shaking. Fog clung to the leaves of the trees like grey wraiths and wrapped itself around their trunks. The last drops of rain dripped from the branches and made dark puddles in the path. The wind was rising, pushing the tendrils of fog to and fro as if they were alive.

After that first time, Cory had sworn never to return. He could still see the hammer in the reaper's hand, hear the weeds moving as the man got closer and closer to his hiding place. He could imagine the feral glint in the monster's eyes, the enjoyment at what he had just done and what he was going to do.

The cat had saved him. Its yellow eyes hung in his memories too, but unlike the vicious joy he imagined in the killer's eyes—a look that pierced into his soul and drained the will out of him—the cat's eyes were golden orbs of light, wise and benevolent. The more he thought about it, it really did remind him of Biscuit, the bookshop cat.

It had known what it was doing, he was sure of it. The cat had been there all along but only moved when the killer started toward the tree behind which Cory stood, trapped and helpless. The animal's race across the path in front of the murderers had changed their focus and allowed him to escape.

He'd run until he reached the MacMillen property. He stood in the bushes looking through the front window at the flickering light cast from the television, where the back of his aunt's head just showed above the top of the couch.

Ruth MacMillen sat there every night watching those mindless reality shows parading across the screen. Uncle Ivor was probably at the pub and wouldn't come in till the wee hours of the morning, scunnered as a weasel. The two barely talked to each other, even when his uncle was home, unless it was a tandem tirade against Cory.

He couldn't face his aunt and uncle, or his friends. Not yet. Not after what he'd seen. *He's dead*, the Vicar had said, with no more feeling in his voice than if he were talking about the weather or shooing away a pesky midge.

I've witnessed a murder. The thought kept repeating in his numbed brain. *I've witnessed a murder.*

GLEN COE, SCOTLAND – PRESENT TIME

It wasn't his father lying there on the path. The dead man had been shorter, not really much taller than himself. A person, someone who had been alive and breathing just moments before, standing in the circle and chanting with all the others. The way he had just…collapsed, like a heap of broken parts, would haunt Cory's sleep forever.

He'd never be able to play at swords again, pretend to kill another human being. He'd never think it was grand fun to parry and stab and fake like he was dead. That was child's play, and Cory had left childhood behind in that clearing.

He'd gone to the small, never-used storage shed in the back of the MacMillen's property and lumped some tarpaulins together to form a bed. He stretched out in the dark and stared at the small hole in the roof of the pitiful dwelling and let the cold and damp of a Highlands summer night seep into his soul. He would never be warm. Maybe he'd never sleep through the night without shaking awake from a nightmare where he was being chased by a man with a metal hammer. Nothing in the world would ever be the same again.

The dead man wasn't his father, but his father was one of them. He didn't want to think his father would do that to someone, though. He was a coward; he'd run away and left his wife and son to die in that car long ago and never looked back. But he wouldn't kill someone or watch someone else do it.

You haven't seen him since you were six years old. How do you know what he's capable of? The thoughts swirled through Cory's brain, always coming back to one answer.

Because he's my father.

Sometime in the early morning, Cory sat up, bleary-eyed and shivering, and made a decision. The new Cory MacMillen—*no, Fraser*—needed to know. Why was his father with these people? Did they really worship fire, like they seemed to? Was his father evil, like the Vicar and the other one?

He remembered a man who laughed, told jokes, smiled a lot. A man who read to him at night, who held hands with his wife and carried his small son on his shoulders. Could a man like that really change so much? Was he really the coward a frightened six-year-old remembered? The need to know was burning a hole in his chest.

So he returned to the circle. He chose a different tree, further up the path, near the place where he and the other Musketeers—*how childish that seemed now*—had first seen the shuffling, chanting line of people. He was pretty sure he could outrun them if they discovered him, and he had the advantage of knowing where to go.

As long as you see them coming, a worried little voice whispered in the back of his mind. *As long as they don't have magic.*

They didn't have magic. He was 99 percent sure of that. They were just your normal, everyday *balaich seòlta*, as his gran used to say. Crazier than bedbugs.

Balaich seòlta who chanted and worshipped fire and killed people. That was all. He could feel his heart clenching at the thought of seeing them again.

So he waited, and when they didn't come, he went back to the storage shed at the edge of the

GLEN COE, SCOTLAND – PRESENT TIME

MacMillens' garden and shivered himself to sleep.

The next night he was back again, and the next. Maybe they had changed their location, found another clearing in which to build their fire. Maybe the act of murder had frightened them, and they'd stopped their strange ritual.

His memory conjured the calm, reasonable tone of the murderer when he said, *He's dead.* No, a man like that wouldn't be frightened by anything. But no matter how little he and the Vicar cared about human life, they had to be cautious, right? They wouldn't want to get caught. Right?

Maybe they wouldn't come.

Then a noise came out of the night. It blended into the soundscape of sighs and whimpers, growing louder. A rhythmic, pulsing moan that could not be a part of nature.

They were coming.

Cory could hear his heart pounding like the drums in his school's pipe band, but after a while it slowed, and his breathing returned to something closer to normal. This was his choice. And it was his last chance.

He couldn't keep going on like this, hiding in the woodshed behind his own house and sneaking in when the MacMillens were out to steal whatever food he could carry. He'd give it this one last night, and then he'd go find Bastian and Donnie. After that, he didn't know what they could do. His friends would believe him, but kids had no power.

Still...

He counted them as they went past. Twelve. Maybe the reapers didn't know that one of their group had been murdered. Or maybe they didn't care. A chill worked its way up Cory's spine and settled in his chest with the cold that had become a part of his existence.

They had trouble lighting the fire tonight; the wood was wet. But eventually the flames rose, shooting sparks into the night air. They stood silently, staring into the fire.

The Vicar spoke. "We have been betrayed," he said in English. "By one of our own." His hood moved from side to side as he scanned the group standing at attention before the fire. "He has been punished, cleansed by the fire that protects us all. There will be nothing more said about him."

The others nodded like robots, and Cory wondered if maybe they were on something. His uncle sometimes looked like that. If Uncle Ivor didn't go out to the bar, he smoked skunk before he turned on the telly and then spent hours staring at the box like a zombie. Sort of like the way these guys stared at their fire.

Cory didn't do drugs, and neither did Bastian and Donnie. Drugs were for losers. But he knew there were lots of things out there that could change people, turn them into someone else. The teachers at school droned on and on about the dangers of illicit substances, unaware that some of the kids in their classes could probably give the lesson better than they did. Drugs would explain a lot about this bunch of nutters.

He felt a presence at his side and stifled a yelp. The cat was standing next to him. The animal's golden eyes stared back at him, unblinking. It really did look like the bookshop cat, but probably all black cats looked pretty much alike. It didn't matter. The presence of the animal grounded him, made him feel less alone in the world.

When it had showed up that first time, he'd worried that maybe it had rabies. Cats didn't get that close to strangers usually. But then it had saved his life, and everything changed. He reached out slowly and placed his hand on the cat's head, and when it didn't move, he scratched behind its ears, feeling suddenly warmer than he had in a long time.

The Vicar switched into Gaelic, and the circle parroted his words while the fire crackled. The ritual hadn't changed, except for that part about somebody being 'punished.' Cory shivered again at the callous cruelty. There was no compassion in these men, and if he was discovered, he knew exactly what they'd do to him.

He eased back into the trees and tried to think. "What should I do?" he whispered to the cat. Its answer was to lift its tail high in the air and saunter away from the light cast by the fire, as if to say, 'Are ye daft? Run!'

Biscuit, if it *was* Biscuit, was right. He was never going to find his father by hiding in the bushes and watching. He was going to get himself coshed, just like that other man. "Thanks," he whispered into the empty woods where the cat had disappeared. "Wait for me. I'm coming."

He turned and made his way deeper into the trees, grateful that the floor at the base of the mountain was carpeted with evergreen needles that muffled sound. He walked faster as he got further away from the clearing with its ravenous fire that sucked the sanity out of men and spit it out as angry sparks.

He could hear Donnie saying, *There are lots of jobs that help people. Why does it have to be a firefighter?*

Because of my mom, he had said. And that was still true. But it wasn't just because of his mom, and it wasn't only a need to help people anymore. Cory thought of what Bastian had said: *Why are you so obsessed with fire?*

It wasn't him. Those people standing around the fire pit watching the fire climb higher and higher... they were the ones who were obsessed. A *'glanadh teine,'* they had chanted. *Belenus* sounded like a person's name. Tomorrow he was going to quit hiding, go to the bookstore, and look up those words. That Miss MacLachlan might help. Maybe she could be a trusted adult.

Lost in his thoughts, he almost missed the rustling of shrubbery behind him. He froze and listened. Something was coming, following the way he had taken. Something too large to be a cat. Sticks crackled under its feet, as if the creature had no concern for stealth. It had to be one of the reapers; no one else was out here. And it was coming after him.

Cory turned and ran for his life, his heart pounding a rhythm to his flying footsteps. Now he could hear more branches crackling further back toward the clearing. They knew he was here! They were coming after him, and this time no cat would stop them. Sobbing and gasping, he redoubled his efforts.

He almost made it. He could see the opening in the trees that led to the bottom of the glen. Just

GLEN COE, SCOTLAND – PRESENT TIME

a few more feet... And then a root reached up and grabbed his foot, and he fell headlong onto a heather bush, scraping his hands on the sharp branches.

An arm snaked around his waist and a hand covered his mouth as someone crashed into him and pulled him off the bush. Together they rolled over and over until they were wedged up against a rock, far off the path.

Strong arms rolled Cory over and he found himself looking into a pair of blue eyes. The man's black hood had fallen back from his head, and bright red hair straggled across his forehead. He had one finger held to his lips, and his other hand pressed against Cory's mouth to keep him silent.

Footsteps sounded in the brush off to their left, one pair, two, three. They went on down into the glen, and after a few minutes they returned the way they had come and the sounds diminished as they backtracked toward the clearing and the fire.

"Can I trust you not to call out?" said the man.

The voice was the same. He'd heard it every day until he was six years old. A tear ran down his face to mix with the snot and dirt.

He nodded, and the man took his hand away from Cory's mouth.

"D-dad?"

"Son," said Benedict Fraser.

CHAPTER 38
FORT WILLIAM, SCOTLAND – PRESENT TIME

An unrequited love is so much better than a real one...as long as something is never even started, you never have to worry about it ending. It has endless potential.
—Sarah Dessen

"Màiri, ye have visitors." Mary's face was creased in disapproval.

"Visitors? Who?"

"Those firefighters." Mary sighed. "Take a wee break. They saved yer life, I reckon we should be hospit'ble. Hmmph."

"Really? I just saw them a few days ago." Màiri looked at the group in front of the desk and clapped her hand to her head. "Oh, I forgot. I invited them. Said I'd treat them."

She smiled at Mackie, Meg, and a man she vaguely remembered from her last visit to the fire station. Peter Campbell was missing. *Not surprising, really, but he always seems to be missing,* she thought. *Coincidence? Or is he avoiding me?*

Mackie gave her a shy smile. She grinned at him and turned back to her boss, who was glaring in their general direction. Standing with her feet planted apart, hands on her hips and arms akimbo, Mary looked as if she were auditioning for the role of Superman. A small, grumpy Superman. All she needed was the cape.

"What're ye grinnin' aboot?" Mary said crossly. "Git."

Màiri pursed her lips in an effort not to laugh. Mary was very definite about those she liked and those she didn't have time for. Apparently it didn't matter if you were a lifesaver or not; her judgements were based on some inner sense that no one understood but her.

Mary liked Adam. A warm feeling spread through her. It was important, for some reason. She liked Myles, too, and Adam's work partner, Jared. She seemed to at least tolerate that fire investigator.

She had made her feelings about Laura Macallan abundantly clear. Màiri grinned. *I don't like her either. She's a twit. A young, beautiful, snooty, wee twit.*

Laura had been in once or twice since that day she'd claimed Adam as her boyfriend. She'd wandered around, had a coffee, and stared at Màiri. She hadn't bought a single book.

Adam had vehemently rejected the idea of a romantic connection to her, even though he admitted he'd dated her a few times. Màiri wanted to believe him, but men were notoriously susceptible to a pretty face.

FORT WILLIAM, SCOTLAND – PRESENT TIME

And how would you know what men are like? The voice was back.

I watch the telly, she told it crossly. *I read books. I date. Sometimes.*

She pulled herself out of her own head and walked over to the group at the desk.

"Welcome to HP Booksellers!" she said. "I'm so glad you took me up on my invitation. Follow me." She led the way to the cafe and asked Bernard to pull two of the tables together. Chairs were shuffled and everyone seated, with Mackie beside her and Meg directly across, next to the man whose name she'd forgotten. Orders were taken and Bernard disappeared behind the counter.

"How is it you're all off duty today?" she asked. "I mean, I'm glad to see you, but…"

"We're not off duty," said Meg. "That's why only a few of us could come." She pulled her mobile out of her pocket. "We're tied to these. If a fire breaks out, we'll have to leave mid-scone and join the others there."

"Which seems likely, given the recent rash of fires," said the man next to Meg.

Bernard came over with their orders, and for a few minute conversation gave way to the enjoyment of HP Sweets' generous scones.

Then Meg resumed, her brows creased. "You're too right, Simon," she said. "I love my job, but I wish they'd catch the lad who's starting these fires before someone else gets hurt." There was a general mumble of agreement.

Màiri glanced at Mackie. He was staring at the tabletop, and his large hands were wrapped tightly around his mug. He looked uncomfortable, as if embarrassed by something. He caught her glance, blushed, and looked away again.

Màiri put a hand on his arm. "Are you all right?" she asked him under her breath.

"Um, uh...aye. Only...I wondered...um...never mind."

How can a man this shy have chosen such a dangerous occupation? she wondered. But then, it took a different skill set to interact socially than to fight a fire. He was probably just an introvert. She gave him an encouraging smile and was rewarded with a smile that transformed his face.

Now that she looked more closely, she could see that Mackie wasn't as young as she'd originally thought. There were lines under his grey eyes which spoke of more years than she'd noticed at first glance. He might be closer to her own age.

"Um," he began again. She nodded, hoping that 'Um' wasn't his preferred mode of conversation. She waited.

"Uh, I was hoping to talk with you about something. Um...without the others," he mumbled, and then pursed his lips and studied the tabletop again.

Màiri felt a small thrill of anticipation. Was Mackie going to tell her something more about the museum fire? Like where Peter Campbell had been?

She spied Eve across the shop and stood up. "Mackie, I want to introduce you to the other girl you saved. She's...um..." — *Oh Lord, I'm turning into him!* — "She's been asking me about the man who rescued us, and I know she'd love to meet you." She

FORT WILLIAM, SCOTLAND – PRESENT TIME

looked at the others. "Do you mind if I steal him for a few minutes? We'll be right back."

"Oh, by all means, take our local hero away," said the man called Simon. "He belongs to the world." The others laughed.

Mackie flushed and started to follow Màiri out of the cafe. Then he turned and gave his colleague the universal gesture of disrespect, and Simon laughed.

Màiri led him to the children's corner. "This is the only place where we can be undisturbed at this hour of the day," she said. "The kids are all in school, so it's quiet." She looked around. "I'm sorry, do you mind sitting in a beanbag chair?"

Mackie laughed and folded his tall frame into the squishy chair. Màiri pulled over another beanbag and sat down across from him.

"Now," she said, "what do you need to tell me?"

"Um...well..." His face coloured.

"Was it something about the fire?" Màiri said helpfully.

"The fire?" He gave her a confused look.

"The museum fire? Did you remember something else about it?"

"Oh." He looked surprised. "No. Not about that." He fingered a fold in his trousers nervously. Màiri waited.

"I was...I was wondering..." he began again. "I was wondering..." He took a deep breath. "If you would like to go on a date with me sometime?" he said, the words seemingly propelled by some sort of desperate need to get them out.

"A-a date?" Màiri said. Never in a thousand years

had she thought this was what he'd wanted to say. Now what was she supposed to do? She'd gotten herself stuck in the children's corner with a potential suitor, with no idea how to handle this. She stared at the seam of the beanbag.

"I-I...um..." — *Oh, Lord. This is getting worse.* — "I'm actually seeing someone now," she said.

She looked up to see Mackie's reaction and realized he wasn't paying attention. He was staring at Biscuit, almost invisible atop a dark wooden shelf in the corner. The cat was nearly motionless except for her tail, which swished slowly back and forth along the shelf, and her golden eyes, brilliant in the dim corner lighting.

"She's harmless, unless you try to pet her." Màiri offered the standard caveat on coexisting with the bookshop cat. "The rule is, she'll decide if you're worthy; we lesser humans must wait."

Mackie didn't seem to be listening. His eyes were wide, and he and Biscuit seemed engaged in a staring contest. Her brain supplied the word she wanted. *Ailurophobia*—fear of cats. It didn't seem possible that a man who put his life on the line every time he entered a burning building could be traumatized by a small black cat, but phobias were weird.

A familiar snuffling noise intruded on the awkward silence and Màiri looked up in relief to see Pearl lumbering into the alcove. He ignored the humans and headed for the corner to meet his cat.

Biscuit leapt gracefully off the shelf and sauntered over to give the dog a gentle swat on his nose, and then she moved to where Adam stood in the archway and rubbed up against his trouser legs. He reached down to scratch the cat behind her ears and she leaned into his hand, purring loudly. Then she led Pearl out of the alcove, leaving behind three awkward humans. Màiri and Mackie extricated themselves from the beanbag chairs and stood up.

The alcove seemed suddenly crowded. A flush coloured Màiri's face as she thought of the half-lie she'd told Mackie. *I'm actually seeing someone now.* Well, she was. She was looking right at him.

Mackie's mobile rang and he pulled it out and scanned the display. "I'm sorry, we have a call." He looked at Màiri and smiled. "I'll be in touch, aye?" And he was gone, hurrying to join Meg and the others who were already headed to the front door.

"Why will he be in touch?" Adam asked. His brows were furrowed, and he wore a frown reminiscent of that first time, when she'd refused to acknowledge her role in saving him. The sulky child was back.

Jealousy was an ugly thing. It pulled the worst of human emotions out of a person and made him do and say ridiculous things. So why did she feel so happy?

He was staring at her, waiting for an answer, so she decided to give him what he wanted.

"He asked me out on a date."

"And what did you say?"

"I said I'm seeing someone."

"What? Who?" Maybe it was the moss-coloured jumper he was wearing, but his eyes seemed to have taken on a tinge of green.

"You." There. It was out. *Take it or leave it.*

Adam's eyebrows raised and then drew together, and he frowned. The bookshop was suddenly very quiet.

"Why would you tell him something like that?" he said, after a moment.

She'd expected surprise, hoped for a smile, wanted verification. Not this. She wanted to crawl under the beanbag chair to hide her mortification.

"I thought..."

"Màiri...I'm sorry. I like you. I really do. But...I can't be with you. I—"

"Stop it." Màiri knew her face was red; she could feel the heat moving up from her neck. "I get it; you don't have to explain, damn it." She looked down at her feet, willing them to move. "I have to get back to work." She pushed past him and made for the front of the shop, keeping her spine straight and her shoulders back.

"Can I use the office for a minute?" she asked Mary. "Just a minute. Please."

Her boss gave her a sympathetic look. "Of course. Take all the time you need."

Màiri closed the door and sank into the leather chair behind the desk. She took a long, shaking breath and put her flaming face in her arms. Her body felt bruised and tender, as if she'd taken a tumble down the side of a mountain.

She wasn't used to rejection. She hadn't experienced much of it, and when it did happen, she moved on quickly. She'd never cared about any of them enough for it to matter.

But this—this was awful. It felt like a searing burn

FORT WILLIAM, SCOTLAND – PRESENT TIME

in her soul, like acid working its way down into her stomach. She sat still and let the misery sink in.

When she finally dared to poke her head into the shop, Adam was gone.

"Gie on home, lass," Mary said. "We're closin' soon, anyway." She patted Màiri's hand and looked at her out of wise little bird eyes. "It'll be awright." She walked her to the door and held out a brown paper package. "Somethin' t' read."

"Oh." Màiri looked into the dark eyes and read the compassion in them. Somehow she knew that if Mary said so, it *would* be all right. It didn't help the ache in her heart, but the words seemed somehow like magic, full of hope.

When had the Duncans and their crew become so important to her? She paused with her hand on the knob and looked around the shop as if seeing it for the first time. "Mary?"

"Aye, lass?"

"What does HP stand for?"

Mary Duncan cocked her head. "Highland Players, o' course."

"Seems an odd name for a bookshop."

Mary smiled. "Well, tis not allus a bookshop, lass." And she turned her back and disappeared into the office.

When she reached home, Màiri tossed the unopened package on the side table, poured a glass of wine, and threw herself into her reading chair.

She hadn't known how she felt, not really. Not until Adam had said those words.

But I can't be with you. Stupid words. Hurtful words. They didn't even make sense. He said he liked her. If you liked someone, why couldn't you be with them? Was it because of Laura?

She glanced at the side table, at the package Mary had given her. Desperate to lose herself in something, anything, she reached for it and tore off the wrapping.

The familiar odour of smoke found its way to Màiri's nostrils, and the title danced off the cover in its Celtic script. *The Witch's Daughter*.

It was just a book. It shouldn't have filled her with revulsion like it did. But her senses weren't in working order right now, and she needed a distraction.

She began to read.

CHAPTER 39
DORNACH, SCOTLAND – 1727

HUGH

Hugh woke to a relentless pounding, as if all the demons of Hell were dancing in his head. He kept his eyes closed and tried to remember, but the images refused to condense into something reasonable. They reached toward him and then fractured and fell away, leaving frustration and a growing panic in their place.

A woman, hands bound in front of her. Another, old and frail, also bound. Hands, lifting him. Swaying, as if he were on a ship. Nausea.

Hugh rolled to the edge of the bed and vomited on the floor. The swaying stopped, and he lay back against the headboard. Footsteps sounded, and then a door opened to admit three people. A man and two women. Ignoring the women, he focused on the man. There was something about him...

"You're awake. Good." There was satisfaction in the man's brusque voice. He approached the bed and stopped short, regarding the floor with disgust.

"Aulay!"

An elderly man in a tan homespun shirt and brown woollen trews scuttled into the room. He sidled up to within a yard of the bed and stopped, hands clasped in front of him. "Aye, sir?"

"Git a mop an' clean this mess up!"

The old man bobbed his head and hurried out the door.

Hugh transferred his attention to the two women. The older one—a pasty-faced lady with faded blond hair and watery brown eyes—was holding a handkerchief to her nose and glaring at him as if he'd thrown up on purpose. The younger one was crying, loud hiccupping sobs that threatened to tear his skull open again. He pushed himself to the edge of the bed again and the three stepped back just as he heaved up what little he had left in his stomach.

"Achh!" The man looming over the bed gave a harsh bark. "Ladies, please go out t' th' sitting room while we get 'im cleaned up, aye?" The two women backed out, looking relieved.

The old man returned with a mop and bucket and set about cleaning the mess Hugh had made. Obviously a servant, which meant the other one was... He wracked his brain, but nothing came.

The man stood staring down at him. It gave Hugh a creepy feeling, as if he were a bug and a decision

DORNACH, SCOTLAND – 1727

was being considered as to the means of dispatching him. He closed his eyes against the dark gaze.

"How're ye feeling?" the man said, finally.

"Wh-wha happened?" Hugh's voice was a croak. His throat hurt from vomiting, and every word was torture. He cracked his eyes open against the light that peeked around the edges of the curtains.

"Ye were attacked." Bitterness oozed from the man's voice. "By that vile witch. Ye've been unconscious for on two days."

Hugh focused on some of the words. "A w-witch?" Even in his muddled state it didn't make sense. He looked around the room, trying to think.

He'd obviously been brought to a home owned by someone of means. Damask curtains hung to the floor, covering large windows with polished wood frames. The wall opposite the bed was lined with wooden shelves filled with leather-bound tomes, protected behind glass. To his left was a grey sandstone fireplace with a blazing fire. Despite the weak light trying to force its way around the heavy curtains, the room was dark and the air stifling. None of it was familiar.

Why had someone hit him? Where was this place? And who was this stern gentleman next to the bed? Hugh struggled to a half-sitting position.

"Wh-where am I?" he managed.

The man's face froze and his eyes narrowed.

"Yer at home, son. In yer own room."

Hugh looked around again. *His own room? How was that possible? He'd never been here before.* Then it hit him, what the man had said. *Son.* Was it just a general term of address? It had to be, because he was sure he'd never seen this man before.

A sharp pain arced through his skull and he grabbed his head with both hands. The other man stood still, watching him.

Hugh looked up and tried to focus. He worked to form the words of his next question, sensing that his future might depend on the answer.

"Who…are you, s-sir?"

The man lunged forward and grabbed him by the shoulders. "Stop it, Hugh!" he said. "I ken ye're not happy with me at th' moment, but dinnae ye dare mess with yer father! Ye nearly died!" He released his grip and stepped back as if afraid he'd do something rash if he stayed too close.

My name is Hugh? Why don't I know that? Why can't I remember?

Hugh closed his eyes against the fury in the man's face and lay back against the pillows again. He let the words he'd been told filter into his broken brain and sit there like the detritus on the surface of a swamp.

His name was Hugh. This man was his father. This room was his. The two women were people he was supposed to know. He'd been attacked…by a witch.

He couldn't remember anything, but that last was beyond ridiculous. He put his hand up and felt around for the area from which the dull throbbing was coming. There was a thick bandage wrapped around his head and a raised place in the back that hurt when he pressed it.

He *had* been hit on the head. So, the rest of it must be true as well. He opened his eyes again. The

DORNACH, SCOTLAND – 1727

man who had called himself 'father' was studying him. Hugh took a deep breath and forced words out.

"Who are those women?" he asked. "The ones who were in here?"

The dark eyes narrowed to slits. "If ye're havin' me on, I swear…" His eyes roved over Hugh's face, and then he turned on his heel and left the room. He returned a few moments later with the two women who had been in the room previously and gestured for them to stand next to the bed, taking a place at the foot so he could watch.

Hugh looked at the younger woman closely for the first time. She'd stopped crying. Her brown eyes were huge in her pale face and she was biting her lip. Pretty, he supposed, but not to his liking.

And how do you know that? he thought.

"This is Ailis MacAllan, son. Your fiancée. Ye're t' be married in April." There was a smug tone in the voice of the man who called himself Father.

"No!" he rasped. *T'isn't right! I would ken somethin' like that, wouldn't I?* Hugh was seized by an unreasoning panic, and he pushed himself back into the pillows. The girl's face puckered and her lip quivered.

The older woman was staring at him with horror. She pulled at the girl's arm and urged her toward the door.

"Let us go home an' let th' lad rest, Ailis," she muttered. "Ye have time t' sort everythin' oot before th' weddin, aye?" Her eyes darted to Hugh's and away again. "I'm verra glad ye're better, Hugh."

The girl called Ailis gave him a fearful look as she was pulled away. The door closed behind them and

WITCH

he was left with the oppressive silence that surrounded the man like a cloud.

"Sir," he asked shyly, "what's our surname?"

"Sutherland." The words were gritted out between clenched teeth. The man pulled an ornate timepiece out of his jacket pocket and grimaced. "Get some rest, son. I have a trial t' oversee." He shoved the watch back into his pocket and strode to the door and out.

Hugh lay back and stared at the ceiling. Fear sliced through him, and he clenched the covers with both fists to keep himself from screaming. Nothing he had heard or seen since he woke up felt the least bit familiar. His memory was a yawning abyss, and he was dependent for everything on what others told him.

Giving in to the fear wasn't helping. He relaxed his hands and closed his eyes. If he lay very still and didn't force things, maybe the memories would come. The thoughts drifted through his mind like clouds over the firth.

The firth. There was a firth. He could smell it, hear the waves crashing faintly and the raucous cry of seabirds. Images came and went, bringing bits of the puzzle closer and then scattering them again. *The firth. A girl sitting on the rocks. Black curls flying in the wind, eyes the colour of a summer sky.* He let himself sink into those eyes and slept.

Sìne.

Hugh sat straight up on the bed. The girl was named Sìne. He had no idea how long he'd slept, but the light beyond the window had dimmed. He pushed himself into a sitting position on the bed,

DORNACH, SCOTLAND – 1727

fighting down a fresh wave of nausea, and eased his legs over the edge. Then he just sat, feet flat on the floor, letting the air go in and out of his lungs. And the memories came.

It was as if the seawall had broken and the tide was flooding in, sweeping away everything in its path.

Sìne. The woman he would battle the whole village of Dornach for, if he needed to. His beloved.

Other memories came. That girl, Ailis. His father, telling him he had no choice. Why? It was almost there, the memory dancing away, teasing him.

What had his father said? *I have a trial t' oversee.*

Ye were attacked. By a witch.

Other words rushed in. *Ye're never t' see that creature again, ye hear? Satan is not welcome in Dornach.*

Hugh struggled to his feet, grabbing the bedframe to keep himself from falling. He had to find her—find Sìne—before it was too late. He made his way to the door and out and began to run, heedless of the fact that he was dressed only in a woollen nightshirt that flapped around his knees.

The village was curiously empty. Where was everyone? Hugh ran as fast as he could on legs that felt like a bairn's. He fell twice, regained his feet, and kept going. He had to find her.

I have a trial t' oversee.

A witch.

CHAPTER 40
DORNACH, SCOTLAND – 1727

SÌNE

Sìne sat in the rickety chair into which they had thrust her with rough, careless hands, and looked out over the mass of people in the town hall of Dornach Village. Those who arrived early had managed to grab chairs; the latecomers lounged against the walls or stood uncomfortably, shifting from foot to foot to maintain their balance while being jostled by the others in the overcrowded room. They pushed and pinched and growled like wild animals, all intent on getting the best view of Dornach's witches.

They weren't animals, though. They were her neighbours, people she'd known all her life. There was Bearnas Graham, the costermonger, her eyes flashing delight at the chaos. Mary MacGregor, their neighbour two doors down, whispering to the

WITCH

woman next to her. Was there anyone here she hadn't said hello to in the market? Anyone untouched by Doirin's healing hands?

Of course, the MacKay family had secured seats right in front. Walter sat beside his mother, both of them wearing identical narrow-eyed looks of triumph. Walter's brother Ronain sat next to him, grey eyes set in an expressionless mask. Their father Alpin looked bored, as if a witch trial was something he saw every day.

Sìne forced her gaze away from the MacKays and searched for a face that might hold a hint of pity. There—there was Aoife Campbell, her eight children ranged on the floor at her feet while she held her six-month-old baby daughter, Ruth. If anyone should be on their side, it would be Aoife. She and her bairn wouldn't even be here if it weren't for Sìne. As she watched, Aoife's eyes met hers for the briefest second and then slid away. She bent over her bairn, fussing with the child's wrapping. Sìne sighed.

Ugh. There was that odious Archie Ross and his mother, both of them with smirks on their faces. Sìne pulled her eyes away from them and stiffened in her chair. Sitting next to Mistress Ross was her husband, Alasdair. His gentle brown eyes met hers and he gave her a sympathetic nod. Here was someone who would speak for her...if he hadn't been dead five years on.

Alasdair wasn't the only ghost in the room. Little Hector Cumming was perched on the edge of a table in the back, next to Eilidh Gordon, who had died of consumption only last year. Eilidh held her stillborn bairn tenderly in her arms and crooned to it, rocking gently back and forth. She looked up and met Sìne's eyes and a sad smile broke out on her pale face.

Sìne's throat closed as she spotted two familiar figures standing in the shadows near the door. Mungo Murray stood with his arms wrapped around Maghread Arthur, whose pudgy hands were fisted at her sides. Fury sparked in the old woman's faded blue eyes and tears streamed down her wrinkled cheeks as she stared at Doirin and Sìne.

If th' others could see the look on Gran's face, they'd be runnin' away like the cowards they are, Sìne thought. She lifted her chin and forced a smile for the old couple who had been her closest family, grateful for the support even if it came from spirits who could do nothing to help.

She glanced sideways at her mother sitting hunched over in her chair. Did she understand what was happening? Doirin's grey hair straggled over her shoulders and there were rents in her filthy gown that spoke of rough handling. The two women had been separated since their arrest two days ago, and Sìne prayed her mother didn't understand any of it. She pulled her eyes away from the pitiful figure and looked out over the room again.

The Grant family stood way in the back. Finola was holding tightly to the hand of five-year-old Askill, who was squirming and trying to wrench free to join the other children running around the hall as if they were at a ceilidh. Finola's eyes met Sìne's and she looked away.

Next to Finola, her eldest son Artur leaned against the wall, scribbling in his journal as usual. Sìne hardly

WITCH

knew Alan's older brother, but he seemed always to be writing in that book, as if the doings of Dornach village were the most important thing in the world. *Well,* she thought bitterly, *he finally had something worthy of his penmanship today. He must be very happy.*

Next to him stood Alan, who had told her only last week that she was beautiful and he thought he might be in love with her. He kept his blond head down and would not look at her—the coward. She didn't care. He wasn't the man that mattered. That one wasn't here. His betrayal had crushed her heart and left it in shards that pierced when she thought of him. Still, she worried. Was he all right?

A hush fell over the room. Sìne turned her head as far as she could to see behind her, and wished she hadn't. Her eyes met those of Dornach's sheriff, Duncan Sutherland, and her heart fell at the naked loathing in them. Hugh's father was dressed in his court robes, all black except for a large, ornate silver cross on the collar. Next to him stood Doctor Albert Wilson, the magistrate from Edinburgh. He was dressed in black, too—the colour of his soul.

"All rise!" Sutherland's voice rang out, and the people not already standing rose obediently. Sìne struggled to her feet. One of the bailiffs who stood on either side gripped her arms and spun her around to face the sheriff. She stood as still as possible, swaying from sudden dizziness. When had she last eaten? She wished now she'd forced down the disgusting gruel they'd served her that morning.

She stole a glance to see how her mother was faring and her heart plummeted. Doirin still sat in

DORNACH, SCOTLAND – 1727

her chair, head bowed. She seemed unaware of her surroundings.

Maybe tis better.

"Get th' witch up!" Sutherland's outraged bellow rang through the hall, and the bailiffs on either side of Doirin jumped. Each put a hand under her arms and yanked her to her feet with a viciousness that made Sìne gasp.

They've already condemned us, she thought. *They're callin' mam a witch b'fore th' trial even begins!* She could feel the perspiration run down her back. This was her village, the only home she had ever known, and it had turned against her. Maybe it had always been that way. She closed her eyes against the malice of the men who would determine her fate, but the image still remained, carved into the backs of her eyelids. *Why? Why do they hate us so?*

"This...*creature*..."— Sutherland pointed at Doirin, who smiled sweetly back at him — "has befouled th' good Village o' Dornach, but rest ye well, her time is over!"

There were cheers from the front row, where Walter MacKay's family sat. Sìne heard a roaring like thunder over the firth during a winter storm. She wanted to put her hands to her ears to shut out the awful words, but her wrists were shackled in front of her and the men on either side had a firm grip on her arms.

"As your sheriff, an' your friend,"— Sutherland smiled benevolently out at the villagers — "tis my sworn duty t' see t' th' spiritual safety o' our village, aye?"

"Aye!" The response rang out from several places in the hall. Sutherland held a hand up to quiet the crowd.

"In order t' see that done," he continued, "I brought th' good doctor here..." he pointed to Albert Wilson — "t' help root out th' evil that was takin' root in Dornach...an' that he has done!" Again he held up a hand to quell the cheers.

"This woman," he spat, "was a harlot when she came t' us. She fooled our dear Maighread Arthur," — he cast his eyes to Heaven — "may her soul rest 'n His glory, for she was a guid woman."

How dare ye! Sine's mind screamed. *How dare ye make a mockery o' Gran, th' kindest soul on earth?* She looked for the figures at the back of the room, but the ghosts were gone.

Sutherland was looking straight at her, as if reading her thoughts. Sine forced her face into a mask of indifference, lest her expression incense the madman more.

"I kent th' truth," Sutherland's voice rang out, "when she gave birth t' an abomination!" He pointed a finger and nodded, and the men forced Sine's hands high in the air so that all could see the fused fingers.

"Th' bairns had th' right of it, when th' rest of us were blinded by pity." He shook his head sorrowfully. "Many o' ye will remember that my own son was corrupted by th' witch's spawn, an' I punished 'im for it, though 't broke my heart." He placed a hand over his heart. "But Satan is clever. He made th' wench comely an' set her t' seduce th' lad awa from 'is own father."

DORNACH, SCOTLAND – 1727

Sìne stared at the monster with horrified fascination. Sutherland was still looking at her, his face now a mask of utmost pity.

"Tis maybe not all th' puir lass's fault," he said.

Oh, s' now I'm a puir lass? A minute ago I was an abomination. Sìne wished she did have the powers he'd attributed to her. She wanted to leap onto the bench behind which Sutherland stood, his dark eyes glinting with satisfied malice, and strangle him with her bare hands.

But she was just a lass. A *puir lass*, with deformed fingers and a mother who had lost her mind. There was nothing she could do against this evil man and his power.

How did Hugh survive? she thought, despite her resolve to never think of him again. *How did he live with this man?*

"Tis not th' lass's fault," Sutherland said again, and now he was looking at Doirin.

Sìne felt cold slither down her spine like a snake. *No! Leave mam be! Please!*

"Th' lass didnae ask t' be born a monster," the sheriff said. "She was made t' be th' witch's plaything. Born t' be ridden like a pony for th' Devil's pleasure!"

There were gasps from the captivated audience. Doirin's head came up, and she seemed to notice the people in the room for the first time. A beautiful smile broke out on her wrinkled face and she giggled and clapped her hands.

"A pony!" she said, her voice loud in the shocked silence. "How nice. A pony!" She turned to Sìne. "Would ye like t' ride a pony, love?"

CHAPTER 41
BALLACHULISH AND FORT WILLIAM, SCOTLAND – PRESENT TIME

Curses and blessings look so much alike, one has got to have a sharp soul to tell the difference.
—Sherihan Gamal

It was going to rain...of course. Adam pulled his rain jacket out of his backpack and shrugged his arms into it. *Bring it on*, he thought crossly. The weather matched his mood.

The look on her face yesterday! As if he'd slapped her. She'd probably never speak to him again.

A loud snuffle broke into his thoughts. "I'm sorry, lad," Adam said to Pearl. They were out for their morning walk around the block and he'd forgotten to match his pace to the bulldog's. Pearl gave him a sorrowful look and sat down on the pavement, tongue lolling.

Adam knelt and scratched the dog under his chin. "I don't think we'll be visiting the bookshop much anymore. Maybe Daniel can take you to visit Biscuit when he goes in to pick up Eve." The bulldog's eyes drooped. "Cheer up, lad," Adam assured him. "It could be worse." *How could it be worse?*

He straightened and began walking again, slowing his steps to accommodate Pearl's lumbering gait. They hadn't gone ten yards when the first drops of rain hit the sidewalk. Adam pulled up the hood of his jacket and kept going. Right now he felt like getting wet, and Pearl liked rain.

A pair of arms went around him. Startled and annoyed, he spun out of Laura Macallan's grip and stood facing her.

"Don't *do* that! You scared the shite out of me!"

Her mouth rounded into an O. "I'm sorry. Are you all right?"

Adam took a deep breath and blew it through his nose. "I'm fine. Please stop asking."

Her lips curved downward in the customary pout. "Why? I worry about you, especially after..." She slid closer and tried to take his hand, but Adam forestalled the gesture.

"Laura..." It was time. She had no idea that this was the worst possible moment for her to show up. He'd thought she'd get the message if he was too busy when she called. *I mean, how many hints does it take to get the point across?* "We need to talk."

Her eyes lit and the pout disappeared like magic. "Okay, sure. Where?"

"Walk with me to the office."

She smiled and fell into step beside him, linking her arm with his and leaning into him. He sighed and let her. It wouldn't be for much longer, anyway. This

BALLACHULISH AND FORT WILLIAM, SCOTLAND – PRESENT TIME

conversation should have been had a long time ago.

As they walked, Adam glanced at Laura out of the corner of his eye. She was such a pretty girl, surely she had lots of lads scrambling to get close to her. Why him? He was five years older than her; they had nothing in common. He was a bore; he knew it. Yet she'd been trailing after him for five years. He didn't get it.

Màiri wouldn't act like that. She was more mature, level-headed, intuitive. She wouldn't chase him around like Laura did, waiting for something that would never happen.

No, she'd kick him to the kerb and forget about him, put him right out of her mind and move on. Like you were supposed to do when someone was unspeakably rude. He flinched at the memory of his last words to Màiri. He hadn't meant to be so harsh. The words had come from a place of anguish and desperation.

Depression filtered into his mind. As soon as he finished the business with Laura, he was going to make Jared go for a run with him so he could clear his mind. He'd rather be alone, but he couldn't. Not after the last time. He was never going to allow himself to be alone on the trail again. A small voice whispered in his mind, *Do you really care?*

No, he didn't. Not really. He was sick of waiting for the Curse to do its thing. Tired of pretending, evading...settling. What he was doing wasn't really living; it was just waiting for death.

You're better than that, he told himself.

He straightened his back. "I am," he said out loud.

"What?" Laura asked.

"Oh. Nothing. Never mind. Here we are." Adam unlocked and pushed open the door to Glencoe Mountain Mystery and turned on the overhead light.

Laura looked around. "I've never been here this early. Where are Jared and Daniel?"

"They'll be in soon. I like to get a look at the day's activities before we open."

"So," she said. A slow smile worked its way across her face and her voice was a purr. "We're alone, then? It's nice."

Adam ignored her and sat down at the small round table where he met clients, pointing to the chair across from him. Ignoring the gesture, Laura pulled the chair around to sit next to him so that their knees were nearly touching.

Adam pushed his chair further away.

"Laura," he said, and took a breath. "You need to stop."

"Stop what?" she said. Her brow furrowed and the pout returned.

"This. Calling me. Showing up here. Asking me out."

"But we're—"

"We're nothing, Laura, and we'll never be anything." The words were blunt, but Adam had a sense that they would have to be to get through to her. *And you've said worse, to someone who doesn't deserve it.*

Her eyes filled with tears. "You don't mean that," she said. She sniffed and a single tear worked its way down her cheek. "Did I do something wrong?"

Yes, he wanted to shout. *You did everything wrong!* He felt moisture gathering at the back of his own eyes. *You're not her!*

Laura's expression changed. Her brows drew

down and her brown eyes darkened. She pressed her lips together and fisted her hands on the table.

"Is it that woman?" she asked. "The old one in the awfy costume, in the bookshop?"

Was she reading his mind? Adam gaped at her. "W-what?"

"Is it her?" Laura demanded again.

"This isn't about her..."

"I knew it! It is about her! I don't believe this!" Laura stood "That bitch!" she muttered and paced an angry circle in the small office. Then she rounded on Adam. "How could you do this to me? You just met her! We've been together for five years; doesn't that mean anything to you?"

Adam stared at her. Red blotches had appeared on her cheeks and her nostrils flared with each angry breath. *She's pure radge*, he thought. A sliver of fear slid into his brain. *Is this my fault? Did I give her the idea...?*

He opened his mouth, but before he could say anything, Laura reached over the table and slapped him across the face. The shock was immediate and sobering. He stood up and pointed to the door.

"I think we're done here," he said, trying to keep his voice steady. "You should leave."

"This isn't the end," Laura said, her voice suddenly calm. She smiled. "I know it's not your fault." She patted him on the arm and walked to the door, her steps light on the tile floor. She turned, one hand on the knob. "You're just confused, Adam. It's probably from that accident on the trail. Don't worry. I'll take care of everything." The door slammed behind her so hard the glass panes rattled.

Adam stood staring after her. A low growl rumbled up from the floor, where Pearl was sitting up straight, watching.

"Aye, lad, you're right. I think I misunderstood her." He bent down and patted the dog's head. "She's off her head."

The door opened again and Jared came in, followed by Daniel and his equipment.

"What's up, kid?" Jared said. "You look like you've seen a ghost."

"Laura was here," Adam said.

"Nothing new there," Daniel muttered. "Don't you think it's time you settled things with her?"

Adam sat down and put his head in his hands. "I did. Didn't work out well." He looked up to see Jared eyeing him narrowly.

"What happened?" his partner said.

Adam ran through the altercation. "She was too calm. She was raging at first, then it was almost like she turned into a different person. She blamed it all on Màiri." He looked at Pearl. "Pearl felt it too. Don't dogs sense things better than humans?"

Jared was quiet for a minute and then he said, his voice tentative, "I know you don't want to start anything with Màiri..."

"Too late." Adam's eyes were bleak. "Something *did* start, and I ruined it. You know why, so leave it, aye?"

"That's not my point," Jared said. "What I'm getting at, if you'll listen, is that you might want to warn Màiri about Laura."

Daniel was nodding. "I'm with Jared. I always thought she was just annoying, but now I think it's

BALLACHULISH AND FORT WILLIAM, SCOTLAND – PRESENT TIME

maybe more. She's a stalker. She's been stalking you for five years, and if she thinks Màiri's in the way, well..."

Adam's brown eyes darkened with alarm. "You really think so?" He started to rise, then sank back into the chair.

"How am I supposed to do that now?" he moaned. "I broke things off with her. She probably won't even talk to me, and if she told Mary Duncan what I did, I don't give two pence for my survival if I walk back in there." He looked at Daniel hopefully. "Can't you tell her?"

"Nae," said Daniel, and eyed his brother with scorn. "Are you really that much of a coward? You remind me of me, back when I was drinking and living in a fog. Come on, Adam, you're better than that."

"I know. I'm just talking out my arse." Adam looked at his best friend and his brother. "It's not that I'm afraid—at least not of that. I'm afraid that if I see her again, I'll say something stupid."

"Like what?" Jared's voice was soft.

"Like I'm in love with her."

The silence in the room stretched for a full minute. Then Jared sighed and looked at the ceiling. "Ahh, I do love a good romance," he said.

"Shut up," Adam said, stung. "I'm serious."

"I know you are, kid. We both do. You're the meff here."

Adam glared at Jared. His friend stared back and there was no humour in the dark face. His liquid brown eyes were full of concern.

"I'm in love with her." His eyes implored them. "What am I going to do?"

Daniel gave a harsh laugh. "Do we have to tell you everything?" He stomped over to the worktable and began to fuss with his equipment.

Jared rounded the desk and sat down. He booted up the laptop and immersed himself in it, ignoring his partner.

Adam sat alone at the round table, staring at the whorls in the wooden top.

I'm in love with her. The realization of what that meant swept through him like a Highland storm, leaving a fresh new world in its wake.

It should have been frightening. It couldn't be, *they* couldn't be, but right now, in this moment, he didn't care. He leapt to his feet, grabbed his rain jacket, and ran out onto the pavement in front of the store. Before he could talk himself out of it, he was angling the car into a spot in the carpark at the end of the High Street in Fort William.

Biscuit met him at the front door of the bookshop and gave him a glare that clearly said, 'Did you forget someone?'

"Sorry, lass, I was in a hurry." He bent to pet the cat and she swatted his hand and sauntered away. *Not the best start*, he thought, and straightened to find himself staring into Mary Duncan's beady little eyes.

"Are ye here fer th' right reason, lad?" Her tone was ominous.

He nodded, and she jerked a thumb toward the office door behind her. "Gie in there. I'll get 'er."

Adam sat in the guest chair in front of the desk and stared across at the empty leather chair. He

BALLACHULISH AND FORT WILLIAM, SCOTLAND – PRESENT TIME

couldn't think. It was as if he had the worst head cold in living memory and cotton wool was muffling all the circuits to his brain.

The door opened and Màiri came in. She crossed to sit in the leather chair, clasped her hands together on top of the desk, and looked at him.

He could read nothing in her expression. She was a blank slate, waiting for him to write his message. He took a deep breath.

"I'm sorry," he began. She said nothing.

"What I said about not being able to be with you..."

Màiri's eyes darkened, but still she said nothing. She wasn't going to make this easy for him.

"I—there's something—I have a...a condition."

"The curse," she said.

Adam blinked. "What?"

"Am I right?" Her voice was polite, distant.

"Y-yes, that's what I call it." He took a deep breath, searched her eyes for...something, and went for it. "I have a congenital illness that strikes once in every generation. I'm going to die, probably before I reach thirty-five." Adam closed his eyes, unwilling to see her reaction.

After a moment he looked up again. Màiri's eyes were damp. "I'm so sorry, Adam. That's why you collapsed here, and then on the trail, right?" She reached across the desk and took his hand in hers. "You were right. They weren't panic attacks, were they?"

Adam felt as if her hand was the only thing tethering him to reality. His brain was swimming in some kind of viscous liquid that turned his thoughts into syrup. He managed a nod.

Màiri removed her hand, and it was as if a door slammed shut. "But what does that have to do with you telling me that we can't be together?"

He gaped at her. "I'm going to die!" *Was she daft?* "I can't be with anyone!"

"Why not?" She was glaring at him now. "You're alive right now, aren't you?" Her voice was a challenge. "Or are you just going to sit around waiting to die?"

That's what I've been doing.

"B-but it's not fair..."

"To me or to you? No, forget about that for a minute." She reached for his hand again.

"I love you," she said softly. The words dropped into the quiet of the small office like a pinball finding its slot. "Doesn't that count for something?"

Adam stared at her, unable to process.

"Do you feel the same way about me?" There was a challenge in her voice.

"I do," he said, before he could let thinking get in the way. Nothing horrible happened, so he stumbled on. "I'm in love with you, Màiri. I shouldn't be, but I am." He could feel tears gathering in his eyes, marking a trail down his face. "I love you."

She was smiling and crying at the same time. "There, then. That wasn't so hard, was it?"

"But how can you—"

She came up out of the chair, rounded the desk, and put a finger to his lips. "Hush. I'm here." She held up her right hand and wiggled her fingers. "Did you forget what I can do?"

Adam stared at her, allowing hope to bloom for

BALLACHULISH AND FORT WILLIAM, SCOTLAND – PRESENT TIME

a few seconds. Then he tamped it down. It wouldn't work. Even with her gift, she couldn't be by his side every minute, and someday the Curse would get him. But maybe they could cheat time, at least for a while. He stood, wrapped his arms around her, and crushed her to him. Then he lowered his lips to hers, and everything disappeared in a blur of sensation.

When he finally regained his senses, he was gazing into Màiri's clear blue eyes. *If this is what I see when I die,* he thought, *it'll be all right.*

Suddenly another thought burst through the embargo in his mind. He put his hands on Màiri's shoulders and held her at arm's length.

"Why did you call it a curse?" he asked. "That's what I call it, but I never told you."

Màiri shrugged. "I read about it in a book," she said. She reached into the pocket of her gown and pulled out *The Witch's Daughter*. "Remember this? You should read it too."

CHAPTER 42
FORT WILLIAM, SCOTLAND – PRESENT TIME

Of all the words of mice and men, the saddest are, "It might have been".
—Kurt Vonnegut

A pain, the like of which he'd never known, sank its talons into his chest. He stumbled, and his knees folded. Shadows crawled from the corners of the room and surrounded him, enfolded him, swallowed him. Everything went black. His eyes stared at the ceiling, seeing nothing. Chief Inspector Harper Beaton was dead.

Myles leaned back in his chair and put his hands behind his head. There. It was done. He'd killed off his cash cow, the character who had been with him for six years. His fans were going to hate him. Still, he felt freer than he had for a long time. Ready to move on, find a new muse.

He clicked on the character list in his database. He already knew who the next protagonist would be. Her name was Moira MacLeod. She had curly black hair, sea-blue eyes, and a smile that lit up the world. She was also a witch, with supernatural abilities that helped her defeat the Devil in her eighteenth-century village.

He was taking a huge risk. Myles Grant was famous for his modern-era, gritty crime novels. Changing genres like this was potential suicide for an author; it could make or break his career. He could add another entire demographic to his readership or lose all his fans with one book. A historical romance about witchcraft? What was he thinking?

He knew what had caused this sea change in his writing. That book, *The Witch's Daughter*, had reached into his soul and taken possession of his pen, and he didn't know why. It wasn't even fiction. The writing wasn't close to brilliant, the facts chronicled in a dry, factual manner that should have been guaranteed to put him to sleep.

But this book was different. First of all, that weird bookseller, Mary Duncan, had given it to him and insisted he read it. Myles didn't mind admitting, at least to himself, that there was something strange about her—about that whole lot that ran the shop. They didn't just dress like the eighteenth century... they *lived* it. Maybe it was his writer's imagination, but it was as if all of them —Mary's husband, the red-headed giant, the plump, happy one, even the cat— had sprung out of the past and taken over the present.

Never mind. It made perfect sense for that strange wee woman to give him a book on witchcraft that had a faint odour of smoke. Right. She might be a witch herself, for all he knew. So he'd read it. And

FORT WILLIAM, SCOTLAND – PRESENT TIME

before he'd gone twenty pages, it had taken hold of him and wouldn't let go.

It took a second reading before he knew what bothered him about it—besides the smoke. One of the characters reminded him of himself. The man wasn't even one of the good guys, which was a bit insulting because he'd always thought of himself as a pretty decent lad. This one was a womanizer, a handsome man who thought a great deal of himself and played with women's affections. The physical description matched what he saw in the mirror and on posters and the backs of his novels.

That in itself wouldn't have bothered him so much. What did was his reaction to the character. When he read of the man's seductive lifestyle, his inability to commit to a woman, it had hit too close to home. It was as if he were reading a cautionary tale about himself. He'd been filled with shame and self-loathing, and he wanted to reach into the book and throttle the bawbag for being such a moral weakling.

Maybe that was why he'd decided to take on this genre and write a fictional account of the happenings long ago in a northern Scottish village. Maybe he wanted to vindicate himself. He closed his eyes. Or maybe it was because he'd fallen in love with the book's protagonist, the witch's daughter.

Myles stood and walked to the window. The waves of Loch Linhe tumbled by, as they always did, in their never-ending march to the sea. It usually calmed his thoughts. But not this time.

Maybe he'd fallen in love with the protagonist... No. Not her. If the womanizing man in the novel reminded him of himself, the protagonist reminded him of someone else. Black curly hair, blue eyes. A smile that lit up the room.

He steeled himself and faced his demons. He was in love with Màiri MacLachlan, a very real woman who lived right here in Fort William, in this century.

Why had it taken so long to realize the truth? Why had he stopped every time just short of telling her how he felt? Why was he standing here right now, asking himself the same questions over and over again?

Myles glanced out the window again. The mountains were swallowed up by encroaching dusk, and the whitecaps had disappeared into the gloom. He grabbed his light jacket and his car keys and sprinted out to his car before he could allow himself to think. He kept his attention on the road while he drove, forcing his mind to empty. It wasn't until he'd pulled into the car park at the end of the High Street that he realized his mistake.

There were no cars in the park. Myles sat for a moment, stupefied, and then looked at his watch and cursed himself for an arse. It was half ten in the evening! The bookshop had been closed for hours.

He pulled out his mobile and scanned his contacts. She'd be home, maybe getting ready for bed. He should wait till tomorrow.

No! If you wait, you won't do it. You know what you're like. His inner voice pushed at him. *Do it now, or you never will.*

Myles took a deep breath and tapped the number he'd saved.

FORT WILLIAM, SCOTLAND – PRESENT TIME

"Hello?"

"Hullo. It's Myles. I'm sorry to call so late. Were you sleeping?"

Her laughter trickled through the mobile. "No. I don't think I'll be able to sleep for a while, so I'm having a cup of tea and reading. What's up?"

"Do you have some time?" He paused. "I'd like to come over and talk to you about something."

"Now?" She sounded surprised. "Well...sure. Give me a few minutes."

He scribbled the address she gave him onto the back of a Morrison's receipt. "See you soon."

He parked in the tiny car park assigned to the residents, as Màiri had instructed, and hiked up the steep hill and around to the back, where outside stairs led up to the top floor. A lamp lit the red door, giving the place a welcoming look.

I hope I'll be welcome, he thought. A sudden nervousness nearly overwhelmed him, and for a moment he thought of turning around and going back. But Myles Grant hadn't gotten where he was in life by being afraid, and he wasn't going to start now. He started toward the bottom step and froze.

The cloud cover had broken, allowing a thin moon to peek through. In its faint light he saw a figure dressed in black, moving up the stairs with exaggerated care as if the person didn't want to be heard. A tiny light from a mobile moved up the steps ahead of the figure.

Definitely not an expected visitor. Myles reached for his own mobile and silenced it. He pulled his hood up over his blond hair and moved forward. It was too much of a coincidence for two people to be visiting Màiri at this hour, and wouldn't she have mentioned it?

The man reached the last step and clicked off the mobile's torch. Myles stopped on the landing and peeked through a small railing. Màiri's flat must have been made from the attic of the original house. It was like a small cottage which sat on a flat wooden veranda. The roof came down on two sides to within three feet of the floor. There was no sign of the man.

He heard a footstep, very faint and moving around the side. Then there was a series of muffled clicks, as if someone were trying a latch. There was no noise from within, but seconds later he felt his mobile vibrate and checked the display. Màiri. He went back down the steps, relieved that his trainers were nearly soundless, and raised the mobile to his ear.

"Myles, are you almost here?" Her voice was a whisper.

"Màiri, there's—"

She cut him off. "I think someone's trying to break in. I thought it was you at first, but he's outside the kitchen window."

"I'm coming. Lock yourself into a room without an outside window and don't move. And call the police!"

Her mobile clicked off. Myles crept back up the stairs and flattened himself against the side of the small building, next to the red door. He eased to the corner and peered around the edge of the wall. Nothing. He slid along to the other corner and peeked.

It was darker on this side, but he could hear the sound of digging into wood, as if someone were prying at something. He eased around the corner and now he could see the vague outline of a man in black working some sort of tool into the wood near a window. A chisel or a knife. His heart was pounding so hard he was sure the man would hear it.

Suddenly something thudded onto the veranda. The man cursed and stooped to pick it up, and Myles took his chance. He leapt forward to tackle him to the ground. They rolled away from each other and regained their feet, and the man charged forward, quicker than he'd thought possible. Myles took a blow to the shoulder and struck out blindly, hearing the satisfied thump of fist on flesh.

Something glinted in the man's hand, and he felt a searing pain along his left forearm. The man pushed past him and raced around the corner and down the steps, leaving Myles clutching his arm and wondering how anything could happen so quickly.

He ran to the edge of the veranda, but the intruder was gone. He watched for any movement, and when there was none, he returned to the side window, pulled out his mobile, and used the torch to search the ground. Nothing. The intruder had taken it with him. Had it been a knife? A screwdriver?

I would've noticed, the husky voice of Inspector Harper Beaton said in his ear. *You probably wish you didn't kill me off now, eh, lad?*

"Shut up and stay dead," Myles told the ghost rudely. He fished his mobile out of his pocket and punched in Màiri's number. Her frightened voice came on immediately.

"He's gone," Myles said. "You can let me in now."

The door opened seconds later and Myles stepped in and closed and locked it. Màiri was standing, blue eyes round with fear, in the middle of a room that on one side was a sitting room and on the other a kitchen. He stepped to the kitchen window and made sure it was still locked, then checked the other windows in the small, cozy space.

"Is that your bedroom?" he asked, pointing to a door on one side of a wall of bookshelves. At Màiri's nod, he went through and checked that the window in the tiny room was also locked. Then he checked the one remaining door, which led to a windowless bathroom.

He came back into the main room to find Màiri sitting on the couch, arms wrapped around her knees. She was shaking, but she managed a smile.

"Thank you," she said. "I can't believe something like this happened." She grabbed his hand. "Myles! You're bleeding! Why didn't you say?" She jumped up and fetched a first aid kit.

"Do you have any idea who it might be?" Myles asked as she wrapped gauze clumsily around the gash on his arm. "I mean..." — he hesitated — "do you have an angry ex-boyfriend or anything like that?"

She looked startled. "No. Don't you think it was probably a burglar?"

"Have any of your neighbours said anything?"

"No." Her eyes went wider. "You think someone was breaking into *my* house, on purpose?"

Myles sat down beside her on the couch and patted her arm, feeling suddenly awkward. "Well, it probably was a burglar. He might have thought that outside staircase was easy access. Do you have an alarm?"

FORT WILLIAM, SCOTLAND – PRESENT TIME

She shook her head. "No, but I'll look into that tomorrow. Oh!" She reached for the mobile lying on her tea table. "I need to call Adam."

"Adam? Adam MacArthur?" Myles frowned. "Why?"

Màiri gave him a shy smile. "We're—we're together."

"As of when?" His own words sounded harsh and grating to his ear.

She glanced at him, startled. "Well, two days ago, officially. You're one of the first to know." Her smile was brilliant.

A dull throbbing was building behind Myles' eyes. He wanted to throw something across the room. He wanted to grab her and beg her to take the words back. He wanted to cry.

Too late. He'd waited and fought with himself and tried to deny his feelings, and now it was all gone.

Sirens sounded in the distance. "The police are coming," he said dully. "I'll wait till they get here."

"Thanks." Màiri smiled at him. "Oh—what was it you wanted to talk to me about?"

"Nothing. It's not important," Myles said. His thoughts were whirling. How could he have been so stupid? What if he'd come yesterday, or the day before yesterday? Would he have had a chance? He looked at Màiri's radiant face and his heart sank.

No, he wouldn't. She was in love. A woman's heart wasn't a commodity, up for sale to the first buyer on the scene. He'd lost.

He managed a smile. "Well anyway, congratulations." *Congratulations, Adam, you lucky bastard.*

CHAPTER 43
FORT WILLIAM, SCOTLAND – PRESENT TIME

I am a book.
I am a tale of woe and secrets...
I am a mystery.
—Lise McClendon

Màiri stood at the bottom of her steps and looked sideways at Adam. It was his first visit to her home, and she wanted him to like it as much as she did. She'd described it to him, told him about the intruder and about Myles Grant's visit, and watched his eyes go dark. *Was he jealous? Of Myles?* The thought made her smile.

He didn't need to be. It seemed ages ago that she'd felt that girlish reaction to Myles' blond good looks, but it had only been weeks. Long enough for her heart to find its place in Adam MacArthur's steady personality, his comforting smile and warm brown eyes. Myles was exciting—she had no doubt—but Adam was...home. Energised by the knowledge, she grabbed his hand and pulled him up the wooden stairs to her flat.

She watched him study the small cottage-like structure perched on top of a hundred- year-old mansion.

"It was a bargain," Màiri told him, "because the other flats have an inside lift and mine doesn't. You have to hike if you want the wrap-around veranda and the view, but it's worth it to me."

"Do you have an alarm?" he asked her, and Màiri knew he was thinking about Laura. He'd told her about their awkward conversation and warned her to be careful and tell him if the younger woman approached her.

Let her try, Màiri thought. She put her arms around Adam and buried her head in his chest, listening to the steady beat of his heart. He was worth fighting for, and no little vixen was going to have a chance at him.

They sat on her veranda and watched the sun set over the mountains on the other side of the firth, and they talked.

Adam had three brothers and two sisters, he told her. It was curious—being an only child, she'd always thought a lot of brothers and sisters would be Heaven on earth. But when Adam described his family dynamic, she realized she might have been the lucky one.

"We've become much closer in the last few years, mostly due to Ewan," he said. "I'll take you up to Inverness soon and you can meet some of them. Ewan and his wife Fiona are still there, and my sister

FORT WILLIAM, SCOTLAND – PRESENT TIME

Sophie—she's a violinist with the Royal Symphony and they're on break for the summer. I don't know about the others. Jonah's all over the place. He's an anthropologist and he goes where the bones and relics are. And Izzy's in Europe, collecting recipes for her next cookbook."

"Where's does Daniel fit in this menagerie?" Màiri asked him.

"Next to youngest, just two years older than Sophie." Adam looked out over the firth. "He was a real mess until he met Eve. He had panic disorder. That's how I know what panic attacks are and why I wasn't having one. He was an alcoholic, or near enough. Selfish to the core. Nobody wanted to be around him back then."

He grinned at Màiri. "Not like me. I'm the family peacemaker because I'm so lovable, as I'm sure you've noticed."

Màiri looked at him, her face serious. "Aye, lad, ye are that."

She shivered, and Adam pulled her to her feet.

"It's getting cold, with the sun gone." He looked at his watch. "And it's half eleven! I should go and let you get some sleep."

She put her hand on his arm and felt electricity arc between them. It gave her courage.

"Can you not? Go, I mean. Can you...stay?"

He hesitated for a second, then cradled her face in his hands. "Aye," he said. "I can stay."

It was that simple. It didn't matter that she had nothing for him to sleep in, or that he didn't have a change of clothes. It didn't matter at all.

The next morning, he showered and put on his rumpled clothes from the night before and they sat on the other side of the veranda and saw the sun come up. She made eggs and toast and they watched the weather on her small television, his feet on the pouffy and her head on his shoulder.

If this is all the future has for us, she thought, *this moment will be what I remember. I can go on, with this.*

Adam turned and met her eyes. He grinned and leaned over to kiss her forehead.

How does he do it? Màiri wondered. *How does he manage to carry on with such sanguinity with the curse hanging over his head?*

"What else am I supposed to do?" he asked, as if he read her thoughts. "Curl up in a corner and cry all day? I tried that, when I first found out." He rested his chin on her head. "I was a miserable pile of shite. Full of self-pity, but snapping at anyone who dared to feel sorry for me. Only my family knows, and Jared—well, he's family, too. And now you." He pulled his head back and captured her gaze. "And dinnae ye dare pity me, lassie, or I'll skelp ye."

"I won't pity you," she said. "But you can't stop me from worrying." She smiled at the stubborn look on his face. "That's what love is. If you care about someone, you worry about them. Whether they're cursed or not."

The Curse. Adam had told her it had a capital letter in his mind, and now it read that way in hers, too. Maybe she was channelling that witch book. She focused on Adam.

"Will you read the book?"

His eyes evaded hers. "I don't want to. It smells."

FORT WILLIAM, SCOTLAND – PRESENT TIME

"Mary says you need to read it, Adam." Her forehead wrinkled. "And I agree with her."

"Why's it so important?" Adam asked.

"I can't explain it, but you'll understand when you read it. And Mary says so." Her mobile rang. Màiri listened for a moment, mumbled, "Aye," and hung up. She stared at the mobile for a second. "How does she *do* that?"

"Do what?"

"It's Mary. She wants us both at the bookshop, as soon as we can get there."

"But you're off today," Adam said. "I wanted to…"

Màiri put a finger to his lips. "It's Mary."

All thoughts of the book fled upon their entry to HP Booksellers. Betty was waiting at the door, an anxious look on her face.

"Finally!" she said. "Come on." She turned the small sign so that the side facing the High Street read, *Done fer today. Hie ye back.*

Màiri exchanged a look with Adam. He shrugged, took her hand, and followed Betty toward the tiny office.

The small space was jammed with people. Mary and Henry stood against one wall. Caomhainn was perched incongruously atop a side table that should have crumbled under his weight. Biscuit eyed Adam narrowly from her perch atop the desk and Màiri stifled a giggle. The look said plainly that if he didn't have Pearl with him, his existence was superfluous to greater beings. The cat sniffed, curled up on the desktop, and closed her eyes.

Màiri glanced to her left and was surprised to see Myles Grant standing in the corner with an odd, guarded look on his face. *What was he here for?* The room was packed, but there was no one in the big leather chair behind the desk or the guest chair that had been pulled up next to it. She could feel anxiety building in her stomach. *What was going on?*

"Ye're just 'n time," Mary said. "We're waitin' fer a few more."

At her words, the door of the shop opened again and four people stepped into the already crowded office. Màiri's mouth dropped open as Inspector Benedict Fraser came in, with Cory MacMillen and his friends Bastien and Donnie in tow.

"Cory!" Màiri gasped. "Oh my God! We thought you were..." Tears sprang to her eyes. "Where have you been?"

The boy flushed. "Well, I..." He looked to Inspector Fraser. "I...he...we..."

"Let's sit down, son," the inspector said. "I'll explain what we know, aye?" He and Cory rounded the desk and sat down in the two empty chairs. Bastien and Donnie leaned against the wall behind them, arms folded over their chests. Both kept their eyes trained on Cory, as if he might disappear again if they looked away.

Something Fraser had just said penetrated Màiri's brain. *Son?* She looked at the two redheads sitting side by side, identical pairs of blue eyes studying the group in front of them. *Well, of course.* How had she never seen that?

"Yes," Inspector Fraser said. "Cory is my son." He looked at the lad and a smile broke out on his normally stern face. "I haven't seen him in nine years."

FORT WILLIAM, SCOTLAND – PRESENT TIME

He reached for Cory's hand, as if he couldn't bear not to touch him. "I thought he was dead."

"He didn't run away, like I thought," Cory said. "He couldn't get us out of the car, so he went for help."

Adam looked confused, but Màiri remembered Bastian and Donnie telling her about an accident that had robbed Cory of his family when he was young. "Tell you later," she whispered.

"I was on the side that got hit hardest," Ben Fraser was saying. "I tried to go for help, but I didn't realize how badly injured I was. I was running on adrenaline. I only made it a few yards and collapsed." His face twisted. "When I woke up, they told me there had been no survivors. I spent the next three months in hospital, thinking my family was gone." Remembered grief shadowed his ruddy features. "When I got out, I moved to Glasgow and tried to put it behind me."

"He became a firefighter—a fire *detective*," Cory said, his face shining with pride. "And all this time I thought he ran out on us." He shook his head. "I was such a bairn."

"Well, you *were* a bairn," his father said, and squeezed his hand.

Adam spoke up. There was ice in his words. "Well, this is all very nice, but...while we were all out searching the woods for Cory, *worrying*, he was with you?"

Father and son exchanged glances. "No," Fraser said. "He was hiding out at the MacMillens." His lip twisted. "If I'd known how they treated him..."

"Hiding out?" Adam said. "Am I missing something here?" He turned to Cory. "All this time, you let your friends and family think you were dead while you were playing hide and seek?"

Mary interrupted. "Let them tell their story, lad. Then you'll understand."

Adam crossed his arms. "Okay. I'm listening."

For the next half hour, Benedict Fraser and his son took turns telling the story of the men in the woods to an increasingly astonished audience.

"I thought Dad was in the cult," Cory said. "I kept going back to try to find him, but I couldn't."

"I was undercover," the inspector explained. "I recognized Cory, even after all those years..." — he shook his head in wonder— "and I thought he recognized me, but I couldn't betray myself." He took a deep breath. "So I had to walk right past him and pretend I didn't see him. It was the hardest thing I've ever done." He sighed. "I stayed in the group and watched, because I was afraid Cory would do exactly what he did and try to find me."

"He was there when they discovered me," Cory said, and a shudder wracked his slight frame. "He saved me."

Benedict Fraser put his arm around his son and looked out at the group in the small office. "Cory's right about it being a cult. Their leader is a charismatic lunatic who has them all praying to some fire god. Part of their worship involves arson, but I wasn't in the inner circle so I couldn't find out what the targets were." He looked at Màiri. "I'm sure they started the fire at the museum, but I can't prove it yet."

"So," she asked slowly, "the dead man was..."

"We're positive he was one of them," Fraser said, his

FORT WILLIAM, SCOTLAND – PRESENT TIME

face grim. "I didn't see it happen; I'd marched ahead with the others. But young Cory saw them kill a man in the woods. We think somehow they got him to the museum and then started the fire to cover it up."

"But that man was a firefighter!" Màiri's face twisted in horror. "How could a firefighter start fires on purpose?"

"Arsonists are attracted to fire," the inspector said. "A very small number of them become firefighters. They might have something called 'hero syndrome' or be angry at society for something that happened to them, or any number of psychotic reasons. It's a mental illness, and in this case, it involves cult worship of fire."

"So why did they kill this guy?" Adam asked.

"Cory heard them say something about betrayal," Fraser said. "Maybe he was trying to get out of the cult. We'll be checking with the police to see if anyone tried to contact them. And we haven't figured out yet who the mastermind is. He could be a firefighter, too."

Màiri looked at Adam, and saw her own thoughts reflected in his eyes.

He went to the fire in his own car. Mackie's words about his grumpy colleague.

Peter Campbell could have gotten to the museum before the others...even before the fire. He had been avoiding their questions that day and hadn't come to the bookshop with the others. Was it possible?

Could Campbell be the cult leader?

CHAPTER 44
DORNACH, SCOTLAND – 1727

HUGH

Hugh stopped twice more to heave his guts into the bushes along the path. Although there was nothing left in his stomach, he couldn't seem to keep it still. His headache was worse; the throbbing relentless. But his memories were back, so he held on to that small victory. He had no time to worry about what it all meant. He had to find Sìne.

The village centre was empty. He could see the looming shadow of the castle, its twin towers black against the darkening sky. He'd never noticed before, but the towers resembled the horns of the devil. It seemed as if the castle was watching him from dark pitiless eyes set into its sandstone face. Judging him.

Hugh shivered and turned toward the pub. At this time of day, that's where everyone should be, quaffing a pint or two before going home to wife and bairns.

The pub was empty, except for the lone barman who looked up from wiping the counters when Hugh stumbled in.

"Young Master Hugh! Good t' see yer better. Terrible thing, that. Dinnae ken what th' world's comin' to these days."

Hugh grabbed the edge of a table for support against a wave of dizziness. "Where is everbody?"

The barman's eyes widened. "T' th' townhouse, o'course. Fer th' trial. Didnae yer Da tell ye?"

But he was talking to empty air. Hugh was already out the door, headed for the town square. He was having difficulty putting one foot in front of the other, and his head felt as if someone had stuffed it with rocks and cotton batting, but he focused on the lights spilling out of the large building in the town centre and kept going.

A long wooden apparatus sat in front of the town house—one he knew well. He'd spent a long night sitting in those stocks while the villagers threw clods of dirt at him and his father watched. If it hadn't been for Sìne...

Sìne! Hugh blinked to clear the dirt that seemed to be gathering before his eyes, and realized it *was* dirt. He was on his hands and knees in front of the stocks. He could hear voices—catcalls, jeers, and cheers coming from the town house door only a few yards away.

He tried to stand, but his knees buckled and spilled him back onto the ground. Hugh focused on the brightly lit doorway, *so close*, and began to crawl toward the stone steps. *Sìne. Have to get to Sìne.*

"*Get th' witch up!*" His father's voice, loud, imperious, laced with venom. The door of the town house was open and pandemonium reigned inside—or was it in his head? He crawled up the stairs until he could grab the railing and pull himself almost to his feet. It took three tries to lift his foot onto the next step, and then he inched his hands along the railing until he could stand. Only for a second, then he lost his balance again and tumbled backwards to land in the dirt at the bottom of the steps.

He must have passed out. He was awakened by a woman's warbling voice calling out in delight, "A pony! Would ye like t' ride a pony, love?"

Shouts drowned out whatever the woman said next. Hugh got to his knees and grabbed for the railing again, and inch by inch he pulled himself to the last step. He leaned against the wall next to the building, spent. Words from inside the hall wove in and out of his ears.

"Ye ken, friends? From th' vile mouth o' th' witch herself—a confession!"

"'At's not true!" A younger voice, choked with desperation.

Sìne.

Hugh tried to move, but his limbs refused to obey. He leaned against the wall, tears rolling down his cheeks.

His father's triumphant voice continued its rant. "Doirin Gilchrist has been workin' th' Devil's magic on this village e'er since she crawled here, bearin'

WITCH

Satan's bairn in her belly. Good neighbours, stand up an' tell us yer stories!"

There was a moment of silence. Then voices began to call out into the stifling air of the room.

"She tried t' kill my wee Askill, abornin'," cried Finola Grant. "I saw her workin' her magic, an' my puir lad was blue!"

"She was talkin' t' young Hector Cumming just b'fore he walked into th' water an' drowned," another voice claimed.

"My Alasdair was fine one minute, an' th' next he just keeled over, deid!" came the sobbing voice of Flora Ross. "Doirin Gilchrist saw him just th' day b'fore!"

Another woman spoke up. "I thynk she kilt Elidh Gordon's bairn, an' when Elidh found oot, she kilt her too!"

The voices rose and called over each other now in their eagerness to have their moment of glory.

"I saw Doirin Gilchrist ridin' her daughter one night. Right doon th' village road!"

"I saw it too! Twas when there was no moon a'tall an' she thought no one could see. Bit I have eyes like a hawk!"

"That's ridic'lous!" Hugh heard Sìne's trembling voice rise above the chaos. He wanted to rush in a comfort her, tell her it was all nonsense, that he was there for her...but he couldn't move.

"My mam healed most o' th' people in this room," Sìne called out. "She birthed yer bairns and patched 'em up when they were hurt. Why are ye tellin' these lies?"

"D' ye thynk that's all we have, lass?" Duncan's voice, oozing poison. "Of course there's more. I'll now turn th' court over t' our witness, Doctor Wilson. Please t' tell th' court what ye saw, sir."

Another voice, oily and repugnant. "I was watchin' the witch's daughter in th' midwifery. I'm sorry t' say it, Mistress Campbell, but ye died on that table. 'An the creature pit her hand on ye, an' ye started t' breathe agin. T'was th' work o' th' Devil, I tell ye!"

There were gasps from the hall. Then Aoife Campbell's voice rang out. "Are ye tellin' me that I was deid an' th' lass brocht me back t' life? Is 'at what yer sayin'? B'cause 'at sounds like th' work o' th' Lord, not th' Devil!"

There was a moment of silence as the crowd took in Aoife's words. Then another voice rose in the stifling air of the room. A young girl's voice, triumphant, familiar.

"She 'as th' mark o' th' Devil!"

"Aye, Miss Ailis?" The silky voice of Duncan Sutherland. "Can ye tell us more?"

"Tis on 'er shoulder. Tis th' cross o' our Lord, but th' Devil pit it upside down!"

There was a scuffle, and Hugh heard a rending sound. The hall became silent. He crawled to the doorway and pulled himself to his feet, swaying. And there was Sìne, her gown torn so that it hung off her shoulder, held in a firm grip by two men so that those closest could see the small mark.

"Aye!"

"Th' Devil's brand!"

"She 'as it. I see it!"

WITCH

"She's a witch, like 'er mother!'

"NO!" The word burst from the open door at the back of the room. His own voice.

People shifted and turned to see from whence the shout came. Hugh Sutherland stood in the doorway of the town hall, clutching the door frame and swaying back and forth. His face was pasty white, his trews covered with dirt and leaves.

"No!' he shouted again. "Tis not th' mark o' th' Devil! Tis not e'en a cross! Look at 't." He raised a shaking hand and pointed toward the front of the room.

"Tis th' sword o' God!"

Someone laughed—a harsh, derisive bark—and others joined in. Hugh locked eyes with his father and the smug satisfaction on the older man's face told him the truth. This had never been a trial. His father and that horrid Wilson had bought their 'witnesses' and the conclusion had been decided long ago. His father's words came back to him: *Ye'll be doin' that wretchit lass no favours by bein' on her side. Ye'll only make it worse fer her.*

He'd thought that if he kept away from Sine, he could keep her safe. But that had never been a part of the plan. He looked toward the front of the room again and saw only self-serving greed and implacable hatred in the eyes of the man who had raised him.

Sutherland looked around the room. He waited for the noise to subside and held up a hand. "The Lord says," he intoned, his voice clear and triumphant, "thou shalt not suffer a witch t' live." He picked up a Bible from the bench in front of him and held it aloft. "And so, I tell thee, the witch an' her unfortunate spawn cannae live." He lowered his voice and said in a voice imbued with sorrow, "This very night th' vile creature will be tarred, feathered, an' taken through the village t' the square, where she will be put t' the flame! An' tomorrow early, her daughter will follow her t' Hell!"

In the ensuing silence, a clear voice rang out.

"This has nothin' t' do with th' Lord, but I do ken there be magick in this world. An' if there be a just God, I call upon him to hear my prayer!" Sìne looked around at the crowd of stunned villagers and lowered her voice so all had to strain to hear her.

"Ye've talked a lot about killin' here t'night, an' twas all lies. Well, here is *my* truth. If ye kill me, I pray ye t' die in turn."

Her voice grew stronger with each word. "No, not pray. I *curse* th' one who stops my heart to burn in agony afore his time, that each generation suffer the flames lit here t'night!" Sìne paused and looked out over the silent crowd. "Only death will end it. Tis my promise t' ye *guid* people!"

Hugh watched in awe. Sìne's black hair straggled over her shoulders. Her fists were clenched at the sides of her torn gown and her blue eyes flashed defiance as she faced her accusers.

She's glorious.

Their eyes met for a brief second. Then the walls wavered and closed in around Hugh. The noise in the room subsided and became a fading echo. His eyes rolled up in his head and he pitched forward into the arms of the nearest villager, who lowered him to the floor gently. The lights, the sounds, even the face of the only woman he would ever love, all faded away.

CHAPTER 45
DORNACH, SCOTLAND – 1727

SÌNE

Sìne crouched in the corner of the small cell and wrapped her arms around her knees to keep herself warm. They hadn't bothered to light a fire on this cold early spring night, but the shivering wasn't coming from outside. It was a pervasive, icy chill that wound itself around her bones and seeped into her heart.

The air in the small prison had changed. Now it was heavy with an acrid, nauseating stench, like all the fetid odours she had ever smelled mixed together into a stew of charcoal and scorched meat. It was so thick and rich in its pungent abhorrence that she could taste it.

She fought to keep her stomach from heaving up the cold porridge they'd given her this morning, because she knew what this smell was. They were killing her beloved mother—burning her, just as they'd said they would.

They called her Waghorn, Clootie, Auld Mistress Sandie—Witch. As if her gentle mother, a healer by nature and calling, would ever consort with the Devil or cast spells to harm. Naming her thus was an abomination, a mockery of justice for which they had no proof.

They had made her watch as they paraded her mother through the town, torches held high—that sweet, simple woman with no harm in her. Covered in an obscene coat of hot tar and goose feathers, forced to hold tight to the insides of a barrel while two mules pulled her along the muddy path. Doirin's eyes had widened when she saw her daughter, and incomprehensible sounds forced their way out through the gag in her mouth, as if to tear out her throat.

And then Sine's captors had yanked at the rope around her neck so she was forced to stumble away, back toward her prison. She could only hear the wretched screeches fade away as they dragged Doirin Gilchrist to the place of her execution, but she knew she would hear those hideous sounds for the rest of her life.

Short as it would be...for she was next.

They unbound her hands before thrusting her back into the tiny hut that had served as her jail since the travesty they called a trial, laughing as she stumbled and fell onto the earthen floor. None of her captors would look her in the eye, but they had no trouble hurling taunts and jeers before they turned away and left her. People she had known all her life, neighbours she had nursed, to whom she brought soup when they were ill.

The villagers had been kind enough when they needed her. No longer; not since the trial. Now she was untouchable, unclean, a child of Satan. A witch. Her mother was Satan's minion, and Sìne her vile plaything.

She and her mother had never really been accepted. The way the village children had treated Sìne was a reflection of their parents' own prejudice. And when Mother began to fail, to stumble in her speech and then to slide slowly into madness, their true feelings had begun to emerge. They stopped bringing their bairns for her healing treatment, avoided the Gilchrist women in the village, whispered behind their backs.

Her mother's words made less and less sense and neighbours' faces darkened when she approached. When Hugh Sutherland was hurt and Doirin discovered crouching over his body, the whispers turned to roars.

The trial was short, presided over by Hugh's father and that odious magistrate, Wilson. There was no hope of reason and no one to stand for them. It was a nightmare of accusation and vitriol that darkened the very air and deepened Mother's confusion, and when Ailis MacAllan hurled her hateful words into the nest of vipers, their fate was sealed. They saw the mark on Sìne's shoulder and were convinced.

"Tis th' Devil's brand!"

"She 'as it. I see it!"

WITCH

"She's a witch, like 'er mother!"

Horrible words, vicious lies, uttered in self-righteous glee. Was it fear that had brought this about? Sine knew that women in other towns and villages had been burned as witches, but this was Dornach. She'd never thought it could happen here. These were her neighbours, no matter that they had no love for Doirin Gilchrist and her daughter. They had known Sine all her life. They *knew* Doirin was no witch.

But the looks on their faces told the truth. They would rather believe the worst than stand against Duncan Sutherland, the man who owned their town and controlled their lives. The only one who had ever stood up for her was Sutherland's own son, Hugh, and he had betrayed her, too, in the end. She had stood alone in that hall, in front of the whole village.

And then, from the back of the hall, she had heard his voice. The man who had abandoned her for another; the one who had broken her heart and left her to face this travesty of a trial alone.

He had cried out in her favour, tried to tell them the mark was not of Satan, but of God. "Tis th' sword o' God!" he had called, and for a moment she thought he was there to save her. But then he was gone. It was all a lie. She had conjured his face and his voice out of a desperate hope that would not die, no matter how she willed it.

Sine hugged herself tighter to keep out the cold. It didn't matter anymore. Tomorrow she would be burned at the stake...alive. Not strangled first, out of some lingering sense of pity. She would feel the fire, smell her own hair as it burned. Would she live long enough to see the skin turn black on her hands and arms, or would the smoke act as a merciful saviour, sealing her mouth and nose and stopping her breath before the inferno melted her skin and left only bone?

Sìne lifted her hands—those horrible, ugly hands—and the guilt rose to lodge in her throat. It was all her fault. She deserved this fate. She was the one who was born imperfect, misshapen. She was the reason for this monstrous perversion of truth, this deception of righteousness. She was different, so no matter that she had saved others and eased their pain. She was what they called her—an abomination, cursed beyond redemption.

Sìne stood in her windowless prison hearing the shouts and jeers that drowned out her mother's shrieks. It was a mercy. She did not want to know when the screams stopped, when the fumes filled Doirin's throat and stole her breath away. She knew she was a coward, but she did not want to recognize the moment her innocent, lovely mother left this unforgiving earth.

Mam would be with God, Sìne knew. There was little mercy in the world, but Heaven would welcome Doirin Gilchrist with open arms. It was small comfort, because Sìne would not see her where *she* was going. The Devil would take her, for some reason known only to himself, but she accepted it because Hell was the only place for one who was born to cause her mother's death. She had no choice. She suspected she had never had a choice.

Tendrils of smoke drifted under the cracks of Sìne's cell and into her eyes. She could taste the thickness of it, the hatred, and she let it wrap around her and fill her heart with its poison. It was as if the fire itself sought vengeance.

The voices outside had died down and the smoke seemed less bitter now. Mam was dead and gone to a better place. The villagers were likely returning to their homes, their unholy lust for killing sated for the moment. They would be back tomorrow though, refreshed by the sleep of the righteous, when it was Sìne's turn to face the unholy blaze.

Her bitter thoughts turned again to the men who had sworn they loved her. Alan Grant was a liar, but he had filled the void left by Hugh's betrayal for a brief time. She'd always known he was a coward, plying her with honeyed words but avoiding her touch. He had never once looked at her during the trial.

It didn't matter...*he* didn't matter. It was easier to think about Alan Grant, though. She didn't want to spare a thought for the one to whom she had given her love unconditionally. He had left her long ago, taken her love with him and replaced it with despair.

A black rage filled what was left of Sìne's heart. She tasted the words of the curse she had thrown into the faces of her tormenters and began to repeat them.

I curse th' one who stops my heart, t' burn in agony afore his time—that each generation suffer the flames lit here t'night. Only death will end it. Tis my promise t' ye guid people.

If they thought her the spawn of the Devil, so be it. If God would not answer her prayer, maybe Satan would listen. She huddled into herself, wrapped the Curse around her like a poisonous blanket, and waited.

CHAPTER 46
FORT WILLIAM, SCOTLAND – PRESENT TIME

Life is pleasant. Death is peaceful. It's the transition that's troublesome.
—Isaac Asimov

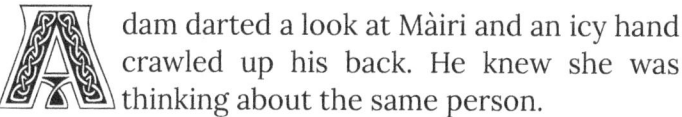

Adam darted a look at Màiri and an icy hand crawled up his back. He knew she was thinking about the same person.

Mackie had seemed evasive about Peter Campbell's whereabouts during the fire. Adam thought Màiri was being ridiculous, wanting to play detective and interview the man who had saved her, but maybe they'd had a clue and never realized it. It wasn't anything Mackie said, but both of them had noticed the flicker in his eyes, as if he suspected something he didn't want to share.

Or as if he was worried.

Did Mackie think something was off about his colleague? He needed to tell Fraser, even if he was wrong.

"Màiri and I..." he said, then stopped as all eyes swivelled in his direction. "We visited the fire station last week. Myles, you were there."

Myles gave a curt nod, his lips pursed and his eyes boring into Adam's.

Why the hostility? Adam wondered, but shook it off. Myles Grant's opinion of him wasn't important right now. He continued. "Màiri wanted to interview the firefighter who had saved her, because we couldn't figure out how he managed to jump off the truck and get through the museum from the back in a matter of minutes."

"Wait." Inspector Fraser put up a hand. "Are you telling me that you suspected something off and decided to play detective?" His face was a mixture of shock and appalled anger. "Are you licenced law enforcement officials? Do you know how foolish that was?"

Adam flushed, but it was Màiri who answered. "It was my fault. I made him do it." Her voice rose. "While you were sneaking around pretending to be a cult member and keeping Cory hidden when his friends were all *grieving*, thinking he was *dead*, we were trying to be useful."

The inspector flushed angrily. "It's my job," he said through tight lips. "And you could have ruined everything I was working on, not to mention getting yourselves hurt—or worse—in the bargain. Have you ever seen a body that's been burned beyond recognition?" His hands were fists on the desktop and he was breathing heavily.

"Leave her alone!" Adam said. "We're sorry. We were wrong. But we may have found out something.

FORT WILLIAM, SCOTLAND – PRESENT TIME

Do you want to yell at us, or do you want to hear it?"

Fraser sat back in the leather chair and blew air through his nostrils. "Okay. What did you find out, Holmes and Watson?"

Adam bit his lip. He deserved the sarcasm. He'd known at the outset that what Màiri was planning was daft. He should've talked her out of it. The inspector was right; he could've gotten her killed. It was like a bucket of ice water dumped on his head.

He took a deep breath and described the interview with Mackie as best he could remember. The retelling made the small flicker in Mackie's eyes seem like a reach across a chasm. A wisp of gossamer, meaningless. But as he told it, more memories came to the surface.

"Peter Campbell didn't ride the fire lorry to the scene," he said. "He could've been there earlier, putting the body of his dead colleague in the basement and getting ready to set it on fire."

A new thought came to him. "Campbell came on one of my running tours, on the same mountain where you say these cult meetings took place." He ignored Fraser's look of condescension and plunged on. "There was a period where he disappeared for a few minutes, with no believable excuse. What if Campbell was looking for Cory?"

"Peter Campbell didn't come with the others when they visited the bookshop," Màiri put in. "I haven't seen him since that day. Oh! I did see Peter and Laura Macallan meeting together at the station the day we were there."

Fraser sat up straight and looked at Màiri with

WITCH

new interest. "Macallan? That's interesting," he murmured to himself. "We've been watching her."

"Why?" Adam asked. "She's just a kid. Annoying, but harmless. Right?"

"Hmmm," Inspector Fraser said. "You say she was talking to Peter Campbell, alone?" He turned to Myles. "Did you see any of that?"

"No." Myles' tone was brusque. "I have the recording of the interviews, if you want it, but I don't think it'll be very useful. It won't show physical reactions or anything."

"I'll get it from you anyway," said Fraser. "You never know." He stood up. "That's all for now. I don't have to tell anyone here that none of what was said can leave this room, aye?"

Adam caught the mutinous look on Mary Duncan's face and smiled to himself. *No love lost there*, he thought. *It's like two alpha dogs squaring off. My money's on Mary.*

The Frasers left the office with Bastian and Donnie in tow. Myles Grant sent another dark look in Adam's direction and followed them out. Mary waited until the bell on the front door signalled their departure, then she closed the office door again, walked around the desk, and sat in the leather chair. She steepled her fingers and closed her eyes. For a long time, no one said anything. Caomhainn and Betty seemed to be waiting.

"Did you read the book?" Mary said suddenly. Her black eyes bored into Adam's.

"N-no, not yet." *What's with that damn book?* "It stinks. I don't like it." He could hear his own voice and knew he sounded like a cranky child. "All right,

FORT WILLIAM, SCOTLAND – PRESENT TIME

I'll read it tonight, aye?" He barely stopped himself from putting up three fingers in the Boy Scout sign of promise.

"It's not Peter Campbell," Mary said.

Adam studied the tiny woman closely. Something about her seemed different...and then it clicked. Her accent was gone.

"What?"

"The cult leader. The arsonist. It's not Campbell."

Adam stared at her, and then he looked around at the others. All of them were gazing back at him with unblinking eyes—even the cat. Suddenly he wanted to grab Màiri's hand and run, as fast and as far as he could, away from these eerie people and their crazy world.

"H-how do you know it's not him?" he said, feeling suddenly short of breath.

"Read the book. He's not in it."

Adam rolled his eyes. Was it just him, or did none of this make sense? Would the Mad Hatter be joining them for tea next?

Mary glared at him. "Either read it or live it," she said. "Your choice." She stood, herded them out of the office and to the door of the shop, and all but pushed them into the street. Adam heard the decisive click of the lock. They'd been dismissed.

"Why is she so insistent that I read that damn book?" he asked, as they walked down to the car park. "You read it. Can't you fill me in?"

Màiri gripped his hand and pulled him around to face her on the street. "No. Mary said it's different for each person." Her eyes were huge and she looked almost frightened. "I don't really understand, but when I read it, I felt sad and sick and angry, all at the same time." She sniffed.

"Are you crying?" Adam asked. "Was her story that sad?"

"It was awful. The things they did to her. When I was reading, her experience filled my head... It was as if I was there, feeling what she felt, thinking her thoughts. They abused her all her life, when all she wanted to do was help them. And in the end, the one she loved betrayed her."

A small sob escaped into the night air. Mairi shivered and buried her head in Adam's chest. "I've never felt so strongly about any other book. And I can tell you this." She raised bleary blue eyes to his. "It must mean something, or they wouldn't be so insistent. The Highland Players, I mean."

"Who?"

"That's what HP means," she said. "Mary told me."

Adam raised his hands in defeat. "All right, all right. I'll read the book. If for no other reason than maybe Mary'll stop nagging me." He punched the button on his key fob to unlock the car door and then turned to face her. "Màiri?"

She gave him a questioning glance.

"What do you think Mary meant when she said, 'Read it or live it'?"

Màiri shrugged. "I don't know, but it sounds ominous. Maybe because it's Mary."

He drove to Màiri's small carpark and walked her up the hill to her flat. At the bottom step he stopped to take her into his arms. "I won't come up tonight," he murmured into her hair. "I've got reading to do."

FORT WILLIAM, SCOTLAND – PRESENT TIME

"That's all right," Màiri said. "We have tomorrow."

His kiss was gentle. "Aye, love. We have tomorrow."

The words played back in a loop as he walked back to his car. *We have tomorrow.* But did they? How many tomorrows did they have before the Curse did its thing?

You promised yourself you wouldn't think about that. Think of the good things. Cory was alive, and he'd found his father. Inspector Fraser was confident that he'd identify the arsonist soon. Màiri loved him. A silly smile broke out on Adam's face, and he hurried the last few steps to his car. *Aye, mostly that last one.*

He stood in front of the door to his flat and rooted in his pocket for his house key, but it wasn't on the fob with the car key. He stared at the ring in dismay. *What the hell?* He could hear Pearl snuffling at the door. *It must have fallen off in the car*, he thought, and retraced his steps to search, using his mobile as a torch. No luck.

"Damn it!" Adam leaned against the car and punched in Màiri's number.

"Miss me already?" she said. "Or are you trying to avoid reading?"

"I'm not even in the flat yet," he growled. "Do you see my house key there anywhere?"

"Wait," she said. She was gone for a while. "Aye, it was on the veranda in front of the door—two of them, in an envelope. Guess you'll have to come back." She didn't sound upset.

Adam sighed. "Dammit. I took it off the ring to make you a copy and forgot to put mine back on the ring. Okay, I'm on my way." He sent a silent apology to his dog and climbed back into the car. He parked again in the small car park and climbed the hill. As he reached the outside steps, he punched in Màiri's number again. "I'm here."

He kept the mobile to his ear as he reached the top and started across the veranda. "Màiri, do you have a spare bulb? Your lamp's out...aye, then." He clicked the mobile off.

Adam sensed a movement to his left and turned as a darker shape detached itself from the shadows and rushed forward, propelling him backwards until he was pinned against the wall of Màiri's flat. He felt a searing pain, heard a grunt as something was withdrawn and thrust into his abdomen again. An arm came across his chest and a voice hissed into his ear. "Sorry, lad. Nothing personal, eh?"

His mobile slipped out of his hand and thudded onto the veranda. Adam's assailant removed the arm that had been holding him up, and he slid down the wall. An odd haze gathered in front of his eyes.

His thoughts slid sideways. His head seemed too heavy; it fell forward, and he saw the handle of a knife embedded in his abdomen. *Stabbed. I've been stabbed.* He raised his hand and stared in confusion at the blood on it.

Adam forced his head up and tried to focus on the face of the man kneeling in front of him. Grey eyes studied him with detached interest. A name rose slowly out of his numb mind, and he fought to hold onto it even as his consciousness ebbed...

No! He had to stay awake! He had to warn Màiri! Out of the corner of his eye he saw his mobile's

FORT WILLIAM, SCOTLAND – PRESENT TIME

display light up with her face. His fingers groped for the mobile, touched it with one bloody finger. *Can't let her come out!*

The man stood up and turned toward Màiri's door.

"I've...called... the c...ops," Adam whispered with the last of his strength.

Alexander MacKay spun around. He looked at Màiri's red door, and back at Adam. "Fuck!" he snarled, and was gone, down the wooden steps and into the night.

Adam closed his eyes and let his head fall forward again. The roaring in his ears was gone now. An eerie quiet had settled over the veranda. *Damn,* he thought. *All this time, waiting for the Curse.* His last thought floated into the night air. *I'm sorry, love. I don't think we have tomorrow, after all.*

CHAPTER 47
FORT WILLIAM, SCOTLAND – PRESENT TIME

*If life transcends death, then I
will seek for you there.
If not, then there too.*
—James S.A. Corey

Màiri opened her door to a world gone mad. Adam lay against the outside wall of her house with his long legs splayed across her veranda, his eyes closed in a face white as paper. Blood pooled around a knife embedded in his stomach and ran in a thin stream across the porch floor. Her knees buckled and she fell in a graceless heap beside him.

Call 999! She stared at the mobile in confusion. *999!* the panicked voice in her head repeated, and she realized it was her own. She raised the mobile and dialed, sure her words would never be understood, and then threw it down and reached for the bloody hand in his lap. There was a pulse, a weak, thready whisper, but it was there.

She opened his blood-soaked shirt and laid her hand on his chest, waiting for the blue glow...

...and nothing happened. The fear rose in her throat and nearly choked off her breathing. She checked his pupils. Fixed and unresponsive. The panic bloomed. She placed a shaking hand on his chest again. Still nothing.

Why isn't it working? Tears streamed down Màiri's face. *Why can't I save him?* She knew he was dying. His skin was already turning blue and the pool of blood on her porch floor was increasing. She pressed harder and began to pray.

It seemed that time had stopped, but then she heard boot steps on the stairs heralding the arrival of two paramedics, who carried a patient trolley up the three flights of stairs as if it weighed nothing. A man and a woman crouched by Adam's side. They assessed him quickly, applied pressure without removing the knife, and affixed a breathing mask before hoisting him onto the trolley and carrying him down the stairs to the waiting ambulance. Màiri followed them, clutching the rail to keep herself from tumbling down the steps.

The woman technician turned to where she stood, hugging herself against the evening chill. "Are you coming?" she asked gently. Màiri blinked, then nodded and climbed into an ambulance for the second time in a month, this time in the front passenger seat.

She sent a terse message off to Daniel and then turned around and watched through the window as the technicians busied themselves placing electrodes to Adam's chest and attaching their lines to a

FORT WILLIAM, SCOTLAND – PRESENT TIME

monitor. Numbers appeared on the left of the screen, and lines began to travel from left to right.

"He's arresting!"

The male EMT pushed the button on the defibrillator. Adam's body arced as the shock coursed through the pads on his chest and then relaxed again. The technician monitoring the screen shook her head.

"Again!"

The electrodes were activated once more. The technician straddled Adam's body and began another round of CPR.

Màiri huddled against the ambulance wall and tried to will away the fear. Her mind kept repeating the scene that had met her eyes when she opened her door, as if her brain was trying for a different outcome than what she had seen on her veranda. But the reality was lying right in front of her, unmoving.

The monitor shrilled. "We're losing him!" said the paramedic. The wavy lines collapsed into a flat stream that flowed steadily across the display, but the technician continued his efforts without a pause.

Màiri looked at Adam MacArthur, the man she loved more than she'd ever thought possible, unable to process what was happening. The technician atop his body kept performing CPR, the straight line continued to flow across the screen, and the monitor shrilled incessantly. A word from television dramas floated into Màiri's mind. *Flatline*, she thought dully. *He's flatlining.*

Seconds later they pulled up to the emergency room entrance. People in white coats rushed out to help, moving Adam quickly off the ambulance and into the hospital, the EMT still straddling his body and working furiously.

Màiri, left alone, climbed out of the ambulance and stood looking at the neon lights flashing *Emergency*. Her world narrowed to the pneumatic doors, sliding open and shut as people rushed through. She looked down at her feet, rooted to the pavement, and then concentrated on picking up one foot and placing it ahead of the other, over and over, until she made her way into the hospital.

He's dead. The thought filtered into her consciousness and she pushed it away, only to have it return to taunt her. *Adam is gone.* She cast her mind back to the one night they'd had together. *If this is all we have, it will be enough,* she had told herself. How wrong she'd been. How easy to think such things, enfolded in the warm arms of your lover. How ridiculously stupid. It would never be enough.

She stood in the middle of the chaotic emergency room, numb with the bitter truth that filled her mind. She was alone, again.

"Màiri." Eve and Daniel were here, and Jared, all of them looking shattered and helpless. Eve folded her friend into her arms and patted her back, and Màiri let the tears come.

After a while she raised streaming eyes to the men who were closest to him—his brother and his best friend. "I'm so sorry," she said. "I'm so, so sorry." They nodded, unable to articulate the grief she saw in their taut faces and swollen eyes. Together they stood, arms around each other, and cried, while trolleys flowed in and people with drawn faces streamed past.

FORT WILLIAM, SCOTLAND – PRESENT TIME

Alexander MacKay stared into the sink in the bathroom of his flat and watched Adam MacArthur's blood wash down the drain. He stripped off his clothes and went into the shower, where the cascading water washed the blood away and allowed his jumbled thoughts to solidify.

He hadn't meant to kill MacArthur. Laura was going to be furious, but there was nothing he could do about it now. She deserved it, anyway. Women were more trouble than they were worth, for sure. She'd been whinging on about the bitch who stole her man for so long he thought he'd go radge, and finally he told her he'd take care of it, just to shut her up. Mackie laughed at the irony.

It had been a lie. He wasn't going to kill Màiri, not even for Laura. When he pulled her out of the fire at the museum, he'd been impressed by her courage in a time of crisis. Then she'd come to the station to thank him. She was charming, and when a beautiful woman brought you biscuits and called you her hero, she was hard to resist. He didn't need to kill her. It would be easy enough to lure her away from MacArthur, and certainly more fun.

He wasn't interested in her sexually. That was reserved for Laura. And it didn't bother him in the least that Laura wanted to use him to get her boyfriend back, because it wasn't about love with them. It was about control. Laura was Belenus' tool, just as the disciples were.

The game had nothing to do with romance; it was

purely seduction and dominance. Alexander MacKay had never lost a woman he wanted. Laura had tried to leave once or twice, but like the planets to the sun, she'd been pulled back into his orbit where she belonged. She'd never had a chance.

So, when she asked him for his help in getting rid of the bitch at the bookshop, he took it as an opportunity to shut her up and keep her in line. He talked his colleagues into taking Màiri up on her offer for free coffee and scones, then pulled out his shy act and told her he liked her. If he could seduce her away from MacArthur, things would go back to normal.

Then he saw that cat, and everything went to shite. It was the same cat that had run across the path in the woods the night they'd done Fletcher, he was sure of it. The animal had stared back at him as if it knew what he was thinking, and for a second a red haze had flooded his brain and he'd barely stopped himself from running over and strangling it. MacArthur's entrance with that pathetic excuse for a dog had probably saved the cat and kept Mackie from making the biggest mistake of his life.

But then he realized that nobody was watching him, anyway. Màiri's eyes were only for MacArthur, who was staring at her with undisguised longing. Neither of them seemed to remember he was even there. And it was then the fire alarm sounded. Mackie had never been happier to respond to a call. He jumped to his feet, made his excuses, and nearly ran out the door after the others.

He would have to change his plan. He suspected he wasn't going to be able to seduce Màiri MacLachlan,

FORT WILLIAM, SCOTLAND – PRESENT TIME

not if what he'd seen meant what he thought it did. Those two weren't just dating; they were in love. There was only one way to separate them. He was going to have to do it Laura's way. Some part of him knew this was a bad idea, but the challenge energised him.

He'd looked up Màiri's address, grateful that the department had Fort William residents on file, and drove by to scout it out. Perfect. It was at the top of an old mansion that had been converted into flats. The security would likely be less than in a modern building. His plan was to make enough noise to scare her, jimmy a window to suggest a burglary, and then present himself at her door. Her hero, there to save the day again. Only this time the outcome would be very different.

When he was ready, he parked down the street and walked to her flat in the dark in his black hoodie and jeans and soundless trainers. He used the torch on his mobile and moved silently up the stairs and around to a side window.

Màiri was inside, talking to someone on her mobile. Mackie moved on to the next window and began chipping at the window frame, making enough noise to attract her attention. So far, so good. But then the knife slipped out of his hands and landed on the wooden floor with a thud.

He cursed and bent to retrieve it, and that was when something came at him like a panther and tackled him. They wrestled in the dark until Mackie managed to slash the man's arm and get away. It was the first time in his life he'd felt fear. The power surged in with the adrenaline, and he embraced it.

Two days later, he was back. He climbed silently to the veranda on the third storey, unscrewed the bulb in the light over her door, then walked carefully around the entire structure to make sure he was alone. He stood for a long moment at the corner of the building and let the anticipation of what he was about to do flow through his body like an electrical current, then took a deep breath and stepped out of the shadows.

MacArthur was standing at the darkened front door, on his mobile.

Fuck. In another moment, the man would turn and see him. The plan changed again. *First him, then the woman.* He pulled his knife out.

Quiet as he was, MacArthur must have sensed his presence because he began to turn. Mackie rushed him at full speed, slamming him backwards into the side of the house and driving the knife into his gut. He pulled it out and pushed the blade in again, surprised that there was no noise and very little resistance. He watched pain fill the brown eyes, felt the body go slack, and let the power roar through his mind.

Mackie pinned the helpless man against the wall with one arm and leaned forward. "Sorry, lad. Nothing personal, eh?" Then he let go and MacArthur slid down the wall. The man scrabbled for his mobile, only a foot away from his body, and got his fingers on it, but then the hand went limp and his head sagged forward onto his chest.

Well, that was a little anticlimactic. Mackie stepped over the man's legs and started for the door.

"I've...called... the c...ops," came a whisper from behind him, and he turned to see MacArthur staring

FORT WILLIAM, SCOTLAND – PRESENT TIME

at him. The man's eyes closed and his head dipped forward again.

Mackie stared at him in astonishment. *No, he couldn't have. But what if he had?* He looked from the dying man to the door of the flat. "Fuck!" he said out loud and ran for the steps.

Now he stepped out of the shower, ready to plan. *Take it slow and think.* He'd already made one error when he forgot to retrieve his knife from the body. He'd worn gloves, of course, so there'd be no prints, but still...he shouldn't have left it. He really liked that knife.

Mackie shrugged. He'd come too far to allow himself to rush into another mistake. He looked at the pile of bloodstained clothing on his bathroom floor. He'd light another fire for Belenus tomorrow night and burn the clothes as an offering. Maybe he should go to MacArthur's funeral, too. It would be appropriate, and it didn't hurt to be nice.

He'd wait a few days, then put in his notice at the station and leave. Join another company, maybe in the islands, and begin recruiting again. Belenus could be served anywhere, and Mackie had the feeling he'd outstayed his welcome in Fort William.

He heard a knock on the door and checked his watch. 11:00. Who would be visiting him at this time of night? What if they'd shown up a few minutes ago, before he washed off the blood? Well, he'd always been lucky...

Two policemen stood outside his door. The older, a middle-aged man with a full head of white hair and piercing blue eyes, gave him a cold look.

WITCH

"Alexander MacKay, I am arresting you under Section 1 of the Criminal Justice Act for arson and homicide, and I believe that keeping you in custody is necessary and proportionate for the purposes of bringing you before a court or otherwise dealing with you in accordance with the law. You do not have to say anything, but it may harm your defence if you do not mention when questioned something which you later rely on in court. Anything you do say may be given in evidence."

Mackie stared at them in stunned disbelief. Murder? But how could anyone know? Then the truth seeped into his consciousness. Not MacArthur. Fletcher.

Laura.

The bitch had betrayed him.

CHAPTER 48
DORNACH, SCOTLAND – 1727

HUGH

Hugh crept through the village, keeping to the shadows and trying to make no sound. He was lucky to be free after collapsing in the doorway of the town house. The villager who'd caught him as he fell had carried him outside, where the March wind blew cool. The man's wife soaked a cloth at the pump and wiped his forehead, and within minutes, his head cleared and he was sitting up, thanking them for their kindness.

Kindness? This couple had been part of the crowd that condemned Sìne and her mother with no evidence. Their kindness to him was only a reflection of their obsequious bending to his father's will. They were monsters, like all the others.

His father! If he were caught now, he would be taken back to that house he no longer called home, imprisoned at the will of the greatest monster of all. He evaded the pressing hands of the couple and stumbled away from the mockery of a trial and into the woods.

He hid in the deepest part of the forest and wept. The air had turned chill, and there was an acrid smell that reminded Hugh of the bonfires lit every fifth of November to observe the execution of the famous conspirator, Guy Fawkes.

As a child he'd thought it thrilling to watch the fire burn higher and higher, consuming a straw effigy of the instigator of the Gunpowder Plot that had nearly killed the king and all his ministers. He'd watched it with Sìne, hurling taunts at the effigy and throwing sticks into the fire.

The smell grew worse, and Hugh gagged as he realized what it was. *They were burning Sìne!* No, not Sìne—he'd heard his father shout out the sentence. It was Doirin who was dying. Sìne's turn was tomorrow. Sickened, he crawled out of his hiding place, brushed the leaves off his filthy trews, and made his way to the edge of the village.

Even this far away, he could hear the cheers from the village green. Hugh knew he could go no further. Surely his father had men out looking for him—men sorely vexed to be taxed with searching for him while the witch was being burned.

He couldn't see the fire, but he could imagine it, greedy fingers reaching into the air and smothering all it touched. He could tell by the horrible smell

DORNACH, SCOTLAND – 1727

that the effigy was no straw man but the remains of what had once been a real person—a villager like those watching with hunger in their eyes. The fun of watching a towering fire was forever gone for Hugh Sutherland.

He crouched underneath the eaves of the blacksmith's shop—a simple lean-to that served as the man's place of business during the day—and thought about how he was going to rescue Sìne.

He hoped Doirin Gilchrist had stopped breathing before the fire reached her. Hoped the hut where they were keeping Sìne was far enough away that she hadn't heard her mother's shrieks, couldn't smell the indescribable odour of a burning human body.

They were going to do the same to her, to his beautiful Sìne, unless he stopped them. He made his way through the empty village, stopping frequently to listen for the sounds of human passage. But they were all at the green, watching the execution of a witch.

Where would they be keeping Sìne? It had to be one of the storage houses at the edge of the market square, which had locks to keep thieves from plying their trade. And they'd be guarded.

He arrived at the site of the three decrepit storage huts, plastered himself against the wall of the nearest one, and peeked out. The hut in the centre had two men stationed outside. The lock looked sturdy, too. Hugh crept around the back, away from the guards.

Each hut had a tiny window, high up near the thatch. These windows also had locks. He moved away and retraced his steps into the woods. Safe under his bush, Hugh made his plan. He would need something to pick the lock on the window, and he had to hope the small aperture was wide enough to allow a person through, because this was Sìne's only escape route.

He made his way through the woods until his own house came into view, and stopped for a minute to stare at the grandiose building. The house where he'd been born and raised, where his mother had died, where he had plumbed the depths of his father's depravity.

He'd never again allow himself to be dragged into that place against his will. He and Sìne would find a new village, far away from the Dornach Firth...maybe on one of the western isles. He would work the rigs and Sìne would heal under his care.

Hugh moved to the front door of his house, put his ear to the door, and listened. He heard nothing. He tried the door, but it was locked, as expected. So he made his way with caution to the back wall of the house. Locked. He listened again, but the house had that sense of emptiness that is palpable. Everyone was at the burning.

A surge of anger coursed through his body. Hugh picked up a nearby rock and smashed the window next to the door. He crawled carefully over the sill and stood up in the kitchen, exactly the place he needed to be. He moved to the pantry and searched until he found a large kitchen knife, stuffed it into the belt of his trews, and made his way back out and into the woods.

His father would kill him for breaking the window, but if all went as he hoped, the bastart wouldn't

DORNACH, SCOTLAND – 1727

have the chance. If Hugh's plan went well tonight, Duncan Sutherland would never see his son again. If it didn't...

Hugh shook his head to clear it. Now was the time, while the villagers were still at the green. He made his way back to the huts at the edge of the village and waited.

His head ached and the nausea was back, circling in his gut like an old friend who has worn out his welcome. The wind blew his hair into his eyes and he brushed it away impatiently. Memories chased each other through his mind, but he had no time to stop and consider them. Sìne was waiting.

Hugh pressed himself against the back of the building and listened to the muffled voices of the men stationed at the door on the other side.

"Wisht we didnae git stuck 'ere watchin' th' wee witch," one grumbled. "She's no goin' enywhere, an' we missed all th' fun."

Fun? Hugh curled his fists and resisted the urge to run around the hut and stab them with his kitchen knife. Burning Sìne's mother was fun?

"Weel, 'is lordship says we can go t'morra. Won't be needin' t' keep guard eny more, aye? 'Ere, I brought some ale."

Hugh pressed both hands to his ears in a vain attempt to drown out the careless words of the guards. He crept to the window and reached up, glad for the height that allowed him to just touch the lock. He pulled out the knife and worked at the flimsy thing, trying to keep the sound down. Every few minutes he stopped to listen for voices or footsteps, but the guards were busy at their ale. Who would expect someone to try to rescue a witch?

The lock clicked open.

Hugh's mouth dropped. The first step in his plan had worked. He pulled the bottom of the window open and gripped the sill with his fingers. Then he pulled himself up until he could raise the window above his head and peer inside. He knew he hadn't the strength he should have, but something was flooding through his body, giving him a strange power when he needed it most. He raised his head and peered into the gloom.

Sìne stood in the middle of the dirty room, staring at him. Her eyes were red from weeping and the tracks of tears wound down her face. Her lips were cracked and blood-filled, and her dirt-encrusted hair sprang up in curls that seemed to have a life of their own. She was the most beautiful thing he'd ever seen.

"Come!" he whispered. Sìne stood still, gaping at him as if he were a ghost. "Come! Please, *leannan!*"

Sìne looked behind her, at the door behind which stood her guards, and then at Hugh. She walked to the window and extended her hands. Hugh grabbed them and pulled, willing his arms to work one more time.

Slowly, painfully, he pulled his love up the wall inch by inch, until she could grab the window frame and help herself through. She fell into his arms and hung there, exhausted.

"Can ye walk, *mo ghràdh*?" He set her gently down and she stood, swaying. Then her knees folded and she sagged in his arms. He scooped her up and walked away from her prison, carrying the only thing in his life that mattered.

DORNACH, SCOTLAND – 1727

He had not planned for this. She was too weak, and he couldn't make it far carrying her. They would be caught. It was over, he knew it...but he would protect her with everything he had until the end.

They reached the barren area west of the village before Hugh heard the baying of hounds. He sat in the road, took Sìne into his lap, and waited for his father.

Duncan Sutherland was accompanied by at least ten of his farm workers, all brandishing swords and cudgels. They stood across the path about ten feet away, legs braced and ready for their master's order.

"What 're ye doin', son?" Sutherland's voice held a note of curiosity. "Surely ye didnae think t' take our witch away, did ye? Bring her here. Now."

Hugh shook his head stubbornly. "She's mine. I willnae give her t' ye."

"Ye have no choice, son." He signalled his men. "Take her. Dinnae hurt her; th' wickit creature put doon a curse. We'll let th' fire do th' work, aye?"

Hugh turned to Sìne, looked deep into her eyes, and took her hand in his. "I'm sorry, *mo chridhe*. I willnae see them burn ye." His right hand moved and her eyes widened. She looked down at the shaft of the knife buried in her stomach, and then back into Hugh's tortured face.

"Why?" she whispered. "Ye heard th' curse! Th' one who kills me..." She coughed and blood appeared at the corner of her mouth.

"I'll bear it, gladly," Hugh said. "I cannae let them put ye t' th' flame." He pulled her to his chest and sobbed. "I love ye too much."

Her hand found his and he gripped it tightly against his heart. "I'll come t' ye soon's I can, *mo ghràdh*. Will ye wait?"

Hugh felt the smallest squeeze of his hand, and then her body went limp in his arms. He rocked her and let the grief take him until a guttural oath broke the stillness. Duncan Sutherland was standing on the path, his face contorted with rage.

Hugh raised defiant eyes to his father. "Ye've lost, ye bastart."

CHAPTER 49
FORT WILLIAM, SCOTLAND – PRESENT TIME

I would not want to live in a world without magic, for that is a world without mystery, and that is a world without faith.
—R.A. Salvatore

"Raise it to 350!"
The doctor lifted the paddles again and placed them against Adam's chest. His body jerked; the shrilling of the monitor stopped. Tiny waves appeared on the screen and began their march across.

"He's back," the doctor said. "Get him prepped for surgery. This lad's just pulled one out of his hat."

❦

Adam woke to semi-darkness. The old-fashioned village was gone. The grieving young man crooning over the body of his beloved was gone. He was floating in a world of darkness.

There was something wrong with his body, he decided. It hurt, but not in the region of his heart. This pain seemed lower, somewhere in his abdomen. A humming sound came from behind him, but when he tried to turn his head to search for the source, the pain rose up and all his nerves seemed to be on fire.

There was a ghost standing by his bed. A white thing, hovering as ghosts are expected to do. *So, I'm dead.* His eyes travelled up its body and found its head. It was white, too, of course, with dark eyes that stared at him through the round lenses of its glasses.

Glasses? Ghosts have glasses?

It reached over his head and suddenly the room was filled with a bright light.

"Welcome back to the land of the living. I'm Doctor Welles, your surgeon. How are you feeling?"

"It hurts," Adam managed. "But it's a different kind of pain. And not in the right place."

"Aye, pain is expected when you've been stabbed, lad. And you don't get to pick the place."

Stabbed? Adam lay back and let the memories trickle into his consciousness. Màiri's veranda. Someone rushing at him, pushing him up against the wall of her flat. Excruciating pain in his stomach, then a weakness that spread through his body. Sliding down the wall. A face looming in front of him.

Mackie. Leering at him as he pulled the knife out and thrust it in again.

He must have passed out, because Mackie had become Màiri, leaning over him, her hand on his chest, crying. Then, nothing.

"Where's Màiri?" he asked the doctor.

FORT WILLIAM, SCOTLAND – PRESENT TIME

"Ach, your lassie has been here since last night, along with your friends. You gave everyone quite a scare, including the ER staff." Doctor Welles leant over, peeled up Adam's eyelid, and shone a small light into it. Then he stood back and regarded him seriously.

"Your heart stopped, lad, more than once," he said. "You were clinically dead for almost five minutes, but our ER doctors never give up, so here you are."

He peeled back the cover and checked something on Adam's stomach. "And because I'm rather good at what I do, you're going to be fine. You'll have a scar, but you should heal pretty quickly. Now, get some rest. You're in recovery, but we'll be moving you to a patient room in a while, and then your horde can come in and visit." He patted Adam on the shoulder and left.

Rest? That wasn't on the ticket. He didn't plan on closing his eyes until he saw Màiri. Adam braced himself against the pain and looked around the recovery room. There was nothing on the walls, and he was alone in the room. The humming was coming from a monitor near his bed, next to a small side table. On the table was a book.

What was a book doing in the recovery room? Adam reached his left arm over, gritting his teeth against the twinge in his stomach, and picked the book up. Even before he focused on the title, he knew what it was from the smell. *The Witch's Daughter. Damn.*

He sighed and began to read. When they came to move him to his room, he put the book under the hospital sheet and held onto it, and as soon as they had him settled, he pulled it out and continued reading. He didn't want to, but he couldn't stop. He felt as if he were stretched between two worlds, trying to fit into both and managing neither.

The door eased open and he looked up from the book, startled. Sìne Gilchrist stood in the doorway, her blue eyes brimming with unshed tears. He blinked and shook his head, and suddenly he was back in his hospital room and Màiri was reaching for his hand.

"Oh, Adam," she breathed. "Oh, oh..." She broke down and let the tears come, wiping them away with the hand that wasn't fastened to his. "Don't you ever do that to me again!" Then she sobered. "I mean...I know you couldn't help it, but..."

"The Curse is gone," Adam said softly.

Her head jerked up. "What?" The light of hope in her eyes almost undid him.

"It's gone, Màiri. I can feel it." He took a breath and focused on his words. "Sìne said it could only be ended by a death, and I died. The doctor said it. I died, and while I was dead, I saw everything."

"W-what do you mean?" Màiri's brows were furrowed.

"I saw my past life...and yours," Adam said. "It was as if I was there, running beside Hugh Sutherland. I knew what he was thinking. I felt his panic and his horror at what he had to do. It was terrible... Màiri, he loved her so much."

Màiri's face was a mask of confusion. "I don't understand."

Adam held up the book. "I read it, just now. But before I did, I knew what happened. I had already

FORT WILLIAM, SCOTLAND – PRESENT TIME

seen everything, and there's so much more than was in the book." He took a deep breath. "Remember when Mary Duncan said, 'Read it or live it'?" Màiri nodded. "Well, I hadn't read it yet, when I was attacked. So I guess I had to live it."

They stared at each other for a long moment, and then Adam said softly, "I'm sorry, Màiri. I'm sorry I put you through that." He could feel the tears running down his cheeks. "But it's over. We have all the time in the world, now. Really."

She took his face between her hands and kissed him very gently, tasting the tears between them...for all of ten seconds. Then door flew open and Jared rushed in, followed by Daniel and Eve.

"Sorry, mate, we couldn't wait any longer," his partner said, looking quite un-sorry. "You have lots of time to get mushy later, eh?" His dark brown eyes were damp and his voice seemed huskier than usual. "And in case you're worried about Pearl, which apparently you're not, I picked him up and took him to my place. He's fine, but he misses you."

"Thanks," Adam said. "You're the best."

Jared handed him a cream-coloured envelope. "Myles Grant dropped this off at the front desk," he said. "I didn't know you two were close."

Adam looked up. "Neither did I." He opened the card, which featured a watercolour of Loch Linnhe and the words, *Be well. You win. Myles.*

"Well," he said. "Nice of him...I guess." He tossed the card onto the bedside table.

Daniel stepped forward and patted his brother's arm. "That was a hell of a thing," he said. "The doctor said it was probably your conditioning that saved you, you know." He let out a shaky breath and grinned. "So you should maybe come home and work those muscles when you get the time, aye?"

"But it's like a party here," Adam said. "Not very restful, what with nurses and doctors poking and prodding and turning on lights all night long, but still so much fun."

On cue, a nurse came in. "I know you lot have catching up to do, but we need to run some tests. You can come back later."

Màiri leaned down and kissed Adam's forehead and then let herself be herded toward the door with the others.

The hours went by in a whirl of tests, liquid meals, prodding, and consultations. After every visit the nurses said, "Get some rest."

Really? Adam thought. *And how do you suggest I do that?* He closed his eyes just for a moment. When he woke, it was evening and Inspector Benjamin Fraser was sitting by his bed.

"Well, lad," said the inspector. "You really know how to grab attention, eh? Also, you snore. So... are you up for hearing what's been going on in your absence?"

Adam fumbled for the button to raise his bed. "It was Mackie, wasn't it?"

Fraser narrowed his eyes. "Well, that's confidential."

Adam pulled a deep breath through his nose and huffed it out. The inspector grinned at him.

"All right. I'll give you the gist, since you're weak and cranky. We've arrested the arsonist and rounded

FORT WILLIAM, SCOTLAND – PRESENT TIME

up his mad crew, and yes, it was Alexander MacKay." Fraser's face creased in a rare smile. "Cory's meddling helped us find the killer. He might actually make a decent cop one day." His eyes darkened. "He's going to need therapy. No lad should ever have to see what he saw, go through what he did. But he's a tough one, my Cory." Pride shone in the blue eyes.

"Anyway," he went on after a moment, "once we knew the dead man was a cult member and a firefighter, it was a matter of narrowing down who'd been on scene at the museum just before the fire started. And that person was our Mister MacKay."

"But what about Peter Campbell? He took his own car to the scene," Adam said.

"Aye, he did. But so did MacKay. You two thought you were so clever, pretending to interview him, but MacKay is a very smart man. He saw an opportunity and threw Campbell right under the bus." He paused. "Your information did prove useful, I'll grant you that."

"So Campbell was just one of the cult members?"

"Campbell was totally innocent," Fraser said. "Just because he's a nasty dobber doesn't mean he's a criminal. On the other hand, Alexander MacKay is a sociopath. He's extremely affable, and he can wear whatever mask he needs. When the police raided his house, they found posters and statues about some ancient fire god, as well as news articles on all the fires in the local area."

"But why did he stab me?"

"You weren't his real target. He was there for Miss MacLachlan, and you were just in the way."

Sorry, lad. Nothing personal. The words whispered into his ear by a killer who didn't even care. *Nothing personal.* A shiver went down his spine. If he hadn't lied to Mackie about calling the police, that monster would still have been there when Màiri came out. *If he hadn't lost his key...* The icy grip tightened.

"Why did he want to hurt Màiri? We were both there that day at the station."

"It had nothing to do with your visit to the fire station," Fraser said. "Mackie targeted Màiri because Laura Macallan asked him to. She turned herself in last night."

"*Laura?* Why?"

Fraser narrowed his eyes. "Apparently you're quite the ladies' man." He shrugged. "I don't see it, but Miss Macallan said she acted out of love. She swore she didn't want MacKay to hurt your lass; she just asked him to scare her, so she'd stay away from you. I don't entirely believe that, and MacKay isn't talking, but that's a problem for the police. At any rate, she'll be going away for a long time."

"She sent a madman after Màiri because she was jealous?" Adam lay back on the bed, exhausted. None of this seemed remotely possible. It was like a bad TV drama.

"But how did Laura know Mackie?" he said eventually.

"She was the reporter assigned to the first fire, months ago. She met MacKay, and they formed some sort of unholy bond. I suspect he was just using her, but a man like that has a lethal sort of charm. It's how he recruited people into his cult, after all."

FORT WILLIAM, SCOTLAND – PRESENT TIME

Ben Fraser stood. "That's about it. I'm due to take the Musketeers to the chippy. Get some rest, eh, Romeo?" And he went out, chuckling.

Adam lay for a while staring at the tiles in the ceiling. *Laura. Who would've thought?* At the time, he'd thought her pestering merely annoying, but now he saw it in a different light. She was a stalker, just like Daniel had said, and worse. He pictured her standing in his office, pouting like a hurt child, and shivered.

Màiri came back an hour later, bringing biscuits and books.

"I took the week off so I can take care of you," she said. "And I was thinking about what you said about Hugh and Sìne, so I brought some more books about witchcraft in Scotland," she said. "Their story is pretty famous because Doirin Gilchrist was the last person to be executed as a witch. They repealed the Witchcraft Act in 1736. There's a stone monument in Dornach; maybe we should go see it."

"No, thanks," Adam said. "I'm all witched out. You can take this book back and tell Mary and Company to resell it, or bury it, or burn it." He grimaced. "Never mind, forget that last one. But here—please take it away." He reached for *The Witch's Daughter* on the side table, and his hand froze in mid-air.

The book was gone.

CHAPTER 50
FORT WILLIAM, SCOTLAND – PRESENT TIME

The greatest gift life can give you today is the promise of tomorrow.
—Matshona Dhliwayo

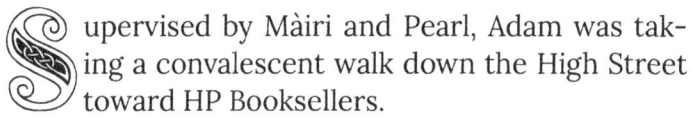

Supervised by Màiri and Pearl, Adam was taking a convalescent walk down the High Street toward HP Booksellers.

"It feels good to be out of that place," he said, looking around at the familiar shops. "I feel as if I've lost about a year out of my life cooped up in there with all those white coats and machines."

"Well, those white coats and machines saved your life, don't forget." Màiri squeezed his hand. "I, for one, will thank them forever."

"Aye, I know that, and I'm grateful." He pushed a frustrated breath out between his lips. "I'm just anxious to get my strength back and start working again."

"Don't push it, though." Màiri stopped and pulled him around to face her. She took both of his hands in hers and studied his stubborn face. His brows were drawn down in that sulky little boy look she knew well.

"I almost lost you, Adam. And I hope you don't mind, but I'm going to make sure you don't rush things. You can go into the office, but that's it. Daniel and Jared asked one of the members of the running club to help, and they can handle the tours for a while longer, aye?"

He grinned and saluted her. "Aye, ma'am. Your word is law."

She harumphed but then returned the grin. Raising a man was harder than she'd ever thought it would be, but worth every minute. *He's so precious*, she thought. *I wonder if he has a clue?*

She decided it was time to change the subject and seized on the first thing that came to mind. "Did I ever tell you what HP stands for?"

"The bookshop name? Aye, you said it meant Highland Players."

"Right," she said. "Which makes sense, when you think on it. They are a bit like actors in a play, aren't they? Not quite real, but somehow wonderful."

Adam nodded. "I always have the feeling they know exactly what I'm thinking. It's a bit off-putting, but I don't really mind because they feel...I don't know... *safe*. Like I know I can trust them with my favourite person." He grinned at her. "I'll admit, I was a little afraid Mary was going to kill me when I acted like an arse and hurt your feelings—ach!" He stumbled and looked down at his feet. "Dammit, Pearl!"

He bent to untangle the leash that Pearl had gotten tangled round their legs, then gave the dog's head a pat. "Sorry, lad. I know I haven't been around to give you much attention lately. I'll do better, promise."

When he straightened, Màiri was staring at him, her brow wrinkled.

"What?"

"Oh," she said. "Well...it's just that..."

"What's wrong?"

"Nothing's wrong. But there's something I've been thinking about ever since—" She took a deep breath and faced him. "I have to tell Mary, but of course I want to tell you first. If you don't agree, then I won't do it. But I hope you do. Agree, that is." She stumbled to a halt and met his gaze with anxious blue eyes.

"Agree with what? Come on, you're scaring me!"

"I want to train to be a paramedic."

His brows went up. "Where did *that* come from?"

"Just hear me out," she said. "You know when I saved you before? The blue light I told you about?"

He nodded. "Aye."

"Well, I tried it again, when Mackie stabbed you, and...it didn't work." Her voice was thick now, memory taking her back to the horror of that night. "I don't know what it was, whether it was magic or some kind of weird aberration, but it didn't happen that time, and I don't think I can do it anymore."

"Oh." He studied her face. "Do you mind terribly?"

"No," she said slowly. "Not since you're okay. But that night—when I needed it most—it wasn't there, and I was so scared I just panicked. I felt so useless! Then the paramedics came, and they knew exactly what to do. Even with the machines screaming that

WITCH

it was too late, that you were..."— she cleared her throat— "that you were gone, they never gave up."

She looked up at him, brows furrowed. "I want to do that, Adam. Save people. Not with some sort of weird magic, but with my brain and my heart and my skills." She stopped and studied his eyes. "Does that sound mental? To start a new career at my age?"

Adam laughed. "Ach, yer nae so auld, lass. I think ye hae a few years left."

"So it's not daft?"

"It's not daft at all. I think you should do it. You'll be brilliant."

The relief was like the flood of water released by the locks on the Caledonian Canal, sweeping all her doubts and worries away. She grinned at Adam, took his arm, and pulled him toward the bookshop, Pearl waddling behind.

"I've been talking to Inspector Fraser," she said, her words picking up speed. "There's a program in Stirling, and some of it's online so I wouldn't have to move, and I really want to do it but I'd have to quit the bookshop and I don't know how to tell M—" The words died on Màiri's lips and she stopped short. Adam followed her gaze, and his own eyes widened.

They had reached HP Booksellers, but the sign above the shop was different. Now it read *High Street Book Store* in modern block letters. Through the display window they could see beige carpeting, IKEA-style bookshelves, and a large central island with three or four cashiers, all dressed in khaki trousers and navy-blue polo shirts.

Inside, a middle-aged woman greeted them with

FORT WILLIAM, SCOTLAND – PRESENT TIME

a warm smile. "Welcome to High Street Books," she said. "Can I help you?"

"Is Mary Duncan in?" asked Màiri.

"Who?"

"Mary Duncan. The own—" She stopped as Adam tugged her arm. He tilted his head toward the centre of the shop, and her eyes grew round with shock.

Employees were shelving books, helping customers with questions, and taking credit cards at the counter. Employees—but not the right employees. She had never seen any of these people before in her life.

"Let's go," she said under her breath, and pulled Adam back out onto the street.

"They're not here!" she said. "Mary, Henry, Betty, Caomhainn—none of them. It's all changed!"

She rounded on Adam and clutched his arm. "How is this possible?" She looked at the door of the bookshop and then back at Adam. "Were-were they even real? Was any of it real?"

He took her hands in his. "Aye," he said. "It was real, I'm sure of it." He looked into her eyes. "And so were Hugh and Sìne." He paused. "You know what I think? I think the Players were here to give us that book. They wanted us to meet Hugh and Sìne, and we did."

He hesitated and lowered his voice. "I'm betting if we walked back into that bookshop right now, there would be no book called *The Witch's Daughter* in the database. But the story was real. It's a part of history."

Màiri glanced toward the High Street Book Store and shivered. "I think you're right." She focused on his multi-hued brown eyes—they were Hugh

459

Sutherland's eyes, though she couldn't have said how she knew—and felt tears welling in her own.

"But it was so sad! He killed her, even knowing he would be cursed. That his descendants would be cursed. He gave his life for her." Her voice was low and urgent. "Adam...If there's an afterlife, do you think she forgave him?"

"Absolutely." Adam's voice was firm. "In fact... Don't think I'm radge, but I think they've been waiting all this time for two people with a love as strong as theirs to make it all come right."

Màiri whispered, "Two people like us, you mean." She put her arms around him. "Let's make their sacrifice worth it, Adam. Let's live the life they gave us, aye?"

Adam looked once more at the bookstore, and then he turned back to Màiri and took her into his arms. "Aye, love, let's do that." He lowered his head and kissed her, heedless of the passersby on the High Street.

Màiri held him tight and returned the kiss with all the passion in her being. *This is what I've been waiting for*, the thought drifted through her mind. *I'll never be alone again.*

A loud snort brought them back to the present. Adam looked at Pearl, who was sitting in front of the bookshop door, snuffling sadly. He sighed and turned back to Màiri. "Are you up for a ride to Inverness this weekend?"

She laughed. "Well, that came out of nowhere, but sure, if you think you're ready. Why?"

"It's time you met my family," he said. "We have a

FORT WILLIAM, SCOTLAND – PRESENT TIME

lot to tell them." He looked at his dog again. "And I need to stop by the SPCA. I think we're going to have to adopt a cat."

EPILOGUE
DORNACH, SCOTLAND, 1737

Hugh sat in his favourite leather chair with a glass of whisky in his hand and watched the stiff back of his wife as she walked out of his life, dragging their nine-year-old son behind her. He'd thought the parting would bring at least some guilt, but he was beyond such emotion.

He hadn't been a good husband. He'd tried to be a decent father, at least for a while, but the child was too much like his mother. Hugh's relationship with his son became more distant as time passed, and he hadn't the energy to try harder. He'd been drifting for ten years, and he didn't care.

His wedding to Ailis MacAllan had been the celebration of the year in Dornach. He was hailed as a hero by the village—after all, he had rid them of the evil that threatened their souls by killing the witch's daughter. Most of his neighbours lauded his courage in capturing the abomination and putting an end to it.

Most.

There were some whose rigid limbs and taut faces belied their disappointment at such an easy death for Doirin's daughter. One was his father, of whom he expected no less. Duncan Sutherland's stoic face had always hidden the monster that lurked within, and obscured a character so depraved that he would hunt down and torture an innocent lass for no other reason than to prove his power.

Only Hugh saw through the mask to the seething fury that lived inside Duncan Sutherland. Had he cared enough, he might have taunted the man for his helpless anger, but he and his father had not exchanged a word since that night ten years ago.

Hugh had expected jubilation from Walter MacKay, but that one seemed curiously subdued, even dismayed, by the aftermath of the trial. He avoided Hugh's eyes when they passed on the road, and the usual caustic jibes were lacking. Perhaps the trial had taught him that there were far worse bullies in the world than he.

But it wasn't Walter whose behaviour had Hugh on the alert; it was his brother, Ronain. The younger man's grey eyes had lit with triumph when the news was presented in the marketplace, as if he knew what this outcome had done to Hugh and nothing could please him more.

There was an evil about Ronain MacKay, despite his innocent look. He liked to hurt people. He was the one, Hugh was sure, who had tried to kill him the night the Gilchrists were arrested and his world fell apart. He was likely also the one responsible when the witches' cottage burned to the ground not long after the execution. Ronain had always blamed Sine for his

DORNACH, SCOTLAND, 1737

brother's embarrassment so many years ago, and he hated Hugh for marrying Ailis, the woman he thought should have been his.

Aye, Ronain had malevolence in him. But as with Hugh's father, it was born of greed, lust and hatred that was all too human. Hugh had pondered long on it over the years, and he was convinced the real evil in Dornach had come from the magistrate, Albert Wilson. A rat hiding in the shadows, delivering plague and then vanishing back into the gutter so none would perceive his part in the calumny and know where the true Devil lived. He had disappeared the night of the trial and was never heard from again.

Hugh's head still ached when the weather was dreich—maybe it was God's reminder that he was the worst kind of sinner, or perhaps it was a foreboding of the curse Sine had delivered to the village at her trial. 'I curse th' one who stops my heart...die in agony afore his time...'

He'd told her he would bear her curse gladly, and he meant the words still. He was awaiting the day it would claim him...looking forward to it.

But until then, he would bide. He went through the motions. Stood in Kirk and repeated the oath of marriage with a smile fixed on his face. He bedded Ailis as a husband should do, but in his mind the bride's hair was black as midnight and her eyes blue as the firth on a summer's day.

In due time, Ailis gave birth to a son, and Hugh never touched his wife again. Ailis went from pouting to complaining to screaming like a fishwife, but Hugh retreated to a place in his mind where he could be safe *from everyone but himself. He avoided the house and spent as much time in the fields as he could. Outside he was closer to the clouds, and somewhere in those clouds, Sìne was waiting.*

He became friends with the whisky bottle. It dulled his senses and muffled his wife's petulant whinging. They lived separate lives in the same house, floating like the ships that plied the waters of Dornach Firth, never getting close enough to make contact.

His father had died two years ago, and Hugh hadn't shed a tear. Duncan Sutherland's funeral had been a milestone in the life of the village, attended by all as though the man still ruled their lives. Hugh and Ailis accepted their neighbours' condolences, standing next to each other like statues, never touching. When it was over, she returned to her rooms, and he to his whisky bottle.

Now Ailis was leaving him, taking their son with her and going to live with her mother, and he felt nothing but relief. He leaned against the back of the chair and closed his eyes, alone now in the great house he hated so much. Free to wait.

He was thirty-two years old. Much had changed in Scotland in the ten years since he stopped caring. A year ago, parliament had passed a new Witchcraft Act, this time making it illegal to execute someone for practising magic.

"See that, leannan?" Hugh told Sìne. "That was yer doin'—yers and yer mother's. Are ye nae glad?" He envisioned her smiling face, and let the tears flow unimpeded.

The light around the edges of the heavy brocade curtains dimmed and the room darkened, summoning another endless night. Hugh sighed and picked up the empty bottle. He stood and swayed for a moment, then found his feet and started across the floor toward the dustbin outside the back door.

He was having more difficulty than usual keeping his balance tonight; maybe a little less whisky was in order. A new warmth crept into his heart and chased the thought away, and he stood still and let it spread through him. It felt good.

The warmth grew hotter, and now it was no longer comforting. It had become like an ember that has burst into flame, scorching everything around it. He clutched at his chest and gasped from the pain, but it grew in intensity, and he was helpless to fight it.

Hugh heard the glass shatter as the whisky bottle fell from his nerveless fingers onto the wooden floor. His legs gave out and he collapsed. A shard of glass bit into his arm, but it was nothing compared to the fire raging now through his body. He rolled over onto his back and stared at the ceiling, and suddenly he knew.

Sìne's curse. It was coming for him, burning him up as her mother had been burned, turning him to ash from the inside out. Just as she had promised.

'Die in agony, afore his time...'

"I'll bear it, gladly." Despite the excruciating pain coursing through his body, a smile found its way onto his face. "Tis time, leannan. I'm coming," he whispered into the silence of the room. He closed his eyes, happy for the first time in ten years, and waited.

His body seemed lighter, and he could no longer feel his back against the floorboards. He rose to meet the dark ceiling, closed his eyes against the impact—but there was none. The ceiling evaporated into mist, and Hugh was drifting up and over the firth. The pain was gone.

The air smelled like Doirin's kitchen, redolent with the scent of fresh-baked oatcakes, and he could hear the waves battering the coastline far below. Wind whispered around him and away, carrying with it the last memories of the horror his life had been.

A figure materialized out of the mist. Tendrils of curly black hair blew around a pale face and into eyes bluer than the sea in summer. She smiled and held out a slender hand. "Took ye a wee while," she said. "Do ye ken how long I've been waitin'?"

Hugh reached out, and five perfect fingers curled into his hand. His voice, when it came, was choked with wonder and pent-up longing, the words barely audible.

"Mo ghràdh," he said. "Sìne."

AUTHOR'S NOTE

The Witchcraft Act of 1563 resulted in a century and a half of witch hunts and persecution throughout Scotland. Thousands of people were burned as witches before the Act was repealed by parliament in 1736.

This novel is based on the true story of the last witch of Scotland, Janet Horne. It is not her real name, because that is unknown, so the name given her in history basically means "Jane Doe." She was, like Doirin Gilchrist in this story, a lady's maid who came to Dornach with her daughter in the early part of the eighteenth century. There is little known about her life in the village, beyond the fact that she was brought to trial in 1727 and found guilty of witchcraft, but modern historians believe she was likely suffering from dementia and unable to defend herself in court. She was burned alive like many of those who came before her. Her daughter, born with physical deformities, escaped and was never heard from again.

The memorial below stands in a small side yard in Dornach. The date on the stone is incorrect, the final humiliation for a woman reviled by her neighbours and put to death for a crime she didn't commit and could not understand.

BOOKS BY M MACKINNON

The Highland Spirits
The Comyn's Curse
The Piper's Warning
The Healer's Legacy

Echoes in Time
Drumossie
Glencoe
Seven
Witch

Made in the USA
Middletown, DE
10 September 2025